"Haley?" 're
all in range, to
hear her respo..., ..., ..., lay
face down in the water, and pushed himself out into the
river with his toes.

The hardest part wasn't being pelted with bullets—
the projectile shield took care of most of that. The
hardest part was not reacting in any way as the bullets
hit him like a thousand tiny hammers. Fortunately for
Allen, mechs were not ones to waste bullets on what
they perceived to be a dead body. Just as he couldn't
bear the pain any longer, the firing stopped. Now all he
had to worry about was drowning.

The sounds of the world came through the water
with otherworldly distortion. Under the murky river, the
noise of servo motors blended with splashes from the
mechs walking toward Allen. Then another set joined
the chorus, farther off. And finally a third set. Together,
they got closer. And closer.

A new sound split its way through the throbbing
noise headed for Allen, like something between a
shrieking cat and an agitated dolphin. At last, the sound
Allen had been waiting for.

Last Hope for Hire

by

Matthew Wilcox

Last Hope for Hire

Cover Art by *Kristian Norris*

The Wild Rose Press, Inc.
PO Box 708
Adams Basin, NY 14410-0708
Visit us at www.thewildrosepress.com

Publishing History
First Edition, 2021
Trade Paperback ISBN 978-1-5092-3559-9
Digital ISBN 978-1-5092-3560-5

Published in the United States of America

Dedication

For Rowan and everyone who loves him.

Special thanks to my family, to editor Dianne Rich, and to all the scientists and health care workers fighting to stop epilepsy every day.

Chapter One

Why are jungles always so damn hot?

This thought had been running through Allen's mind for the past hour as he set up his firing position. He didn't remember it being so hard when he was younger. But now that he was in his forties, a few pounds heavier, and years removed from being a super-soldier operator for hire, putting together a stealth deflection shield and high-powered pulse rifle was a real struggle. Doing it all in a steamy Central American jungle while squeezed into hardened body armor wasn't helping things either. As Allen wiped sweat from his brow yet again, his radio crackled in his ear.

"I can hear you breathing all the way over here," a young woman's voice said in a deadpan tone.

"Well, I'm almost done, so you don't have to hear me dying much longer," Allen replied. He finished the final connections on the stealth shield, which in its deactivated state was just a large oval frame with a thin layer of white pixel-film covering it, and moved on to adjust his rifle. "Are you done?" Allen asked.

"Been done for a while now," the voice said. "I started counting mosquitos until I thought I heard a bear. Then I realized it was you."

"Hilarious," Allen said with as much sarcasm as he could muster between heavy breaths.

"Like a bear with asthma," the young woman

1

continued, "having a really bad day."

Allen guided his pulse rifle onto its tripod mount. He checked the battery and confirmed it was fully charged, everything from its core power cells to its nano-battery molecular structure holding as much energy as possible. Satisfied with his weapon, Allen turned his attention back to the shield. He sat back and brushed dirt from the wrist of his left arm to reveal a digital control pad built into his armor.

"Now you see me…" he said as he pressed a key on his control pad, "now you don't." Allen saw a small flash of light from the shield before the frosted white film shifted and became transparent. He looked downhill through it as the activated pixel-film created a video window that displayed the jungle and river valley below. After stepping around to the opposite side of the shield and confirming that its camouflage projection system was blending it in with its surroundings, Allen crouched back behind it. "How do I look from there?" he asked.

"Like a bunch of nothing. You're good. Now we just hide here?" the woman asked.

"I wouldn't call it hiding," Allen replied. "I'd call it 'tactically waiting.' " Moving back to his pulse rifle, he pressed a small button on the side of the stock that activated a tiny pulse beam no more powerful than a laser pointer. Though weak, the green dot he saw on a nearby tree told him that the beam was passing through the shield and reassured him that his high-energy fire would do the same. It had been over seven years since he'd set up a one-way energy shield and thought it best to make sure his pulse fire would pass through instead of bouncing back into his face. Allen's radio crackled again.

"Did you and my dad 'tactically wait' a lot when you were younger?"

"On the good jobs, yeah," Allen replied. "C'mon, Haley, did you think your dad was going to let me take you out on your first mission to some run-and-gun firefight?"

"No," Haley replied. "But I also didn't know you usually just waited to massacre a bunch of people."

"People?" Allen scoffed. "They're a bunch of robots. Terrible, soulless mechs controlled by an evil dictator going village to village killing people."

"I meant other times."

"Other times, what? Other jobs?"

"Yeah. Other times you did this."

"I'd rather not go through my career mission-by-mission to see if each one passes the Haley Morality Test, thank you very much."

There was a long pause. Allen worried either he or Haley had gone too far but couldn't decide which one of them was to blame. He looked ahead to his right across the ridge to where Haley was dug in behind her own cloaking shield and pondered what to say next.

Finally, Haley broke the silence. "Just doesn't seem totally fair."

Allen slumped his shoulders. "Yeah, well, nothing feels very fair lately."

"Sorry...is Benjamin still in the hospital?" Haley asked sympathetically.

"The cold he caught is doing a number on him, so he's still on oxygen. Last I heard from Kelsey, anyway." Allen leaned his weight into the end of his rifle and stared off, imagining his son lying in a hospital bed connected to wires and oxygen tubes. Again.

"Sorry," Haley repeated. "But I thought insurance was cutting you off."

"They're still covering illness. For now, anyway. The other stuff..." Allen trailed off, the humidity sapping his will to discuss the intricacies of his son's insurance policy. He flinched as a mosquito bit him on the neck. After vainly slapping at it, Allen decided heat was less annoying than insects and pulled a cloth collar up on his armor before strapping on his helmet. "You sure you turned the signal on?" he asked.

"Turned it on twenty minutes ago. The mechs should be reading fifty refugees camped down by the river on their sensors," Haley said. "Honestly, who sends a squad of mech soldiers to kill innocent people?"

"Jerk dictators," Allen answered. He put his eye up to his rifle scope and scanned the trees and vines on the other side of the river. Then something changed in the air. The steady ambiance of insects and bird calls dropped away, replaced by rustling in the canopy from an unseen rush of animals passing by.

"They're coming," Allen told Haley. "Fire in bursts and watch for overheating. Aim at their waists. That's their weakest point, but a good shot to the chest can knock them down."

"Okay," Haley replied. There was a jump in her voice, a blend of nerves and excitement, just the way Allen had felt on his own first mission. As his eyes swept side to side across the river, he caught a faint sound of motors on the wind. Finally, the mechs stepped out from the jungle's shadowy curtain. Five dark shapes stopped and stood on the far riverbank. They were roughly modeled after humans, with two legs and two arms, but their sensors and cameras were clustered between their shoulders with additional cameras on the ends of their weapons.

"They don't have heads," Haley observed.

"No, they do not," Allen replied flatly, now serious.

"Or pulse weapons," Haley continued. "Looks like they're carrying standard automatics."

"Yeah, well, nowadays a single pulse weapon costs as much as all these mechs," Allen said. "Hold on until they cross the river and I give the order to fire."

They waited. The mechs stood there, making occasional fidgeting motions, searching for the dozens of refugees their sensors told them were there but that their cameras couldn't find. Then, a single mech jumped down from the bank and waded into the shallow, muddy water. Their movements were human-like and yet, not. Allen's skin crawled. After the first mech was halfway across the river, the other four made their way down, crossing in a fanning-out pattern. When they had nearly crossed the river, Allen heard Haley in his ear again.

"Now?" Haley asked.

"Keep watching the far bank," Allen told her.

"For what?"

"The rest of them."

The five mechs halted on the nearside bank, weapons drawn, turning slightly left and right looking for targets. Allen swallowed the anxiousness rising in his throat.

"How you doing?" Allen asked, as much to himself as his partner.

"I'm all right," Haley answered, her voice thinner

but steady.

"Any more on the far side?"

"Maybe…"

Allen waited. The mechs were still swaying back and forth with guns drawn, aiming up the hill in his general direction. Then they froze. The sudden absence of motor and servo sounds combined with the lack of animal noises made the jungle eerily quiet. Allen brought a hand to his mouth to dampen the relatively deafening volume of his own breathing.

Haley whispered over the radio, "There they are."

A second line of mechs emerged from the edge of the jungle on the far riverbank. About two dozen walked in a wide arc toward him and Haley, probably to cast a wide perimeter for attacking the fictitious refugees. The rear group of mechs entered the river and crossed without pausing while the forward mechs covered them, watching for an attack. When the rear mechs were about halfway across the river, Allen looked over at Haley's position. She was hidden behind her cloaking shield, but he imagined her at the ready waiting for his signal. She could do this, he reminded himself. Too late to turn back now.

"Okay, Haley," Allen said, raising his pulse rifle and taking aim at the nearest mech. He put his finger on the trigger and turned off the safety. "Fire."

Haley's pulse rifle erupted with bursts of pale green energy bolts firing at the mechs, taking out three before they could return fire. The remaining mechs fired blindly in the direction of their attacker. Every shot Haley fired would let the mechs home in closer on her position. Even behind the cloaking shield, she wouldn't last long once they all got a bead on her.

Which was why it was especially terrifying to Allen that, no matter what he did, his pulse rifle simply would not fire.

Haley couldn't help but notice. "Why the hell aren't you shooting?" she yelled.

"I don't know!" he shouted back. Allen looked down at his pulse rifle and the small display screen built into the side. It cycled between flashing ERROR and INTERFERENCE, though it failed to say in what way or from what. The mechs advanced on Haley's position, firing as they moved. Haley knocked out two more while Allen worked on his pulse rifle, each evaporating moment bringing the mechs closer to when they would inevitably split off to flank her.

"It says 'interference,' " Allen told Haley, his voice cracking with urgency.

"Is the wiring shielded?" Haley asked between bursts of fire.

"Shielded from what?"

"From *interference*!" Haley screamed. "Old pulse rifles could be jammed by some kind of, I don't know, jamming field thing! That's why the wiring on the new ones have special coatings!"

"Well, that wasn't an option when I bought this one," Allen said, throwing his pulse rifle to the ground in disgust.

"You're still using your old one?"

"As I explained, they are very expensive," Allen said. "I wasn't just going to toss it out." He lifted his arm to look at the control pad on his wrist. He toggled to a different status display, which also flashed INTERFERENCE. "Damnit," he said.

"Why are *you* swearing? I'm the one they're

shooting at," Haley yelled back.

"My signal to the charges is blocked, too."

"Your signal to the *what*?" Haley asked, fear creeping into her voice.

"I set up a line of explosives on our side of the riverbank," Allen explained. "This whole thing was to give you real-world practice, so if things got tricky I was just gonna blow up the mechs."

Haley had taken down two more of the mechs, but the rest were still closing in. They had quickened their pace, and Haley's shots grew more scarce as the mechs moved behind the cover of jungle growth.

"You could have blown them up this whole time?" Haley asked in disbelief.

"Well, apparently not, because I can't get a signal through to set them off." Allen's mind raced as the mechs split into two separate groups and began to come around Haley on either side. It was just a matter of time until she was surrounded. Allen looked to his wrist again and toggled his control pad to a new function screen, relieved to see that it had no notification of interference. "I'm going to get closer to the charges to set them off."

"And how exactly are you going to do that?"

"Well, you wanted a fair fight," Allen replied as he tapped an ACTIVATE option on his wrist.

"What does that mean?" Haley asked.

In response, Allen stood up from behind his cloaking shield. "Hey, death bots! Shoot at me!"

Allen dove downhill as the mechs obliged him by firing a barrage of bullets that shredded the vines and branches where he had stood a fraction of a second earlier. Shards of trees filled the air as he slid down the muddy bank. He struggled to get his feet under him until the trunk of a tree stopped his descent. After finding his footing, Allen continued down the steep hill, forced to run nearly sideways to keep his balance as heavy mud clung to his boots.

Allen looked to see how many mechs were coming after him. Most had taken the bait, but a small squad continued after Haley. Just as he turned to look back down the hill, a bullet caught him in the right shoulder, spinning him around. He landed on his back with his head downhill from his feet. Allen rolled onto his side and felt a numb buzz in his right shoulder where the bullet hit him. He checked his control pad again. The projectile shield he activated right before standing up and taunting the mechs was still active and working normally, though the hit had cost him some shield energy, dropping its charge to seventy-eight percent. He hoped it would be enough.

Allen scrambled back to his feet and continued down the hill, running from tree to tree, taking cover for random lengths of time to keep the mechs guessing what he'd do. His strategy had limited success. His right thigh flared from the pang of a bullet, and he almost lost his footing again. Another bullet caught him under his right arm in his rib cage. It knocked the wind out of him for a few steps, but he forced himself to keep running through the pain. He had to get closer to the line of charges strung together at the edge of the river where the water met the jungle. Every few paces, Allen glanced at his control pad to see if he could get a signal through the jamming to the main detonator. It was still coming up negative.

Twenty feet from the river, a bullet struck Allen's

right calf and knocked him off balance. He tumbled headfirst, still churning his legs trying to recover, and landed on his chest. He slid down the hill all the way to the riverbank, emerging from the jungle and falling into the shallow, muddy water. Looking up, Allen saw two mechs had broken away to try and cut him off. As they took aim at Allen, each abruptly blasted apart one after the other as Haley took them out. He glanced up the hill to see how she was doing, but a spray of gunfire forced Allen to dive into the filthy river and take cover behind a tangle of roots from a fallen tree.

Allen checked his control pad again. Finally, he had a signal to the charges. He tapped the ARM command. The display changed from green to red and a DETONATE button filled the screen. Allen took a peek over the tree roots to see how close the mechs were, but as soon as his head poked out from cover, bullets pummeled the tree. He ducked back down and realized he needed someone else's eyes.

"Haley? You okay?" Allen asked over the radio.

"Better than you," she yelled. "There's only two mechs coming at me, but they're moving from tree to tree and I can't get a clear shot."

"I need you to say when the mechs over here are all within ten yards of me."

"I see about half wading into the water to get a better shot at you. The rest are on their way down the hill—"

Haley's voice was cut off by incoming gunfire. The sound of her returning fire was the last thing Allen heard before the radio signal automatically muted itself. It was just as well. Better to let Haley focus on her problem while he figured a way out of his.

Some of the mechs had fanned out to flank him. More were on their way. The clock was ticking. And Allen had no weapon. Other than the string of six explosive charges buried along the river, of course. On top of it all, he was still really hot. Simply being in the jungle was bad enough, but running through the thick air took his discomfort to a whole new level of awful. And now he was soaking wet. These were not things he missed from his younger days of work. He longed to be able to lay in a pool all day, forget about his broken weapons, his son's medical problems and expensive treatments, and just float in the sun.

Then, Allen realized that was exactly what he had to do.

"Haley?" Allen called on the radio. "When they're all in range, just scream at me." Allen didn't wait to hear her response. Instead, he took a deep breath, lay face down in the water, and pushed himself out into the river with his toes.

The hardest part wasn't being pelted with bullets—the projectile shield took care of most of that. The hardest part was not reacting in any way as the bullets hit him like a thousand tiny hammers. Fortunately for Allen, mechs were not ones to waste bullets on what they perceived to be a dead body. Just as he couldn't bear the pain any longer, the firing stopped. Now all he had to worry about was drowning.

The sounds of the world came through the water with otherworldly distortion. Under the murky river, the noise of servo motors blended with splashes from the mechs walking toward Allen. Then another set joined the chorus, farther off. And finally a third set. Together, they got closer. And closer.

11

A new sound split its way through the throbbing noise headed for Allen, like something between a shrieking cat and an agitated dolphin. At last, the sound Allen had been waiting for.

Hearing Haley's screams underwater, Allen reached his arms up over his head and pressed a finger to his control pad to activate the explosives. The blast blew a surge of water toward him, pushing him clear across to the far riverbank. After rolling onto his back, he was immediately forced to dodge a spattering of metal robotic pieces falling from the sky. On the far shore where the charges had been, vines had caught fire and brackish water quickly rushed in to fill a series of large craters.

Allen's head rang and his body was numb from bullet strikes. Removing his helmet, Allen was fairly certain he was about to throw up. A moment later, his suspicions were confirmed. After emptying his lunch into the river, Allen remembered the two mechs still headed for Haley.

"Haley," Allen croaked, looking up the hill toward her position. "What's happening?"

"The mechs are down," Haley replied. "I'm okay." Allen saw movement far up the hill, but it wasn't until Haley pulled off her camouflage helmet to reveal a head of black hair that Allen clearly made her out. "The explosion knocked out so many of the others, they must have calculated they needed to retreat and they ran off. So I shot them in the back."

"Doesn't seem very fair," Allen said.

"Well, after watching you fall down a hill and get pummeled with bullets, I now agree that being unfair is the way to go."

"Glad to hear it," Allen said as he turned his helmet over in his hands. It looked old to him now. As did his body armor. He thought leaving them in storage over the years meant they wouldn't age. But no matter how pristine their condition was, the world had still moved ahead, and being out-of-date was just as bad as being worn out. If Allen was going to keep doing this as a way to earn money and help his son, he needed to upgrade.

"At least the projectile shield held up," Allen said out loud to himself. He looked at his control pad and read that the projectile shield had survived with two percent energy remaining. Then, as he watched, it flashed ERROR, REPLACE UNIT over and over. "Fine, control pad, I will," he promised his expired gear. "I will."

Chapter Two

"Next stop, Medical District: Children's Hospital."
Kelsey was tired of this train station. She was tired
of cramming into the train with all the people going to
work, going downtown to sightsee, going out on dates,
or going to do any other normal things she herself
couldn't do because she was on her way to the hospital
again.

As the train slowed, Kelsey stood and headed for
the doors. After they opened, she walked out and
passed a pregnant woman on the platform waiting to
board. Kelsey thought back to her own pregnancy and
how normal it had been. She thought back on all the
firsts: the first time coming home, the first night getting
up to breastfeed, the first bath, the first time her baby
took a bottle. She was excited for the woman. Having
only the normal responsibilities of parenting would feel
like a vacation to her now, but Kelsey tried not to dwell
on self-pity. Though she allowed herself to envy the
woman just a little.

At the top of a set of escalators from the train
platform, Kelsey came to the hub of Chicago's Medical
District Complex. The children's hospital was the
centerpiece of a massive collection of buildings,
including a general hospital, veterans' hospital,
women's hospital, and various clinics and offices. After
the collapse of the national economy when the dollar

was no longer seen as a stable form of currency, skyrocketing inflation sent most traditional hospitals into bankruptcy. Especially after government health insurance went broke. Thus, corporations stepped in with their freshly minted International Financial Units to jockey for ways to project a warm feeling of caring to the people of Chicago. With that goal in mind, it seemed like a smart idea to put the children's hospital at the center of things.

Kelsey made her way through the two-story archway that served as the main entrance. Carved into the archway were scenes of physicians performing kind, doctorly tasks for children, like bandaging broken arms, using tongue depressors to peer down throats, checking heartbeats, and so on. The easy stuff. No carvings of the pediatric intensive care unit. No scenes in the epilepsy center showing brainwave patterns causing brain damage. Nothing of what Kelsey and Allen had experienced for the past two years.

Kelsey took her place at the end of the line to check in through security. It was long that morning. Kelsey sometimes forgot that even typical kids had to go to the doctor. She stood patiently and fell into a daze staring at the exotic fish tank built into the wall until she noticed a check-in attendant waving at her from the head of the line.

It was Monica, one of the regular attendants and the only one Kelsey knew by name. Then again, Monica was the only one who ever introduced herself. After seeing Kelsey come through more times than she could count, Monica explained that exchanging names only seemed proper.

Kelsey walked over as Monica held out a security

badge. "Here you go, dear," Monica said. "Say 'hi' to beautiful Benjamin for me."

Kelsey took the badge with a smile. "Thank you, I will." After briefly flashing the disposable badge to a security guard, she loaded into a packed elevator and hit the button for the ninth floor out of habit without thinking. It was very much like her workday routine had been once upon a time. Take the train downtown, maybe grab a coffee before getting to the office, scan a badge through a turnstile, then huddle inside a cramped elevator in silence. In her previous life, that would have been followed by highly complex computer programming and software development. Now her routine led her to highly complex medical problems for her two-year-old son.

At the ninth floor, Kelsey got out and walked through the pediatric intensive care unit. She passed identical room after room with monitors displaying vital signs, televisions mounted on the wall playing movies, and parents looking nervous or just bored waiting for updates. At least, those were the scenes in the rooms she could actually see into. In others, she caught the sounds of wailing behind closed curtains, or heated arguments between parents and administrative staff members over coverage and expenses. It was better not to think about the latter rooms. Things were stressful enough.

Kelsey reached Benjamin's room and walked inside. A nursing assistant that Kelsey swore had to be a teenager was using a stethoscope to check his heart rate. She looked up as Kelsey walked in.

"Hi," the nurse whispered. "He's still sleeping. I'm just checking his vitals. Did you get everything you needed from home?"

"I just took a shower and changed my clothes," Kelsey replied. "I'd spent two days in the same outfit, couldn't wait any longer."

"Oh good," said the nurse. "Well, the doctors will be rounding in a couple of hours. Your little guy's lungs sound a lot better, oxygen levels look stable. Fingers crossed that he'll be going home today."

"Yeah, that's what I'm hoping, too," Kelsey said, sitting on the convertible couch/bed near the window. "My husband is out of town, so it will be nice to bring Benjamin home."

"Is he out of town for work?" the nurse asked.

"Yes. It was a bit of a last-minute trip," Kelsey said.

"What kind of work does he do?"

"Consulting," Kelsey answered. Luckily the nurse didn't ask any follow-up questions. Being a mercenary still existed in a bit of a legal gray area. But between the multiple loopholes corporations insisted on having for private military operations and thin law enforcement budgets, any prosecution was virtually nonexistent. All the same, explaining that Allen had to earn high-risk money because their insurance would soon consider Benjamin too difficult to treat wasn't an appropriate subject for small talk.

The nurse finished confirming Benjamin's vital signs. "Need anything else?" she asked.

"Do you know if Doctor Ellis is stopping by today? She's Benjamin's neurologist," Kelsey explained. "Someone told me she would visit to work on our insurance appeal, but that was two days ago. We still haven't seen her."

"Oh," the nursing assistant replied, reacting with hesitation. "Yes, I've seen her on the floor. I'll ask somebody about it."

"Thanks," Kelsey said. "Somebody" never got back to her the last time she asked.

After the nursing assistant left, Kelsey walked over to the bed to say good morning to her son. Benjamin's hair was matted down from lying in bed twenty-four hours a day, and even though his thumb was out of his mouth, it still stuck out from his balled fist resting on the pillow. The fact that the thumb was out of his mouth told Kelsey he was fast asleep. As soon as Benjamin woke up, the thumb would swiftly return.

Kelsey grabbed Benjamin's blanket from around his feet and pulled it over his body up to his shoulders. As she finished, he let out a heavy sigh. Kelsey stood frozen until he settled again, then sat on the vinyl guest couch under the window and looked out over downtown. She was tired of being in the hospital. But even worse, she was tired of Benjamin's need to be there.

Thinking back, she remembered when it hadn't always been like this. When Benjamin was born, everything went as expected. Other than him having a full head of hair. She didn't see that coming. Benjamin did everything like the parenting books said he would until he was about six months old and couldn't roll onto his belly like the developmental checklist predicted. His pediatrician said every child was different, give him time. By eight months, Benjamin hadn't learned to sit. Again, they were told to give him time. Fortunately, Benjamin continued to develop in other ways. He learned to eat like other kids, making a typically terrible mess. He giggled when his belly was tickled and laughed out loud when he was bounced on Allen's knee.

Then, at ten months, the seizures began.

Back then, Kelsey and Allen were both working, she writing software for large infrastructure projects and Allen stuck in middle-management at a logistics company. Years of working as an international soldier of fortune apparently made Allen good at getting freight and equipment from one place to another. It was a bad economy and their salaries were far lower than they used to be, but they felt lucky to earn enough to live and still afford daycare. It was actually there, at daycare, that the seizures first started.

When Kelsey picked up Benjamin that day, the infant teacher said he had been having some odd head movements. His head thrust ahead and down a few times, ten or twenty seconds apart, over the course of a few minutes. It didn't seem voluntary, she said. Later at home, Benjamin did it in front of Kelsey and Allen. Benjamin cried as he fought it, as if someone else was forcing his body to move. Kelsey and Allen rushed to the emergency room.

In the waiting area of the ER, Benjamin had the movements again, that time throwing his arms out as well as thrusting his head forward. It must be some kind of seizure, though neither Kelsey or Allen had heard of that type before. They recorded the seizures on their phones, and when at long last they were taken back to meet with a pediatrician, they showed her the video. The doctor immediately admitted Benjamin to the epilepsy unit. The sudden intensity in the way everyone cared for Benjamin after that point was frightening. In the back of their minds, Kelsey and Allen had still held out hope that their worries would be brushed aside and they would all go home with a simple prescription. Instead, Benjamin was brought to a hospital room and, kicking and screaming, had dozens of wires pasted to his head to monitor his brainwaves. First for an hour. Then two. Then three. Until a final diagnosis was confirmed.

When the doctors first mentioned "Infantile Spasms," it sounded like something harmless, on the same level as fussy eating or colic. Instead, the spasms Benjamin had were a type of seizure caused by a much bigger problem. His brainwaves were chaotic and wild, with too many random discharges and activity. The connections in Benjamin's brain that were supposed to let him learn and develop like every other child were being damaged, the likely cause for his delay in learning to sit up. If not treated, the intense activity would begin wiping away the skills and abilities he had already learned, not to mention prevent him from learning new ones. Even within the range of epilepsy, this was at the bad end.

And so began a parade of intense treatments. High-dose steroid injections. Medications that could cause liver failure or blindness. A high-fat diet that threatened to destroy his kidneys. When those didn't work, combinations of all three were tried. In the early weeks of treatment, Benjamin could still smile and laugh. Until he didn't anymore. The steroids made him cranky, then later medications made him sleepy. Things would seem to get better, then they would get worse, back and forth. Benjamin slowly slipped behind. Now two-and-a-half years old, he still couldn't sit. He couldn't speak.

Where once Benjamin could eat finger food by himself, he now had to be fed puree with a spoon. His already low muscle tone grew even weaker, lacking the strength to cough mucus from his lungs when he got sick. Simple colds led to multiple hospitalizations throughout the year.

Kelsey and Allen both quickly ran out of time-off at work. With her making more than he did, Allen quit his job to stay home. But Benjamin didn't get better, and treatment co-pays got more expensive. With fewer projects at work, Kelsey's salary was cut even more. More and more layoffs swept through her company. When Kelsey and Allen got married, they'd decided it was time for a quiet life. That meant Allen being home, safe, and not traveling around the world fighting dangerous people in foreign countries. But with mounting medical bills and Kelsey's layoff fears soon confirmed, their plans were forced to change.

A gentle knock on the hospital room door interrupted Kelsey's wandering thoughts. The physician in charge of Benjamin's epilepsy treatment, Doctor Ellis, stood in the doorway. Kelsey stood to greet her, but the doctor waved her to sit back down as she entered the room and moved the guest chair closer to Kelsey before sitting down.

"How are you?" Ellis asked in a mumble, looking at her feet. She took a breath and sighed before looking Kelsey in the eyes as if digging deep to find the will to meet her gaze.

"What's wrong?" Kelsey asked.

"Nothing has changed with Benjamin," Ellis assured her. A ring of creases and puffiness hung around the doctor's eyes.

"Then what is it?" Kelsey replied.

"The hospital will be sending a letter out," Ellis said, "but I wanted to let a few people know ahead of time. Um…" she stammered, looking around the room trying to find the words. "Did I ever tell you I was actually born in Sweden?"

Kelsey blinked. "What?"

"My dad is from there," she explained. " 'Ellis' is my married name. I grew up an Eriksson."

"The hospital is sending out a letter to explain that your maiden name was Eriksson?" Kelsey asked.

"No, I'm sorry," Ellis answered, rubbing her forehead. "This is the third time I've had to explain this, and I've failed horribly every time."

"Just say what's going on," Kelsey demanded.

"I'm leaving," Ellis said. "I'm here through the end of the month. The hospital will let you know who your new epileptologist will be."

Kelsey swayed and grabbed the edge of the couch for balance. "But…why?"

"We're just not surviving anymore," Ellis said. "My family, on my salary, that is. I'm the only one working, but the hospital…" Ellis stopped herself. "All I can say is, with cutbacks in insurance payments to the hospital, salaries have been cut as well."

"So you're moving to Sweden," Kelsey finished for her.

"I'm sure whoever gets assigned to Benjamin will give him excellent care," Ellis said with practiced ease.

"But he's still having seizures," Kelsey argued. "And you talked about new medicine. So what about our HAPA appeal? Would the new doctor help us with that?" Kelsey took in air with quick, shallow breaths.

Doctor Ellis looked down to the floor again at Kelsey's mention of the HAPA appeal. The euphemistically-named Healthcare Assurance and Preservation Act was designed to help private insurers cover more people once everyone who was on public insurance had lost coverage. To do that, insurance companies needed the government to pave the way to prevent litigation for their planned coverage stipulations, of which there were many. The most pressing stipulation to Kelsey and Allen was the restriction that any person with a rare medical problem that could not be controlled after three different treatment plans would lose coverage for any further attempts. Benjamin was on his third treatment plan, with no clear benefits.

"I understand," Ellis said, still dodging Kelsey's gaze. "I think, for now, we can keep his medicine where it is until Benjamin gets a new physician."

"You said every day with these seizures costs him IQ points," Kelsey said in a raised voice. "But now it's okay to wait for the next doctor?"

"I feel, in the aggregate, it's the safer course," Ellis answered. She had been Benjamin's doctor for well over a year but now talked as if speaking to a stranger.

Kelsey squirmed in her seat. Each fresh question and argument trickled to a mumble before they were halfway out of her mouth. Her shoulders dropped in defeat. "Okay then," she simply said.

Ellis got up and walked out of the room, wishing Kelsey and Benjamin luck on the way out. The sound barely registered as a murmur through the pounding of blood in Kelsey's ears. It had been over a year and a half since Benjamin's diagnosis. A year and a half. And after all that time, Doctor Ellis was still on the hunt for drugs that might stop his seizures, despite the insurance limitations. Now, with a new doctor, it was like starting over again.

Kelsey looked up at the clock on the wall. It had only been fifteen minutes since she'd come in the room. She hadn't expected her day to be ruined until well after noon.

She took her phone out of her pocket and pulled up Allen's number. She had to tell him about Doctor Ellis leaving. The news of it felt like a weight on her shoulders that she needed help carrying. It wasn't until she started putting the call through that she remembered he was on a mission. He said it would be a simple ambush against early-model mech soldiers, no sweat. She hoped he had been right.

Chapter Three

They couldn't pick us up any closer?

Haley couldn't get over the fact that, with cloaked aerial hovercrafts existing in the world, their client insisted on picking her and Allen up over five miles away from where they fought the mechs in the jungle.

"Exactly how much farther do we need to lug this stuff?" Haley asked as she and Allen trudged through the jungle hauling gear on their backs, both still sweltering in their body armor.

"It's not much more. Besides, it builds character," Allen said.

"Ugh, you're such a dad," Haley replied.

"Yeah, yeah," Allen responded. "Wait, stop, oh crap."

Haley spun around as fast as she dared with her heavy gear, already reaching for her weapon. "What?"

"I forgot to put on my stupid Healthy Helper," Allen answered, strapping a small biometric tracking device to his wrist.

"If you hate it, why do you use it?"

"I have to if I want to keep our insurance," Allen grumbled. "Now I won't get credit for all the walking we did."

Shortly after Allen tightened the wristband on the Healthy Helper, an artificial voice spoke to him in a soothing tone. "Allen, you seem quite exerted. Be sure to consult your doctor before starting new activities."

"Uh-huh," Allen said to the device, grabbing the shoulder straps of his gear and moving forward.

"May I suggest other more age-appropriate exercises?" the tracker asked.

"No," Allen growled.

Haley smiled. "See, your tracker doesn't think we should walk either." She turned and moved slowly through a small stream. She had almost slipped twice on the soft ground and was just one bad step away from lying on her back like a flipped-over turtle.

"It's necessary," Allen said behind her. "Clients need to be able to deny they had anything to do with us, which means we go in and out on our own."

"Maybe next time we can 'go in and out on our own' with some kind of vehicle," Haley said over her shoulder.

"Sure thing. Right after I pay off the medical bills, I'll pick up something cheap like a luxury air yacht. We can even sleep while it takes us out."

"Fine by me," Haley replied. "If it serves drinks, that would be even better."

"Well, that I can help you with," Allen said. Haley turned and looked back at him with a raised eyebrow, but he only gestured ahead in the direction they were walking. Haley took slow, deliberate steps and leaned to see around a tangle of vines. Ahead, as if appearing from thin air, stood a man wearing a white short-sleeved shirt and matching shorts. He held a serving tray with two drink glasses.

The man smiled as they approached and stepped forward to present the drinks. Haley picked up a glass. It was ice cold and covered with condensation from the jungle heat. She looked the server in the eye searching for an explanation, but he only smiled and bowed his head in silence. She held the drink up to her nose. It smelled like cucumber.

"The nice man didn't come to the jungle with drinks to poison you, Haley," Allen said, catching up. He grabbed the other drink and brought it to his mouth in a single motion. After guzzling it down, he returned the empty glass to the tray.

Both the server and Allen watched Haley closely as she took an exploratory sip. The coolness of the water alone was enough to convince her that even if it was poisonous, it was still worth drinking. Once Haley finished and returned the glass, the server turned and began walking away.

Allen immediately followed. "Come on," he said, as if walking into his own kitchen instead of after some silent jungle beverage elf. Still, Haley figured it best to follow along.

The trio walked down a path cut into the thick jungle. Because there was a slight curve to the path, Haley's view was still filled with jungle growth stretching up toward the sun, but she caught the sound of splashing water wafting in the air. A few steps later, muffled voices seemed to come from both sides of her. The path finally broke through the dense rainforest and, an instant later, Haley collided into a different server carrying a tray full of frozen daiquiris.

Tall glasses of frosty red, white, yellow, and blue smashed across the tiled pool deck. The unfortunate server carrying them spun from the impact before tripping on a deck chair and crashing to the ground as well.

"Oh my God, I'm so sorry," Haley said, rushing to the fallen server. She repeated her apologies as she helped untangle him from the crumpled chair. Once he was back on his feet, the fallen server simply smiled and waved away her concern as he began cleaning the destroyed daiquiris. Haley looked around at the dozens of disapproving scowls from the resort guests. They were not the kind of guests she remembered seeing at the family resorts she visited as a kid. These were rich-people guests. Their furrowed brows and piercing go-away gazes let her know that they were part of a class she was not a member of. She instantly hated them all.

"Don't worry about them," a stranger's voice said to her. "Personally, I'm glad for the excitement." Haley turned toward the voice to find a plump older man with white hair, light blue shorts, and a drink in his hand. What she did not see on him was a shirt. Before Haley could suggest for everyone's sake that he put one on, Allen stepped in.

"Mister Richter," Allen said, reaching to shake the man's hand. "Sorry for the dramatic entrance."

"Like I said, don't be," Richter replied, giving Allen's hand a crisp, well-practiced shake. "A little drama breaks up the day." Richter eyed up Allen, who was still covered in dried river mud. "You look a little messier than you used to after a mission."

Allen laughed. "Yeah, well, we had a little excitement of our own."

"His equipment wasn't shielded against jamming," Haley blurted out. Allen glared at her, virtually stabbing her in the face with his eyes.

Richter raised his eyebrows. "Your pulse weapons stopped working?"

"Yeah, but that's what explosives are for," Allen replied.

The concern on Richter's face melted as he began to laugh. "Well, the best backup weapon is a bigger weapon," he said, chuckling at his own joke. It made his belly bounce in disturbing ways.

Richter motioned for them to sit down at a nearby table. After removing the gear from their backs, Allen and Haley fell heavily into their seats. As soon as they sat, a servant appeared out of nowhere. Richter took the lead.

"A pitcher of water, a refill on my vodka and soda, and, I don't know, a couple of those tall fruity drinks for these two. The ones with the pineapple spears sticking out," Richter ordered without even looking at the servant. No "please," no "thank you," no small talk. With such a high price and exclusive clientele, the resort came with the option of leaving all feigned consideration of others at the door. Richter turned to Allen as the servant left.

"Mission summary, Mister Moran," Richter said.

"Yes, sir. We lured a squad of sentry mechs to our location. Operator Eckland here laid down fire from her position while I maneuvered toward the river bank and detonated explosive charges. In all, thirty-two mechs confirmed destroyed."

"Hot damn," said a satisfied Richter. "If you didn't look so filthy, Allen, I'd say it was a walk in the park. This is fantastic."

"I'm glad we could help," Allen said.

"You called for a job at just the right time, Allen. It was great to use you again." Richter finished his drink before continuing. "The way this Vargas guy keeps getting uppity, there may even be steady work in it for you."

"Vargas…that's the dictator?" Haley asked.

"Yeah, he's a real piece of work," Richter answered, shaking his head. "We come in here, my company that is, we set up a telecom network, power grid, food supply chain, and everything. All with the understanding that he gets a little personal income in exchange for not rocking the boat. And then he rocks the hell out of the boat with this ethnic cleansing crap."

"Yeah, people running for their lives can't spend money," Haley said sarcastically.

"Exactly!" Richter bellowed, oblivious to Haley's tone. "They can't gas their cars or watch TV or text or do anything. And then the Europeans start talking about humanitarian intervention, and we all know that's just code for a slow-burn war that takes forever. You two really got us out of a pickle. Those mechs were a little older but still expensive for Vargas. He should at least answer our phone calls now." Richter laughed again at his good fortune before getting distracted by something blinking on Allen's wrist. "Speaking of…"

Allen followed Richter's gaze to his control panel where a notification flashed with an incoming call. He fished the handset from a pocket on his arm. "Sorry," Allen said, "it's Kelsey. I better take it." Allen walked away, only answering the call when he was well out of earshot.

Richter and Haley looked at each other across the table. Haley tried to conjure up some small talk but was too distracted by Richter's unpleasant shirtlessness. Thankfully, Richter spoke first.

"How's the boy?" he asked.

Haley didn't understand. "Who?"

"You know," Richter said, nodding in Allen's direction. "His son."

"Oh, *Benjamin*," Haley stressed. "I'm not sure. He's back in the hospital, caught a cold."

"He's in the hospital for a cold?" Richter said with disbelief. "Good lord, that's shitty."

The servant returned with drinks. He placed the water pitcher down at the center of the table, the vodka and soda in front of Richter, and the most elaborate tropical drink Haley had ever seen right in front of her face. The virtual fruit basket of multicolored spears jutting out from the top of the glass made the blended frozen drink inside seem more like an afterthought. Haley inspected the fruit, planning her eating strategy as she spoke. "Why don't you ask Allen yourself?"

"No, no, that's not a good idea," Richter replied.

"Why not?"

"When a man retires from this business, he only comes back because he's desperate," Richter said. He took a sip of his drink, then continued. "Some miss the thrill, some can't make it in the regular world, whatever. But desperate to earn money for your sick son? That hurts in ways I can't even imagine. I'm not going to bring it up. Allen deserves to keep his pride."

Haley studied her drink and decided to try a piece of watermelon while she processed Richter's comment. Allen wasn't ashamed of his son—he talked about Benjamin all the time. But maybe "ashamed" wasn't what Richter meant. With so many ways to injure male pride, it was difficult to know for sure what Richter was talking about. "I think the fact that his insurance is going to cut off any new treatments is his biggest concern now."

"Right, right. 'To preserve assets for those most likely to benefit, while fulfilling shareholder obligations,' as the law says." Richter shook his head. "The insurance guys make Vargas look like a saint." Then, out of nowhere, Richter asked, "How's your dad?"

"What?" Haley replied, pink chunks of watermelon flying from her mouth.

"Your dad," Richter repeated. "I knew him back when he and Allen were doing this gig together. Before your dad's accident, obviously."

"Right, sure, that makes sense," Haley said. "I just didn't think…"

"That I knew who you were?" Richter said with a smirk. "Of course I do. I don't hire people without knowing who they are. Allen told me your name, I recognized your last name, and put two and two together. Even before the background check."

"Background check? I didn't know being a gun-for-hire operator had a formal HR process."

"Well, it's more of a private investigation than a background check," Richter conceded. "A lot of violent crazies try to get into this business."

"Good to know you've decided I'm not violent and crazy," Haley replied.

"Well, you're violent and thoughtful. Personal combat training, international studies major, a hobby in weapons modifications. Very promising." Richter took another swig from his drink, keeping his gaze on Haley. The judgement of this half-naked older man, even if it was only about her background and education, made her skin crawl. "So, like I asked, how's Daryl?"

"Dad's okay. Stays around the house. Takes odd jobs here and there, mostly making custom equipment."

"Good. Crazy thing, to blast his way out of hotspots around the world just to have a drunk driver put him in a wheelchair." Richter shook his head.

"I'm happy to still have him around, wheelchair or not," Haley told him. The accident had taken a lot away from her dad. But between him being away most of the time when she was little and her parents' eventual divorce, getting her dad back in her life as a teenager had been for the better. There was a lot to appreciate about that.

Haley moved on to a melon spear, hoping Richter wouldn't ask her any more questions while she had food in her mouth. He inhaled sharply and was about to disappoint her by speaking again when Allen reappeared at the table.

"Sorry for that," Allen said. He somehow looked even more haggard than he did when he'd left.

"Everything okay on the home front?" Richter asked.

"We'd better move things along," Allen answered.

"Yes, yes, no need to keep you waiting," Richter said, gesturing to a servant behind the bar. The servant nodded and came over to the table with a tablet device, placing it in front of Richter before moving a few steps away to stand in waiting.

Haley looked at the screen of the tablet. It read CONFIRM TRANSFER with all three of their names displayed below it. Allen stepped closer and put his thumb against the screen. Richter did the same.

"I need your thumb, dear," said Richter with a smirk. "It doesn't work until we all do it together."

"Why together?" Haley asked.

"Because I don't pay anyone unless they come back alive," Richter said.

"And I don't trust anyone to pay me later," Allen added. Once Haley put her thumb on the tablet, the onscreen text changed to read PAYMENT CONFIRMED.

Richter handed the tablet back to the servant, stood, then extended his hand to Allen. "A driver out front will take you to the airport."

Allen shook Richter's hand. "Thanks, appreciate it."

"Stay safe, you two," Richter said. "At least until I need you again."

After Richter walked off, Haley stood as well, expecting that she and Allen would head straight for the car. But to her surprise, Allen sat down. "We're not going?" she asked.

"I'm going to drink this drink," Allen said. "Then we go. Unless you're in a hurry to spend seven hours bouncing around a cargo plane." Allen took his beverage from the table, leaned back in his chair, and took a long drink from his straw.

"Everything okay?" she asked him.

Allen swallowed hard before answering. "I just need to catch a break," he said, shaking his head. "Just need something to change."

As Allen took another drink, Haley considered asking more but decided against it. Allen didn't look to be in a talkative mood, and she figured there wasn't much she could say to help anyway. Besides, sipping an expensive tropical drink with no small talk sounded like a good idea to her, too.

Chapter Four

Damn rich people and their fancy drinks...

Allen woke with a jolt as the plane touched down in Chicago. He was greeted to consciousness with a splitting headache. As bright runway lights broke up the nighttime blackness out the window, he reached up to massage his temples until a different pain diverted them to his neck instead. He had slept strapped upright into a no-frills jumpseat mounted to the wall outside the cockpit, leaving his head to hang straight down to his chest for the entire flight. Allen let out a groan as the plane came to a stop inside a cargo hangar.

"Well, you look terrible," Haley said, unbuckling herself from a seat across the aisle.

"I didn't realize how much tequila was in that drink," Allen croaked while trying to rub the misery from his eyes.

"Mezcal," Haley corrected him.

"What's the difference?" Allen asked.

"Mezcal is the one with the worm in the bottle," Haley responded.

"I don't think a worm did this to me," Allen said, wincing as he released his seat harness and stood. He pulled out his phone to check the time and add up the hours of sleep he might still catch at home, but the battery was dead. Maybe there would be more time for rest before the work of fatherhood began when

Benjamin woke up. He and Kelsey should have left the hospital by now.

Allen and Haley walked out of the plane and down a set of wheeled stairs. Squinting from the bright lights of the cargo hangar, Allen stumbled his way behind Haley into a large black SUV that sat waiting for them. Once the driver and a crew member loaded their gear from the plane into the vehicle, they were driven out of the hangar and onto the freeway toward the city. Allen's stomach protested the motion of the car, and he forced himself to look straight ahead through the windshield to avoid car sickness.

"Any other jobs lined up?" Haley asked after some time.

"Not yet," Allen said. "I've been reaching out to old contacts, but only a couple replied. Though most were never very chatty to begin with. The best I can do is let them know I'm back." Not having another job right away was fine with Allen. He'd learned a lot from this mission. Even if he hadn't been hurting from his deceptively strong drink, his body was still feeling the physical tolls of the job. He would need some time to recover, not to mention hit the treadmill. And there was still the issue of his outdated equipment. Going back to mercenary work was turning out to be a much more complicated plan than he originally thought.

Allen and Haley rode in silence the rest of the drive into the city until they reached Haley's apartment. As the car pulled up to the Chinese restaurant Haley lived above, the street lit up with flashes of sparks from an elevated train passing by. The noise of it all was like a knife to Allen's temple.

Haley opened her door and Allen called to her. "In

a couple days," he said, "let's meet up at your dad's place. Maybe ask him to start thinking of some new gear for me. I guess I'm ready for some updates."

"Okay," Haley responded.

"And Haley," Allen added, leaning toward her as she was about to close the door.

"What?"

"When you tell your dad about the mission, maybe downplay the amount of…I don't want to say danger you were in but, maybe like, the peril of the situation."

Haley reacted with a confused yet thoughtful expression, as if Allen had thrown an algebra problem at her and she was trying to solve it without understanding why.

"Please?" Allen pleaded.

"Sure, no problem," Haley told him before quickly closing the door. After she retrieved her gear from the back, the driver put the vehicle in gear.

"Let's wait until she's inside," Allen told him. The driver complied and put the vehicle back into park. The weight of what had almost gone wrong in the jungle still clung heavily on Allen. It was a big deal to him that Daryl had asked him to take on his daughter as a partner. No doubt she had begged Daryl to let her try the business as badly as Allen had begged Daryl when Allen was her age. It also didn't hurt matters that Allen was in dire need of a partner at the time. And although Haley was far more capable than Allen remembered being at her age, Daryl still expected Allen to protect her, whether it was chauvinistic or not. So even though she could bludgeon any attacker to within an inch of his life without breaking a sweat, Allen sat in the car until Haley unlocked the street level door to the stairs of her apartment and went inside.

The driver put the car back into gear and pulled away. For the rest of the ride, Allen alternated between fighting fatigue and battling nausea.

His Healthy Helper was all too eager to help. "Allen, you seem ill at ease. Perhaps you can make time to meditate or find shapes in the clouds and journal about them."

When the vehicle finally pulled in front of his condo building, Allen popped open his door for fresh air before it came to a complete stop. The drive home was part of the payment from Richter for the job but getting his gear into the house was not. Allen built up a clammy sweat transferring his gear from the back of the vehicle to the curb, and the very moment he closed the hatch, the driver pulled away. Allen walked into the building like a teenager sneaking home after curfew, making his way slowly up the stairs to his unit with gear in each hand. After getting to the second floor, he turned, set his gear down as gently as he could, tapped in a code to unlock the door, and entered his home.

Stepping into the small entryway, Allen put the cases inside the door before walking the short distance to the living room and slumping into his reclining chair. He sat motionless and looked around the room. There were toys and therapy gear strewn around the floor by the television. The dining room table had papers on it, probably discharge instructions from the hospital. The only thing resembling food in the kitchen was an empty bread bag and a couple of paper coffee cups on the counter. With Kelsey and Benjamin having spent most of their time in the hospital, the condo looked much like it did when Allen left, making it feel like he'd only been gone for a few hours.

Allen struggled from the chair to his feet to seek the proper respite of his comfortable bed. On his way to the bedroom, he filled a glass with water and drank it all while standing at the sink before continuing down the hall, removing and dropping pieces of his outfit as he went. He stopped at the door to Benjamin's room and looked in. His son was asleep. Allen sneaked into the room, holding his breath to be even quieter and not wake him. Other than a bandage on his hand where the IV had been placed, you wouldn't know anything was different about him. He looked like any typical sleepy boy. Allen yawned, then left the room. He had his own sleep to catch up on.

In the master bedroom, Kelsey lay wrapped with the entire blanket around her. Allen saw no way to claim his own piece of it without waking her, so after removing the rest of his armor down to his underclothes and pulling his phone from his pocket, Allen tried his best to enter the bed like a ghost and settle in, blanket-less, next to his wife. He put his phone on the nightstand where it immediately began to draw power from the wireless charging surface. Allen took a deep breath, rolled to his side, and began to drift off when Kelsey's voice broke through the silence.

"How was the trip back?" she asked, not bothering to roll over to face him.

"I slept through the flight," Allen said.

"Did you leave your stuff in the entryway?" Kelsey asked.

"Yeah, why?" Allen replied.

"Physical therapist is coming tomorrow morning. Probably shouldn't have weapons and explosives in the living room."

"I used up all the explosives," Allen said through another yawn.

"Still," Kelsey mumbled.

Allen could move his gear in the morning. Now was the time for slumber. He grabbed the end of the blanket and tugged it toward him. Kelsey grumbled and pulled some blanket from underneath her while Allen took up the slack to cover himself. He had just started drifting off again when his freshly revived phone lit up. Out of habit, he reached out, tilted the phone toward him, and checked for any notifications from his encrypted inbox. To his surprise, he had indeed received a message, but when he tried to read it, his eyes refused to bring it into focus. Giving up, Allen returned his phone to the nightstand and fell asleep with his hand still reaching out.

****

Allen woke to the sound of cheering. He sat up in bed and was greeted by a chorus of cracking joints. Grimacing from sore muscles throughout his body, he changed into a fresh T-shirt and a pair of sweatpants, grabbed his phone, then left the bedroom and followed the sound to his living room to see what all the commotion was about.

Allen found Stephanie, Benjamin's physical therapist, on the floor making his son lie face down with a pillow under his chest while Kelsey also sat on the floor and watched. With one hand on his lower back, Stephanie used her other hand to gently tap Benjamin under his arm. After a few taps, Benjamin reacted to the cue by lifting his head up from the pillow and holding it parallel to the floor.

"Yay, Benjamin!" Stephanie and Kelsey cheered in unison. After just a few seconds, Benjamin lowered his head back to the pillow, squirming and fussing, wanting to be left alone.

"I know, bud, it's too early for all that," Allen said, wiping the sleep from his eyes before pulling out a dining room chair and taking a seat.

"He lifted his head up three times!" Kelsey said.

"Wow, that's awesome," Allen said, half-heartedly.

"Well, I think it's exciting," Kelsey replied, rubbing Benjamin on the head, "even if Daddy doesn't."

"I didn't say it wasn't exciting," Allen grumbled before plastering a smile on his face as Stephanie looked up at him. He wasn't sure what was expected of him. Benjamin had been doing the same head control and strength exercises for over a year and still wasn't any closer to sitting up on his own. The physical therapy was necessary and he couldn't think of a better alternative, but Allen still watched every session with slumped shoulders, counting the minutes until it was over.

Stephanie looked up at Kelsey. "So try this position with Benjamin and see if he'll raise his head five times for you. Do that every day and also that sitting exercise I showed you, and I'll see how he's doing next week."

"Sounds good, thank you," Kelsey said before picking Benjamin up off the floor. She smiled at him while rocking him back and forth. "Do you need a diaper change?" she asked, already heading down the hall toward Benjamin's room and the changing table.

On her way down the hall, Kelsey passed Allen's weapon cases sitting neatly against the wall. Allen mentally scolded himself for not getting up in time to move them himself. Between that and being allowed to sleep in late, he had surely used up all the passes Kelsey would give him on account of his just coming back from a mission. Allen's phone chirped for his attention in his pocket, reminding him of the incoming encrypted message he still hadn't read from the night before. He pulled his phone out and called up his inbox, but before he could read the message Kelsey placed their son in Allen's arms.

"Here you go, Benjamin. Snuggle with Daddy while I finally make myself some breakfast," she said, walking into the kitchen after handing the boy over. Her tone confirmed that Allen was definitely not receiving any more passes.

"I missed you, I missed you," Allen told Benjamin, kissing him on the cheek. He squirmed a bit before putting his thumb in his mouth, then looked up at Allen and made eye contact for a few seconds before his eyelids grew heavy. "Okay, pal, just hold on for a second," Allen said. Lowering Benjamin to his lap, Allen balanced his son while gently prying his phone from beneath the boy's legs.

As Benjamin drifted off to sleep, Allen read who had sent him a message. "Holy shit."

"Please don't talk like that around him," Kelsey said, standing over the toaster.

"Huh?" Allen replied.

"You swore," Kelsey said.

"I'm sorry, I'm just surprised," Allen explained. "But, c'mon, it doesn't matter."

"Yes, it does matter."

"How does it matter?" Allen asked, his voice

rising. "He can't understand any words. He doesn't know what I'm saying."

"He understands in some way," Kelsey countered. "He at least understands the tone. Besides, when he does learn to talk, I don't want the first things he says to be swear words."

Allen scoffed. "If we can't get his seizures under control, he's not going to be saying anything. I don't care how much therapy he gets."

"Well, I love him anyway, so don't swear around him," Kelsey said through a clenched jaw.

"What, and I don't love him?" Allen snapped. "Just because I don't think he's going to get better unless we stop his seizures?"

Kelsey sighed. "Medicine isn't the only thing that can help him," she said as she carried her plate of toast and sat down next to Allen at the dinner table.

Allen ground his teeth. There was no way to win the argument. He focused on his breathing and calming down instead.

Kelsey was nearly finished eating her breakfast before she spoke again. "So, what surprised you?"

"Someone who sent me a message," Allen replied, grateful to move on.

"A work message?" Kelsey asked. "So what was the name, 'Santa Claus'?"

"Eamon Tor," Allen said.

"Shut up," Kelsey said with a laugh. Allen turned his phone toward her. Even after reading the name on the screen, Kelsey still shook her head. "No way. You sent him a message and he replied just like that?"

"No, this is him starting a message to me."

Kelsey laughed again, finished her last bite of

toast, then continued. "So, the world's first trillionaire heard you were back on the operator market and just sent you a message begging you to take his money?"

Allen chuckled. "No, not exactly."

"Then why would he be messaging you?"

"Maybe because he was my college roommate," Allen admitted.

"I thought you went to Chicago University," Kelsey said, confused.

"Yeah, and so did Eamon. He could only afford public college, just like me."

"And the whole time we've been together," Kelsey said, "you never thought to mention this."

"You understand that I've met a lot of rich people over the years, right?"

"I suppose," Kelsey conceded. "But still, college roommates?"

"Yeah."

Kelsey leaned forward intently. "Did you know back then he'd be super rich one day?"

"If I did, I would have stuck by him closer after we graduated." Allen chuckled. "Though he did insist on driving outside the city to buy beer just to save on the liquor tax. Before we sold the beer to freshmen."

"At double the price," Kelsey said.

"Exactly. So I should have known he'd make it big. And one time we forged IDs," Allen said, smirking.

"To buy beer?"

"No, to sell again," Allen corrected. "That's how we got into the football stadium when the Bears played the division game our senior year. We sneaked in as beer guys."

"Like good capitalists," Kelsey said, smiling.

"Made a hundred bucks in tips, too."

Kelsey stood up from the table to bring her plate to the sink. "So you and Eamon Tor were roommates, and now he's shooting you a message because, why?"

"The message doesn't say." Allen looked again at his phone. "It just says he wants to meet, then lists his building with a date and time."

"Without giving a reason?"

"Nope," Allen said, scrolling through the message yet again to check for more information he may have missed. "I guess I'll find out."

Chapter Five

Disgusting, disgusting, disgusting...
Daryl did not enjoy plumbing. He liked to tinker with electronics, custom weapons, computers, and such, and if he felt like doing a little garden work, that would be fine, too. But plumbing was not the kind of work he got excited about. However, he hated the idea of paying someone to do something he knew he could handle on his own. A clogged kitchen sink drain was certainly something he could handle, no matter how nasty it was, though nobody would have blamed him for having someone else do it. But in that moment, lying with his back on the floor below his kitchen sink, holding a loose S-bend drain pipe while filthy water poured out, it felt like his independent spirit had backfired on him.

Daryl pulled the S-bend away from the other drain pipes and dropped it into a bucket he had positioned to hold it before putting his arms down to rest. After catching his breath, Daryl used only his arms to pull himself out from underneath the sink and turn himself sideways. He craned his neck over his shoulder to look behind him at the wheelchair sitting a few feet away.

"Closer, please," Daryl called out. Hearing his command, the wheelchair obeyed and rolled itself closer, stopping over him with its front wheels on either side of his head. After the wheelchair self-locked its wheels, Daryl grabbed the frame and pulled himself up to sit on the floor with his back leaning against the chair for support. Then, holding the chair with his left hand to anchor himself, he used his right arm to reach under the sink and pull out the bucket. He grimaced as he beat the detached piece of pipe against the inside of the bucket to release the disgusting contents of the clog. Daryl had seen a lot of action around the world with Allen back in their heyday, but none of those experiences disturbed him as much as the sickening mixture of rotting egg shells and decomposing vegetables that he had just cleared from underneath his sink.

Having removed the revolting cause of his troubles, Daryl got back under the sink to tighten the S-bend back into place. As he began to tighten the pipe, the noise of rattling keys came from outside the front door. The deadbolt turned free and the door opened before the sound of light footsteps entered the kitchen. After a beat of silence, a familiar voice asked an obvious question.

"What are you doing down there?" Haley asked.

"Clogged sink," Daryl told his daughter matter-of-factly.

"Yuck." Haley groaned before putting her satchel on the kitchen table and sitting down.

"Don't sit down yet," Daryl said as he finished tightening the drain pipe. "I need you to help with the non-disgusting part."

Haley stood up and walked over. "What?"

"Just turn the water on," Daryl requested. As Haley obliged, Daryl winced at the thought of water leaking onto him. He was relieved when the only thing that came from the drain pipe was the sound of flowing water. "That's enough, thanks."

After Haley turned off the water, she grabbed an apple from the fridge. As Daryl extracted himself once again from below the sink, Haley sat at the kitchen table without asking her father if he needed help into his chair. At Daryl's insistence, she had long since stopped offering.

With one hand grabbing his wheelchair as high up as he could and the other hand braced against the floor, Daryl used his chin to keep his knees in place before he push/pulled himself off the floor and up into his wheelchair. After getting comfortable in his seat, he wheeled himself around and joined his daughter at the table.

"So, how was the mission?" Daryl asked.

"Good, good," Haley mumbled absently before taking a bite from her apple.

"What went wrong?"

Haley finished chewing and replied, "It was fine." She kept her eyes on the apple.

"Okay, so I'll have to guess," Daryl said. He leaned in closer with a suspicious stare, examining her face. Haley only returned her father's gaze for brief, scattered moments.

"It wasn't your fault," Daryl divined. "It was...Allen... Wait, did he remember to upgrade his pulse rifle?"

Haley only looked at her father silently and took another large bite from her apple.

"I told him!" Daryl said, moving away from the table to wheel around the room. He always paced when he was angry. "I even offered to fix him up for free! But he was too proud. Pride is a killer—you remember that."

"I wasn't supposed to tell you," Haley admitted, confirming her father's intuition.

"Well, you're his partner now, and that means keeping secrets. Technically you didn't tell me, anyway." Daryl looked at his daughter again. He could already tell from her changed body language that he had uncovered the only secret she was holding back. Which meant that the mission had otherwise worked out. Daryl calmed down and returned to the table. "I'm proud of you," he told his daughter.

Haley, still chewing her apple, broke out into an over-the-top smile so big that bits of apple spilled from her mouth. Daryl chuckled at his daughter. She'd been doing that silly move since she was four, and it still got him every time.

"Anyway," Haley said after swallowing her food, "Allen wanted me to ask if you had any gear in mind for him. He decided he was"—Haley made air quotes—" 'Ready for some updates.' So if he asks, that's what I said."

"Uh-huh," Daryl replied, "like I wouldn't see through that line, either." He pushed himself back from the table and wheeled into the adjacent room. Having a more spacious house was one of the advantages of living in the Washington Heights neighborhood on the south end of Chicago. His house sat on a wide double lot big enough for a driveway to run from the street to the back of his house, a rarity for most of the city. Not only did it make his house more accessible, but it also meant more space on the first floor without having to use his wheelchair lift to go upstairs, which was nice. Daryl preferred to have his workshop as close to the kitchen as possible. Some people have their best ideas while taking a shower. Daryl had his best ideas while sitting at the kitchen table eating a simple cheese sandwich.

Once inside his living room turned workshop, Daryl navigated a narrow path between tables that were actually hinged panels attached on the room's outside walls that could be pulled down when needed. At the moment, they were all in use. Once on the far end of the room, Daryl reached a table covered with new weapons he was ready to put finishing touches on.

"Luckily, I didn't wait for Allen to ask before I started working on his new gear," Daryl said over his shoulder. "What do you think?" There was no reply. Daryl turned, assuming Haley was right behind him. Instead, Haley had stopped at the threshold of the room and stared at her father's latest creation, which stood prominently in the center of his workshop.

"What in the world is that, Dad?" Haley asked.

His pet project was impossible to ignore, and he had been looking forward to seeing Haley's reaction to it. In fact, he stayed up late the night before to assemble it into a standing position in anticipation of her coming over. Looking at Haley's face, he barely stifled a grin.

"Oh, that?" Daryl asked innocently, gesturing toward the eight-foot-high robotic walker exoskeleton standing in the middle of the room. "That's just an accessibility project I'm working on."

Haley stepped forward to get a closer look. The walker had two legs and two arms but looked more like a robotic vehicle than a suit. Its feet resembled the curved prosthetic blades that amputee runners used to run. The blades attached to a pair of sockets on the outside of a large central ball joint. Above that the suit had a seat and a frame to protect the rider, with controls near both hand positions on the arms.

"Accessibility, huh? The wheelchair's just not doing it for you anymore?" Haley asked.

"I'd like to get back into jogging," Daryl said, still feigning innocence.

Haley's gaze moved down the arms of the machine and settled on a piece of hardware not appropriate for a neighborhood jogging path. "Most joggers don't carry a six-barrel high-rotation minigun."

"*Pulse* minigun," Daryl corrected. "Three thousand pulses per minute." Daryl's daughter gave him a skeptical look and he returned it with as serious an expression as he could muster. "What can I say, I don't like slow people."

Daryl's joke got a chuckle out of his daughter, instantly making his late-night work session worthwhile. "Anyway," Daryl continued, "I'm just about done with Allen's new pulse rifle. I just stuck with the basics on it, assuming we can reuse his pulse core. Anything more and I'm going to need to get paid. A man's gotta eat."

"Thanks, Dad," Haley said.

"Tell Allen to thank me," Daryl countered. "Where is he, anyway? He hasn't called me since you got back."

"Said something about having a meeting today." Haley walked over to her father to take a closer look at the pulse rifle he made for Allen.

"Here in the city?" Daryl asked.

"Mm-hmm."

"That's interesting."

"Yep."

As Daryl watched, his daughter looked over the components on his work table with a slow gaze while her expression grew vacant. "It's okay to be scared when you're out there," Daryl reminded Haley, once again seeming to read his daughter's mind.

"So you've told me."

"It's also okay not to do it anymore. There's plenty of work out there for a genius," he offered.

"I know."

"And you could always help me around here."

"I get it. If I want to stop, I'll let you know." With her gaze still fixed on the components on the table, Haley put her hand on her dad's shoulder and gave it a little squeeze to know that she meant what she said.

"So, where are you taking us?" Daryl asked, changing the subject.

Haley looked her father in the eyes. "Taking us?"

"For your celebratory lunch? Your first mission deserves a celebration," Daryl declared as he turned his chair and wheeled out of the room. "I want pancakes!" he bellowed over his shoulder. Sensing that he wasn't being followed again, Daryl went back to the living room.

Haley stood in the workshop looking at him, a quizzical look on her face, until he pulled the keys to his vehicle from a pocket and gave the most doe-eyed look he could muster.

"Then I guess we're having pancakes," Haley said, walking toward her father to gather her things. "I can't think of a better way to celebrate my success than eating whatever food my father demands."

Chapter Six

Glass, glass, and more glass…

Allen was not much of an architectural aficionado, but even he took note of the central theme of the Tor Building's ultra-modern design. From the outside, the building didn't have the traditional grid of windows with clearly-defined borders like all its other downtown neighbors along the Chicago River. Instead, the entire structure was concealed behind an iridescent sheath of glass, with curves instead of sharp corners at the edges, and reflections that morphed and changed like flowing water as one looked at it. Allen had seen it many times from the train or walking along the river, but he had never gone inside before. The thought of walking in and trying to talk his way into a meeting with Eamon had crossed his mind every once in a while over the years, but he figured too much time had passed to pull it off. Now, having been summoned, it occurred to Allen that maybe Eamon had been wishing for him to do just that.

As he approached the entrance, Allen brought his gaze down from gawking at the building and instead looked straight ahead. The last thing he wanted was for anyone to think he was a tourist. He navigated the bottleneck of people waiting to pass through the revolving doors and pushed his way inside.

The lobby was much more vast than Allen expected. It was five stories high with multiple levels of walkways ringing the outside, exotic plants lining both sides of each walkway. Employees filled the space, some fast-walking to meetings, others strolling around casually enjoying the landscaping or huddling in conversation. The vastness of the space reminded Allen that the Tor Building wasn't called that just because Eamon's company bought the naming rights or was the majority tenant. The Tor Corporation was in fact the only tenant, housing offices for the hundreds of smaller companies it owned. It was a long way from the beer schemes Eamon ran with Allen in college, but Eamon's nose for opportunity gave him a knack for acquiring companies at the right price at the right time and growing them into empires. Because of that, the Tor Corporation wasn't so much a producer of goods as it was a business of making businesses.

Allen wandered, sweeping his gaze left and right, searching for any signs of a security desk. Instead, the only objects of interest were several white, vertical panels about seven feet high, positioned at odd angles from each other, spaced across the entire floor of the lobby. Probably some kind of sculpture garden or bit of Feng Shui he didn't understand. He started walking through the sculptures to examine them closer when someone called his name.

"Mister Moran," said a female voice over Allen's shoulder, "I can help you over here."

Allen turned toward the person's voice but it wasn't a person at all. Not in the traditional sense at least. Instead, a projected image of a woman materialized onto the nearest white monolith and greeted Allen. The surface of the monolith protruded and receded to give her form and dimension. The virtual assistant wore professional clothing, a collared shirt and dark skirt, and greeted him with a smile. "I understand you're visiting the top floor today."

Two employees passing by overheard and snapped their heads around to see what kind of bigwig was headed to the top floor. They looked Allen up and down with furrowed brows. When they met his gaze, Allen couldn't resist giving them a little wink just to mess with them.

The virtual assistant continued. "If you could please follow me this way, Mister Moran," she said as she walked to her right and disappeared off the side of the panel. Allen turned to see where she would reappear and found her projected on a panel at the far end of the lobby, waving to him. He walked the distance across and followed the assistant as her image hopped from panel to panel. Around a corner and down a short hallway, her projection waited on the surface of an exclusive elevator door.

"This elevator will take you directly to the executive level. See you up top," she said, the doors opening on cue the moment she finished her sentence. Allen walked inside and faced the doors as they closed. The elevator began to rise as expected, but shortly thereafter continued to accelerate faster than any elevator Allen had been in before. With the rush of speed came a sudden change in air pressure that pushed against his eardrums. The floor numbers counted up with the dizzying speed of a stopwatch until the eightieth floor, where it began to slow down to finally come to a stop at an even one hundred.

The doors opened, and Allen stepped into the executive level. The design themes of the lobby continued on the top floor. It felt more like a botanical conservatory than a reception area, except that here there was no one else besides Allen. From the elevator, he followed a path through exotic plants around a short bend to a small receiving area with two simple wooden benches, a koi pond, and a lone white projection panel where the virtual assistant waited for him.

"Please take a seat and enjoy your surroundings while you wait for Mister Tor," she said, then faded away. Allen's posture relaxed. He had been worried that the virtual thing was going to try and make small talk with him. Chatting about the weather with a stranger was hard enough, much less with a computerized one.

In the quiet of his calm surroundings with nothing but the gentle sound of water to distract him, a queasiness burrowed into his stomach. Allen hadn't seen Eamon in twenty years, and after all that time, what did he have to show for it? Plus with Benjamin's health struggles, Allen had a tough enough time catching up with friends as it was. It was difficult to explain his son's situation from scratch, especially when things weren't going well. That's why he usually just skipped over it if he ran into any casual acquaintances around the neighborhood. It was much easier to say "good" when asked about his family than "struggling with intractable epilepsy and global developmental delay."

Allen paced around for a while, taking things in. He stopped at the raised koi pond, which was elevated to about knee level and edged with some kind of molded artificial rock. He stared down at the red and orange striped fish for a long time, watching as some swam leisurely in the shallow water while others seemed to hover in place. Allen patted his pockets for something he could feed them to pass the time. A voice broke him away from his search.

"Allen," the quiet voice called. He turned to see Eamon standing there, seemingly out of thin air, dressed casually in light earth tones like he was on vacation instead of in an office building. Eamon smiled when Allen met his gaze. There was more wear on his face around his eyes than Allen remembered from college, and the hair was a bit thinner, but the youthful smile was the same. These were the small differences that the images in the news rarely captured, which had been the only way Allen had seen Eamon over the years. It was like seeing a celebrity in person, both familiar and different than expected. Allen stood motionless. A quietness settled between them, broken only by the babble of the water circulating in the pond. Allen took a step forward and nearly stumbled while reaching out his arm to shake his old friend's hand.

Eamon took Allen's hand firmly before pulling him closer for a hug. Allen had wondered if this was going to be a hugging occasion. The two exchanged firm slaps on the back before stepping away from each other.

"This way, please," Eamon said, gesturing to a walkway behind him that Allen hadn't noticed. After a short distance, they stepped through a pair of automatic glass doors and into Eamon's vast office. It was mostly empty, with the entire room leading toward a desk with multiple screens near a set of expensive-looking chairs that combined deep leather, a carbon black frame, and a minimalist design that balanced almost in defiance of gravity. Floor-to-ceiling windows overlooked the river and the forest of skyscrapers along its urban banks.

"I hope your trip up was easy enough," Eamon said, leading Allen to his desk.

"It was good. I wasn't sure what to expect when I came in, but somehow I wasn't surprised by what I found."

"Exactly. I've got a reputation to keep up," Eamon said with a smirk. "It does more than give a fancy impression, though. I find regular lobbies with security desks boring and antiquated. And have you ever gone in to meet someone and had to wait until they came down? It always makes me feel like a child."

Allen raised an eyebrow with a playful grin. "Oh yeah, I'm sure people keep you waiting all the time."

Eamon laughed as he walked around his desk and sat. "No, not so much anymore."

Allen sat across from Eamon. The fancy guest chair was as comfortable as it looked. Now that they were both seated, looking across from each other, there was a pause. Allen tapped a finger against his knee and looked around the room. Luckily, Eamon was more practiced in the art of conversation.

"How are you?" Eamon asked warmly.

"I'm…okay. Not falling apart yet."

"And your wife, doing well, too?" Eamon continued.

"Kelsey, yes. She does kickboxing and stuff, definitely in better shape than I've kept," Allen replied. Next was the part he hated. Time to explain the complete medical history of his son. It had been two years since Benjamin's epilepsy diagnosis, and Allen had long since decided against keeping it a secret from anyone. But it's easy to feel like a rude guest by coming into a fresh conversation and dumping a pile of personal troubles onto it. But Eamon was ahead of him on that as well.

"I know about Benjamin," Eamon said.

Allen's eyes narrowed. "You know…"

"I know he's been having problems," Eamon finished.

"Oh. Yeah, he's—you know. Good days and bad. To be honest, the seizures have taken a backseat lately. He keeps getting sick with colds and gets stuck in the hospital. We have to use a suction machine to suck the snot out of him because he can't clear it out himself. It's really nasty," Allen said. He laughed at the absurdity of it all. "Seriously. It is so disgusting."

"I'm sorry. That's hard," Eamon said.

Allen looked at Eamon. It was strange to have a friend from college acting so mature now. Allen had kept himself isolated from friends in the past couple of years and wasn't used to sympathy for himself personally, as a father. With the risk of tears welling up in his eyes, Allen looked down and shifted in his seat. "Thank you," he said before clearing his throat. "But how did you find out? About Benjamin's epilepsy?"

Eamon stared back at him. Allen was about to repeat the question when Eamon turned and looked at one of the monitors on his desk. He tapped a few keys on his keyboard before reaching up and pressing a button on the monitor itself. The black backside of the monitor facing Allen dissolved to show what he assumed was the same screen Eamon also saw on his side.

It was an online operator message board, the one Allen used, *Sentinel*. It had no public web address—it was a site on the dark web to chat with other freelance operators in the world. It was also connected to *Operator Exchange*, or *Op-X*, where clients from around the world could connect with operators-for-hire. On the monitor was a single message dated a few months earlier by a user with the handle "Mystic." It read, *MYSTIC: Back.*

Allen stared at the screen and the message—his message. To his trusted, long-time clients, ones like Richter, he was Allen. But to new clients and the operator world at large, he was known simply as Mystic. It wasn't a terribly original name. Allen wasn't even the first operator to use it, but he was able to put his flag in the sand as the best one to go by it. The name also happened to be accurate. Allen's greatest professional joy was getting in and out of a job without leaving a trace or even a logical clue about how he got things done. His style earned Allen a loyal following in the operator community. So when he was forced to go back to work, Allen's pride wasn't sure how to advertise the fact without coming off like he was begging. In the end, *Back* was all he could stand to write to announce his return.

Allen's surprise at seeing his message on Eamon's screen quickly passed when he remembered that his friend was now a trillionaire. "You a fan?" Allen finally asked.

"Of course," Eamon said with a grin. "I couldn't help but wonder why though."

"Because I'm good," Allen said.

"No, I mean why you came back," Eamon said. "After college, I knew you were going to do something more exciting than push papers around. When I became aware of this world"—Eamon gestured toward the monitor displaying the *Sentinel* message board—"I noticed this Mystic character getting mentioned. Especially right after you came back from one of your frequent, random trips."

"You had me followed?"

"Not recently. This was, like, fifteen years ago," Eamon answered.

"I'm not sure how that's supposed to make me feel better."

"I don't expect you to be very sympathetic to this," Eamon said as he sat back in his chair, "but after college when I had a few successes under my belt, every social occasion eventually turned into someone asking me for money. So I started keeping to myself. I would go down these online rabbit holes, especially this operator stuff. I got curious about this Mystic person and I had a hunch it was you. But I wasn't about to call you up and ask you about it. It would've been weird."

"So having me followed was the normal choice," Allen said flatly.

"The more normal of the two options, yes."

It didn't bother Allen that Eamon had him followed, at least not as much as he was letting on. It was the explanation he hadn't heard yet, of how Eamon knew about Benjamin's condition, that made him clench his jaw. "So you had your people dig around about me again, after I posted my message."

"Yes."

"And you found I had a young son," Allen continued.

"Yes."

"Then discovered he was having problems," Allen

finished.

Eamon nodded.

"How much of his medical record did you read?" Allen asked, his voice rising.

Instead of answering, Eamon leaned forward in his chair again. "I'm sorry. This must feel like an invasion."

"I would have told you. All you had to do was ask."

"It wasn't my intention to go that far into your life, but my investigators are thorough. As is the HAPA data collection network."

Allen's stomach lurched like he was in freefall. He studied Eamon's face and the cool expression that had now overtaken the easy smile reminiscent of their college days. Having people followed and investigated was one thing, but being able to tap into the slush of personal data and pool of mass surveillance footage that insurers were allowed to use for tracking, recording, and predicting health outcomes put Eamon on a whole new level. And it all seemed completely normal to him. "Why am I here?" Allen asked.

"How much do you know about Olivia Rusk?" Eamon asked in return.

"What are you talking about, Olivia Rusk? You dug into my personal life because of some old, dying, rich woman?" Allen stood from the chair. "Whatever you two squabbling oligarchs are fighting about, I doubt I can help you." Allen turned to leave, but Eamon reached out his hand and gestured for Allen to stop.

"She's not dying," said Eamon.

"Stage four brain cancer isn't dying?" Allen said, nearly yelling.

"It's *grade* four, not stage four. Brain cancers are rated in grades—"

"She's in hospice care," Allen interrupted. "The news wouldn't stop talking about it. I understand that Rusk Corp runs most of the internet access in this country, but they acted like she was everyone's mother. They were crying actual tears on-air."

"Well, Rusk owns most of the news outlets, too," Eamon reminded him.

"Then they'll be very happy to hear about her amazing recovery," Allen replied with an acerbic tone. "This has nothing to do with me." Allen turned again and walked toward the door.

"They call it 'Eden Therapy,' " Eamon cried out, rising to his feet. Allen stopped and faced him.

"Who calls what that?"

"The treatment that cured Rusk. It's some type of cell editing technology," said Eamon, walking toward the wall to Allen's right. The light in the room dimmed automatically and a projection appeared, covering the wall with a variety of information. The projection included technical diagrams, engineering formulas, DNA helices, and various intricate waveforms.

Allen walked toward the display without thinking, mesmerized by medical information that wasn't simply more bad news about his son. "What, like gene therapy?" he asked.

"Somewhat, though that's more for curing defects or problems people are born with," Eamon explained. "Eden can heal both genetic problems as well as other kinds of diseases."

Allen continued to look over the diagrams and animations but felt no closer to understanding. "So it's a catch-all miracle machine? How could this possibly work? I see radiation on the screen, chemicals, and all kinds of drugs. That image there looks like some kind of microscopic robot..."

"I'll spare you the exact techno-babble details." Eamon's voice rose with a sudden burst of agitation. "It took years to build the system. The superconductors for the imaging system alone took three years to fabricate. So yeah, it's complicated."

Allen rubbed his temple. This was not how he imagined this meeting going. "So Olivia Rusk dumped millions of dollars into researching this Eden Therapy technology, a treatment was developed, and now she's secretly cured of cancer."

"Billions of dollars," Eamon corrected him. "Tens of billions. And it did more than just stop the cancer." Eamon changed the display to show some grainy photographs taken at a distance.

The location was a resort somewhere in an unlabeled mountain range that looked like the Alps. Two people were in the photograph standing outside on a balcony.

"Olivia Rusk had also developed Parkinson's disease," Eamon continued. "Normally with modern treatments that wouldn't be an issue, but she's allergic to the frontline drug we developed to stop it."

"Congratulations on your Nobel Prize, by the way," Allen said.

"Thanks," Eamon said absently as he changed the display to zoom in on the figures on the balcony. "But look at her now..." The figure on the right was a man dressed in black with outstretched arms holding something Allen couldn't make out. The figure on the left was dressed in purple and frozen in the still image with her upper body tilted back while standing on one leg. It took Allen a moment to find the other leg frozen in mid-air.

"She's kickboxing?" Allen asked in surprise.

"She and Kelsey could practice together," Eamon said as he adjusted the photograph and enhanced it further. Even with the blurry image quality, Allen made out Olivia Rusk dressed in purple athletic wear mid-kick, striking the hand of a trainer wearing target gloves. Thanks to the news networks treating each of her birthdays like a holiday, Allen knew Olivia Rusk was over eighty. Unless her hospice featured end-of-life kickboxing therapy, her recovery seemed incredible.

Allen paced in a slow circle. Neither man spoke for a few moments. Inside Allen's head, he struggled to bring his thoughts into focus and winced as he fought back confusion. A miracle cure had saved an old billionaire from cancer. His mind jumped to his son, both how Benjamin was now and how he may be in the future. He thought about Eamon, both the good friend he had been in college and now the changed, detached man presenting a high-tech slideshow that could end the pain for Allen's family.

Once Allen was able to finally wrangle his thinking into something comprehensible, he turned and faced Eamon. When discussing a job with a potential client, Allen had found it best to be direct. "Are you asking me to break into wherever this Eden Therapy stuff is and steal it for you? Then you'll use it to help Benjamin?"

"No," Eamon responded. "I'm asking you to destroy it. Then I'll help Benjamin."

Chapter Seven

I miss being hungover.

Allen wasn't thinking of the relatively mild hangover he experienced from Richter's complimentary drink in the jungle. Instead, he remembered himself and Eamon back in their dorm room in college, lying in their beds groaning with nausea and the consequences of heavy drinking from the night before. With bleary eyes, they would get themselves up and stumble over to Franny's, a greasy spoon diner just off campus. There they would down cups of coffee and eat bacon and hash browns in silence, assuming their stomachs had settled enough to eat. It felt like torture. It felt like the worst thing in the whole world, the ultimate misery. Then Allen got older. His son was diagnosed with destructive epilepsy. And that same level of pain, now emotional instead of physical, hurt him every day. At least a hangover was a result of too much fun, a price paid for a good time. The pain he felt now, having just been told of a possible cure for his son that he was being asked to destroy, made him feel just as nauseous as those late nights many years ago.

Allen looked Eamon in the eyes a long time before asking, "What in the world are you talking about?"

"There's no such thing as a miracle cure, Allen. Every treatment has side effects."

"You don't think I know that?" Allen shot back.

"We have to watch Benjamin to make sure his drugs don't destroy his liver or make him go blind. I understand medicine has goddamn side effects."

"These side effects can be especially dangerous," Eamon replied.

"Oh yeah? Like what?" Allen challenged. " 'Cause I gotta say, old Missus Rusk looks pretty good in that picture."

"The connections between the brain cells can get disrupted in a way that isn't fully understood." Eamon changed the projection on the wall to images of brain scans and chemical formulas Allen didn't recognize. "The symptoms start as behavioral problems. Paranoia, anxiety, megalomania, authoritarian tendencies…"

"Oh my, it's turning rich people into assholes?" Allen said, feigning shock.

"It's progressive," Eamon continued. "Some patients develop psychosis. They lose touch with reality and, eventually, all higher brain function."

"How do you know all this?" Allen asked. "You've never even seen it work."

"I have a guy on the inside," Eamon answered, displaying a new photograph. "Emmanuel Sloan. Doctor of neurology, with a Ph.D. in neuropharmacology. He was brought on to study the side effects when they started popping up. Not that they told him that. He assumed the conditions were naturally occurring, as of course any doctor would." The photo Eamon displayed on the wall was from some kind of ID badge. A man in his late forties to early fifties with graying hair smiled out at them. "Sloan has been holed up at an off-the-books research facility for almost a year."

"Because they've been testing it in secret," Allen said, unsurprised. It was a typical mega-corp operation. Why bother getting the proper government approvals when you can just do things under the radar and buy everyone off?

"Yes, but he isn't allowed to leave anymore. He has essentially become a prisoner, though for the moment he can still communicate with the outside world. He reached out to a former colleague that works for me here. The message was vague, but my employee knew something was wrong and brought it to my attention."

"And he told you all this? That the technology has psychotic side effects?"

"Not directly, no. He just wants to be rescued." Eamon pulled up some satellite images on the screen that showed a facility surrounded by a bleak, brown landscape of scattered rock and snow. The location stamp in the corner identified it as Alluttoq Island, Greenland. "We traced the message to its source after hiding a data-mining program into an email reply. That's how we stole these fragments of medical data."

Allen didn't respond. He looked at the surveillance photo of the research facility for a while, then turned and slowly walked back toward Eamon's desk.

After Allen sat and still hadn't responded, Eamon followed him and continued. "I want you to go in, destroy the equipment, copy the technical plans, and bring Doctor Sloan back here to me. In return, I'll cover the costs of Benjamin's medical treatments, therapies, all of it."

Allen looked off into space. It was everything he needed—unrestricted access to the best medical care and specialists for Benjamin and a life without having to worry about providing for his son. But Eden could be a cure. "I've got a better idea," Allen said. "How about I just wait it out until this therapy hits the market?"

"It'll never hit the general market," Eamon said, shaking his head. "Putting aside the risk of side effects, this technology will only be available to those who can afford the price."

"I'll pay whatever it takes," Allen said. "And the side effects can't possibly be worse than what my son already faces."

"I disagree," Eamon said, looking down at his desk and typing on his keyboard. Instantly, a collection of images appeared, projected on every wall. They were pictures taken in the snow, with the same landscape as the research facility. In the wide shots, Allen saw dark mounds spread out at a distance. When the images got closer and showed more detail, the contents of the mounds became clear and only added to Allen's nausea.

"Almost a hundred people killed," Eamon said. "Shot in the back, shot as they ran, shot as they slept, as they ate dinner, just living their lives." New scenes of horror continued to cycle around the room with victims of all ages.

"Who did it?" Allen asked.

"Rusk," Eamon replied. "She said she could hear them breathing, said the noise was keeping her up at night. The village is a mile away from the research facility. But hey, if the boss says the whole village has to die, who's going to argue? Good jobs are hard to come by nowadays."

Allen watched the images flash by on the walls, the victims looking at him with lifeless eyes. Then all at once they disappeared. Allen continued to look at the wall as he spoke. "Why do you care?"

"I just showed you why I care."

Allen turned to Eamon. "Give me a break. Of all the terrible things going on in the world, you just happen to care about these people?"

"More people will suffer and die if Rusk isn't stopped," Eamon said.

"Again, why do you care?" Allen yelled.

"Because somebody has to give a shit occasionally," Eamon shouted back.

"Oh yes, well done. You want me to sabotage a competitor and steal her product, a treatment that every patient with a HAPA restriction would pay anything to get. But you also slightly give a shit about people so that makes you a saint."

"That tiny bit of caring by people like me is the only thing keeping the world from becoming a total nightmare," Eamon replied, his face turning red. "You think medicine like this should only be in the hands of the rich? Because I don't."

Allen shook his head. "Stop. I still don't buy it. This is a business move."

"Yes, but one guided by principle."

"If you care about people you've never met," Allen said, "then why not care about me? Or my son? If you really cared, you'd just give us the money we need."

"I think we can help each other out. That feels better to me than charity."

"I'm beyond pride at this point. Please, Eamon."

"It's just…" Eamon began. He took a breath and was about to continue before he stopped again and seemed to change his mind. His face became expressionless. "I need this done," Eamon explained. "And you seem best suited for it. Do the job, destroy what they've built, and bring their plans back to me so we can perfect it the right way. For everyone who needs it, including your son."

Allen fell silent and slumped in his seat. He desperately wanted to keep arguing his case. Unfortunately, he could also tell it would be hopeless.

****

Later that afternoon, as Allen sat at his kitchen table fidgeting with the salt and pepper shakers, Eamon's words echoed in his mind as he watched Kelsey feed Benjamin at the highchair.

"Nice lateral tongue movement!" Kelsey cheered as Benjamin mouthed a small bite of instant oatmeal. She dipped a tiny toddler spoon back into the bowl, dug another small pea-sized dollop out, and brought the spoon back up to Benjamin's eye level. His eating skills had declined steadily for months as the uncontrolled seizures damaged his brain's ability to coordinate the simple motions of chewing and swallowing. Feeding therapists had shown Kelsey and Allen what types of foods to try and where to place them in Benjamin's mouth to help build his skills back up.

"Here comes another bite!" Kelsey announced as she presented the oatmeal. Benjamin didn't seem to be paying attention to her, his gaze looking both beyond her and nowhere at the same time. Still, in the last moment, Benjamin opened his mouth just as the spoon was about to touch it. Kelsey unloaded the small amount of oatmeal to the front of Benjamin's mouth and was pleased that, as in the bite before, he used his tongue to push the oatmeal sideways to sit on his molars where he could chew it.

As Kelsey waited for Benjamin to finish chewing, she continued the conversation she and Allen were having. "I just don't get it. One of the richest men in the world hasn't seen you in like twenty years and you're the one he calls. Conveniently, at a time when you're clearly desperate for work."

Allen sighed. "I know. He's always had a way of getting the biggest gain for the smallest amount of effort."

"How many other people did he approach for the mission?" Kelsey asked.

The question took Allen by surprise. "I don't know. I didn't even think to ask. I assumed just me."

"Uh-huh," Kelsey said as she loaded another small bite of oatmeal and presented it to her son. "Or you could have been the last of a dozen people who thought it was crazy." Kelsey brought the spoon to Benjamin's mouth. Again, he took the small morsel of oatmeal into his mouth and used his tongue to push it sideways before chewing. "Good boy!" Kelsey said with sing-song excitement.

"It wouldn't be the most dangerous mission I've ever done," Allen said, thinking out loud.

"Just the most dangerous mission you've ever done over forty with a family," Kelsey pointed out, more of a statement than an argument.

"See if he'll close his mouth around the spoon," Allen requested, referring to Benjamin.

"Isn't that what he's been doing?" Kelsey asked.

"You're kind of placing it in his mouth. I'm wondering if he'll close on the spoon and suck in the food," Allen explained.

Kelsey prepped the spoon and held it up to Benjamin's mouth, pressing the bottom of the spoon just slightly on the top of his lower lip. "There are plenty of relatively safe missions out there that pay pretty well," Kelsey suggested while waiting for her son. "It may take longer, but maybe that's okay. Getting our mortgage payments back up to date definitely bought us some time, and we can pay for new treatments as we go."

"Maybe if you tip the spoon up more," Allen said as Benjamin kept his mouth shut tight. Kelsey tipped up the handle of the spoon until the end was touching Benjamin's mouth at a forty-five-degree angle. He parted his lips but otherwise didn't seem to understand what was expected of him. Feeling she had given him enough time to try, Kelsey moved the spoon inside Benjamin's mouth and wiped the oatmeal from the tip of the spoon to the inside of his upper lip. Once he felt the food inside his mouth, Benjamin began chewing it. "Oh well," Allen said.

"It's okay—he's doing a good job," Kelsey said before leaning in closer to her son's face. "Aren't you, sweetie?" Benjamin continued chewing and looking off to the side without reaction.

"The thing is," Allen said, "I'm not sure how many missions I have left in me. Good ones, anyway."

Kelsey looked up while she prepared another bite. "You are not that old, Allen," she said with an annoyed sigh.

"Not at the moment, no," Allen explained, "but what if Benjamin doesn't get better? What if he stays like this? I can't keep going out there for ten more years or whenever this Eden Therapy comes out on the black market. If they even bother trying to make it safe."

"He'll get better. We just have to find the right plan," Kelsey said as Benjamin ate another spoonful.

"I hope he gets better. I want him to get better, but what if he doesn't?" Allen countered. "And what if I get hurt, then where would he be once he's HAPA-restricted? That's what I'm worried about. And it wouldn't be a bad thing to be first on the list whenever Eamon perfects the treatment."

Benjamin began to retch, the oatmeal triggering his gag reflex.

Kelsey stood up and gently patted her son's back with one hand while supporting Benjamin's head under his jaw to keep it straight while he coughed. Allen stood, grabbed a paper towel, then walked over and wiped the saliva and tears from Benjamin's face as he worked to clear the food. After another minute of Benjamin's coughing, Kelsey unbuckled him from his high chair and sat before leaning him forward to let gravity help. Gradually, the wetness in Benjamin's coughing cleared. The child settled and, exhausted from the effort, began to doze off in his mother's arms.

"I understand what you're saying," Kelsey said in a whisper. "But I also think you need to focus on loving the son we have, not getting killed on risky missions chasing the one we wish we had."

"This is not me rejecting my son," Allen said sharply. Benjamin stirred at the sound of his father's voice. After he settled again, Allen continued. "This is about giving him the best chance we can."

The two sat in silence as Benjamin's breathing slowed, eventually becoming a gentle snore. "If you do this mission," Kelsey whispered, "I want to be involved. You need new armor. I took a look. It barely made it through the last mission."

"It's the first thing on a wish list I'm putting together for Daryl," Allen said.

"But I want to design the software for it. You know, put together some features we always talked about you having. Make it more intuitive, integrated with your weapons, predictive..." Kelsey slowly stood and gently rocked her son as she walked by Allen and sat on a recliner a few feet away. "I need to use that side of my brain again."

"Okay," Allen agreed. He sat there looking at the floor, his mouth dry after winning the discussion. He still wanted to move ahead, but part of him wished Kelsey had talked him out of it. Allen looked up at his wife to say more, but in the short time he had been thinking, her eyes had closed as she joined Benjamin in taking a nap. Allen stood, took his phone out of his pocket, and quietly walked down the hallway into the bedroom before making a call.

"Hello?" Haley answered.

"Are you and your dad open to meet tomorrow?" Allen asked.

"You're the only employer I have right now. So, yeah," Haley answered.

"Well, I just wanted to make sure in case you had something fun planned."

"Nope," Haley confirmed. "No fun Wednesday morning plans."

"Then ask your dad if he's free, and we'll get together."

"Is this about whoever you met with today? Are they still 'whoever' or are they a client now?"

"Yes, *he* is a client now," Allen said. "And yes, it's about that."

"Exciting," Haley said without much excitement in her voice.

"It is exciting actually. It won't be like the last one. There's real money behind it."

"Okay. Is that it?"

"Not quite," Allen said. "For this one, we're going to need remote support."

"Are we breaking in somewhere? Like stealing corporate secrets?" Haley genuinely sounded intrigued.

"I'll tell you tomorrow," Allen said. "So what about it? Do you know someone?"

Haley responded with a heavy sigh.

"What? What's wrong?" asked Allen, sitting on the bed.

"I know a guy," Haley said, somehow annoyed at the fact.

"Is he any good?"

"He's very good. It's just…" Haley trailed off.

"Just what?" Allen prodded before standing and rigidly waiting for a straight answer.

"It's just," Haley continued, "he's got a really stupid name."

Chapter Eight

"Meat-Taaaaaaaaaank!"

Kyle Thomas "MeatTank" Johnson held up both arms in celebration. Inside his virtual reality headset, an avatar of himself mimicked his movements. Like the real-world Kyle Johnson, the virtual-world MeatTank was tall, lanky, and oozing with victorious swagger. Kyle's electronic caricature stood atop a winner's podium in first place, though in reality he actually stood in a sparse efficiency apartment mostly filled with electronic equipment. The closest thing he had to furniture was a pair of laundry baskets, one for clean and folded laundry and the other for dirty, as well as a roll-out sleeping pad and blanket. The lack of furnishings was necessary to make space for his virtual gaming setup. The way Kyle played, he didn't need a whole lot of room, just enough to turn a complete 360 degrees and to sidestep from time to time. VR gamers with far too much money on their hands bragged about their fully-immersive open-run spaces. Serious gamers knew their own legs were far too slow when winning or losing often came down to the distance of a single pixel. That kind of precision was best left to handheld controllers.

Kyle's victory was just the latest in a string of deathmatch wins in *Annihilate '98*, his latest gaming obsession. It was a traditional first-person shooter with maps featuring locations from all over the world, but unlike most modern games, the graphics and content were based on the world of the late 1990s. A mixture of good level design, balanced weapons, and its setting in a legendary time of prosperity far before most gamers were even born had made the game a hit. Playing as his online alter ego, MeatTank had won a "Cellphone Slappers" match, defeating all other players without anyone killing his character even once in a match where the only weapons were giant 90's-era cell phones to beat each other with.

Kyle continued his MeatTank victory dance on the podium until the image transitioned to the lobby screen for the next round. As he began choosing his weapons for a match on the Mir Space Station map, a notification screen popped up indicating he had an encrypted voice call coming in. The only calls that came in like that were work calls, so a battle aboard a recreation of a Russian space station would have to wait.

Kyle removed the VR goggles from his head, walked over to his main computer setup, and tapped a button to accept the call.

"This is MeatTank!" he said with excessive pleasantness. Excessive for most people, anyway. Kyle had the rare quality of actually being very interested in just about everything he did. Most people found his earnest enthusiasm charming, though not everyone.

"Ugh." Haley's voice groaned on the other end of the call. "You seriously need to change that name."

"Better to have a codename that people feel strongly about than no name at all, Miss Still-Has-No-Name," Kyle teased.

"Everything I think of sounds stupid."

"You've always had that problem, even in middle school," Kyle told his friend. "You'd judge everything you did before you did it. Like in art class, you kept smashing your pottery projects before they got cooked in the oven or whatnot."

"It's called a kiln. And whatever, I'm sorry for wanting things to be good."

"There's always someone who thinks good things aren't good," Kyle replied. "When Da Vinci painted the Mona Lisa, I'll bet there was at least one person who said, 'Ew, boring. She's just sitting there. Blah!' "

"Yes," Haley answered skeptically. "The name 'MeatTank' is truly the Mona Lisa of codenames."

"Thank you," Kyle said as he put his VR goggles down on the desk next to his keyboard before walking to his refrigerator. "So, did you ever cook a piece?"

"What?"

"In the kiln. Did you ever finish a piece after I moved away?"

"Yes, I made a cup for my dad," Haley said with pride. "So there."

Kyle opened the fridge and considered his beverage options. "Very nice. So, what can I do for you today?"

"I'm actually calling about a job."

"Ooo, a job," Kyle said, still deciding between an orange-flavored energy drink and a mango-infused aloe water. "I like jobs. What is it?"

"I'm not sure yet," Haley admitted. "All I know is my partner said he needed someone for remote support and asked if I knew anybody."

"And you know me!" Kyle exclaimed as he

decided on the orange energy drink and took it from the fridge. "Well, you're in luck, I'm available." Kyle cracked open the can and took a deep drink.

"Good. We're meeting about it tomorrow," Haley said. "I'll send you the information for the video call."

"Man, this is awesome!" Kyle burst out.

"Yeah, it'll be nice to work together."

"That too," Kyle said. "I meant this drink I was having. It's concentrated orange with B12 and stuff. It just lit up my mouth."

Haley laughed. She couldn't help herself.

"But working together is awesome, too," Kyle clarified. "It's a double-awesome situation."

"Well, I'm glad the day is working out for you so well."

Kyle carried his drink back to his computer and sat at the desk. "And how are other things going? I'm excited to learn about this partner of yours. Have you done a lot of missions?"

"Just one," Haley said.

"Was it what you expected?"

"At first, yes," Haley replied. "Then everything changed all at once. It worked out, but it was like all that planning went out the window in a heartbeat."

"Oh yeah," Kyle said, putting his feet up on his desk. "Most of my job is prep work and loading up every single bit of data I can scrub together. It's like the games I play. Each one starts out with the same basic situation every time but it never plays out the same way twice."

"Well, improvising has never been my strong suit," Haley mulled.

"C'mon, Negative Nancy, bashing yourself isn't

going to make you better.

"Thank you, Counselor O'Reilly," Haley said, referring to the guidance counselor from their youth.

"Well, he was right! The simplest advice usually is. That way, there's less chance of being wrong."

That made Haley chuckle again. "You're like a living, breathing motivational poster."

"I know," Kyle said with pride. "I find it easy to give people advice on success because I'm very successful."

"Well, I'm glad you're working with us then."

"Me too," Kyle said with a smile. "See you on the video link tomorrow?"

"Yes," Haley said.

"Are you going to have a cool secret codename by then?" Kyle asked before taking a final, long drink of his energy beverage.

"Don't think so. But I get the sense you'll have some suggestions."

"I'll have *tons* of suggestions," Kyle said as he stood and picked up his VR goggles. "I find giving suggestions to be intensely rewarding."

"Great," Haley replied. "See you then."

"Bye," Kyle answered. He disconnected the call and put the goggles back on his head. It was time to get back into the game. These online players weren't going to beat themselves.

Chapter Nine

"I feel like the broccoli is muscling out the cauliflower."

Haley had been watching her dad distress over the vegetable tray for the past five minutes. Every time he added more of one thing, another got crowded out. "But maybe that's just because I'm staring at it," she admitted.

"Well, I don't get guests very often—just trying to get it right," Daryl said, his gaze never leaving the tray of food sitting on the kitchen island. He stood with the assistance of his wheelchair in vertical mode so he was tall enough to cut vegetables at the counter.

Haley hadn't been sure it was necessary to arrive early to help her dad out before the big team meeting, but his knotted brow told her she had been right to come. "There's still more cauliflower in the fridge, but I think the tray is fine the way it is."

"You only think that because you hate cauliflower," Daryl accused.

"I only hate it because it's disgusting," Haley replied with a smile. She watched her dad's face as he continued to examine the vegetables. He didn't appear to find his daughter's answer satisfying.

"Can you...?" Daryl requested, gesturing toward the refrigerator.

It took a second for Haley to realize he was asking

her to get the cauliflower for him. "Oh, yeah," Haley said before walking around the kitchen island. She had forgotten that it was the wheelchair that was allowing him to stand, not his own legs, and it didn't turn while in the standing position. She retrieved the cauliflower and put it down where her dad could reach it, then put her hand on Daryl's shoulder. "It's okay, Dad."

"I just want to do it right, that's all," Daryl said as he put what was left of the cauliflower on the cutting board and began cutting it into smaller pieces. After slicing and positioning additional pieces into just-right places, Daryl finally looked satisfied. "Okay, you can put it on the table now," he declared.

Haley took the tray to the kitchen table while Daryl lowered himself into a seated position before following her. Haley stepped back, and she and Daryl inspected the table arrangement, which also featured napkins, bottled water, and a small video teleconference monitor.

"Quite the little conference setup," Haley said with satisfaction.

"We are professionals, after all," Daryl replied, his voice less strained.

Soon after everything was arranged, a car pulled into the driveway. Haley opened the front door of the house to go outside and help, but by that time Allen had already gotten out of the rideshare car, made his way to the trunk, and was unfolding Benjamin's stroller while Kelsey got out with Benjamin in her arms. Haley held the front door open as the car pulled away and Benjamin was put into his stroller.

While the family made their way to the house, Daryl parked himself closer to the front door and elevated himself back into a standing position. "If people are going to hug me, I'd rather be standing," Daryl said, answering a curious look from his daughter.

Daryl was right to be prepared. Even though Allen had texted or spoke on the phone with Daryl on a regular basis while bringing Haley on, he hadn't visited for months. And Daryl couldn't remember the last time he had spoken with Kelsey. So it was only natural for Allen to greet his friend with a full two-armed bearhug and a macho back slap before Kelsey did the same, replacing the back slap with an affectionate kiss on the cheek.

Turning his attention to Benjamin, Daryl returned to a seated position to get closer to the child. "Look at this handsome little man," Daryl gushed. Benjamin ignored the comment and instead looked off into the distance. Daryl reached in and gave him a little tickle on the chin, but Benjamin's only response was to fidget in his seat a bit before resting his head against the side of the stroller.

"He's pretty sleepy most of the time," Allen explained with a sheepish grin after his son didn't respond. But Daryl wasn't bothered.

"Tell your dad not to worry about it, young man," Daryl told Benjamin. "That's what happens when you fight the good fight."

As the old friends chatted and made pleasantries, Haley busied herself with chores. She cleaned up the vegetable mess on the kitchen island and took out the trash while her dad and the others took a casual tour through the workshop. It seemed like an easier choice than trying to hold her own in a conversation with people over twenty years her senior, no matter how well she knew them.

When Haley came back inside, her dad, Allen, and Kelsey were still in the workshop. Daryl and Allen were telling a story of some kind, talking in turns with one another between occasional laughter, reminiscing about some old mission. Haley made herself scarce until it was over. Between growing up with her dad and training with Allen, she had heard enough stories about their exploits to last a lifetime.

She took a seat at the kitchen table and served herself a hearty sampling from the vegetable tray. The table setup reminded her of her first job right after college working for an international relations think tank in Washington DC. One of the odd takeaways she got from that job was how uncomfortable people were to be the first one to take something from a snack tray at a conference table. She sat through entire meetings watching people eye up various muffins and fresh fruit without taking a single piece. She noticed meetings went much better if she bit the bullet and demonstrated that it was acceptable to eat food that had been placed there for that explicit purpose. Plus, she usually got tired of waiting for someone else to do it first.

While snacking on a miniature carrot, Haley heard a small noise next to her and turned to see Benjamin stirring in his stroller. Haley hadn't noticed him before she sat down and only then remembered that he had been falling asleep right before everyone else moved into the workshop. Benjamin was awake but looking drowsy, grimacing and rubbing his eyes. Haley watched him work to get comfortable, but the more he tried to settle himself back to sleep, the more agitated he became.

After a few moments of this, the awkwardness Haley felt by simply watching him fuss and doing nothing overcame her discomfort of interacting with children. She pulled her chair closer to Benjamin and figured she had watched parents shush their kids enough times for her to try it herself. She leaned closer to Benjamin's face and began shushing softly, cupping the top of his head and rubbing it as soothingly as she could muster. In a short time, Benjamin's eyes closed and his breathing slowed. Haley pulled her hand away and sat up straight before quietly scooting on her chair back to her original place at the table.

Haley's eyes went wide. *Holy crap, it worked!* She returned her attention to the vegetables and spent the next few minutes continuing to watch Benjamin for any new signs of restlessness in case her services were needed again. Haley rolled her eyes at herself. Five minutes earlier, she hadn't even thought to look at Benjamin and now she was watching after him like a mother hen. Kids were insidious.

Benjamin continued his nap as the rest of the group came out to the kitchen to start the meeting. Kelsey checked on Benjamin and, seeing that he was still asleep, rolled him away from the table to just inside the workshop so he could still be seen without the meeting disturbing him. As everyone took a seat at the table, Haley noted with satisfaction that Allen and Kelsey wasted no time taking healthy samplings of vegetables for themselves.

"Okay," Allen began, still crunching broccoli between his teeth, "let's get started." He pulled his phone out of his pocket and placed it down on the table before turning to Haley. "Is your guy ready?"

"He should be," Haley replied before tapping the teleconference monitor to wake it up. The display confirmed that a remote participant was standing by on the other end of the call.

"This is the remote support guy?" Kelsey asked. "Does he have a name?"

"Yes..." Allen replied, his voice trailing off without elaborating.

"Well," Kelsey said with confusion, "what is it?"

Haley tapped the monitor to connect the video call. Instantly, the room filled with the sounds of loud rock music. On screen, animated text displayed the name *MeatTank* with the kind of motion effects more in the style of introducing a professional wrestler than a clandestine technical support specialist. The animation faded away and was replaced with the face of a young, pale man wearing large over-the-ears headphones with an attached microphone. He bobbed his head up and down to the music still playing in the background.

"Hey! How's everyone doing today?" Kyle asked with an exuberance unfit for casual everyday life.

The group at the table stared at the screen with their mouths open until Kelsey spoke up. "Cut the music!" she commanded before turning to look toward Benjamin in his stroller.

The music stopped. Kelsey took a half step up from her chair, her gaze locked on her son, scrutinizing for any signs of wakefulness. She paused mid-step for a few moments and, not seeing any indication that Benjamin was stirring, sat down again, letting out a relieved breath.

"Kyle?" Daryl asked, confused.

"Hi there, Mister Eckland!" Kyle said with a wave.

"How are you?"

"Fine," Daryl replied as he shot Haley a puzzled look.

"He's the best remote guy out there," Haley explained.

"Though there could be better remote *gals* out there," Kyle added.

"Be a feminist later," Haley commanded.

"The best remote operator out there is my daughter's friend from grade school?" Daryl asked, his eyes narrowing.

"I'm sorry," Kelsey cut in, "is his name Kyle or MeatTank?"

"We were actually friends until middle school, then I guess we became penpals," Kyle said.

"His online handle is MeatTank," replied Haley to Kelsey. "And yes, Dad, he is the best."

Daryl pointed at the video screen. "This guy, the kid who got himself stuck in our doggie door?"

"In my defense," Kyle interrupted, "you had a small dog."

Haley cracked a smile. "I forgot about that."

Daryl looked at Allen for backup. Instead, Allen gave him an expression that indicated he and Haley both agreed on this one. "Okay," Daryl said, "okay. I'll try to keep an open mind, but I can't promise it."

Allen reached out to his phone still lying on the table. "All right then," he said as he opened an app on his phone. After a couple of taps, Allen activated a projection function that displayed a mirror image of his screen onto the surface of the table surrounding it, filling the space with surveillance images and technical information. "Let's start. The first objective is to rescue this man, Doctor Emmanuel Sloan," Allen said as a photo of Sloan appeared.

"If this is the first objective," Daryl interrupted, "what's the second?"

"Well," Allen stammered. "The second one...requires a bit of explaining. But first, let's talk about Sloan."

Chapter Ten

They know, they know, they know...

Doctor Emmanuel Sloan wiped sweat from his palms onto the knees of his pants as he sat at his work terminal in the patient observation bay, five stories below Greenland's arctic surface. He stole glances around him at medical technicians and security personnel who sat at other workstations or walked through the bunker-like space around him, looking for cues that anyone was onto him. He tried to remind himself that he still had deniability. He could always say that he'd only emailed a former colleague. Sloan's excuse did seem reasonable, but he had learned long ago that he wasn't working for reasonable people. The massacre of the nearby village taught him that.

Sloan turned his attention back to his computer, but the text of the patient chart seemed to swim on the screen. He thought about the wording of the message he had sent as a kind of SOS to his former colleague, Eric Baner, working at the Tor Research Institute in Chicago. The two had gone through medical school together and had a running inside joke that came from an attending physician they had studied under. The attending physician had an odd way of using lavish descriptions for patient symptoms. Rather than saying a patient was bleeding badly, he would say the patient was "hemorrhaging with profusion worthy of concern."

Instead of having a bad cough, a patient "coughed with unrelenting fervor." Baner and Sloan never quite knew if he used these descriptions seriously or as a way to entertain himself, but either way, the habit caught on to describe everything from dinner dates to the flavor of a new beer.

The two friends had also decided that using the technique was a good way for Sloan to let his friend know that he was in trouble, though this had been thrown out as a joke by Baner right before Sloan left for Greenland. Now, with all travel away from the research base forbidden, that simple throwaway joke became the only lifeline Sloan had.

Giving up on his patient charts, Sloan pulled up his email and reread the reply he had gotten from Baner. In response to Sloan's message that used five hundred words to elaborately describe what he'd had for breakfast, Sloan received a suspiciously dull reply:

Sounds good. Pretty much the same around here. Glad all is well.

Take care,

Eric

He had to be up to something, Sloan hoped. Though he worried that he may have an inflated sense of his friend's ability to get Eamon Tor's attention.

Sloan shook his head. Why wasn't *he* working for Eamon Tor? *Midlife crisis*, Sloan reminded himself. The research job in Greenland seemed so exotic when it had been offered to him. In his mind, he'd imagined he would spend every late afternoon hiking through a beautiful, pristine landscape after working easy nine-to-five hours. Plus, with traditional medical research jobs like the one he lost in Baltimore drying up, Sloan was desperate. So when he got a message out of the blue offering a cushy corporate gig in an exotic, remote locale, one that included free room and board, he ignored the red flags and saw only possibilities. Maybe he would learn the language, train in local customs and cuisine, and return to Baltimore to open a Greenlandian restaurant with all the money he would make. Maybe he would even grow a beard. But instead, he was rarely allowed to travel outside the research facility even before the shutdown, the local delicacy was fermented birds packed five hundred at a time into seal skins, and his facial hair was too spotty to look like anything more than an uneven shave job.

And then, of course, there were the deaths.

As it was originally explained to him, Doctor Sloan's role was to evaluate patients with a wide range of psychiatric conditions and then track the progress of experimental treatments. The fact that this was being done in the middle of nowhere only told Sloan that he would be working for a large corporation with deep pockets, one that didn't feel like being restricted by, what some called "traditional roadblocks to drug development" and others referred to as "safety regulations."

When Sloan first arrived, all twelve rooms in the semicircular patient bay were full and a variety of treatments were already underway. Then there was an incident with the patient in Room Eight, Ellie Barker. Ellie was schizophrenic with bouts of paranoia and rage. Her symptoms had been improving until, one afternoon, she accused an orderly of taking her bedsheets so he could steal her DNA and clone her. She shoved the orderly, and he fell down to the floor against the door to the room. Ellie then grabbed a metal wastebasket and smashed it against his head over and over, continuing long after he had stopped moving. As other staff members pushed against the door with the orderly jammed against it, Ellie ran over to the sink, grabbed it with both of her hands, and swiftly brought her head down straight onto the steel faucet.

The facility was not equipped to treat severe head injuries, and Ellie died a couple of hours later. When Sloan brought up the idea of evacuating Ellie for emergency care, his suggestion was curtly dismissed. The issue didn't seem to be that there was no emergency evacuation plan. It was that the emergency evacuation plan was to not evacuate at all.

In the week following the incident, Sloan felt as if he were the only one who knew what had happened, based on how quickly everyone around him had moved on. It was obvious the incident had not been the first patient death, but Sloan couldn't find the courage to ask anyone about it.

Soon, a new patient took up residence in Ellie's former room. Charles Dahl entered Room Eight with a strolling ease Sloan didn't usually see in patients. Most were agitated, emotionally numb, or at the very least apprehensive about their new surroundings. But Charles seemed more appreciative than anything.

At his workstation, Sloan pulled his focus out of his memories and brought up Charles' medical chart before looking across the row of one-way mirrors and settling his gaze on Room Eight. There, Charles lay on his medical bed reading a book.

"Call me Chuck, please," he had insisted when Sloan first introduced himself a few weeks earlier.

Chuck was in his early fifties with thinning hair and a Florida accent. "I'm from Crawfordville, born and raised. Usually I tell out-of-state folks I'm from Tallahassee 'cause it's close enough and people know it, but you're a doctor so I figure I better be honest."

Sloan ran Chuck through the standard questions and physical tests. He came without any previous diagnosis, and the only instructions in Chuck's medical chart simply read, *assess and observe.*

On the second day, after the first wave of tests and blood work was completed, the doctor returned to speak again with his newest patient. "I appreciate your patience, Chuck," Sloan said while looking through results on a tablet. "It's not often I get a patient in here that doesn't come with a clear diagnosis."

"Don't worry, doc, I don't mind at all," Chuck answered with a smile. "I'm just so appreciative for everything you guys have done for me."

"I'm not sure we've done much of anything for you yet," Sloan replied.

"Well, maybe not you personally, but now that I've gotten my life back, a few extra medical tests don't seem so bad."

Sloan looked up from his tablet. "What do you mean?" he asked.

"I mean the melanoma!" Chuck said with a laugh, then quickly took on a hushed tone. "Unless I'm not supposed to say anything. I don't want to ruin some double-blind situation or whatever it's called."

"You had melanoma?" Sloan asked.

"Bad," Chuck confirmed. "Stage four, spread all over. Docs told me I was a goner."

"That's a harsh way to put it," Sloan said.

Chuck laughed again. "Well, I guess they put it a little more delicately than that, but it's not an easy thing to sugarcoat."

Chuck went on to tell Sloan the story of his diagnosis and aftermath. Chuck had gone through multiple bouts of skin cancer in his life and usually had regular follow-ups with his local oncologist. But as the economy got worse and medical care got more expensive and harder to find, his check-ups grew farther apart. By the time he noticed the return of his melanoma and had it looked at, it had spread throughout his body. Doctors were not optimistic about treatment, but they did lay out a plan of surgery, drugs, and chemotherapy. Chuck wasn't very excited about the idea of spending the rest of his remaining days weak and nauseous but found it hard to tell that to his wife and children.

"My sons are all grown up, but when I told them about the cancer, all I could see were my little boys," Chuck said. "Figured I had to at least try."

Chuck and his wife, Amy, went to the hospital one morning for a final wellness check before surgery. But when they arrived, a woman from the billing department came into the waiting room and took them to a small office. Chuck said the woman seemed in a daze, like going through the motions of a routine she had done a thousand times. She never even gave Chuck her name. As Chuck and Amy sat down, the woman pulled out forms from a folder while reciting a pre-written statement in monotone from memory. She informed Chuck that due to the shortages in insurance coverage generally, as well as HAPA predictive outcome models about Chuck specifically, the hospital required a form of collateral before any major medical procedure. "She wanted me to sign my house over before they treated me," Chuck told Sloan.

Chuck and his wife took the forms. After his appointment, when Chuck and Amy got home, he carried the forms into the house and threw them straight into the garbage. "That pissed Amy off something fierce," Chuck said. "I didn't know a woman could cry and cuss so hard at the same time, but Amy pulled it off." Chuck wouldn't risk their house to pay for treatments that only had a small chance of working. "So, that was that," Chuck recalled. He was angry and disappointed, but, he said, the decision made sense. He wouldn't bankrupt his wife and leave her homeless, and he wouldn't allow his sons to do it either. "I couldn't let them sign away their futures and pay for failed treatments long after I'd already died." Instead, Chuck decided to enjoy things while he could. He went on long walks with his dog. He went fishing. He and Amy went out to dinner to the fancy restaurants she had always wanted to try. "I'm not a fan of the wine-drinking restaurants," Chuck admitted. "But if you order an ice water and slip a couple ice cubes into a glass of red wine, it goes down a lot easier." Chuck did all the things he'd put off in his life. Until the time came when he couldn't.

Chuck grew more confined to his house as his cancer got worse. He felt it most in his lungs, gasping for air after short walks and getting weaker and weaker every day. A dull pain became ever-present, he had spells of confusion, he slept more and ate less. No more walks with the dog. No more dinners with his wife. He needed help going to the bathroom. He started using an oxygen tank. And even through all that, Chuck said he still wasn't sure how to feel. "I didn't want to go on, but I still wasn't ready to go," he said. "That's when they knocked on my door."

"Who were 'they?' " Sloan asked.

"Two guys wearing suits," Chuck answered. "At first I thought they were Mormons, but then they introduced themselves as researchers." Chuck told Sloan that on the day the two men came to the house, he couldn't even stand up to greet them as Amy led them into the living room. Chuck sat in his recliner breathing with an oxygen mask while the men described their research into treatments for complex, intractable diseases, including stage four cancers and other various HAPA-restricted conditions. If Chuck participated in the study, he would be flown by private medical transport to an independent facility for experimental treatment. Due to corporate confidentiality, he and his family would not be told where he was going, and he would have to go alone. Chuck was nervous about traveling and potentially dying surrounded by strangers, but the men had one more surprise to sweeten the deal. "They offered us a six-figure payment if I agreed to go," Chuck said. "But they didn't call it a payment. They called it an 'honorarium.' Pretty fancy stuff."

So, in spite of their concerns, Chuck and Amy decided he should go. After a tearful goodbye with his family, he was moved to a medical facility a few hours' flight away and brought to a nondescript hospital room. Chuck wasn't told where he was, and all he could see through the windows were light panels that generated artificial daylight. He underwent tests, then more tests, and more tests after that. Chuck was able to exchange recorded video messages with his family, but he couldn't talk with them live. The video messages kept him from feeling lonely, though not entirely entertained. "Not that fighting for my life was boring, but still, there's only so much TV a guy can watch." After days of this, Chuck was relieved to finally receive his actual treatment.

"They took me to a room with a machine. It was a long metal cylinder, a little bigger than me, with a metal platform that rolled in and out for me to lie on," Chuck recounted. "It looked like one of those iron lungs they used to put polio patients in when their lungs were paralyzed. I watched a history show about it once. Polio, I mean." The treatment session sounded very mundane as Chuck explained it. He lay down on the metal platform, was given an injection, then had a number of sensors stuck onto him before being pushed inside the chamber. He stayed inside listening to music for about an hour. There was no noise, no pain, no poking and prodding, just sitting and waiting for whatever was being done to finish. Then he was taken out and returned to his room where he stayed for three days. "That was the worst," Chuck remembered. "Different medical people came in to check this and that, ask me questions, then they'd just disappear. The whole thing felt like a mistake. Until day four."

Chuck said day four was when he woke up feeling different. He said it was like waking up in the morning when you're just getting over the hump of a nasty cold—it's still there, but you can tell you're past the worst of it. "I wasn't one hundred percent, but I felt like I'd turned a corner. I actually wanted to get out of bed instead of wishing I could sleep more."

The medical staff put Chuck through physical tests, which he termed "The Terminally Ill Olympics." He blew air as hard as he could through a tube to keep a ping pong ball afloat, walked as far as he could down the hall without taking a break, and lifted a variety of weights over his head. Gradually, day by day, he was able to do more and set new personal records. After a week of this, Chuck underwent a full body scan to check on the cancer. "The tumors started shrinking," said Chuck, a hint of tears in his eyes. "I'd given up on the whole thing. I guess I got used to the idea of dying. I couldn't believe it."

Two weeks later, after surgery to remove tumors on his skin and multiple follow-up scans, Chuck was declared to be in remission. Through video messages, plans were made for a party and a vacation with his wife. But all those plans had to wait for more tests. "So I guess that's why I'm here, doc," Chuck told Sloan, finishing his story. "You gotta keep watching me to make sure I'm okay, and I'll just sit tight and stay healthy until I can go home."

While Sloan remembered their past conversations, he continued to watch Chuck reading. Chuck was the perfect patient, one without anything wrong, and yet he hadn't been sent home. Still, Sloan wasn't sure what to think about Chuck's story of being cured of cancer by secret therapies.

As he mulled his thoughts, a shadow spread across Sloan's desk and the sense of someone looming over him pulled him fully back into the present. He didn't need to look up to know who it was but forced himself to do so anyway.

At over six-and-a-half feet tall with a muscle mass somewhere between a professional wrestler and a rhinoceros, Hanspeter Jodock towered over Sloan. The doctor began to stand to greet his immediate supervisor until Jodock put a massive hand on Sloan's shoulder and effortlessly pushed him back down.

"Please, doctor, no need to get up," Jodock said. His Swiss accent was always jarring. To Sloan's ear, its mixture of European influences and German undertone made Jodock sound highly intelligent yet brutally intimidating, as if he could perform Hamlet while bashing someone's skull with his bare hands and succeed brilliantly at both.

"Okay, Mister Jodock," Sloan replied, his entire body tense with Jodock's hand still on his shoulder. "What can I, I mean, do you need something?"

"I've just read your latest update on Mister Dahl," Jodock said. "I wanted to talk with you about it."

Jodock's role at the facility seemed an odd mixture of responsibilities to Sloan. He was Sloan's immediate superior and the person who took Sloan's findings to the higher-ups at the company, but Jodock also personally directed security as well as the transfer of patients, and his daily wardrobe was the same kind of utility clothing and body armor the security forces wore. Even for someone with the job title Head of Operations, Jodock was incredibly involved in everything that went on.

"Well," Sloan stammered, "in my last report I noted that I haven't seen any signs of mental illness."

"Yes, I just want to be sure you're being as thorough as possible," Jodock said.

Sloan decided to take a chance and put Chuck's

story to the test. "I don't know. It looks like after his treatment at the other facility, he's stable and holding his own."

Jodock was silent for a moment. His hand, still on Sloan's shoulder, tightened slightly before he replied. "Yes, well, we've been here before with other patients, and it's important that we don't let our guard down."

It took everything Sloan had not to flinch at Jodock's grip. "Yes, sir, I understand."

Jodock smiled. "Thank you, doctor, I knew you would." He removed his hand from Sloan's shoulder and walked away without another word, heading to the back of the room and the set of stairs that led up to his office.

Sloan's breath rasped out of his control as he looked out over the patients in the observation bay, confused about the truth of what he was doing and where his patients had come from. He stood and walked through a short hallway that split the two halves of the observation bay and into an inner ring hallway that allowed access to a line of doors to the patient rooms. He went to Room Eight and waved his security badge across the access panel to unlock the door before letting himself inside.

On the bed, Chuck glanced up from his book. "Hi, doc, what's the good word?"

"Nothing new yet, sorry," Sloan replied, walking over to Chuck. "I just had a quick question."

"Shoot," Chuck said, so used to people coming in and out that he didn't even bother sitting up from the bed.

"When you got your cancer treatment," Sloan began, "did you see any other patients there?"

"I never met any other patients," Chuck answered.

"But you think there were other people there?"

"When they rolled me away for the treatment, we went past a bunch of doors that all looked the same," Chuck remembered. "There were some folks in one of them, cleaning it up. It was a room just like mine, looked like it was getting a new guest."

"How many doors like that did you see?"

"I don't know, maybe a dozen," Chuck guessed. "Why, you planning on moving?"

Sloan forced a smile. "No, no, just trying to think of, you know, budget planning. Ordering supplies, stuff like that."

"Okay, then, glad I could help," Chuck said before returning to his book.

Sloan left the room and made his way back to his workstation. A dozen rooms in the mysterious treatment area. Twelve patient rooms in his observation bay. Maybe there was a link between the two. Or maybe both areas just had the same numbers-obsessed architect. In either case, neither changed Sloan's desire to get away. He tried to go back to his work and think of other ways of being more thorough, as Jodock had suggested, but came up empty. Instead, Sloan pulled up Baner's email and read it yet another time, checking for any hidden meaning he may have missed.

Chapter Eleven

"Slow down, nobody here is fluent in 'conniption fit.'"

Haley had hoped her joke would calm her father down, but Daryl's hands were still clenched.

"I'm just having a hard time understanding this," Daryl said to Haley before turning back to Allen. "You're being hired to destroy something that could cure your son, and you're okay with that?"

"That's not what we're doing," Allen said.

"Isn't it?" Daryl replied, his voice rising again. "Because I'm pretty sure folks down at the spinal cord clinic would find it awfully useful."

"Please, Daryl, it's not like that," Allen pleaded. "It's not safe to use."

"And who came to that conclusion?" Daryl shot back. "You and Eamon Tor decided it's too dangerous so we should just blow it up?"

"You'd be playing Russian roulette," Allen said. "Except instead of killing yourself you'd become a monster before going insane. I'm not going to trade Benjamin's epilepsy for some other brain disorder."

"But what about other people, Allen?" Daryl said. "Thousands of people deemed unworthy for medical care. We forget about them, too?"

"Once Eamon has the research, he can make it safe," Allen assured Daryl. "Like every other drug."

"And what about those of us who might not want to wait a decade or so for that to happen?"

"Read the medical files," Allen said sternly, picking up his phone. The projection on the table disappeared as Allen handed the phone to Daryl. "They're all there. Read how Rusk is acting. See if that's someone you want to become."

Daryl clenched his jaw and looked through the files while the rest of them sat in uncomfortable silence. Haley studied her father's hands as he interacted with the projections on the table. He clawed with his nails to enlarge documents to read them before viciously flicking them aside as if trying to wipe them from existence. She wasn't sure she'd have the courage later to ask about his feelings. And even if she did, what could she say to him?

After a few more minutes, Daryl spoke while still looking over the medical files. "And what if your buddy Eamon Tor has you rescue Doctor Sloan just to build his own Eden Therapy and charge millions to use it, just like he said Rusk would do? What if this is all just one big story to help a rich man get richer?"

"Eamon could have said the technology works fine and I would have done the job for free," Allen answered. "I think in his mind, he feels it's some sort of cosmic balance that he can prevent Eden from hurting people while eventually making money at the same time."

"Yeah, well, it must be easy to understand the universe when you're richer than God," Daryl grumbled, handing the phone back. As Allen returned the phone to the center of the table and reactivated the projection, Haley watched her father again. His breathing had slowed and his scowl had relaxed, as if he were coming around to Allen's rationalizations. But that didn't necessarily mean he liked the situation any better.

As if to confirm her suspicions, Daryl spoke up again. "Still, I have concerns. We're talking about infiltrating a virtual bunker in a remote part of Greenland to rescue a doctor we don't even know how to find."

"We're just going to have to work the problem," Allen said.

"Sure, but then there's Olivia Rusk," Daryl countered. "Normal places we break into are usually run by people who are greedy and evil but more or less sane. Apparently she's all of some and none of the other."

"What does that matter?" Allen asked.

"She slaughtered innocent people over nothing," Daryl explained. "Lord knows what she has planned for people actually working against her. For all we know the facility is filled with booby traps from floor to ceiling."

"She has a private army as well as staff in the facility. That forces her to keep some basic level of rationality to things," Allen reasoned.

"An army?" Kelsey asked. "These are private contractors, not mechs like that Central American job?"

Haley had the same question. It was one thing to mow down a unit of artificial soldiers. It was another to fight real people.

"No mechs," Allen confirmed. "Things being what they are, Rusk can hire desperate people cheap. Intel is limited, but Eamon figures the top two or three people running the show are former military with experience, and the rest are basic guns for hire or newbies. Probably just trying to keep their heads down and follow orders, no questions asked."

"Which is not as easy as it sounds," Kelsey said.

"Right," Allen said. "Some of the bodies in the village were Rusk's own forces. It looks like they were executed, presumably for not following orders."

"That's the kind of stuff I'm talking about," Daryl said, growing agitated again. "You're not robbing one of Rusk's forgotten summer homes—this is serious for her. And she's gone completely insane. She obviously doesn't care about her people. There's a real chance she could blow the entire facility sky-high rather than let anyone get out."

"Daryl," Allen said in a calming voice. "It's not like Haley and I are just going to walk in there without a plan."

"I have concerns about Haley walking in there at all," Daryl said.

Haley straightened up and looked at her father. She had been intentionally silent, waiting for Allen and her dad to figure out a game plan while she took it all in. She hadn't expected the discussion to turn into a full-on argument. Getting brought into it caught her off guard. "Excuse me?" was all she could get out.

"This is not a mission for a rookie," Daryl said to her. "Even in our prime, Allen and I would think twice before taking this on."

Allen jumped in before Haley could respond. "I wouldn't have brought her in on this if I didn't think she could do it."

"Wouldn't you?" Daryl challenged. "No offense,

but I'm not sure you can be totally rational here."

"I am not so desperate to help my son that I would sign up for a suicide mission," Allen replied, his voice getting louder.

"All I know is," Daryl said, "if I were in your spot, I don't know how clear-headed I would be."

Once again, Haley tried to speak for herself. But once again, Allen beat her to it. "You asked me to take Haley on as a partner," Allen said to Daryl. "That means she can make her own decisions about what missions she will or won't take."

"Not if she's so desperate to prove herself that she'll walk straight into a death trap," Daryl argued.

"That's not fair..." Allen countered. And on it continued.

Haley's mind drifted. With the noise of Allen and her father arguing in the background, Haley looked at the mission briefing displayed on the table. It showed the research facility, which looked isolated but not impossible to break into. Getting in wasn't as dangerous as what might happen if they were caught underground with no way out. This was not a mission about brute force. It needed patience and intelligence, and right now Allen and her father were showing neither.

Haley closed her eyes and visualized herself and Allen breaking into the base, gauging the level of fear she felt at the idea. Was that something she could handle? She had definitely been afraid in the jungle when the mechs were bearing down on her. Afraid, but not paralyzed. Haley found hope in that. Still, she couldn't help but wonder if her father was right. She did want to prove herself, prove that she could be a great operator like she wanted since she was a teenager. But her father had yet to understand that it was herself she was trying to convince most of all.

Through the sound of arguing, Haley heard another sound. She turned and looked into the other room where Benjamin sat in his stroller. His eyes were still closed but he was fussing. His body twisted in discomfort while he rubbed his eyes with balled fists. Then Haley saw it, Benjamin's arms springing with a jolt from his body, the classic sign Allen said was Benjamin having a seizure. It was subtle and quick, but Haley had no doubt of what she saw. Benjamin grew quiet and his eyes fluttered. Just when Haley thought it was over, Benjamin's arms sprung out again without warning and the boy started to cry.

"Guys, I think Benjamin…" Haley said.

Before Haley could finish, Kelsey was on her feet heading toward her son. Allen and Daryl fell silent while Kelsey knelt by Benjamin to comfort him.

Haley had never seen Benjamin have a seizure before. She had always thought of his condition as a problem that Allen was going through, never thinking about it from Benjamin's point-of-view. She wasn't even sure what level of point-of-view he had. She knew from her own curious online searches that Benjamin's condition disrupted his brain waves, limiting how he could learn. Even how he could think. Haley had just been trying to judge her ability to control her fear, but would Benjamin ever feel fear? Or joy? Love?

Unexpectedly, Haley's thoughts turned to the best night of her life. It was a friend's birthday during her junior year of college. It was November, but it was hot for that time of year, so everything was outside. Her friend had a patio and they were having drinks outside. A mutual friend came. Her name was Lilah, and Haley had a mild crush on her. They sat together. They talked. The group went out to dance. Haley drank through the night, just enough to feel a subtle electricity. She and Lilah kissed on the dance floor, then went back to her apartment and spent the night together. It wasn't the start of a beautiful relationship; the two never really became a couple, but that wasn't the point. It was the best night of her life because it was perfect and effortless and could never happen again.

Would Benjamin ever experience a night like that?

It wasn't Benjamin's inability to walk or talk or even make eye contact that was suddenly bothering her. It went further. He wasn't just fighting for his life or his soul—he was fighting for the ability to even understand that he had a life and soul. And if that small two-year-old could fight for that, maybe it was time for her to cowboy the hell up.

Haley turned back to the table. Allen's eyes were locked across the room at his son. Daryl turned and looked at her. "I'm in," she said to her father.

"Let's just talk about it," Daryl suggested.

Allen's head turned. "I'm sorry, what now?" he asked Haley.

"I said I'm in," she repeated.

Kelsey walked back to the table, leaving Benjamin still in the stroller. "He fell back asleep," she said with a sigh as she returned.

"You have a choice," Allen told Haley. "You can feel free to say no."

"I know," Haley said. "I just don't feel like saying no."

Daryl looked at his daughter sternly with a quiver in his eyes only Haley could detect. But knowing that no explanation or assurance could completely erase his fears, Haley offered none. Daryl also held his tongue, though he didn't look away from her either.

"Well, I'm in too if anyone was wondering," Kyle declared through the tinny monitor speaker.

"Thank you, MeatTank," Kelsey responded. "We're glad to have you on board."

"Well, thank *you*, ma'am," Kyle replied. "See how effortlessly she used my codename, everybody? It really is that easy."

Daryl finally broke his silence. "I don't like it," he said, still looking at Haley. "And since I don't like it, you're going to have to work, train, study, and plan until I do like it."

Haley nodded her understanding to her father, then Daryl turned to Allen and got the same nod from him.

"It seems to me," Kelsey said, pointing to an image of the research facility, "the first big problem is to figure out how to get into the place."

"I actually have an idea about that," Kyle said from the monitor. "But I have a question." The group all turned toward the monitor as Kyle continued. "What kind of takeout do rent-a-cops eat?"

Allen shrugged his shoulders. "Is that a real question or are you asking some kind of riddle?"

"It's a totally real question," Kyle said. "And the answer might just get us inside that facility."

Chapter Twelve

You'd think performing rogue medical experiments would at least earn me some coffee.

Doctor Sloan stood bleary-eyed at the water cooler for his third cup of water that morning. He had not been able to sleep the past few nights and relied on frequent trips to the back of the observation bay for tiny portions of cold water to keep from falling asleep at his workstation. Coffee, he was told, was being rationed.

After downing his drink, Sloan crushed the tiny paper cone and tossed it in a wastebasket on his way back to his desk, checking his email the moment he sat in his chair. Still no more word from Baner. Sloan wasn't sure what he expected from his friend, but he definitely thought it would have happened by now.

The sound of a loud, unknown voice interrupted Sloan from his obsessive worrying. He looked up from his computer and saw a new yet somehow familiar face. Flanked by a pair of personal security guards, Olivia Rusk walked with purpose through the observation bay, heading toward the back stairs that led up to Jodock's office.

"He'd better be here," Rusk said with a snarl. Sloan recognized her from the news over the years, but instead of the grandmotherly demeanor he was familiar with, Rusk seemed transformed into an entirely different person. She moved in a flustered rush, her eyes darting around the room. Instead of the kind of modest dresses Sloan had seen her wear in pictures over the years, Rusk now wore an ensemble that blended the fit of athletic wear with the boldness of experimental fashion. Her jacket was made of squares of multifaceted microbeads that made sections appear to change color depending on the angle they were seen at, and the fabric of the outfit hugged her body like a second skin. Somehow Sloan doubted the physique of a woman in her eighties was the frame the designers had intended their outfit for.

Rusk and her guards walked up the back stairs and disappeared through a doorway at the top. A moment later, Sloan heard the door to Jodock's inner office slam shut. Even with the door closed, Rusk's muffled yelling drifted through the walls, and Sloan along with everyone else working in the observation bay listened intently while trying to act as if they weren't. A cold sweat broke out on Sloan's forehead as his mind raced to understand what he had seen. A multi-billionaire supposedly on death's door and considered one of the sweetest women to ever walk the planet had just strolled through his workspace looking ready to knock somebody out. The similarities to Chuck and his miraculous recovery, as well as the familiar on-edge behavior he'd seen in so many of his patients, were inescapable. The room spun around him.

Rusk's voice grew louder as she came out of Jodock's office onto the top landing of the stairs. "...and I want real progress! Not these dingle notes from blind, pencil-pushing dung bags!"

Rusk cursed as if she'd only begun to dabble in it recently, and then only learning from books. Sloan would have laughed about it if the sight of Jodock appearing through the door hadn't made his blood run cold.

"Yes, madam, of course," Jodock replied, stopping just outside the door to watch as Rusk stomped down the metal stairs with her guards close behind. After Rusk stormed out of the observation bay the same way she'd come in, Sloan turned back toward his computer but stopped short when he caught Jodock looking at him. Without a word, Jodock motioned with a hand for Sloan to come up to him before turning and disappearing through the door.

Sloan's legs were like rubber and he swayed as he walked toward the stairs. A pounding in his head grew louder and his chest tightened with each step. He took a deep breath. Panicking wasn't going to help anything.

Going through the door at the top of the stairs, Sloan entered a small outer office that was both a reception area and guard post. A guard stared absently at several video monitors from behind a small, simple desk. He looked up at Sloan and waved the doctor on to the main office. Sloan sneaked a glance at the monitors as he passed, recognizing feeds from the patient rooms as well as a wide shot of the observation area where he and the other medical staff members worked. The guard at the desk started to look up again at Sloan, and the doctor quickly turned away and rushed into Jodock's office before he was caught peeking.

Once inside, Sloan stopped and waited. The situation would have been far less awkward if Jodock immediately said what he wanted without delay, but sadly that was not to be. Instead, Jodock sat at his desk and typed on his computer, both of which looked absurdly small in comparison to Jodock's size. Without his presence being acknowledged, Sloan was forced to wait in nervous silence until Jodock completed his task.

Finally, Jodock finished. "Doctor Sloan," he said, gesturing for Sloan to come closer.

Sloan stepped forward and stood in the general area he imagined a chair would be if Jodock had ever cared to put one there. "Yes, sir?"

"I wanted to speak to you about Charles Dahl."

"Yes?" Sloan repeated.

Jodock looked up from his computer. "You haven't noticed," he said as a statement rather than a question.

"No, I haven't noticed anything," Sloan said, a wave of heat coming over him. "What happened?"

Jodock pointed across the room over Sloan's right shoulder. The doctor turned and saw a bank of video monitors against the wall that he hadn't noticed before. He walked over to the monitor for Patient Room Eight. On the screen, Chuck stood smiling and gesturing in wide motions as if telling a story. But Sloan saw no one else in the room.

"He's talking to himself?" Sloan asked.

"You're supposed to tell me, doctor," Jodock said coldly.

Sloan looked around the video image again, confirming that no one but Chuck was in the room. "I'll go talk to him, do a complete workup."

With his attention on the video screen, Sloan hadn't noticed Jodock get up from the desk to stand only inches behind him. The doctor stifled a gasp as Jodock spoke. "I don't appreciate having these kinds of problems being pointed out to me by Madam Rusk."

"I apologize," the doctor said stiffly, still looking

straight ahead. "I'll get answers for you. I won't stop until I know something."

"Happy to hear it," Jodock replied, though his tone was anything but joyful. He continued to stand there. A hot bead of sweat ran down the back of Sloan's neck behind his right ear. Finally, Jodock turned and walked back to his desk. "Thank you for coming by, doctor," he said dismissively as he sat and resumed working at his computer. "I look forward to learning what you find."

Sloan left Jodock's office as fast as he could without breaking into a full run. At the bottom of the stairs, he paused for a moment, leaning his full weight against the railing, before wiping the sweat from his face and continuing on to the central nursing desk where most of the medical staff was based.

Angelina, the nurse manager on duty, greeted him with a smile. "Good morning, Doctor Sloan. Are you feeling okay? You look—"

"I need a blood tech and somebody from pharmacy to meet me in Room Eight," Sloan ordered.

"I didn't see any orders in the system. Did you want to add some at my station?" Angelina asked helpfully.

Sloan walked away before she finished her sentence. "No, I'll just have them draw a few vials," Sloan said over his shoulder. "I'll figure it out in the room."

Sloan quickly rounded a corner before Angelina could ask him anything more. The doctor's mind raced to think of rational reasons for Chuck to be speaking to himself. Sloan hadn't realized until that moment how much his hope for escape was tied to Chuck also getting out. So, as Sloan turned into the corridor of doors leading to the medical rooms, his fear for himself transformed into an urgent need to speak with his patient.

Sloan reached the door to Room Eight, unlocked it with his keycard, and gently knocked before slowly opening it and looking in. Chuck sat on his medical bed with his hands held in fists in front of his body, rocking back and forth as if hauling in a fish with an invisible fishing rod.

"...Damn thing nearly pulled me in the water," Chuck explained, tilting his head toward an empty chair. "Took me an hour to land her. That swordfish was a beast." After a short pause, Chuck nodded and laughed at a comment only he could hear. As Sloan walked into the room, Chuck looked over and greeted the doctor. "Hey there, doc. Hope I wasn't being too loud, just swapping fish stories."

"No, it's all right," Sloan assured him as he glanced around the room. "Just wanted to see how your day is going."

"Good, good," Chuck answered before turning back to the empty chair and pausing as if listening to someone. "Oh yeah, okay," Chuck said to the unseen friend. "I'll catch up with you later." Chuck's gaze seemed to follow someone leaving the room, and as that person apparently walked out through the door, Chuck turned back to Sloan. "He's a good kid."

Sloan decided to play along. "Yeah, seems so. I'm embarrassed to say that I've forgotten his name."

"Eddie," Chuck said. "Don't worry. I won't tell him you forgot. It must be hard keeping all the names straight when you're in charge."

"Does Eddie come in here a lot?" Sloan asked, walking farther into the room.

"Just in the past few days," Chuck replied as he picked up a glass from his overbed table and brought it to the sink. "Today was the first time he spoke to me, though."

"And what did he say?"

"Just introduced himself, asked where I was from, you know. Small talk." Chuck filled his glass with water and took a drink before walking back, pulling the wheeled table over to the reclining chair where "Eddie" had been, and sitting down. Sloan watched Chuck carefully as he put the glass down next to a book of sudoku puzzles, then picked up the book and opened to a page where he had put a pen as a bookmark. To Sloan's experienced eyes, there was no doubt that Chuck believed he had just been speaking to a real person.

"How are you feeling, Chuck?" the doctor asked.

"Same as I feel every day, doc," Chuck replied as he grabbed his pen and continued his puzzle.

"And how is that? Specifically?"

"I feel fine," Chuck answered with a hint of a scowl. "I just want to go home."

"Well, we're doing everything we can to—"

"Damnit," Chuck blurted out, eyes still on his book.

"What? What's wrong?" Sloan asked, stepping closer.

"Nothing, doc, just this sudoku," Chuck answered with a sheepish smile. "I've got two more to solve before I finish the book, and this one here is a nightmare."

The door clicked behind Sloan, and he turned to see the blood technician enter the room. A slight man in his thirties, the technician wore hospital scrubs and carried a metal tray with supplies. Sloan wasn't familiar with his name. There was truth to what Chuck had said about being in charge. "I have trouble with number puzzles myself," Sloan admitted. "Working here, I've had plenty of time for crosswords, though."

"Yeah, well, I'm usually...wait, here we go," Chuck said, scratching out numbers on the paper and marking spaces with new ones. A moment later, he burst into a sudden rage. "No! Of course not, still not right!" Chuck slammed the book against the table, sending the glass of water flying.

Sloan turned his body away from the glass as it shattered on the floor, spraying water along with it. Chuck's pulse throbbed in his neck as the doctor tried to calm his patient. "It's okay, Chuck, just take it easy. I'll get something to clean up the water."

Sloan headed for the sink and its paper towel dispenser but stopped short as Chuck stood and shouted again. "No, you've done enough! Just get me out of here, that's what you can do for me."

"I understand, Chuck, I know," Sloan said. "Let's just take a deep breath and sit down."

Chuck looked as if he would argue more, but then it passed. He sat back down and took slow, even breaths. Soon, his face softened. "I'm sorry, I don't know what's going on with me," he said before letting out a small chuckle. "I feel like I'm possessed today."

"I understand," Sloan assured him. He stepped back from Chuck to make room for the blood tech. "We're going to draw some blood and see if we can figure out what's going on."

"Okay, doc. Okay," Chuck replied.

Sloan looked over at the blood technician and nodded. Taking his cue, the technician stepped forward and put his tray on the table before taking a blue disposable tourniquet out of its sterile packaging and wrapping it around Chuck's upper arm.

"It won't take long, Chuck," Sloan reassured. "We all just want to make sure you're well."

After swabbing the crook of Chuck's arm, the technician pushed a small needle into his vein and drew blood. "That's right," the technician told Chuck. "We're doing everything we can to make you feel better so you can return to your family."

The mention of Chuck's family set him off again. "Don't talk about my family!" he spat, grabbing the technician by the shirt with the needle still in his arm.

Tiny drops of warm blood hit Sloan's face as Chuck grabbed the technician by the shirt and threw him against the wall. The technician hit face-first before crumpling to the floor in a daze. As Sloan lurched to intervene, Chuck raised a leg and stomped full-force onto the technician's head, releasing a disturbing crack.

The technician's neck lay at a ghastly angle, and the remaining strength in Sloan's legs evaporated completely. While fighting to get back to his feet, Sloan felt himself lifted and brought face to face with Chuck.

"I want to go home!" Chuck bellowed. The raging blood vessels in his eyes and contorted expression made him unrecognizable.

Behind him, Sloan heard the door open and turned. A young woman in a white pharmacy coat stared wide-eyed at the technician on the floor. She slapped an emergency panic button located on a panel next to the door before racing away. Sloan turned back to face Chuck. "Please, sit down. We'll figure this out," he begged.

"Liar!" Chuck screamed before something over Sloan's shoulder caught his gaze. Chuck spun Sloan around and held him by the back of the shirt as three security guards now stood in the small room with guns drawn.

"I'll kill him!" Chuck threatened, squeezing an arm around Sloan's neck.

Sloan tried to order the guards to back down, but the words wouldn't come out. His vision filled with static and stars. The yelling sounded muddled and far off. Hot spit hit his neck as Chuck screamed at the guards. The barrels of the guns loomed heavy and inescapable.

Then a shot rang out, the sound panging through the room like a mallet. Sloan, instantly released from Chuck's grip, fell to the floor with Chuck landing on top of him. The doctor's ears rang intensely as he squirmed to escape Chuck's limp body. Once free, a guard pulled Sloan to his feet and rushed him out of the room.

In the hallway outside, Sloan crumpled back to the floor. He sat up as medical staff came to his aid to inspect his wounds and give him oxygen. As he was being cared for, Sloan looked through the propped-open door at Chuck's body lying in an ever-growing pool of blood. His face was not calm or at peace, nor did it have the hint of a smile Sloan was accustomed to. It was frozen into a glare of pain and anger, with an equally unfamiliar bullet wound in the left temple.

Sloan stared at Chuck for a long time, refusing to move even after the medics left and the clean-up began. He shook his head, struggling to reconcile which way to die was better for Chuck, by cancer or by the bloody mess in front of him. As a team of orderlies in sanitary jumpsuits started cleaning the floors and loading Chuck's body onto a gurney, a prickling feeling came over him. It alerted him to the fact that Jodock stood over him long before he looked up to confirm it.

After wordlessly entering the room, Jodock went over to Chuck's body on the gurney and inspected the wound at his head. Jodock let out a sigh and stepped away to allow the body bag to be sealed before noticing something on the floor. He reached down and picked up Chuck's sudoku book, as well as the pen lying nearby.

Jodock thumbed through the book, stopped, and began writing in it as he walked over to Sloan. "It's a real shame, doctor," he said without looking up from the book. "We could have gotten a lot of data from examining his brain." After writing a bit more, Jodock placed the pen inside and dropped the book into Sloan's lap before walking away without saying anything more.

Sloan picked up the sudoku puzzle book, its corners soaked in Chuck's blood, and opened it to the page Jodock had finished. It was the puzzle Chuck had been struggling with, his writing scratched out and replaced with Jodock's answers, filling every open space and correcting several others to complete it.

The doctor stayed until Chuck's body was taken away. Then he finally stood and made his way out of the corridor. Instead of going to his quarters, he headed for his workstation. It was time to leave. Now. He fell into the chair at his desk and opened his messaging program. He began typing but almost immediately deleted what he wrote. He tried again and once more cleared his screen before slamming his fist on his desk. Nurses and technicians turned toward the sharp noise but Sloan ignored them. He closed his eyes tightly and hovered his fingers over the keyboard. It was time to somehow, directly yet descreetly, craft an email that made it painfully clear he needed to get out.

Chapter Thirteen

I knew I should have brought earplugs.

Allen winced at the overwhelming high-pitched whine assaulting his ears from all directions. He wanted to plug his ears with his fingers, but his hands were already occupied with gripping a pair of handlebars in front of him. Seated on his drone-cycle, its motor and whirling propellers running, Allen hovered three feet above the floor of the concrete storage garage he usually kept it in. Along with the rest of the gear from his previous professional life, Allen had thought about selling the flying machine a few times over the years but never had. Now his procrastination had paid off. The motorcycle-like frame of the drone-cycle felt sturdy and familiar, and as he glanced down at the propellers in front and back of him spinning within their safety cages, the drone-cycle seemed none the worse for its lack of use. The thick walls of the storage unit provided an excellent level of privacy, just as the owners of the facility had advertised. But it also amplified the whir of the cycle through the confined space like an acoustic pressure cooker. Allen cringed again at the pain in his ears as he went through a final test of the controls. He slowly rolled the cycle left, the propellers tilting to the side together in perfect unison. After making the same move to his right, Allen gently brought the cycle back to the floor and powered it down.

A muffled voiced called out behind Allen, and he turned to where Haley and Daryl waited in the corner of the room, both bringing their hands down from their ears.

"What?" Allen yelled, his ears still buzzing.

"Looks good," Haley said, matching Allen's volume. Allen stood, swung his leg over the seat, and stepped down from the cycle as Haley walked over. While she took a closer look at the cycle, her father wheeled over and took readings with a handheld maintenance computer.

"The batteries are holding up," Daryl commented. "Doesn't look like we need to replace anything."

"Unlike the rest of my gear," Allen replied. "How is it coming?"

"I have all the parts I need, but it's only about half assembled," Daryl told him. "Right now I'm loading your armor with stock software until Kelsey gives me a final build."

"So for our next outing, I'll be donning my vintage attire?" Allen asked.

"Yeah, but I shielded the electronics, so at least you won't get jammed again," Daryl confirmed as he moved to put his tools away in a case near the opened overhead door.

Allen walked over to Haley, who was sitting on the drone-cycle examining the controls. "So you told him?" Allen asked in a strained yet hushed voice.

"No, but...have you ever tried to keep something from him?" Haley stammered out.

"Hmm..." Allen grunted knowingly before changing the subject. "You ready for tonight?"

"The hardest part is thinking about food every time we go over the plans," Haley said, still eyeing up the controls in front of her. "I keep craving Italian. Otherwise, the rest of it seems straightforward."

"Well, they're still security guards, even if they're just chair-riding camera watchers. But yes, it is straightforward," Allen agreed. "That is if our buddy MeatTank comes through." It was hard enough for Allen to put faith in someone he didn't know well, much less someone who used such an unfortunate name, but Allen couldn't deny that the plan Kyle had come up with was solid.

"I think Kyle can handle hacking into a food delivery service," Haley said dismissively. "I wish it was you delivering the sandwiches," she grumbled. "I'm not very good at, you know, dealing with people."

"Consider it a chance for personal growth. Besides, to the security guards, a dude in his forties delivering a pair of parmesan sandwiches is a lot more suspicious than someone in her twenties. You're all supposed to be broke."

"Everybody's broke nowadays," Haley responded.

"Yeah, but people my age have a harder time admitting it," Allen said, kneeling to pack up his own tools. "And let's be honest, for me they would only open the door a crack, but for you they'll probably fling the door open and invite you to eat with them."

"Well, that's nice and creepy."

"And yet true." Allen closed his tool kit and stood. Though he was ready to go, Haley still sat firm on the drone-cycle.

"When am I going to take this thing out for a spin?" she asked.

Allen gave Haley a look as if she were a toddler. "We'll talk about it when you're older," he teased.

"It's incredible how you've made it this whole day without being punched," Haley said, stepping off the cycle.

Allen picked up a pair of wheel attachments, brought one to each end of the cycle, then moved to the front to place one underneath the front propeller. Haley stood by the rear of the cycle and did the same at her end. The two then pushed the drone-cycle on its new wheels through the overhead door to where Daryl waited for them in the hallway. Allen took a moment to pull the overhead door closed and lock it before he and Haley pushed the cycle past dozens of identical storage units to the oversized elevator at the end of the hall, with Daryl following close behind.

As the three crammed into the elevator with the cycle and pushed the button for the ground floor, Allen looked over at his old partner. Daryl had been quieter than normal lately. A little silent treatment after an argument was nothing new between them, but the lack of cheer and even eye contact made a ghost of Allen's former partner. The plan for stealing blueprints of the Greenland facility from the company that designed it should have earned Allen a small amount of approval. Instead, Daryl had only spoken in short, matter-of-fact sentences and hadn't laughed or joked at all since the kitchen table meeting a couple of days earlier. Could it be the real problem was that Daryl hadn't expected him to take Haley on any serious missions, assuming they would stick to safe errand work to satisfy Haley's need for excitement and Allen's need for money? Not that Allen necessarily had a problem with that idea. It just wasn't what was happening, and Allen couldn't sacrifice an opportunity to cover Benjamin's needs just to meet Daryl's expectations. But feeling in the right wasn't much of a consolation if it meant losing his mentor and closest friend.

"Thanks for helping us out with this, Daryl," Allen said while the elevator slowly brought them down. "It would have taken me half the day to get the cycle running again."

Daryl turned his head slightly and replied with a hard look. A dismissive comment appeared imminent, and Allen withered. It still stung to see any disapproval from the man who taught him how to be a hired gun.

"Come on, Allen," Daryl said to Allen's surprise. "Don't sell yourself short. I'm sure you would have taken the whole day to get it working." Not the most original joke in the world, but it added air to Allen's deflated posture. Like Daryl always taught him, it was the right tool for the job. "I do have to ask something, though," Daryl added.

Allen's posture sank again. "Yeah?"

"We're hiring Kyle, and he's a world-class hacker, remote support guy," Daryl said. "But you have to physically break into a building downtown to steal Rusk's blueprints?"

Allen took a breath to defend the reasoning, but Haley beat him to it.

"The design files are stored in a digital vault," she explained. "Kyle's program traced the construction shell companies back to the architecture firm downtown, but all the records refer to the digital vault for the actual blueprints."

"And the vault isn't connected to any network,"

Allen added.

"Hmmm," Daryl grumbled. "I just don't like it."

"At least it's here in town," Allen said with forced cheeriness. "That's pretty great." He let his grin linger. Maybe his optimism would transfer to Daryl. Instead, Daryl delivered another hard look that brought Allen's smile to a quick end.

Once on the ground floor, Allen and Haley pushed the cycle into the parking lot while Daryl went to his SUV and used its built-in wheelchair lift to get into the driver's position. By the time Daryl was set and started the engine, Allen and Haley had gotten the drone-cycle to the middle of the parking lot and disconnected the wheels. Haley brought the attachments to her dad's vehicle, dropped them into the back, and got in on the passenger side, while Allen pulled out a helmet from his drone-cycle's under-seat storage compartment, put it on his head, and took a seat.

Allen fired up the cycle's propellers, hovered a foot above the ground, and held it there while he waited for the cycle's onboard navigation system to acquire a GPS signal. He looked over and waved goodbye to Daryl and Haley. As they pulled out and turned into the street, his drone-cycle's console display confirmed it was ready for flight. Allen climbed the cycle quickly up into the sky, a move his stomach instantly regretted. It had been quite a while since he'd ridden, and while his spirit assumed he could move as nimbly as he once had, his body needed more convincing.

Allen leveled the cycle to a more gradual climb until he reached the appropriate altitude. The City of Chicago had designated altitudes in its airspace that Allen could fly in depending on the direction he was going, and Kelsey had reminded him not to get a ticket. With his home to the northeast, Allen stopped climbing within the two- to three-hundred-foot zone reserved for travel in that direction. All personal flying was restricted downtown, but Allen was going to have to bend that rule later on that evening.

Settling in with the cycle on a straight bearing toward his condo, Allen relaxed and looked around. Personal aircraft were a lot more popular back when Allen bought his own machine, but with the downturn in jobs and the basic value of the dollar, personal luxuries like drone-cycles were the first things people sold for money. Even the company that made Allen's machine had gone bankrupt. So as Allen admired his view of the city in the late day sun, he was greeted with open sky with the exception of a few city airbuses flying above the freeway. At that time of day, the freeway was busy in all directions. Allen didn't envy the drive Daryl and Haley had to take to get back to Daryl's house, but he put the thought aside as he took in the view of downtown. This was Allen's favorite direction to see the skyscrapers from. The buildings were roughly clustered north to south following the coastline of Lake Michigan, and Allen's view from the southwest made the buildings appear stacked on top of each other to form a faux mountain of structures against the painfully-flat Illinois landscape. The golden light of the setting sun even gave it a majestic feel.

After passing downtown, Allen continued his diagonal path from the far southwest side of the city up to the northwest side. Out of curiosity, he descended as low as he was allowed. His drone-cycle had been in storage longer than he and Kelsey owned their condo, and he had never seen their neighborhood from the air before. Finally, his condo building came into view, and he circled it once before flipping a switch to extend small landing struts from the bottom of each propeller assembly and setting down on the roof deck.

Allen got off the cycle, removed his helmet, and headed for the door that led to the interior stairwell. The wood of the roof deck looked more worn than he remembered, and Allen realized he hadn't been up there since before Benjamin was born. All the parties and outside time he and Kelsey thought they'd have had been pushed aside with many of their other plans. Allen made a mental note to make new plans for being up there once the Greenland mission was over. It would be nice to have something fun on the agenda for once.

After going through the door, Allen walked carefully down the stairs. The back stairwell connected all the units in the building to the shared roof deck, but it was also used as an unofficial storage space. He navigated his way around golf clubs, drink coolers, and bicycles on his way to his back door and entered into his kitchen. The counter was littered with dirty toddler bowls and bibs, as well as an assortment of medication bottles and oral syringes for Benjamin's liquid medicines. By the look of the counter, it had been a busy day at home.

Allen made his way to the dining room table where he found Kelsey sitting in front of her laptop typing away with Benjamin fast asleep across her lap, his head resting in the crook of her arm. Kelsey didn't look up as Allen approached and only acknowledged his presence when he was standing right next to her.

"Hey" was all she said, her eyes fixed on her

screen and lines of computer code.

"You want me to take him?" Allen asked, already moving to pick up their son.

"Not yet," she replied. "It feels nice to have him cuddled here."

"What are you working on?"

"Daryl showed me the specs for your new body armor," Kelsey said. "It's got motion-assist, built-in motors, and whatnot. I'm streamlining the functions to help you run, aim, dodge, stuff like that."

"How about something to help my back," Allen suggested as he stepped into the kitchen area.

Kelsey thought for a moment. "I could probably put in some kind of lumbar support," she said.

"Hell yes, lumbar support," Allen said, opening the refrigerator. "Did you eat?"

"No, but I'm fine," Kelsey replied.

Allen put together a sandwich with some leftover chicken, poured a glass of milk, then brought his food to the table and sat. "How was his day?" he asked, referring to Benjamin.

Kelsey kept typing without answering. Allen repeated his question, assuming Kelsey hadn't heard him. She didn't answer for a long time again until she eventually took a deep breath and responded. "Stephanie's agency is dropping our insurance."

Allen dropped his sandwich hard on the table. "We're losing Benjamin's physical therapist? Why? When?"

"End of the month," Kelsey said. "She says our plan doesn't pay enough, and when it does, the money comes six months to a year late."

Allen scoffed, and his face turned red. Kelsey took

another deep breath but kept her gaze on her computer screen. Allen left dozens of questions hanging on the tip of his tongue. The answers wouldn't change anything. Kelsey's explanation of the situation was open and shut as well as familiar. With nothing else to do, Allen returned to his sandwich.

"Goddamnit," he muttered before taking a bite. Allen spent the rest of his modest meal mumbling more profane curses under his breath about Benjamin's insurance. With restrictions on Benjamin's coverage soon to come in the months ahead, it was becoming obvious that more money was needed.

"She felt really bad about it," Kelsey mentioned as Allen finished his sandwich.

"Yeah, everyone feels bad," Allen grumbled. "But guilt and condolences aren't much help."

"Stephanie cares. It's not her fault," Kelsey said. "Don't be angry with her."

"Why? What's the point of being nice when, apparently, what we really need is a huge pile of cash?"

"Lower your voice. Do not wake up Benjamin," Kelsey instructed.

Allen ground his teeth as he put away the dishes. When he was done, he looked at the clock. It was time for Benjamin's evening medications. So much for letting him sleep.

Allen lined up syringes of different sizes on the counter and drew up the appropriate meds. Three-point-five milliliters of this, five milliliters of that, and so on, Allen prepared doses of three different seizure medications as well as two more to offset the side effects from the others. When he was finished, Allen took all the filled syringes and placed them on an end table next to the recliner on the other side of Kelsey. Then came the worst part—having to wake Benjamin just to put sour medicines into his mouth. Allen went to Kelsey and picked up their son as gently as he could. Allen carried Benjamin to the recliner, calling his son's name in a singsong voice while rocking him until the boy's eyes fluttered open as they sat down.

"Sorry, buddy, sorry," Allen apologized, picking up the first syringe. He tucked the end into the inside of Benjamin's cheek before squirting some medicine into his mouth and pulling it away. Benjamin winced at the taste before reflexively swallowing. The pharmacy added cherry flavoring to everything, but it wasn't enough to make it taste anywhere near good. Allen went to put the syringe back into Benjamin's mouth to finish the dose, but Benjamin jerked his head to avoid it.

"Sorry," Allen apologized again as he tucked the syringe into Benjamin's pursed lips. The boy opened his mouth just enough for Allen to get the rest of the dose in. Back and forth it went with the other syringes until Allen finished, interrupted a few times by short outbursts of coughing and whining. Once done, Allen comforted his son in his arms until Benjamin calmed down. Then Allen carried him down the hall to his room, changed his diaper, swapped his clothes for pajamas, and sat with him in the gliding chair until he fell asleep.

As Allen stood and put Benjamin into the crib, he wondered how many more years his son would need it. Was there a weight limit to cribs? How expensive was a special-needs bed? Putting aside these dreaded questions, Allen covered his son with a blanket and left the room, trying not to think about them more than he already had. Better to focus his thoughts on breaking into an office building.

But before he did that, there was one daily question he had to ask Kelsey. "How many seizures did he have today?"

"Three clusters," Kelsey said flatly, "all about ten minutes each."

Allen's shoulders went heavy, as happened every day when he got his answer. He glanced at the counter and saw Benjamin's seizure log where Kelsey wrote information about his spasms. It was just a typical spiral notebook, but Allen stared daggers at it. He couldn't stand leafing through the pages filled with days' and days' worth of seizure clusters, their frequencies and durations slightly different from each other yet always with the same endless persistence week after week. Enduring Benjamin's daily seizures was hard enough without looking back on the past ones.

Allen spent the rest of his prep time putting on his body armor, checking its systems, and reviewing the building layout Kyle had given him. The offices of Castile Architecture, the firm responsible for designing and building the Greenland research facility, were on the top floor of the Nolan Building. From the roof, there were two stairwells Allen had to navigate to get to the server room that held the digital vault. Allen studied his route to know what to expect, then turned his attention to the device Daryl had packed with his refurbished armor. It was a black cube, slightly bigger than Allen's fist, with a small handle at one end. Allen inspected the side opposite the handle and found the compartment he was told to look for. Inside was a cable attached to the device with a series of six different types of connectors. It was a basic data-cloning device, designed to function as a massive portable hard drive that automatically copied data from whatever it was plugged into. To speed up the process, Kyle had modified the data cloner to crack into the system and pull information specific to the Rusk facility, shaving the copy time to a mere one to two minutes instead of the hours and multiple devices it would take to clone the entire archive.

Allen stood up in his full armor, clipped the data cloner to his utility belt, and packed a small pulse pistol into his holster. Like his armor, Daryl had also shielded Allen's pistol from interference. Allen nodded at the reassuring improvement hidden inside. He preferred to use the pulse pistol more as a tool than a weapon, manipulating its power levels and beam shape to do everything from taking out locks to cooking food. It seemed like the perfect accessory for the late-night theft of intellectual property.

Emerging from the bedroom, Allen saw that Kelsey hadn't moved since he went in except to put on a pair of headphones. Allen walked over to his wife, and as he bent down to give her a goodbye kiss, he winced at the volume of the electronic music pouring out. After the kiss, Kelsey reached out and grabbed Allen by the neck before he could fully stand up straight.

"Come back, okay?" she said.

"Yep," Allen answered, reaching up to touch Kelsey's hand on his neck. He loosened her fingers and held her hand for a moment as he stood, then gave her a smile and let go before heading for the door. Kelsey put her headphones back on, and Allen made his way up to the roof as quietly as he could. The last thing he needed was one of his neighbors popping out into the stairwell with inconvenient questions like, *what are you doing?*

Allen emerged onto the roof and immediately looked toward the downtown skyline. With nightfall, the skyscrapers glowed from thousands of windows and exterior lights. Allen resolved that if he couldn't motivate himself enough to have a family activity on the roof during the day, he would at least try to enjoy the view at night. He mounted up onto the drone-cycle and activated a secure satellite connection. Once connected, Allen saw that another user was also connected, so he put in his wireless earpiece and activated it.

"MeatTank, Mystic," Allen said, greeting Kyle.

"Read you, Mystic," Kyle replied. "Hey, did you and, uh, our other team member decide on a codename to use?"

"No, I forgot. I better text it," Allen answered before using the control pad built into the wrist of his armor to send Haley a message.

"It's not like we totally need codenames, you know," Kyle said. "This line has maybe the best encryption I've ever seen. Your friend Mister To—I mean, Rich Dude, really came through."

"Yeah, but the encrypted line isn't connected directly to my brain," Allen said, grabbing his cycle controls after sending his message. "If somebody hears me talking and saying names, things could get complicated."

"Oh, right," Kyle said, laughing nervously. "I didn't think of that."

"Most remoters don't," Allen assured him, using

the shorthand name for remote-support specialists. Allen powered up the drone-cycle and put it into a one-foot hover. Out in the open air, the sound of the whirling propellers was only a modest whine. Around him, the roof deck lit up as the drone-cycle's underbelly strobe beacon fired off at regular intervals. Allen grabbed his helmet resting on the console and put it on, then reached below his seat and flipped a switch. The strobe lights and visual displays on the cycle instantly went dark as a heads-up display on his helmet activated.

"I'm connecting my systems to you now," Allen told Kyle.

"I see you," Kyle confirmed. "I'm putting the roof of the Nolan Building into your nav system. You want me to fly it from here?"

"No, I got it," Allen said, securing his feet into the stirrups before grabbing the handlebars. The navigation display in Allen's helmet lit up, with a three-dimensional arrow showing him the direction he had to travel as well as the distance to his destination. Allen gained altitude to climb clear of his condo building, then headed straight toward downtown, about four miles away. He tried to find a good height to give him the best chance of not being seen. Too low and he risked being caught in the glow of the streetlights. Too high and he could be seen and tracked from a distance. The Chicago police certainly had their hands full on any given night, but as he headed downtown Allen still preferred to avoid any 911 calls in case the cops decided it was time to start vigorously enforcing the city's aerial ordinances.

When he got above the freeway, Allen turned south until he reached the commuter rail tracks, then followed them east into the city. As he got to a cluster of high-rise condo towers, he banked and turned, using the towers as cover against any onlookers that might spot him. He then leapfrogged from tall building to tall building until he crossed the Chicago River and officially entered downtown. After the river, he slowed and followed the alleyways, keeping an eye out for windows with lights on that could reveal him in the shadows. He slowed even more when he hovered above people cutting between buildings or smoking cigarettes, holding his breath a bit as he floated past them to his next turn. Finally, Allen caught sight of the slate-gray-and-glass honeycomb pattern that distinguished the Nolan Building from its high-rise neighbors. Only a spattering of lights shone through the floors as Allen got closer, like the building itself had to catch some sleep before its work day started in the morning. Allen zipped through the last gap between buildings and set the drone-cycle down on the roof just outside the doorway leading inside.

"I'm on the roof," Allen reported.

"Copy," Kyle confirmed. "Did you get a response to your message about the codename?"

"No," Allen said.

"Because it's stupid." Haley's voice cut in with a surly tone.

"Then you should have come up with a better one," Allen told her as he got off the drone-cycle and removed his helmet.

"We didn't use codenames on the last mission."

"Yeah, but we should have."

"But, c'mon, my codename is 'Temp'? It may as well be 'Pending' or 'TBD.' "

"Those have too many syllables," Allen said dryly. " 'Temp' is nice and short."

"And annoying."

Allen chuckled then moved on to business. "MeatTank, are we just waiting now?"

"Yep, I'm hacked into Carl's phone and spoofing the EatFleet delivery service, so when he puts in the order, I'll make it look like it's going through. Then Haley can walk in and order it instead," Kyle explained.

"Carl?" Allen asked. "You're on a first-name basis with our target now?"

"Carl is just the one who does the ordering," Kyle said, unaffected by Allen's mocking tone. "Carl Davis and Desmond White are the two guards. They share a meal break every time they work together. Two chicken parmesan sandwiches with sweet peppers and a single order of french fries."

"So now you know what rent-a-cops eat," Allen said, answering the question Kyle had at their kitchen table briefing. "It's a nice way to catch both guards in the same place," Allen admitted.

"*Gracias,* sir," Kyle replied.

"I'm already here at Vito's Italian. I'm going to smell like a deep-fried pizza when I get out," Haley complained.

From there, the chatter stopped as the team waited for their targets to get hungry. After an hour, Allen's own meager dinner failed him, and his stomach growled. He considered asking Haley to pick up some extra food from Vito's while she was at it, but Kyle spoke up before he had the chance.

"They're ordering," Kyle announced. "Carl's typing in the order and—" He paused for a moment before finishing. "—they've ordered."

"Okay," Haley said, "I'm going up to the counter."

As Allen stood there waiting, he had a thought. "Hey MeatTank, you said you were spoofing the food delivery service, so what happens to the payment these guys think they're making?"

"They're making it to me," Kyle said proudly. "Why? You want a piece of the action?"

"No, that's okay, you've earned it," Allen replied with a smile. "It just makes me wonder why you even bother doing remote work when you can make money like that."

"I don't mess with people's money," Kyle answered. "These guys are still getting their sandwiches, so it works out. Plus, if you steal from the wrong people, things tend to get a bit murder-y."

A few minutes later, Haley updated the group. "I'm walking out the door now."

Allen made his way to the edge of the building and peered over the side to look for Haley down below on the street. Soon she came into view. "I see you from the building," Allen said. "Good luck, Temp."

"Shut up," she replied.

Chapter Fourteen

Easy breath in, easy breath out.

Walking toward the Nolan Building, Haley reminded herself to play it casual. She looked up toward the top of the building to see if she could spot Allen before realizing it was probably too dark to see him at that distance. *Just act natural, don't freak out.* It was a bit silly for her to feel so nervous about pretending to work for a food-delivery service, especially because she was actually delivering food. It barely met the requirements to qualify as acting. Still, she was out of her element. As she got within sight of the main entrance to the lobby, Haley forced herself to smile. When she was a teenager, she bussed tables and occasionally took orders at a small diner by her house. She quickly lost count of how many times she was told to smile more. Whether because of her gender or just working in service, people seemed to expect more joyous enthusiasm as she cleared away their half-eaten Salisbury steak. She'd hated that job.

"I'm here," Haley told Allen and Kyle as she crossed the street and arrived at the main doors. She tried the revolving door and found it wouldn't budge, so she stepped back, moved to one of the standard doors, and peered through the glass at the lobby beyond.

The walls of the lobby were covered in grayish stone tile lit dimly by sconces set to after-hours brightness. At the back near the elevators sat the security desk. Two men in blue security uniforms were near it, one sitting at the desk while the other walked toward Haley with a set of keys in his hand. The walking guard gave Haley a half wave and quickened his pace to a light jog to close the distance, the embroidered name of "Carl" becoming legible on his shirt as he came closer. Haley smiled her fake smile as she waited, hating it just as much as she did years before.

When he got to the door, Carl bent down and used one of his many keys to unlock the bolt holding the door in place, then stood and pulled the door back.

"Hey there, good evening," Carl said with his own friendly smile. He pulled the door a bit wider, then stopped and set his foot in the doorway to prevent it from closing on him. The door was only open enough for Haley to pass the sandwiches through to him, and Carl put his arm out for her to do just that. So much for Allen's theory about an older guard throwing the door wide open for a younger woman.

With her fake smile frozen on her face, Haley looked down at his outreached hand and tried to think. Carl cocked his head to the side and flexed his fingers—each one yearning for the bag of delicious sandwiches not yet within their grasp. "I can take it," he offered.

"Right, but, ah…" Haley stalled, looking past Carl to where Desmond still sat at the desk. "Is this order for him, too?"

Carl looked puzzled, then answered, "Yeah."

"I just need to confirm the order with both of you," Haley said as she turned sideways and pushed herself through the small opening Carl held open. He moved his body away from the door without pulling it open any larger, forcing Haley to slither through until she was inside.

"With both of us?" Carl asked.

"Yep," Haley said, already walking toward Desmond at the desk. "New policy, gotta make sure you're both getting exactly what you ordered." Haley sped up to make the desk before Carl could catch up to her, stopping just shy of breaking into a run. As she approached the desk, Desmond stood and gave Carl a questioning look.

"She says she has to make sure we both got what we ordered," Carl told him.

"We both ordered the same thing," Desmond responded with a laugh.

"I know, but I need to, like, confirm your satisfaction," Haley stammered as she set down the bag of food. Carl caught up and stood to Haley's left while Desmond remained standing on the other side of the desk. She opened the bag and carefully took out each wrapped sandwich.

When the guards tried reaching for their food, Haley stopped them. "Just a second, got to be official," she told them, setting a sandwich on the desk in front of each of them. She tore the pieces of tape that secured the white paper around each sandwich in quick succession, then put both hands into her pockets as she waited. Both men leaned forward to inspect their respective chicken parmesan dinners.

"That's what I ordered," Carl confirmed.

"Me, too," Desmond agreed.

"Great," Haley said with genuine happiness. Then,

as both men stood bent over their sandwiches, Haley pulled her hands out of her pockets and gave both men a hard pat on the back at the same time. Their startled expressions were quickly interrupted by high-voltage electrical charges from the stun buzzers Haley had slapped on their backs. Carl and Desmond dropped to the floor and writhed for a few seconds before falling unconscious and going still.

"Guards are down," Haley reported before grabbing Carl under the arms. She dragged his slack body around behind the security desk to be with his partner, out of view from anyone walking by on the street.

"Copy," Allen said through her earpiece. "Nice job."

After making sure the guards were out of sight, Haley sat at the desk to inspect the security console while Kyle gave her instructions.

"You need to open the roof access door and all the doors on the fortieth floor, sections four through twelve. That last section is where Castile's digital vault is," Kyle told her.

"Gotcha," Haley replied. She called up the security access screen on the desk console and navigated to the alarms and access screen. Digging around the menu, she found the areas Kyle mentioned, then silenced each alarm and unlocked every door to give Allen a clear path. "I'm done. Everything's open."

"Roger that," Allen said. "Keep up the good work, Temp."

Haley shuddered in annoyance. She tried to think of a good comeback to Allen's continued use of her terrible codename but didn't have the chance. Before she could respond, she felt a sharp pain in the back of her head and could only wonder what was happening as the world went dark.

****

This isn't so hard, Allen thought as he passed through the rooftop door. He took the stairwell down to the fortieth floor, then walked casually through the empty, dim hallway. It really was going well. Kyle knew his stuff. Haley seemed to be coming into her own. And the Greenland mission was starting to feel like something they could actually pull off. Sure, he had a long way to go before things would be over, but it reminded him of the first time he ran a marathon. Once he started running on the road, the challenge didn't seem so impossible.

Turning a corner, Allen saw a bank of elevators and, across from them, a pair of doors to an office suite with "Castile Architecture" etched into them. "I'm at the office," he said.

"The vault should be two doors farther down the hall, Suite Four-Twelve," Kyle told him.

Allen continued down the hall reading signs on the doors until he found the room he needed and went inside. Upon opening the door, Allen was greeted by scores of quickly blinking LED lights flashing from floor to ceiling. He pulled out a flashlight to make sense of what he was looking at and found that the blinking was coming from rows of data servers and network routers, each connected to its neighbor by blue data cables. "MeatTank, what am I looking for? There's a ton of stuff in here."

"Yeah, it's Castile's network server room," Kyle said, "but the vault is a standalone system. Look for a computer that isn't connected to the others."

Allen sighed. He had assumed the vault would be a single monolithic computer in an otherwise empty room. He scanned the computers with his flashlight and followed the flow of cables, trying to find which device was not like the others. "Would it have flashing lights like everything else?" Allen asked.

"No, the lights you see are blinking to show that data is being transferred, so the vault shouldn't have any," Kyle answered. "None that blink, anyway."

A minute later, Allen caught sight of a standalone device on a shelf that fit the bill with no blinking lights, just a solid blue one, and a single data port.

"I've got it," Allen said, unclipping the data cloner from his belt. He opened the compartment to release the cloner's data cable, found the appropriate connector, and plugged it into the port on the vault. "It's working," Allen reported a short time later as the cloning device began to blink a small green light of its own. Allen stood in silence waiting for the small cube to complete its task. While waiting, his stomach growled, the seriousness of the situation apparently failing to suppress his appetite.

"Hey, Temp, what else did that Italian place have, anything good?" Allen asked Haley over the radio. After ten seconds without an answer, Allen tried again. "Temp? You copy?" Again, no answer came. " 'Tank, did she go off comms?"

"She didn't say anything to me," Kyle replied.

"See if she left the building," Allen ordered. He reminded himself that Haley was still new at all this. Maybe she didn't realize she was supposed to stay in touch until everyone was out.

"I'm already looking," Kyle answered. After several more tense seconds, Kyle finally came back. "Her earpiece is still on the ground floor."

"But what about her? Where is she?" Allen asked, disconnecting the data-cloning device after its indicator light held steady and confirmed its task was complete.

"The earpiece is out, so it automatically went on standby mode. I activated it from here, but she's still not answering," Kyle explained, tension creeping into his voice.

Allen walked out the door and into the hallway, heading back toward the roof. "Check if there are any street cameras you can access. She still could have left."

"Okay, but..." Kyle replied doubtfully.

"I know, but it's still worth checking," Allen said, heading up the stairs two at a time. He burst through the door onto the roof and paced quickly in a circle waiting for Kyle to get back to him. "Come on, Haley," he said impatiently to himself. "Where did you go?"

****

Haley woke with a ringing in her ears and a sense that the room was spinning before she even knew exactly what kind of room she was in. She tried to open her eyes but felt a searing pain from the light like she'd never felt before, preventing her from making anything out in the blinding glare. As her head cleared, Haley realized she was sitting on the floor with her arms behind her. She tried bringing a hand up to feel the back of her head where it was throbbing, but her hand caught on something. She tried her other hand but couldn't move that one either. Her breathing quickened. Her hands weren't just stuck behind her back—they were tied.

Through the ringing in her ears, Haley focused on a repeating electronic sound in the background. It finally dawned on her that it was the sound of an elevator chirping each time the car passed a floor.

The elevator stopped, and someone grabbed her under her arms. When the doors opened, she was turned and dragged backward, the movement making her motion sick. Through half-open eyes, Haley struggled to focus on glimpses of ladders and utility lights. Then the arms dropped her hard on the floor. Haley opened her eyes a bit more to look around, still trying to clear out the fog. She saw sheets of clear, waving plastic hanging from the ceiling, and metal frames dividing up an open space. It occurred to her that she must be on a floor being renovated for new office tenants, only then remembering what building she was in and why.

Haley closed her eyes again and focused on her hands. They were bound by something wider than a rope. Bending each thumb toward the opposite wrist, she felt the edge of whatever material they were tied with. She ran both thumbs down and around until she touched something cooler and smoother than before, and all at once the image of a belt buckle flashed into her mind. She moved her wrists in opposite directions to begin prying them free when she heard a voice frighteningly close to her ear.

"You look so stupid here on the floor," the male voice snarled. "Just as dumb as those two idiots you knocked out. You're all so pathetic."

Haley didn't reply. She stayed still with her eyes closed while straining to listen if the man remained next to her or if he had moved somewhere else. The next sound Haley heard was the noise of metal tools clanking and the man's voice again. "Come on, where is it? They're all supposed to have some." Haley recognized the sounds of a toolbox slamming shut and the man rummaging through another. "These guys are all idiots, too. They look at me like I'm the loser, the homeless loser who sleeps in his father's building. Never mind that I'm a better security guard than his actual ones!" The man went on to a third toolbox. "Finally!" he bellowed before making his way back to Haley, stomping like an angry toddler.

Haley kept pretending to be unconscious as she felt the man get closer and kneel above her. She heard duct tape being pulled and torn before a length of it was slapped over her mouth.

"You're going to wish those morons stopped you instead of me," the man said, still rubbing the tape back and forth with his fingers. His hand pressed against Haley more heavily and she felt the heat of his face move close to hers. "I just hope you wake up before I start."

With the man's creepy statement bringing her patience to a sudden end, Haley drew both knees and kicked the man back as hard as she could. The man's surprised eyes stared at her as he flew back and landed against a utility light, knocking it over.

Haley scrambled to her feet and struggled against the belt around her wrist, freeing her hands as the man stood. He didn't look much older than Haley, with a lean build and a face covered in scraggly facial hair. He wore jeans and a T-shirt covered in food stains, looking well past due to be thrown out.

The man bellowed and came at Haley. The

wildness of the attack caught Haley off guard, but she was able to pivot to avoid him. The sudden movement gave Haley a swell of vertigo, and she steadied herself on a nearby ladder.

Haley readied herself for another attack, but the man was gone. Her eyes unable to pierce the shadows, Haley decided to make a run for the elevators. She moved deliberately and paused between each step, both to be ready for an attack and to keep her balance, straining the limits of her hearing for any signs of her attacker.

Haley closed half the distance to the elevators when she was stopped by an attack from behind. The man tried to wrestle her down, but Haley countered with a punch straight to his nose. As the man howled and stumbled away, Haley delivered kicks to his torso and head, causing him to crash into a row of aluminum studs and slump to the floor.

The man groaned in pain, and Haley ran toward the elevators. But soon, the room began to tumble again, and she grabbed the nearest stud to steady herself. She kept her eyes on the elevators and willed herself forward through the dizziness. Slowly, her feet complied, stomping heavily one after another, but not before the man appeared again, swinging something at her like a bat. Haley ducked away at the last moment, but the metal object still caught her in the shoulder and sent her down. She looked up to see the man raising an object over his head, a metal stilt workers used to make themselves taller for ceiling work. He brought the stilt down with a chopping motion, and Haley rolled to avoid it.

The man screamed with rage and lunged on top of

Haley, putting his full weight on her chest. The edges of her vision soon grew dark. The man's face was covered in blood, with more pouring from his nose. He smiled as he put a hand over Haley's nose, the only source of air she had with her mouth still taped shut. She balled her hands into fists and delivered blows to the man's head, but between her injuries and lightheadedness, she lacked the strength to knock him down.

This is it, Haley thought. She hoped that passing out from a lack of oxygen would feel peaceful. Also, why was this man so mad and what kind of life made him this way? But she could see in his face that whatever was going on it had convinced him that Haley had to die.

A blast of air and flying glass stopped him before he could go through with his decision. The burst of debris flew into his eyes, forcing him to throw his hands in front of his face. Haley sucked in precious oxygen and rolled to the side, knocking the man off her. Haley crawled away, the man still clawing at her, and looked up to see Allen on his drone-cycle flying in through the hole he had just blown through the window.

The man stood to confront the new threat. Allen continued forward, and just as it looked like he was going to run the man down, he turned the aircraft sharply to point the full force of its propellers at the man to blast him back several feet through the air.

Allen leveled the drone-cycle into a hover as Haley got to her feet. Once she made her way onto the seat behind him, Allen hit the accelerator and flew back out through the broken window into the night air. Haley fought her nausea as Allen banked hard to avoid running into the building across the street before snaking between skyscrapers until they got close enough to the river to make a straight shot over the freeway toward his home.

Allen and Haley made a hard landing on Allen's roof, lurching forward and almost falling out onto the deck. Allen stood and turned around to his partner while Haley clawed at the duct tape still stuck over her mouth. Allen reached out to help, but she swung at the flash of a sudden hand coming toward her and swatted it away. Struggling for composure, Haley reached up to the corner of the tape, pried an edge loose with her thumbnail, and pulled it from her face. She flung it away before getting up from the seat and stumbling a few steps before bracing herself against the barrier at the edge of the roof.

Allen stepped away from the drone-cycle but kept his distance. "Are you okay?"

"He had me," Haley croaked without looking at Allen. "I couldn't stay on my feet, and I couldn't stop him…" She trailed off as she fell short of breath.

Allen pulled a lounge chair from the other side of the deck and put it next to her before going back to the drone-cycle and returning with a small zippered pouch. Opening the pouch, Allen retrieved what looked like an alcohol wipe. But when he tore it open, it revealed a thin square inside that was light blue and semi-transparent. "Here, put it under your tongue," Allen instructed, handing it to Haley.

She sat, pulled the small blue square from its package, and did as she was told. It tasted of medicine and artificial sweetness, and quickly dissolved away in a few seconds. Allen pulled a second item from his pouch, a small, curved device in the shape of a half-circle. He placed the device over the top of Haley's head and pressed a small button on the side. An amber light on the device blinked slowly, then faster and faster over the next two minutes before changing to green and holding steady.

"There's no bleeding in the brain. You should be okay," Allen announced while putting the device back into his bag. "That dissolving tab I gave you will help with the nausea and headache."

Allen's mention of a headache along with her decreasing levels of adrenaline made Haley's pain swell from a dull ache to a full migraine in only a moment's time. She bent over in the chair and put her head in her hands while she waited for the medicine to kick in.

"Can you tell me what happened?" Allen tried again.

"I took out the guards, and then...I don't remember," Haley said. "After the guards, I woke up in an elevator with my hands tied behind my back, and that sick freak dragged me out, and..." Haley trailed off again. Allen waited for her to continue, but she couldn't find the words to explain more.

"It was Ernest Nolan," Kyle's voice interjected from a speaker on the drone-cycle's console. "Thaddeus Nolan's son."

Allen turned toward the cycle. "The owner of the building?"

"Yeah, looks like ol' Ernie broke out of rehab," Kyle replied.

"How did you find me?" Haley asked, staring down at the deck.

"Kyle used your earpiece to connect to the building's security system," Allen said.

"The earpiece could read what the wireless sensors were telling the security desk," Kyle explained. "I couldn't control anything, but I picked up the signal of Ernest Nolan using his access code to take the elevator to the twenty-ninth floor."

"But we still couldn't open any doors," Allen added, "so once I caught sight of you through the window, I had to blow it out."

Haley looked off toward the city skyline glowing in the distance as panic boiled up inside her. "I was going to die," she said with a shaky voice. "He had me. It was over, and there wasn't anything I could do."

"Well…" Allen said, avoiding her gaze, "that's why we go in teams."

"He was killing me," Haley continued, the fresh memory flashing before her eyes. "I was about to die, and I couldn't stop him." A wave of heat burned through the nerves in Haley's legs. She heeded their urgency to move by standing and pacing.

Allen walked after her. "It's okay. You're fine now."

"Fine?" Haley fired back. "I can still feel where his hand was pressed against my face, and I'm supposed to be fine already?"

"No, I mean, you're safe now," Allen stammered. "It's okay to be scared. But now you've learned something for next time."

"Next time, sure," Haley said, getting angrier. "Next time I only die half as much. Or maybe someone else dies instead."

Allen's phone started buzzing. He reached into a compartment on his armor, took out the phone, and tapped a button to silence it. "That's not going to happen. You'll recover from this."

"I don't know," Haley told him. "I don't know about this anymore."

"You don't know about what?" Allen asked, getting closer.

"This!" Haley yelled, gesturing at Allen and herself. "Us...me, doing this anymore."

Allen's phone started buzzing again. He tapped the screen and put it up to his ear. "What?" he screamed at the unknown caller.

"Good evening, Mister Moran, this is Carol." The woman's voice on the other end of Allen's phone was loud enough for Haley to hear.

"Who?" he asked impatiently.

"Mister Tor's assistant," Carol answered. "I showed you to his office." Her helpful tone seemed to imply, *remember me?*

"Oh, right...Carol," Allen replied. "What is it?"

"Mister Tor needs to see you right away," Carol said.

"I can be there first thing in the morn—"

"Mister Tor will see you tonight," Carol interrupted. "It's quite urgent."

Chapter Fifteen

Come on, Haley, don't quit now.

Allen replayed the conversation he and Haley had up on his roof in his mind as he sat in the back of the luxurious and driverless town car Eamon had sent to fetch him. He was having a hard time understanding, much less accepting, Haley's sudden change in attitude. Sure, she had just had a brush with death, but that's what the job was. And Haley seemed born for it. She wasn't a poser looking for thrills or an egotist with an oversized sense of how tough she was. She was a good operator and just needed to get past her little hump of almost dying. If only Allen could figure out a more inspiring way of telling her that.

Sensing Allen's conflicted state, his Healthy Helper offered a suggestion. "Allen, does stress and depression have you down? Try a one-week trial of prescription Melifuzam. Just ninety-nine dollars. Even out those odd feelings with Melifuzam. This has been a paid advertisement."

Allen let out a deep sigh, as he did every time his health tracker spoke. Outside, the town car had come off the freeway and entered downtown. As the car turned north, finely dressed people walked around, laughing, heading into restaurants. When was the last time he and Kelsey had gone out to dinner? The closest thing he could think of was when they shared a meal in the hospital cafeteria while Benjamin got an MRI of his brain. Their son had to be sedated so he didn't move, and the couple spent nearly two hours waiting for the procedure to be over. They split a bland turkey burger.

Reflections of pulsing blue light from multiple police cars cascaded up the windows of the Nolan Building as the car passed Washington Street. The cops would likely be too busy fighting street crime to mount any serious investigation into the break-in, but with his recent luck Allen wasn't so sure.

The town car got within a block of the Chicago River, then turned down an alleyway before reaching a small garage door next to a loading dock. The car stopped to have a digital conversation with Eamon's security system. After clearing the car, the garage door opened, and the car made its way down a tight ramp to a small parking area where two other identical cars sat next to each other. The car parked in front of a single elevator door where a familiar artificial face waited.

"Good evening, Mister Moran," Carol said as Allen approached, her image projected on the elevator. "This will take you directly to Mister Tor's private penthouse." She disappeared as the door opened. After it closed again, the car quickly accelerated upward with so much speed that Allen's knuckles turned white gripping the hand rail to keep his knees from buckling.

Once the acceleration leveled out, Allen's thoughts turned back to Haley. He rushed off while she was still upset, but maybe it was for the best. Allen and Haley worked well together, but he couldn't say they were close. She needed to spend time with Daryl and work things out instead of arguing with him. Hopefully then she would realize she was fine and get back to work.

Allen couldn't afford to be sympathetic, not now. Once the mission was done and Benjamin had what he needed, Haley could have all the time off she wanted.

The elevator slowed to a stop and opened its doors. Allen stepped out into a vast open floor, dimly lit with occasional lamps. The open floor plan of Eamon's residence closely mimicked that of his office. There were no typical walls. As his eyes adjusted to the dim light, Allen studied the furnishings. Traditional living spaces like the dining room, kitchen, and bedrooms were grouped into distinct clusters around the space. One could easily imagine where walls would normally go, as if they were simply removed and never replaced. Freestanding cabinets in matte gray with dark wooden trim rose and connected together with a horizontal section to form a kind of archway over a cluster of sleek appliances and an island counter. Beds and accompanying furniture were minimalistic but oversized and larger than Allen had ever seen before. The headboards were equally as large and upholstered with various materials as if each were simply a canvas to show off their workmanship. Small benches with artful curves sat seemingly at random around the space. Maybe Eamon liked to rest on long hikes inside his home.

"Eamon?" Allen called.

"Over here," Eamon replied in the distance. A moment later, a series of track lights high up in the industrial ceiling turned on to project a path on the floor to follow. Allen walked forward, continuing to look around. Two small walled-off areas caught his eye. Looking through an open door of the nearest one, he saw a toilet and his apprehension eased a bit.

Something about the familiarity of a private bathroom made the space feel less alien.

Rounding the kitchen area, Allen caught sight of Eamon making his way to a seating area with a couch and several chairs over a large hand-knotted wool rug woven with a complex geometric pattern that gave it a false sense of depth as if it were carved into the floor. Motion-activated floor lamps lit up as Eamon passed and revealed he was using a cane. He winced with every step.

"Are you all right?" Allen asked his friend as he came closer.

"Oh, yeah," Eamon assured him before slowly sitting down into a sleek, modern armchair. "It's stupid. I did it to myself. I got angry and took it out by kicking the fridge."

"Like after an argument with someone?"

"No, no. But never mind," Eamon said, gesturing for Allen to sit down on an identical armchair across from him. "We've gotten another message from Doctor Sloan and it doesn't look good," he continued, getting right to business.

"Another email?" Allen asked, sitting down.

"Yes, but not coded very well. It's not going to take a genius to figure out he's asking for help." Eamon turned and spoke as if talking to someone invisible. "Carol, could you read the email, please?"

In the direction Eamon spoke, the image of Carol materialized into the room like a ghost. Allen looked up and saw a pair of thread-like cables coming down from the ceiling, a faint glimmer of thin material strung between them. It now made sense why Eamon's space was so open and dim. Carol's image could be projected to any part of the penthouse at any time. Allen's appreciation for the walled-off bathrooms grew exponentially.

"Yes, Eamon," Carol answered, speaking in a more familiar tone than she had used in his office. She turned to Allen. "The email from Doctor Sloan to his former colleague at our company opened with the typical pleasantries, but it was the following passage that caught our attention: 'Eric, the work here is overwhelming. I could really use some help. I wish I could help myself, but I don't know how. I need help from the outside, but I'm not sure how to get it. If you can help, or know of anyone available to help, please send them my way.' "

"Well, he only said 'help' like five times. Hard to know what he wants," Allen said with a groan.

"Obviously, he's scared," Eamon said. "Thank you, Carol."

"Of course," the virtual assistant replied. Carol locked eyes with Allen as she faded away, and though he wasn't quite sure what to make of it, he got the distinct feeling of being a third wheel.

"How close are you to being ready to go?" Eamon asked, repeatedly tapping his thumb on the arm of his chair.

"I was planning on another week. We only got the layout of the facility today," Allen replied.

"You mean tonight," Eamon corrected him.

"You were listening in?"

"It's my mission and my data lines," Eamon said, his tone cold.

"Then you know we haven't had time to unpack the files and figure a way in. And we're still working on equipment."

"I'll have a private plane fly you to Greenland—there's an airport at Ilulissat. From there you can bribe someone at the port to get you on a ship to Alluttoq Island," Eamon said, ignoring Allen's protest.

"We need more time," Allen implored.

"No!" Eamon screamed in a flash of anger. His eyes were wide for a brief moment before he composed himself enough to continue. "You will gather your team and leave tomorrow, or I will find somebody else to go."

Allen was tempted to take a pass on the mission with Eamon forcing his hand, especially without a clear plan. His friend had become cold and obsessive, a bad combination for dangerous work. Then the weight of everything waiting at home hit him. Hospital bills, insurance that would soon run out, therapists leaving, doctors fleeing the country, medicines Benjamin couldn't get, and the inevitable result of all these problems—a son with little hope of recovery.

"We'll go," Allen said.

Eamon leaned back in his seat. "Good," he said before closing his eyes and sitting motionless. Allen understood from many years of working with the ultra-rich that a sudden tuning out of his presence meant it was time to show himself out. He stood and made his way out to the elevator. On his descent back down to the garage, Allen tried to mentally put together a list of things he would need to somehow pull the mission off. But no matter how he arranged things, the list always started with Haley. At least Kyle was on board. Kyle…

"Hey, MeatTank, did you hear everything that just happened?" Allen asked into the earpiece he had only then remembered was still active in his ear.

"Yes," Kyle said sheepishly. "You were still broadcasting, so…" He trailed off. Allen had forgotten that remoters were all just high-functioning voyeurs of one type or another.

"It's fine. Forget it," Allen told him. "Just tell me, where's Haley?"

****

Allen spent the whole ride from downtown to Daryl's house trying to figure out what he would say to Haley. The fact that she had chosen the supportive comfort of her father's house instead of her apartment dashed Allen's hopes that the solution would be something quick like, "You good?" He was no closer to an answer when he was dropped off by Eamon's driverless car, and he was still trying to figure it out as he rang the doorbell. After ringing two more times without an answer, Daryl came to the door wearing a white tank top and boxer shorts, reminding Allen that it was the middle of the night. Allen apologized as he walked inside, his eyes cast down toward the floor mumbling potential arguments to himself that might convince Haley to join him on the mission. Even as Haley came downstairs and sat on the couch, Allen was still no more certain of what to say than when he left Eamon's building.

"A message came in from Doctor Sloan," Allen began, sitting on the far end of the couch from Haley. "He's in danger, and I've been told that we have to leave tomorrow." Haley looked away but otherwise had no reaction.

Daryl, on the other hand, made a face like someone had asked him to tie a knot using his elbows. "You can't be serious."

"I understand," Allen said calmly.

"But—" Daryl responded.

"I understand," Allen repeated. After Daryl softened his expression, Allen continued, "Can the new gear be ready by tomorrow?"

"Yes, if I get to work now," Daryl answered. "But Kelsey is still days away from finishing a version of the armor software."

"The stock software will be fine," Allen said.

"I can talk to her," Daryl offered. "If she has some features ready to go, I could try to integrate—"

"No, I'll talk to her," Allen interrupted again. "Just focus on getting everything together. That'll be complicated enough."

Daryl nodded then looked at his daughter as he wheeled closer to Allen. He spoke in a whisper only his friend could hear. "Are you sure about this?"

Allen gave Daryl a defeated look. "There isn't a better way, I'm sure of that."

Daryl moved away. "I'll get to work," he said, heading into his workshop. Allen listened to the sounds of Daryl working for a while before gathering the courage to talk to his partner.

"How are you?" Allen asked Haley.

"Better," she answered, sounding more confident than she had on the roof. "Sleeping helped, until I got woken up."

"Sorry about that. I wouldn't have come so late if I had a choice."

They were both silent for a long time until Haley continued. "I'm still not sure how I feel about going."

"And I'm not sure what to say about that," Allen

told her. "I feel like anything I say will just be me trying to convince you to go, whether it's the best thing for you or not." Allen squirmed on the couch. If only he could find a comfortable position for this uncomfortable conversation. "I just know I need you. And I need..." Allen struggled for the words. "I need Benjamin to get better. I can't stand watching him fade away anymore. It has to change. So we'll do this mission, get Benjamin more help, maybe even get him cured, and then...well, I'd owe you big for the rest of my life, basically."

Allen wasn't used to asking for help and he had the sinking feeling he was doing a lousy job of it, especially when Haley stood from the couch without saying anything.

"I'm going either way," Allen announced. Haley turned with wide eyes. "I know," Allen said, acknowledging the message Haley's expression sent. "But Benjamin's losing too many doctors and therapists, and at some point they'll just cut us off. He needs better care now. Waiting isn't working."

"It just doesn't make any sense," Haley said.

Allen looked off for a moment, searching for more words that could explain to his partner how he felt, but no more came. With nothing else to say, Allen simply gave a defeated shrug and left Haley to herself. He walked into Daryl's workshop to see if he needed to do anything more before leaving.

Daryl was hunched over a work table, a pair of glasses propped at the end of his nose with a work apron across his lap, assembling pieces of armor onto an arm section. "Get over here," he said, hearing Allen enter the room. "I need to take your measurements with the scanner."

Allen obediently walked over. As he did, he looked at all the pieces of armor plating, motors, and mechanisms laid out across the workspace taking up a whole side of the room. "It's a lot to put together," Allen noted.

"So let's scan you and make sure I do it right the first time," Daryl responded, removing a small device from a pocket of his work apron. The device had a grip handle and trigger as well as a tiny display screen at the top with a laser emitter at the end. Daryl pointed the scanner at Allen. "Close your eyes, and put your arms to your sides."

Allen did as he was told, and Daryl pulled the trigger, sweeping him slowly with the laser from his feet and working up. "So, what did you do, give her an ultimatum?"

"No, I just said I was going with or without her," Allen said, holding still with his eyes closed to avoid looking directly into Daryl's laser.

"Great, I'm sure that won't traumatize her at all," Daryl said.

"I don't have time to beg. I need this mission to happen."

"Now put your arms out," Daryl instructed. Once Allen did so, Daryl continued his scan. "You need help for your son, yes, but getting that and finishing this mission aren't necessarily the same things."

"I don't know how to help him any other way," Allen said, scowling. "The money I've made so far isn't getting it done. Once he's HAPA-restricted, it'll get worse. He's already being written off as it is like he's just too hopeless to help."

"Turn around, away from me," Daryl demanded. "Keep your arms out to the sides." Allen turned away and stared at the wall. Daryl worked in silence for a minute before continuing. "You've only started working again, Allen. You can pick up more jobs, appeal to the insurance company, pay when you can. You still have options."

"The seizures are too strong. They're scrambling his brain. That's why he can't do anything." Allen closed his eyes even though he wasn't facing the laser. "Getting more insurance won't cut it. It's still the same problems."

"But losing you would only make things worse," Daryl replied.

Allen scoffed. "Okay, mister drama. I'm talking about real issues."

"I understand the issues, and I'm just saying that, seizures or not, Benjamin is better off with you around."

"You use the word 'seizure' like it's just a little hand tremor or something," Allen said sharply. "They're nonstop in his head, burning away brain cells."

"Still, he needs you," Daryl said before finishing his scan. "You can put your arms down now." Allen complied and turned back toward Daryl but did not speak. "You disagree?" Daryl finally asked.

"Best case, I finish this mission and Eamon gives Benjamin what he needs to stop his seizures. That's what I'm focused on now."

Daryl reviewed the measurements before putting the device on his lap. "Okay, I got it. What are you going to tell Kelsey?"

"I'm not sure," Allen admitted, "but thanks for having a practice argument with me first." Allen smirked at his joke, but Daryl didn't return it.

"Just make sure you're not so desperate to help your son that you get my daughter killed," Daryl said coolly.

It was a reminder of the understanding the two had when Haley started out as Allen's partner, and Allen knew he was dangerously at risk of failing to live up to it. "I won't," Allen told his friend. "I promise."

With that, Daryl returned to his work table and the stitching and construction that lay ahead of him. Allen left the room and walked out the front door of the house, planning for the equally difficult task that lay ahead of him as well.

Chapter Sixteen

There's just no way...

Kelsey stared at the laptop screen in front of her on the dining room table, her cursor blinking halfway through a line of code she had been typing before the realization of the situation overwhelmed her. There was no way she could finish the armor software in time. She still had half a dozen different features only partially written, and at least as many more not even started. She could use off-the-shelf software to fill in the gaps, but she'd still have to write some kind of interface program to tie everything together, and there was no way the whole Frankenstein mess would work perfectly on the first try.

"You're sure you have to leave tomorrow?" Kelsey asked her husband.

"Yes," Allen said from his seat across from her at the table. "Eamon threatened to fire me if I didn't."

Kelsey stared at her screen in a daze. She cursed herself for not starting with pre-written software and simply modifying it, then changed her mind and decided that she was right to start from scratch. Her programming was better than the software that was out there, and she had made good progress. She needed more time, that was undeniable. And she wasn't the only one.

"You're not ready," Kelsey said absently. "You're

just running into this with some pieced-together gear and an untested partner."

"I still think it's the best way to help Benjamin," Allen said.

"I understand the situation, Allen," Kelsey shouted. "Just because I disagree with you doesn't mean I'm confused."

"I'm the one going, you know," Allen replied. "Both you and Daryl are keen on telling me how much of a bad idea it is for me to go when I'm the one taking the risk."

Kelsey looked up from the computer to glare at her husband. "But you're not going alone. You might understand what you need to do, but Haley needs to be taught."

"Well, she might not even go, so…" Allen trailed off.

"So you might go alone?" Kelsey asked incredulously.

"She'll be at the plane. She just needs time. Something happened at the office building, but she'll be fine."

"You don't know that," Kelsey said, jabbing a finger toward Allen. "You don't know what she'll do. Your entire plan is just hoping things will work out."

"Well, that's all we've been doing with Benjamin, isn't it? For over two years now, we've been trying things and hoping it'll all just work out."

"What's your point?" Kelsey asked.

"My point is, leaving in the morning might not have been my plan, but it's still better than turning it down and not going at all."

"So now a half-baked attempt is better than a

thought-out plan?"

Allen threw up his arms. "I don't know, Kel. I just don't know what else to say."

The two of them sat in silence for a time. New arguments popped into Kelsey's head, but she imagined each one would only anger Allen even more and get her nowhere. Kelsey had long since realized that having anything close to a logical argument between them was impossible when every day felt like the most stressful one of their lives. Especially when the bar for what qualified as the most stressful day of their lives kept getting pushed higher and higher.

Once her breathing had slowed, Kelsey decided the only thing she could do was to be straightforward. "I don't want you to go," she said.

Allen looked at her. She desperately wanted the lines of resolve on his face to soften. She wanted him to laugh it off, admit he wasn't thinking clearly. Or at least say he'd talk to Eamon about a delay. But he didn't. Instead, Allen got up without saying a word, walked over to the living room, and sat down on the recliner before turning his back to her to look out the front window. It was clear that he would go, and more hours of arguing about it would not change his mind. It seemed like yet another thing beyond her control. Time and her husband's mind had joined her son's seizures in a brutal conspiracy to defy her.

Kelsey closed her laptop as she stood from the table. She glanced over at Allen briefly before walking in the opposite direction. She passed by the kitchen, walked down the hall, and stopped at the slightly open door to Benjamin's room. She slipped in through the small opening and walked gently to the side of the crib.

He was deep asleep, lying on his side, without a hint of the troubles he fought.

Kelsey moved from the crib and sat on the nearby gliding nursery chair. In the calm of darkness and the sound of Benjamin's white noise machine, her mind wandered. What would it feel like if her family was reduced to just her and Benjamin, without Allen? Her eyes welled up. She exhaled with the sharpness of a curse and wiped her tears away. There were victims in the world, but she refused to count herself among them, not with her son lying right there in front of her. Her emotions reminded her of the way she felt in the days following Benjamin's diagnosis. It was an odd mixture of sadness and acceptance, like a small child eating a mouthful of vegetables with tears streaming down her face all to finish dinner and earn a treat. Kelsey still believed, even two years later, that a treat in the form of no more seizures was coming for Benjamin. Until then, she just had to push through the sadness and rage as best she could. Still, it would be nice if the situation didn't suck so bad.

Kelsey rested her head against the soft raised back of the chair. Even in the dim light, she fixed her gaze on a pair of parallel cracks in the wall where tape under the paint covered a seam between two drywall panels. She had watched the vertical cracks grow over the months, the bulging, detaching tape a symptom of quick work from a shoddy developer. Its repair had been put off month after month—a glaring problem that had somehow grown acceptable. Kelsey scowled at the thin lines and dug her nails into the arms of the chair. She leaped up and reached as high as she could on the wall, clawing through the paint to dig up a loose end. With a jagged edge revealed, she pulled the tape down top to bottom and tore it away. Paint split and chunks of dusty drywall fell, leaving a thick stripe of jagged white material bare for all to see. Kelsey breathed heavily as she made her way back to the chair, glancing at Benjamin to see him still asleep. Kelsey admired her spontaneous renovation and nodded. Sometimes raw and exposed was better than being ignored.

Kelsey had only been asleep for about an hour before Allen had come home and woke her up, making her rush to her computer to take stock of her work. Now, with the even rhythm of her son's slow breathing, she drifted off to sleep.

Hours later, Kelsey woke with a start. The light through the blinds of the nursery window told her day had come, though it wasn't the sunlight that woke her. A noise had interrupted her sleep, but the fog of waking prevented her from remembering what it was. She stood and crouched over the crib to check on Benjamin and saw he wasn't there. At the same time, the noise that woke her came again and instantly jogged her memory. It was the sound of Benjamin crying in the next room.

Kelsey stumbled groggily out of Benjamin's bedroom, into the hallway, and past the kitchen, following the sound until she saw her son. Allen held Benjamin in his arms in the same recliner he had sat in the night before. Allen rocked and made soothing sounds in an attempt to calm their son. Benjamin was not a child who cried often. In fact, he showed very little emotion at all. But the one thing that always made him upset were seizures.

As Kelsey watched, Benjamin's arms jumped straight out in front of him involuntarily while he simultaneously took a sharp intake of breath. Nobody had ever been able to definitively tell Kelsey or Allen if Benjamin experienced pain during his infantile spasms. Regardless, whatever Benjamin felt was at the very least upsetting to him and at the worst terrifying. Tears and mucus poured out of his eyes and nose, and Benjamin let out a fresh scream as his arms relaxed. Allen used a burp cloth to wipe his son's face as he continued to rock back and forth trying to calm the child.

Kelsey walked up to her husband and son, crouched down, and kissed Benjamin on the cheek. "I'm sorry, Benji," she said before giving Benjamin another pair of kisses for good measure. She stood back up and patted the top of her son's head. "How long has it been going on?" Kelsey asked Allen.

"A little over twenty minutes," Allen replied. "I didn't want to wake you." His eyes were puffy with a tinge of redness that mirrored their son's.

A few minutes later, the cluster of spasms ceased. There was never any clue as to when they would end, just as there was usually no hint as to when they would begin. Afterward, Benjamin quickly fell asleep. Allen put him back into bed while Kelsey dutifully noted the time and duration of the spasm cluster in Benjamin's seizure log. Allen and Kelsey spent the rest of the morning in relative silence, each doing their own separate chores and routines without involving the other. As Kelsey worked on cleaning up the clutter around the house, Allen posted a sticky note on the refrigerator.

"What's that?" Kelsey asked.

"Tail number of the airplane Eamon's flying us in,"

Allen said.

The reality of Allen's intent to follow through on his plan made Kelsey's stomach drop. "What if you do this and, God forbid, get hurt or die and his seizures stop anyway?" she asked. "How am I supposed to live with that?"

"What happens if I quit and his seizures never stop?" Allen countered. "I'm sick of already living that now."

"His seizures may never stop," Kelsey said almost in a whisper.

Allen didn't reply, though Kelsey noticed the color in his face drain before he eventually walked away. Over the next hour, Allen got odds and ends ready for his trip while Kelsey finished getting their home ready for a visit from Sidney, Benjamin's occupational therapist. Luckily, Benjamin woke up on his own before she was forced to end his nap. Kelsey changed his diaper and already had him in his highchair by the time Sidney rang up from the main entryway. As Allen came out and prepared to leave, Sidney had placed an assortment of small toys in front of Benjamin on his highchair tray, encouraging him to grasp and hold different ones to work on his skills using his hands.

Kelsey stood nearby watching her son when Allen headed for the door with his gear. He stopped and watched his son for a time while Benjamin struggled to grasp a small ball, forcing Sidney to put her hand over his to help. Kelsey stepped in closer. Sessions like these were her son's last lifeline for development. Hundreds of hours would be spent making tiny, incremental steps just to learn things as simple as holding a spoon or picking up food. That was the grinding work that needed to be done, and she resented Allen for running off to try and be the big hero while leaving her to tackle the equally important yet far less dramatic challenges alone.

Kelsey turned to look at her husband to see if he'd had a last-minute change of heart. Though his expression was sad, he showed no signs of reconsidering.

"Bye," he said quietly.

"Bye," Kelsey said back. The two looked at each other for a moment more before Kelsey returned to watching Benjamin, avoiding her desire to scream at her husband at the top of her lungs. Still, she couldn't help but listen as Allen turned the handle of the front door and quietly left, closing the door gently behind him.

****

Inside a driverless town car identical to the one he rode in the night before, Allen felt a heavy weight on his body as he was driven to Eamon's private airplane hangar. He tried to shake away the feeling by focusing on the mission ahead, but that only reminded him of his struggles with Haley. His emotions volleyed back and forth, from Kelsey and guilt to Haley and worry. With nowhere for his concern to escape, Allen attempted to preserve his sanity and mindfully pause for the time being. After all, the ride in the car was probably the last time he would have any peace for the next few days. So he tried to make the most of it and rest his weary brain cells by simply thinking about nothing.

After forty-five minutes of actively thinking about not thinking, Allen arrived at the outer security gate of the private airfield. Like the secluded garage entrance to Eamon's personal elevator, the security gate was automated. But unlike Eamon's gate, it failed to open automatically after a minute of waiting. Allen lowered his window to get a closer look at the control box attached to the gate arm. It had a numbered keypad, a sensor for detecting wireless access passes, and a small camera. As Allen was about to speak up to see if somebody was watching him through the camera, a small light above it flashed green. A moment later, the gate opened. The problem had been resolved so easily. If only the rest of the world responded to him so well.

It didn't take long for the car to make its way up the driveway, past the airport control tower, and into a private hangar where a small passenger jet waited. Allen got out of the car with his bag of gear and looked around. There was no one else in the hangar. He felt especially lonely walking inside such a large open structure by himself, the plane notwithstanding. It became even more so when the driverless town car backed out of the hangar without warning and abandoned Allen by driving away. He walked forward and dropped his bags absently with a heavy sigh. He said he'd go it alone, but actually standing by himself next to an empty plane with no sign of the new armor Daryl was supposed to have waiting for him made Allen tremble in a way he couldn't walk off. Seeing no other way forward than the one he'd already set for himself, Allen boarded the jet. At least his stubbornness and depression could travel in luxury accommodations.

The door to the jet had already been pulled down, exposing a set of stairs on the inside of the hatch for Allen to step up into the aircraft. As he reached the top step and prepared to turn into the passenger cabin, a dark blur jabbed out straight toward his face. Allen pulled back, forgetting about the stairs behind him. Gravity swiftly reminded him of his error and pulled him stumbling past the first two steps. Allen was able to take hold of the narrow cable acting as a railing and twist his body to balance his weight under his feet before taking the last step down to the hangar floor. Then he spun around to look back up the stairs to face his attacker.

At the top step, Haley stared down at him in shock. "What just happened?"

"How long have you been in there?" Allen asked, trying to catch his breath.

"Five minutes, maybe. I was checking out the jet. Now I'm going to see if my dad needs help."

"Yeah? Is he going to jump up through the floor?" Allen shouted, pacing quickly from a mixture of adrenaline and bruised ego.

Haley laughed, her own shock melting away. Allen shot her an angry look, which made her laugh harder. His sternness only lasted a moment more before his scowl transformed into a grin as he chuckled at himself. His shoulders rose from their slump. His partner was with him. "I know this wasn't an easy decision for you," Allen said once their laughter died down. "Thank you."

Haley looked back at him and shifted her weight between her feet. "I'm willing to do this because I said I would," she said, "and to give myself a fair chance. But saying anything more than that makes me feel super uncomfortable, and I desperately want this conversation to move on."

"Okay," Allen agreed. The partners stood

awkwardly without a smooth transition out of their tender moment until a noise from the far end of the hangar gave them one. They both turned to see Daryl coming toward them on his wheelchair. Behind him, a man in a pilot's uniform pushed a pallet dolly stacked with dark cases and a pair of large black duffel bags. As the pilot made his way to the other side of the plane to load the gear into the cargo hold, Daryl approached Allen.

"Everything's ready, just under the wire," he said. Once Daryl was close enough so only Allen could hear him, he asked, "How did Kelsey take it?"

Allen just shook his head in response.

"Hmmm," Daryl replied, thoughtfully. "Well, maybe you can bring her back a souvenir."

Allen remained stoic. "Yes, frozen rocks will win her back."

Daryl gave Allen a smile, then reached out his arm. "Help me up." Allen held Daryl's hand to support his weight as he activated his wheelchair's standing mode. Once fully upright, Daryl pulled Allen toward him and the two embraced. "Make it back so you can apologize. She'll forgive you," Daryl assured Allen.

"I know," Allen said as he pulled away to look his friend in the eye. "I just wish I didn't make her have to. And…I need to ask you to do something for me."

"Yes, yes," Daryl said, anticipating Allen's request. "If something happens to you, I'll watch out for Kelsey and Benjamin."

"Um…yes, that too. But also…" Allen said, removing his Healthy Helper from his wrist and handing it to Daryl. "If I have this off for more than a couple days, we could lose coverage. Could you wear it if things run long?"

Daryl stared at the fitness tracker dubiously as if he were being asked to eat it. "Sure," he said, reluctantly taking the device.

Allen moved back, and Haley took her turn to say goodbye to her father. As the pair hugged, Allen stepped away to give them privacy and made his way into the jet.

Allen wove past a pair of thick leather seats in the first row before taking a seat on the far side of a small table, facing forward toward the cockpit with a matching seat across from him. There he waited until Haley finished her goodbyes to her father and boarded the aircraft to sit on the other side of the table.

Before the pair began to speak, a pilot, different than the one Allen had seen with the luggage, came onto the plane.

"Good afternoon," said the crisp man in his thirties. "I'm Captain Keller. I'll be flying today with my co-pilot, First Officer Maitlin. He's outside loading your things. Food and drinks are in the refrigerated compartment behind you. We'll be taking off shortly." With that, Captain Keller entered the cockpit and got to work. It was time for Allen and Haley to do the same.

Using a small set of controls built into the table, Allen activated a double-sided monitor that rose up out of a small sliding compartment in the center. Once up to its full height at eye level, each side of the monitor lit up to show Allen and Haley the same identical standby screen. Allen removed a small case from his pocket, retrieved his earpiece, then put it in his ear.

"MeatTank, I'm going to pair my earpiece with the system here so you can transmit to our monitors," Allen told Kyle on the other end of the line.

"I'm ready!" Kyle replied with trademark enthusiasm.

Allen placed the earpiece on the table, digitally paired it with the monitor system, and waited. Ten seconds passed. Then twenty. Allen reached out to examine the earpiece when the cabin lights inside the jet blinked and went dark. Just as Allen began calling out to the pilots, lights in the floor and ceiling lit up to shower the cabin in colorful light, accompanied by booming electronic music.

Now inside the world's most compressed rave venue, an animated character began dancing on the screen. With the body of a human and the head of a unicorn, the animated creature wore clothes that glowed with all the colors of the rainbow and spoke in a voice that was instantly recognizable as Kyle's.

"It's mission tiiiiiiiiiiime!" announced the one-horned abomination, gyrating its body with no detectable rhythm.

Allen looked toward the cockpit in time to see First Officer Maitlin enter before Captain Keller reached to close the cockpit door. "Sorry!" Allen yelled right before the captain slammed the door shut.

"We've got big things planned, so let's get to it!" the Kyle-voiced unicorn continued. On the screen, the dancing character disappeared, replaced with a top-down satellite image Allen recognized from his own mission prep as the airplane hangar where he and Haley were located.

"This is you, waiting for your personal aircraft to fly you to the isolated yet beautiful town of Ilulissat, Greenland." As Kyle spoke, images on the screen changed to match his narration and pulsed to the beat of the music still blaring throughout the cabin. "You may be interested to know that the name 'Ilulissat' literally means 'iceberg,' " Kyle explained to Allen and Haley. Neither found the fact interesting in any way. "That's because the town is surrounded by icebergs and glaciers, making it the most popular tourist destination in all of Greenland."

Allen looked down at his earpiece and was tempted to smash the device with his fist in order to cut off Kyle's feed but reconsidered at the last moment. Instead, he silently cursed Eamon for inexplicably having multi-colored party lights installed in his aircraft.

"From Ilulissat, the plan *was* to bribe the crew of a supply ship to transport you up to Alluttoq Island, but I've got a surprise! Did somebody say 'whale watching'?" The screen filled with what looked like a hundred different photos of whales, each image flashing for only a brief moment before being replaced by another. "Yes! From Ilulissat, I've booked you on a tour boat that will take you on a virtual whale safari up the coast and drop you off at the small dock at Port Avannaata, just a few miles' trek from Rusk's research facility. How magical is that?"

" 'Tank!" Allen yelled over the music, "can we pause this for a second, please?"

In response, the music stopped—much to the relief of everyone with ears.

"Thank you," Allen said. "Maybe we can simply talk through the plans from here on out."

"Sure thing, Mystic," Kyle replied, unfazed by the requested change. On the screen, the images of the presentation faded away and were replaced with a live video image of Kyle at his computer station.

"Good to see you," Allen said. After the music and lights stopped, the windows flared with sunlight off concrete as the plane passed from inside the hangar out onto the tarmac.

"Did you book a two-way whale tour?" Haley asked Kyle. "Seems like a fairly conspicuous way out after blowing up Rusk's stuff and kidnapping one of her doctors."

"That's true," Kyle agreed. "That's why your transport out will be a little more private."

On the screen in front of Allen and Haley, two photographs popped onto the screen but appeared to be two different shots of the same person. It was a man around Haley's age in his twenties.

"Oh, great, Daryl got them," Allen said.

" 'Them'?" Haley asked.

"John and Jacob Zielinski," Kyle announced. "They'll be waiting with a boat at the coast to get you out."

"They've been shooting messages to your dad for years," Allen told Haley. "I even took a couple calls from them. They offered to pay us to ask questions about the business, and we happily obliged them."

"So they're twins," Haley said.

Allen shook his head. "No, actually. And don't say that to them—they hate it. They were born ten months apart."

"But they look identical," Haley said, pointing to the photographs.

"One is, like, two inches taller than the other."

"Which one?" Haley asked.

"I have no idea. They both look the same," Allen admitted, shrugging his shoulders. "They introduced themselves collectively." Allen felt a shift in the pit of his stomach and looked out the window again to see the scenery outside passing by at ever-quickening speed. A moment later, the aircraft pitched upward and gained altitude.

"In any case," Allen continued, turning back to Kyle on the screen and Haley across from him, "let's talk about how we're getting this thing done."

Chapter Seventeen

"Doctor Sloan, can I help you find something?"

Sloan turned around from the drug supply locker to find one of the floor nurses staring at him. "No, Shawna, thanks. I'm just getting a diazepam dose for Mister Hodges in Room Three. He's especially agitated today."

"Do you want me to bring it to him?"

"No, no," Sloan assured her. "He's a bit paranoid today. He's expecting me to come right back with it. I'm afraid he'll refuse it unless I'm the one who gives it to him."

"Okay, just let me know if you need anything," Shawna offered cheerily before returning to her duties. Sloan took a deep breath and went back into the locker. After entering his security code, Sloan removed two pills from the diazepam container then closed it again. He had only planned on taking one out for himself, but since Nurse Curious had caught him he had to at least make an appearance of telling the truth. Sloan slipped a pill into his mouth and swallowed it dry while he put the other into a small plastic cup. After walking to Room Three and surprising Mister Hodges with an unexpected bonus dose, Sloan went to his work station and logged the administration of two anti-anxiety pills instead of one.

Sloan wasn't even sure why he was covering his

tracks. He was already terrified Hanspeter Jodock was going to drag him outside in the middle of the night and shoot him for sending secret messages asking for help, so what did it matter if he was stealing pills? After all, he was only taking them because memories of Chuck basically being executed in front of him kept flashing in his head. Maybe the trauma would help him only get fired instead of killed. If only he could be so lucky. Sloan finished submitting the false drug order into the computer.

It had been three days since he sent his latest message to Baner asking for help. Sloan had grown more anxious each day since. He felt watched and judged everywhere he went and found an excuse to leave whenever Jodock got anywhere near him. Living in an underground research facility had been fairly claustrophobic even before Sloan had any reason to panic, but lately it was so stifling Sloan could barely breathe.

While his mind raced, the doctor stared at his computer screen and waited for the medication to kick in. He cycled between video feeds of his patients and pretended to read progress notes, all the while trying to think of ways he could get away. As he thought more and more, and as the relaxing effects of the diazepam slipped over him, it occurred to Sloan that the realistic chances of somebody coming to rescue him were slim. And if nobody was coming to save him, then what?

A soft buzzing sensation crawled over Sloan's body, and he was suddenly compelled to stand. He was forced to brace himself against his desk for a moment to steady his sedated muscles. He turned and cautiously made his way out of the observation bay and into the main elevators at the center of the facility. From there he went up two floors to the medical staff habitat level and into his quarters. Once inside, Sloan closed the heavy metal door behind him and allowed himself the luxury of letting out a sigh. He had to get outside. He strained to think of logical alternatives, but the individual thoughts evaporated as soon as they formed.

By necessity, the research facility was not relatively far from the small harbor they relied on to bring in people and supplies. It would be a long hike for Sloan, but doable. He went to his closet and pulled out the parka that was issued to him when he had first arrived. Although it was spring, it would still only be about twenty degrees Fahrenheit outside during the daytime and much colder at night. Next, Sloan opened a small personal safe and tucked as much cash as he could from his monthly stipend into every pocket he could. There weren't many places to spend cash even before the lockdown, and Sloan hoped his stockpile of money would be enough to buy his way onto a boat. The type of people who brought supplies to such a remote location were not known for their charity. Finally, Sloan gathered his winter boots and emergency rations, then got dressed into his last-minute escape ensemble.

Sloan looked in the mirror. The sight of himself wearing a large, puffy jacket indoors made him doubt his chances. He unzipped the coat, removed it, then held it under his arm to try a more casual approach. It looked better, but not by much. Sloan tapped his foot and inspected his closet until his gaze reached his laundry bag. He quickly retrieved the nylon sack and stuffed his coat inside, resulting in a less suspicious, yet still ridiculous, look.

Sloan took one last glance at the small quarters he had called home for the past few months, excited at the idea of never seeing them again. He opened the door and checked both directions down the hallway before stepping out and heading back to the elevator. He hit the button to go up and waited self-consciously, clutching his plump bag with one hand. After a painfully slow thirty seconds, the elevator arrived. He promptly entered, pressed the button for the surface level three floors above, and repeatedly pressed it until the doors finally closed.

Sloan watched the numbers change as he passed each floor, hoping upon hope that nobody else boarded the elevator. When the car reached the surface level, Sloan released a sigh of relief as he stepped out into the hallway leading to the main doors. The ceiling was covered with ductwork, pipes, and cables for carrying fresh air and water to the floors below, as well as connections to communications equipment located on the roof. The dull hum and rumble of the various utilities made the hallway feel far more foreboding than Sloan had remembered.

He walked forward on the concrete floor with as much confidence as he could muster, trying to project the sense that he belonged there rather than the reality that he was running for his life. The hallway was empty. Twenty steps later, there was still no one in sight. Up ahead, a bluish glint of sunlight poured in through the porthole-like windows of the thick main doors. There was no security guard. Sloan picked up his pace with the thought that the guards must all be outside rather than in the hallway. Also, his parka was the same design as the ones they were all wearing. Sloan would look like a guard, and he was only a quick game of *Name Your Price* away from bribing one of them to let him walk away forever.

Sloan grinned as he closed the remaining distance to the doors. He took a look out one of the small windows and got his first glimpse of the outside world in weeks. There were patches of snow on the ground between stretches of rock on the lichen-covered landscape. Sloan couldn't wait to breathe in the cool air with a touch of breeze on his face. It would feel like heaven.

As Sloan put his hand on the handle of the door, a low voice froze him where he stood.

"There you are, Doctor Sloan."

Sloan turned slowly and looked into the eyes of Hanspeter Jodock with as much bravery as he could muster. "Mister Jodock," he croaked. "Good afternoon."

"Good afternoon," Jodock replied with a casual smile as he walked up to Sloan. "A lovely day outside."

"Oh, yes," Sloan stammered, looking out the window again before turning back to Jodock. "I just really wanted to take a look."

"And yet that is against the rules at this time," Jodock said, walking past Sloan to take his own look out the window.

Sweat beaded on Sloan's forehead, the sudden presence of Jodock rendering the diazepam useless. "Yes, well, I figured I could enjoy a little 'privilege of seniority,' let's say."

Jodock turned from the window to face Sloan again, so close that the doctor was forced to crane his head up and lean back to look him in the eye. "Of course," Jodock said before moving even closer to speak in a hushed tone. "We'll keep this just between us." He laid his hand on Sloan's shoulder for a moment before turning the doctor away from the main doors. "I'm glad I ran into you," Jodock said, stepping forward to return to the elevator, pushing Sloan with him.

Sweat now ran down Sloan's temple. "Oh?"

"Yes, there are a few housekeeping items I wanted to go over with you. Just to clear up some odds and ends."

As they walked, Sloan looked up at the ceiling to avert his eyes from the depressing sight of the approaching elevator door. Above him he caught sight of a security camera, only then realizing that Jodock could have watched him from any number of cameras placed throughout the facility. The two men reached the elevator, and Jodock pressed the call button. While they waited, Jodock calmly reached out and took the laundry bag stuffed with Sloan's coat out of the doctor's hand without saying a word.

The elevator arrived, the doors opened, and the two walked inside. Sloan fixed his eyes on the hint of bluish sunlight still faintly visible at the far end of the hall. He clung to the sight of it right up to the moment the closing elevator doors stole it away.

Chapter Eighteen

"Come on, admit it."

"Hmmm," Allen grunted in response to Haley, taking another case of equipment from a deckhand on the ship and placing it on the dock next to the others.

"Come on…" Haley prodded beside him.

"Fine, the whales were cool, okay?" Allen confessed as he grabbed the last case from the ship.

"The ride up wasn't as bleak as I thought it'd be," Haley said, looking out onto the water. "Although the random floating ice chunks made me a bit nervous." She bent down, stacked her cases edge on edge, then locked them together into one tall pack before pulling various straps from different compartments to combine the two cases into a single large backpack.

Allen picked up his cases and moved to the side of the dock to get clear of a relatively small yet unexpected crowd of people. "Yeah, I didn't realize Greenland had become a regular tourist destination." A group of campers lined up and waited to get onboard the modest whale-watching ship they had arrived on, which also doubled as a daily passenger ferry. As they did, one of the campers waiting his turn struck up a conversation.

"How many nights you staying?" asked the scruffy young man, a large camping pack of his own strapped to his back.

"Oh, just a couple nights," Allen answered as casually as one can when bundling weapons while chatting with a stranger.

Haley finished preparing the harness on her pack and hefted her gear onto her back. While she finished buckling the straps, Allen watched the young man glance back and forth between Haley and himself, clearly trying to mentally fill in the gaps of how Allen and Haley were both there together. Being over twenty years apart in age and showing no family resemblance, Allen couldn't blame him.

Haley looked up from her buckling and locked eyes with the young man looking at her with a furrowed brow. She turned to Allen, flustered. "Yes! Are you ready to go, hun, or uh, honey, I mean…Uncle Ted?"

The shaggy man slowly shifted his gaze between Haley and Allen as if he struggled to make sense of the words that had just come from Haley's mouth. For his part, Allen just stared down at the dock, unable to look either of the other two in the eye.

"Almost, my darling…niece," Allen replied. He flashed a smile to diffuse the suddenly creepy vibe, but he could instantly tell it had only made things worse.

Finally it was time to board the ship, and the young man quickly bid goodbye and left. The ship soon cast off from the dock and pulled away, leaving Allen and Haley by themselves. With gear loaded on both their backs, the two hiked inland toward the location Kyle had decided would make a good base camp. After almost thirty minutes without speaking, Haley was the first to break the silence.

"Are you going to say anything?" Haley demanded to know.

"I just feel gross now, and I didn't even do anything," Allen said, shaking his hands as if trying to remove the feeling by force.

"Stop. It wasn't that bad," Haley said defensively.

"Naw, dude, it was super creepy," Kyle's voice broke into their ears. Both Allen and Haley jumped with the startling addition of Kyle to the conversation.

"You were listening that whole time?" Haley asked.

"Yep," Kyle replied cheerfully.

"Maybe you should play a gentle warning tone before you speak after a long while, MeatTank," Allen grumbled.

"I'll think about it, see what I can come up with," Kyle answered, enthusiasm filling his voice at the prospect of another project. "Changing subjects a little, are we keeping the same codenames on this mission that we used on the last one?"

Allen looked over at Haley for her opinion, but she remained quiet. A weight came over her face, the same expression of doubt and fear she had the night she was attacked in the Nolan Building. "Haley, listen. You can't...you..." The words he tried to use to ease Haley's doubts kept catching in his throat and retreating.

But in that moment, he realized there might be a single word that could do the trick.

"MeatTank—Codename: Temp will now go by codename: Specter," Allen announced.

Haley turned to Allen at the sound of her father's codename. "I can't," Haley told him.

Allen stopped walking. As Haley faced him, anger welled up in his voice. "If you didn't deserve it, I wouldn't use it. This isn't some pity move. You've earned it, so that's what we're going to call you." Allen glared at Haley for another moment before wondering if he had maybe jumped the gun on forcing a name on her. "Unless you already had a name in mind. I'm not trying to be a jerk. You—just looked like you didn't have one."

Haley laughed. "Okay, fine," she said reluctantly, "but only until I come up with a name of my own."

Allen smiled. "Did you copy that, 'Tank?"

"Copy that," Kyle replied. "Good to have you with us, Specter."

"All right, all right," Haley replied.

"We could keep 'Darling Niece' if you wanted. Or 'Uncle Ted?' " Kyle joked.

"Stop talking," Haley commanded.

Allen and Haley finished hiking the remaining two miles to their campsite by midday. They set up on the shore of a deep-blue glacial pool, putting up a tent and a series of solar panels for remote power. The site was about a mile off the coast and less than a mile away from the research facility. The two had hiked a diagonal path from the dock to remain off the roads and to position in an area that put a gentle rise between them and the facility, blocking direct line of sight in the bleak landscape. The area had its fair share of campers coming through, so Allen and Haley's presence by itself wasn't suspicious. Still, they didn't want to be within sight where someone could watch them at length.

While they waited for nightfall, the pair split their time between resting and preparing their equipment. Their pulse weapons were already charged and limited to small arms since they weren't planning on an open firefight. But the remaining gear needed to be connected to the solar panels to have their energy cells topped off. Allen took his new set of armor out of its case and spent the better part of the afternoon putting it on and testing its features. After briefly checking through the same functions he had in his old suit, Allen familiarized himself with the new series of motors built into the suit that Kelsey told him about. The motors provided mechanical assistance to all his movements, making walking and running easier as well as helping carry the weight of the armor. The helmet was also more lightweight than his old one and came with a pair of thin protective glasses instead of his old attached pull-down shield. The glasses used small emitters to project images directly onto the contours of his eyes, saving valuable space and weight on display gear.

Allen ran through the basic tutorial included in the system software to check for any differences in what he was already used to. As he did, he couldn't help wonder about the work Kelsey had been doing. For all the features his suit had, it definitely lacked the level of intuitiveness that she always seemed to bring to her programming. The software for much of Allen's equipment was generally programmed by the same engineers who designed the gear in the first place. But using weapons, gadgets, and body armor all at the same time when people were trying to kill you was difficult to simulate in a lab. Still, the software lived on. Daryl himself had been using the same basic open-source programming in all of his projects for years. On one hand, that level of consistency let any operator learn to use nearly any piece of equipment almost immediately.

On the other hand, certain quirks and unnatural controls had been passed down through generations without ever being improved. Much like the standard QWERTY keyboard, it was flawed but familiar.

Allen sighed. It was too late to change anything now. There was no sense in dwelling on what could have been, no matter how much he regretted leaving without waiting for Kelsey to finish her work. He had the sudden urge to call his wife and check in on her but fought it. He may have regretted leaving the way he did, but he still felt that leaving was indeed the right call. Whether it actually was or not, getting into a fight over the phone wouldn't be helpful for anyone.

As the sun set, Allen and Haley assembled the gear that would get them from the campsite to the facility. Three personal octocopters, small eight-propellered drones, had to be unfolded on the ground and prepared for flight. The devices were a zero-frills affair, just simple platforms with propellers, pulse power cells, circuit boards, and wires with harnesses attached. Still, they would do the trick to cover the mile's distance. Allen and Haley would use one drone each while the third would carry a small amount of gear on the way in and Doctor Sloan on the way out. Luckily the octocopters had a follow mode and could match the flight path of the other two copters, saving Sloan the need to become an expert pilot in just a few minutes.

With the octocopters ready and the gear packed, Allen checked in with Kyle to do a comms test and make sure he could see Allen and Haley through the satellite feed that had been made available through Eamon.

"Yep, I've got eyes on the two of you as well as the

target facility," Kyle confirmed. "The guard patrols around the perimeter are sparse, and as we saw in the architectural designs, their security lighting is focused on the building and the area around it, not the sky." It sounded somewhat ridiculous to hear Kyle say the last part out loud, considering that lighting up the sky was not a typical building feature. But for their purposes that evening the last detail was vital.

"There's one final thing before we get started," Allen said. Haley stopped checking her gear and turned to her partner as he continued. "If you…" Allen paused, searching for his words before continuing. "When we're over there, if you feel that I'm not thinking clearly, that I'm too obsessed about finishing the mission…then you're allowed to end it."

Haley seemed surprised by the sudden responsibility thrown on her, but she quickly understood Allen's meaning. "Just don't make me have to, okay?"

Allen nodded his agreement, and the two were ready to go. He and Haley attached their harnesses, and the two copters hovered above their heads, while the third did the same. After exchanging a thumbs-up with Haley, Allen reached up to his controls before putting his full faith in his straps and lifting off the ground.

Behind him, Allen barely made out Haley's silhouette in the growing darkness. The moonless night revealed only the barest outline of a horizon as the final touches of sunset bent around the Earth. They were lucky that the mission was taking place at a time of year when night even occurred. In just a couple of months, it would be light twenty-four hours a day inside the Arctic Circle.

As if sensing his blindness, Kyle cut in through Allen's earpiece. "I'm bringing your displays up now." A topographical overlay displayed in Allen's glasses, showing him the terrain in the darkness below as well as his altitude and distance to the facility.

A minute later, Allen saw the lights of a building, and his breath quickened. The risk was real now. As were his doubts. He understood the rational reasons for destroying Eden and developing it safely, but it was different now that Allen was about to have a hand in it. His doubts confirmed the wisdom of Haley's suggestion that she be the one to go down to the central procedure bay to destroy the Eden servers and equipment. He had assumed Haley just didn't want to babysit Sloan, but maybe she saw his desire for a cure for Benjamin could be a fatal distraction.

Allen climbed to a thousand feet. Down below, he could see the guards patrolling the building by the long shadows they cast from the security lights as they walked. He slowed his forward speed and stopped in a hover directly over the roof.

"Confirm that the roof is clear," Allen requested.

"Confirmed, roof is clear," replied Kyle.

Allen dropped in the darkness, descending smoothly as if in an elevator. As he got closer to the rooftop, satellite dishes and ventilation machinery came into view until he finally got low enough to identify a space to land. Once his feet touched the roof, Allen quickly stepped to the side and killed the power to his octocopter. He had just lowered it to his feet and unhooked himself as Haley touched down behind him. By the time the third drone arrived, Allen was ready and cut the power to its propellers as soon as the gear touched down.

"How are we doing, MeatTank?" Allen whispered.

"No change in movement from the guards," Kyle assured him. "When you get the bridge hooked up, I can tell you more."

Allen dug into the case of gear and removed two pieces of equipment—a pulse pistol and a small combination antenna and communications device. After holstering his weapon, Allen put the base of the antenna down on the roof next to a large metal cabinet that was as tall as he was. He unfolded a series of panels on the antenna that together formed a small satellite dish, then pointed it south and powered it on.

"Bridge active, searching for satellite," Allen reported.

"Checking, stand by," Kyle responded.

While he waited for Kyle, Allen approached the large metal cabinet. Maybe, just maybe, it had been left unlocked considering how remote they were located. A quick attempt at turning its handle disappointed him. Allen pulled his pulse pistol from his hip and set it on the lowest setting before placing the muzzle flush with the keyhole and pulling the trigger. The beam gradually heated the metal of the lock cylinder until it glowed red hot, then Allen pulled the pistol away. He turned the handle and felt some resistance from the lock pins inside before the soft metal gave way. Allen swung the panel open to reveal the communications hub inside.

"The signal bridge is solid," Kyle confirmed. "I should have a good line to you now all the way to the bottom of the facility."

"Good God…" Allen responded with awe.

"Right?" Kyle said. "I kind of forget how

impressive modern technology is. I mean, think about a hundred years ago—"

"No, not that," Allen clarified as he stood in front of the open cabinet staring wide-eyed at the dizzying collection of wires and connections. "This thing has like a million wires. How am I supposed to know which ones to connect you to?"

"Is there a really big one that looks like it's headed to the main satellite dish?" Kyle asked.

Allen took a look at the hub and reported back. "Yeah, it looks more like a cable than a wire."

"Follow it until it connects to a circuit board with a few ports on it. You're going to plug me into that."

Allen found the circuit board, grabbed an appropriate connector from the signal bridge, then used a data cable to complete the link. "How did you learn to hack this stuff?" Allen asked.

"Two years of stealing internet," Kyle answered. "Before I started getting paid for being awesome, that is. Except today we're kind of hacking internet in reverse, pushing an outside connection in instead of pulling one."

Haley came over to Allen, a weapon and explosive charges clipped to her armor. "You ready for this?" Allen asked her.

Haley balked. "Kinda have to be at this point, right?"

Allen nodded, then the two stood in silence while Kyle worked over two thousand miles away. "All right, I'm connected to their data network," Kyle announced. "I've got security camera feeds and door access. I just need another minute to set up the ol' camera loop trick. Which, for some reason, the bad guys haven't figured out a way of stopping yet."

Allen and Haley walked over to a circular hatch a few feet away and stared at it. Aside from the main roof access door, the small hatch and the maintenance tube below it were the only other way into the building from the roof.

"I'm all set. You can go when ready," Kyle said.

Allen drew his pistol while Haley reached down and opened the maintenance hatch. After checking for the unlikely presence of a technician puttering around in the middle of the night, Allen put his weapon away and climbed down the ladder. Haley followed and the two made their way through the narrow walkway lined on all sides by power conduits, data lines, and sprinkler pipes. The crowded maintenance corridors were not only used for maintenance access but also as an alternate escape route in case of fire. With so much of the building underground and no windows to use as fire escapes, it acted as a secondary way out. Even as a secret base, it met the highest level of safety codes.

After a few yards, the two came to another hatch. They repeated the process of going down just as they had on the roof, with Allen checking for anyone below before descending with Haley following close behind. At sublevel three, Allen opened the next hatch and checked below one last time before parting ways with his partner.

"Four more levels down, the procedure bay should be right across from where you come out. After you clone the data, set a charge on the main device and the data drives," Allen instructed. "The fire from the explosion will do the rest."

"I know," Haley told him. "I was in the meeting,

too."

Allen held the hatch open as Haley descended the ladder. At the bottom, she took a deep breath and walked out of sight down the corridor without looking back. Allen waited a moment longer, studying the emptiness, like a parent the first time a kid runs into school without turning to wave goodbye. Just in case she came back.

Allen moved farther down the narrow corridor until he reached Habitat Maintenance Door Three, the door the design plans showed as being the closest to Sloan's quarters. Unfortunately, there was still a wide main hallway and four other living quarters to get past.

"MeatTank, I'm outside Door Three," Allen informed Kyle.

"Hold on, you got a couple of staffers walking by," Kyle warned him. Allen waited. A moment later, footfalls and muffled voices grew louder before drifting away. "Any chance this Doctor Sloan could just freak out when you enter his quarters?" Kyle pondered.

"I'm working on the assumption that he's asleep," Allen whispered back. "But thank you for considering more unpleasant possibilities." After another minute went by without Kyle giving the all-clear, Allen started tapping his foot. "What are they doing?"

"I think we're witnessing the end of a late night romantic rendezvous," Kyle answered. "They're hovering outside one of the habitat doors. They've said goodbye like four times, but the woman still hasn't gone inside."

"Do they have line of sight to Sloan's door?" Allen asked.

"No, it's hidden by the curve of the hallway. You

want to make a run for it?"

"I can't stand here forever," Allen replied. He closed his eyes and took deep, even breaths. There really wasn't a rush, but after five more minutes of painful waiting, Allen's restless foot got the better of him. "What are they doing now?"

"They're talking lovey-dovey and like half-kissing the whole time, it's repulsive," Kyle said with disgust. "It's your call to go or wait."

Allen's hand was already on the knob of the door before Kyle finished speaking. "I'm going," he reported. Allen opened the door gradually to avoid making noise, then stepped out into the hallway. He squinted as he adjusted to the light and began to walk to his right down the hall when Kyle's voice cut into his ear.

"Shit, he's walking your way! The dude is coming back!"

Allen double-timed his pace down the hall, counting the doors as he walked. At the fourth door, he stopped. "I'm at Sloan's door, open it up," Allen commanded in a whisper, looking back down the hall.

"It's still processing," Kyle said.

"Open the damn door," Allen growled through clenched teeth.

"I've sent the command, but each door has its own code and encryption, so it just takes a bit," Kyle explained. "I was going to do it ahead of time, but I forgot."

Allen pressed back, trying to make himself as much a part of the doorway as he could. "No, you were distracted by the kissing couple."

"Probably," Kyle conceded.

The footsteps of the male staffer came closer. There was nowhere to go. Allen lowered his hand, unfastened the strap on his holster, and slowly drew out his pulse pistol. As he moved, every minuscule sound from his shifting clothes felt like a thunderclap in the heavy silence of the hallway, with a slumbering worker behind every door.

Raising the pistol to eye level, Allen took shallow breaths. The man appeared in front of Allen, walking with a smirk on his face, clearly lost in a daydream. Allen froze and simply watched as the staffer moved right to left through his field of vision and away down the hall. The footsteps faded and blended with the sound of blood pumping in Allen's ears.

As his muscles began to relax, Allen heard the staffer come to a sudden halt. Then a clear sound of a shoe twisting on the floor and steps coming nearer. Allen adjusted his grip on the pistol and flicked the safety off. He reminded himself to aim for the chest, imagining the area he needed to hit and the motions he would use to do it. Another few steps and the staffer would be in sight.

"Got it, door's open," Kyle declared.

Allen leaned his weight into the handle of Sloan's door. Once it released, he opened the door just enough to shuffle sideways through the gap, then closed it as gently as he could. In the darkness of Sloan's room, Allen took a moment to take a slow, deep breath before returning his pistol to its holster while waiting for his eyes to adjust to the darkness. Once he was able to make out shapes in the dark and identify a small cot, his posture relaxed as he recognized the form of a person lying under a blanket. He had made it in and found the doctor, whose presence in the room felt like the last major variable in the plan. Now Allen could shift his thinking to the best part of any mission—getting out.

Moving carefully, Allen approached Sloan. The doctor was on his side, turned away from Allen and facing the wall. Allen placed his hand in front of the doctor's mouth in case he decided to yell at the presence of a stranger in his room, but hovered just short of actually covering it. Waking up to the sound of your own name was usually less terrifying than by someone palming half of your face.

"Doctor Sloan," Allen whispered. "Are you awake, Doctor? I've been sent to get you out of here." Sloan's form remained still. "Doctor Sloan?" Allen repeated as he drew closer. He froze and watched for any signs of Sloan waking up. Still, he did not move.

"Doctor?" Allen said again before grabbing Sloan by the shoulder and gently shaking him. Immediately, something seemed off about the way it felt to shake him. Allen couldn't place what was wrong, but when he tugged to roll the doctor toward him, the problem became clear. The doctor's body was rigid, moving as a single inflexible form as if frozen. The telltale sign of rigor mortis sent a bolt of panic through Allen's mind.

Sloan was dead.

"Get out!" Allen cried into his earpiece. "Specter, get—"

Allen was hit on the left side of his head, sending him against the wall.

"Say again?" Haley's voice asked in Allen's ear as pieces of crushed shelving and personal items dropped on top of him. "Mystic, what—"

The sound of gunfire over the radio cut off Haley's

response.

Allen tried to shake away the fog and get back on his feet when a massive hand gripped his neck under the jawbone and pulled him up.

"Good evening," the hulking form told Allen with an accent he couldn't place. The pleasantness of the greeting gave Allen the briefest sense of calm before he was once again thrown across the room. Allen's vision cleared just in time to see his attacker reach down, grab the collar of Allen's armor, and pull him halfway to his feet. As the man pulled his other arm back and made a fist, Allen had the clearest vision of Kelsey in his mind, back at the condo telling him she didn't want him to go on the mission. He wished he had listened as the man's fist landed hard against Allen's head and made the world go dark.

Chapter Nineteen

"Get out! Specter, get—"

Haley had just reached the second-to-last level of the facility when Allen's panicked voice screamed for her to leave. His voice sounded so different the command didn't seem real.

"Say again?" Haley's asked. "Mystic, what—"

Gunfire tore through the narrow, dark corridor, filling it with flashes and deafening noise. Haley felt stinging pangs all over her body where the bullets struck her armor, her projectile shield automatically activating with the sound. The shots were coming from the other hatch at the end of the corridor. Haley returned fire with her pulse pistol, aiming at the muzzle flashes. She heard a man's voice cry in pain, the clank of a dropped gun, and the sound of the metal hatch falling shut. Muffled yelling told her that another attacker would soon be taking the previous one's place.

Haley scrambled up the ladder. "Somebody tell me what is happening!"

"I don't know," Kyle responded. "Mystic entered Sloan's quarters, then a little while later started yelling."

"Mystic, status check!" Haley yelled as she popped up through a hatch and ran through the tight corridor to make her way back to the roof.

As she climbed up the next ladder, Kyle updated

her. "He's not answering comms or visual alerts." Haley had forgotten about the visual communication functions, but now that Kyle reminded her, she became even more worried.

"I'm going to his position," Haley informed Kyle as she reached another level.

"That's not the plan," Kyle said with unusual sternness.

"I'm one level below him!" Haley yelled through the corridor, halfway to the next ladder.

"Specter, make your way to the roof and get out of there."

"Just let me look," Haley said, reaching sublevel three where Sloan's quarters were.

"You have to keep running," Kyle said with rising urgency.

"Damnit, just let me—"

"They're coming for you!" Kyle yelled. "Three guys with machine guns. They're running down the hall of the habitat level."

Haley stood at the same door Allen had used to enter the hallway, the closest one to Sloan's room. "But I'm right here," she said desperately.

"It's too late," Kyle said. "You need to go. Now."

Haley stared at the door another moment.

"Please," Kyle pleaded.

Haley finally peeled herself away from the door and up the next ladder, digging into her supply bag as she went. Below her, the door burst open. A guard fired at her as the others piled in behind him. Haley climbed up the next two levels never looking back as the guards chased her up to the roof, hitting her with bullets as she went.

Just before crossing outside into the night, Haley took the fire charge she had pulled from her supply bag and tossed it behind her. She closed the roof door and leaned hard against it before hitting her remote activator. The blast shoved the door and pushed her forward into the nearest octocopter. As Haley strapped herself to the flying device, she checked the status of her projectile shield. She had fifteen percent power remaining.

"You're going to have to help me see the guards," Haley told Kyle.

"I'll give you night vision," Kyle answered. "Just punch it."

Haley hoisted the octocopter over her head and ran toward the edge of the roof. When she couldn't run any faster, she activated the propellers. But instead of the pure darkness she had enjoyed on the way in, the night air was now filled with searchlights.

Gunfire echoed all around. Haley looked down and saw running guards and muzzle flashes. She felt more stings as bullets shattered against her armor. Haley gripped the control arm of the octocopter and twisted it, flinging herself sideways through the air. She felt yet more deflected bullet strikes as she pitched the octocopter forward and increased speed. However, while she herself was protected by a quickly-draining projectile shield, her octocopter was not.

A shot struck the copter, shattering a propeller. The flying machine dropped a few feet before the remaining propellers adjusted for the extra load. Haley was getting farther from the searchlights, but the strike on the copter made the guards realize the failure in their aiming strategy.

The shots became more spaced out as the guards took more careful aim at the octocopter instead of Haley herself. Another propeller shattered, dropping Haley again before the device counteracted the loss of lift. Haley's descent had slowed, but she was still dropping. She reached again into her supply bag and pulled out another fire charge before looking up at the octocopter to check the amount of light it was still catching from the searchlights. Just as she thought she may have gotten enough distance, a final shot tore through a propeller as well as part of the control platform.

Haley fell quickly before the octocopter tried once again to correct itself, but the device's power now came in spurts, causing it to fluctuate between a steady drop and a sudden one.

Finally, the octocopter was totally encased in darkness, out of range of the searchlights. Haley dropped the fire charge and did the best she could to bank away before activating it. She didn't know how smart the guards were or if they realized there wasn't anything remotely explosive about the octocopter she was flying, but hopefully they had watched too many movies and would go to the location of the fireball instead of wherever she was landing.

The ground approached far too fast for comfort. The bobbing and sudden drops continued as the power was randomly interrupted. She was now twenty feet from the ground, and while the rate of fall had gotten manageable, her forward speed was too fast. She watched her altitude get into the teens, then terrifying single digits. The windswept rocks and thin vegetation moved by in a grainy, green-tinged blur as she waited for the inevitable moment her body made contact with it.

The first thing to hit was her right foot. Her toe bounced off the ground and sent her spinning back up into the air. She came down once more and her right foot hit yet again, this time with the heel. It caught the ground and dragged her just long enough to leverage the octocopter forward and slam onto the rocky surface, crushing itself and sending pieces flying in all directions. Haley tumbled, striking the ground hard with all sides of her body. She bounced along until, at last, her movement became a sideways roll that slowed to an eventual stop.

Haley lay in the dark breathing heavily, her eyes spinning wildly to discern up from down. She reached out with her hands and laid her palms on the ground, giving her enough orientation to attempt to sit up. She winced as she pushed up with her left arm, and her hand snapped to her right knee as soon as she moved it. She gingerly tested the joints in her arms and legs and found she could move every appendage, though each trial evoked a different level of heavy groan.

Feeling a rush of urgency, Haley sat up. "Where am I, 'Tank?"

"You're half a mile from the pickup point. It's roughly due west of you," Kyle answered. "You need to get moving—a pair of vehicles just left the facility."

Haley got to her feet and took a few ginger steps. Her knee hurt, but her elbow was worse off. She took the straps of the harness that were still attached to her armor and fashioned herself a crude sling. "Where do I go?" In response, Kyle activated a beacon on Haley's visual display that showed her where to go and how far she was from her destination. After a few minutes of walking, sunlight started creeping over the horizon. With less than three hours of darkness, it was both the shortest and longest night of her life.

The daylight exposed Haley's distance to the coast, and her muscles shook at the sight of it. She gritted her teeth and quickened her pace. With halfway left to go, the sound of an engine cut through the air. "Is that them behind me?" Haley asked without turning around.

"Yes, the other vehicle went to the explosion," Kyle told her. "The extraction crew just got ashore. You should be able to see them soon."

Haley sped up into a limping gallop. A minute later she saw the Zielinski brothers up ahead. Their rubber raiding boat was pulled up on the rocky shore and two figures scanned the landscape looking for her. Not long after Haley spotted them, they saw her. As did the guards behind her.

"The guards are making a run at you," Kyle said. "I'll tell the guys. Just keep moving."

Ahead of her, the Zielinskis paused, listening to Kyle for a few seconds. Then they sprang into action. One brother turned the boat around to face the water and held it against the surf while the other pulled out some kind of long gun and crouched down with it. The whine of the vehicle behind Haley got closer and closer, but she locked her gaze ahead on the boat and her escape.

Just as the roar of the engine bellowed close enough to run her down, the brother with the long gun fired a burst of pulsefire screaming past Haley's head. The vehicle reacted by tearing up the ground, swerving from its course. The brother fired again as she closed to less than a hundred feet from the boat. As Haley passed him, he fired another barrage before turning to follow her. When he caught up with Haley, he grabbed her under her arm with his free hand and threw her into the boat.

Once onboard, Haley looked back for the vehicle. She caught sight of it just as it came out of a turn to make a run straight at the water. The brothers jumped into the boat, the one with the weapon landing nearest Haley. He took control of the boat's motor and opened it up full throttle, sending them crashing forward through the waves out to sea. By the time the guards got out of their vehicle, the boat was too far away to do anything more than take potshots at.

As the boat carried Haley away from the island, it was hard to feel lucky or come up with a plan to care for her injuries. Explanations, reasons, and details would be required back at home. Like what she would tell her father, what she would say to Kelsey, and how in the world she could possibly rescue Allen. If he was even still alive.

Chapter Twenty

I'm alive.

Allen held on to his pleasant realization as long as he could before opening his eyes after regaining consciousness. He was lying down and thought he heard wind. He listened closer and grimaced at his error. The constant, unwavering rush of air was actually coming through ceiling vents—the kind found in an underground structure in Greenland. But he didn't want to think about all that. He wanted to focus on the fact that he survived—the last victory he might experience for a while.

"I know you're awake," a voice said. Allen recognized it as the man who had warmly greeted him in Sloan's quarters before beating the snot out of him.

Reluctantly, Allen opened his eyes. The room around him was bright, with a mixture of white and metal surfaces. Combined with the presence of medical monitors and other equipment, plus the fact that he was laid out on a medical bed, Allen quickly surmised he was in the procedure bay on the lowest level of the research facility.

To Allen's right, the man from the night before stood looking down on him with a familiar, pleasant grin. "My name is Hanspeter Jodock."

Allen found the name painfully appropriate. "Well,

at least your name explains your accent."

"Clever," Jodock commented. He bent down and checked an intravenous line running into Allen's right arm. As he watched Jodock, Allen became aware that he was dressed in a hospital gown instead of his body armor.

"I don't suppose you want to tell me where my stuff is," Allen ventured.

"Not unless you feel like telling me your real name," Jodock countered.

"Fair enough," Allen admitted. As far as being captured went, it wasn't going half bad. Allen tried to come up with his next line of banter when Olivia Rusk charged through the double glass doors at the end of the room.

"What kind of happy horse-hockey is going on around here?" she demanded to know.

For a terrible moment, Allen thought the question was directed at him and was relieved when Jodock answered instead.

"His accomplice made it to the coast and escaped out to sea," Jodock replied.

Haley had escaped. Allen was mistaken earlier. This news was better than realizing he was alive.

"Christ on a cracker, Jodock, I thought you had this covered!" Rusk yelled.

"Do you not see an intruder before you on the bed? Is the Eden technology and research not still safe?" Jodock asked with measured irritation.

"More prisoners means more intel. And don't get snide with me. We need to know what Tor has been up to."

Allen's heart sank. They had known he would be

coming to the facility. Considering Sloan's clunky final message asking for help, the fact they had been suspicious wasn't a shock. But somehow they knew Eamon was behind the mission. Even though Sloan was messaging a friend at Tor's research institute, it was a big leap to connect it directly to Eamon.

Rusk bent low to growl in Allen's face. "How is my friend Eamon, hmm? Notice anything odd about him lately?" she asked.

Allen decided there was no point in pretending he wasn't working for Eamon. "Well, Mister Tor is a unique individual."

"Uh-huh," Rusk said mockingly. "And how would you rate his behavior on a scale from eccentric to insanely deranged?" She held up both hands on either side of herself as if balancing the choices on a scale.

"It's not helpful to use such harsh terms," Jodock told her as he made notes into a computer about Allen's medical status.

"No?" Rusk shot back. "That's what all your guards call me behind my back, I know it. I use Eden Therapy and get called insane; Eamon uses it and he's just America's quirky trillionaire."

"What?" Allen blurted out before he could stop himself.

"Yeah, that's right," Rusk said with a grin. "Sorry to upset your innocent vision of the incredible Eamon Tor. What did he tell you, that he wanted Eden destroyed for the safety of the world? Well, maybe he shouldn't have helped us create it then."

"Bullshit," Allen said.

"You got that right. That two-faced diaper stain gets...gets..." Rusk turned to Jodock. "What's it called?"

Jodock sighed. "Amyotrophic lateral—"

"Lou Gehrig's disease," Rusk bellowed, cutting off Jodock once she remembered. "He reached out after my cancer diagnosis, tells me we have a mutual interest. The technology was just fine to use on him the first chance he got. But I get Parkinson's and suddenly it's all, 'Sorry, Olivia, the risks are too great.' Hypocrite jerkhole." Rusk paced back and forth and had worked herself into a sweat. Jodock opened a cabinet and retrieved an oxygen mask, connected it to a feed on the wall, and handed it to her.

"Here, slow deep breaths," he told her. Rusk put the mask to her face and complied, muttering to herself between inhaling and exhaling.

While Rusk took time to recover, Allen thought through the recent time he had spent with Eamon. Did the changes in his friend come from years of wealth and power or from Eden Therapy? Allen was doubtful it was the latter. Compared to Rusk's behavior before him, Eamon was a shining example of calm.

After another minute on the oxygen, Rusk dropped the mask to the floor in a kind of inconsiderate way only the very young or filthy rich can manage, then stood over Allen at the bed. "I want to know how Tor has been controlling his side effects, you little wet-rag turd."

"You're wasting your time," Allen said with a smirk. "If Tor cured himself like you say, then he didn't get any side effects. Sorry you rolled the dice on that gamble and lost."

Rusk laughed, an almost pleasant sound if her expression wasn't so menacing. "More lies, I see.

Eamon is nothing if not creative."

"The mental side effects are not a gamble, they're a certainty," Jodock said flatly as he completed his notes. "Everyone who undergoes the treatment gets them."

"Everyone except Eamon Rat-Face Tor," Rusk spat. "And you're going to tell us how. There's no way I'm letting that worm control the entire medical industry."

Allen's vision blurred. His chest felt heavy and there was a sudden pressure in his head. Eamon could have cured Benjamin at any time, but instead had dangled the possibility in Allen's face to lure him into a job no rational person would take. And he had been stupid and desperate enough to fall for it.

"So," Rusk went on, "you'll have a chat with Mister Jodock. If you're helpful, maybe he'll only give you a mild condition to treat." She finished by giving Allen a pat on the arm. The coldness of her bony hand sent a chill through his entire body.

Rusk turned and left the room. While Jodock picked up the discarded oxygen mask from the floor and resumed his tasks, Allen's curiosity about what Rusk had meant overcame his confusion and rage. "What did she mean by giving me a mild condition to treat?"

"Most of our patients come to us with a preexisting condition. We treat them with Eden technology before testing new ways of managing the side effects," Jodock answered with cold precision. "If subjects come with no condition, we give them one."

Allen's head bobbed and settled hard on the scratchy synthetic material of his pillow. He was barely aware of what Jodock was doing around the room and was only mildly aware of other people coming in to draw his blood and confirm his vital signs. The detached feeling was not entirely unpleasant considering the unfortunate things Allen imagined lay ahead of him. It was a shame he couldn't save the feeling for later when he would actually need it.

Satisfied with his preparations, Jodock returned to Allen's bedside. "I am now going to ask you questions. The more truthful you are now, the less pain you will suffer later. However, if you lie, there will be greater pain later."

"Is there an option for zero pain later?" Allen asked.

Jodock shook his head. "There is not."

****

Haley looked out the window of the private jet as it taxied toward the aircraft hangar. The flight had been harshly silent riding in the main cabin alone, especially compared to the lights and sounds of Kyle's presentation when the mission first started. Haley imagined Kyle had created an even more bombastic follow-up show for their successful return. At that moment, she would have done anything to suffer through Kyle's celebration program instead of the reality she was forced to face.

The jet turned into the hangar. As it stopped, Haley saw her father already waiting for her. The pilots got out and simply walked away toward their offices in the back. There was no luggage to remove from the jet, just Haley and what she had on her. She walked down the steps of the aircraft gingerly. Medication from an emergency kit on the plane had taken care of most of her pain, but her knee and elbow still felt tender and weak.

Daryl wheeled up to her as she stepped down to the floor. On her brief call with him before the plane took off from Greenland, Haley had only told him that the mission had not succeeded, she was coming home, and Allen had been taken. It took everything she could muster just to get even those short details out. Now standing in front of her father, she wasn't sure how she would get through a telling of the whole story, especially when he had been against the mission from the beginning.

Before she could speak, however, her father held out his arms to his daughter. Bending low, Haley accepted her father's hug. As it turned out, there was no I-told-you-so. Daryl simply led Haley to his vehicle and the two rode in silence to his house. Haley tried protesting to be brought to her own place, but her words came out as a mumble. She couldn't muster the air into her lungs to put up much of an argument.

Once inside, Haley headed toward the stairs and up to an area that had been hers in high school and left unchanged since moving out. The first floor of the house was where her father had created his living space, and although he had a chairlift to get upstairs, he rarely used it. The arrangement back then meant they each enjoyed their own areas under the same roof, which had been useful for a man adjusting to life in a wheelchair and a girl adjusting to high school as well as her parents' divorce. During that time, they had both learned when it was better to talk about what was going on and when to give each other a break.

"Take a shower, come down for some dinner, then we'll figure this thing out," Daryl said as Haley climbed the steps to the second floor. Heading straight to a small bathroom across the hall from her bedroom, Haley removed her beat-up armor and ran the water in the shower. The mirror had fogged over by the time she took off the last piece and got in. She focused on the sound and sensation of the running water to keep her mind away from thoughts of Allen and what had happened. She tried to maintain her thoughtless state as she got out of the shower, dried off, and covered herself with the towel before walking across the hall to her room. But thoughts of what could be happening to Allen and what she could have done differently kept intruding.

After getting dressed in some workout clothes still in her dresser from college, Haley sat down on the bed and stared at the wooden floor. Dried dots of different colored paints were scattered around her feet from the many times she had painted her room. White, green, purple, and even black over the years. When she was younger, she painted the walls when she needed to calm her mind and escape her worried thoughts. Yet at that moment she couldn't recall what would have been so stressful in those younger days. It hadn't been losing a friend and a mentor, a man with a family who needed him. It hadn't been thinking about how she had personally killed people. And it certainly hadn't been contemplating if she was strong enough to handle the consequences of those events and move forward.

The last thing Allen said to her at the facility kept replaying in her head. His fear was obvious. Yet Haley couldn't help but wonder, if she had been better and more skilled, would he have asked for help instead of telling her to go? If she had been stronger, could she have taken down the guards outside Sloan's room instead of running?

Haley pounded her fists on the bed in frustration, feeling all the world like a failure. Allen should never have taken her on as a partner. Someone had to go back and help him. Surely her father must know someone who could get it done. She had to ask him to contact someone as soon as possible and fix what she had messed up.

Haley got up from the bed, left the bedroom, and started down the stairs. "Dad!" she yelled, nearly in a panic. Halfway down, she could see into the entryway. Standing next to her father was Kelsey, who stared up at Haley while Benjamin sucked his thumb in his stroller. Haley froze midstep, surprise gripping her stomach.

"Come down, Haley," Daryl said.

Haley slowly descended the rest of the stairs and waited at the bottom, looking at her father for guidance. For her part, Kelsey looked only at Haley.

"Let's go in the other room," Daryl directed before wheeling into the living room toward the couch. Kelsey put her hands on her son's stroller but waited until Haley moved ahead before following. Even after Haley sat down, Kelsey stood in the center of the room focusing only on her.

"Kelsey, I'm sorry," Daryl began. "There were complications with the mission."

"What are you going to do?" Kelsey asked, still looking squarely at Haley.

"I'm not sure," Haley replied.

"You didn't have a backup plan in case this happened?"

Haley swallowed hard to prevent another wave of frustration. "I don't know."

"Well, now is a good time to start figuring something out," Kelsey said.

"Kelsey," Daryl tried to jump in again, "if we're going to try any sort of rescue, we need to be smart about it."

"Are you implying I'm being stupid?" Kelsey asked.

"Of course not. And I don't appreciate you putting words in my mouth."

"This is a fun argument," Kelsey said with a sarcastic smile. "I'm sure Allen really appreciates us wasting time on it."

"He told me to leave," Haley blurted.

"So you just did what he said?" Kelsey asked.

"No, I tried to get to him," Haley said.

"And what stopped you?"

"Guards opened fire and cut me off."

"Are those guards here now?" Kelsey asked.

"What?" Haley asked, her emotions swelling again.

"Those guards who stopped you back in Greenland. Are they here at this moment preventing you from helping your partner now?" Kelsey asked, her voice rising.

Haley looked over at her father. "Dad…"

"He's not going to have a plan for you," Kelsey said coolly. "He doesn't want you to go back."

"Allen was my partner before you two even met," Daryl countered. "How dare you say I don't want to help him."

Kelsey sat down on a worn recliner across from the couch and slumped into it. "I didn't say you don't want to help him. I said you don't want your daughter to go back. I get that. I didn't want Allen to go either. And while I'm at it, I don't want Benjamin to have his problems. But unfortunately, we all have shit we have to deal with now, whether we actually want to or not."

Haley looked at her father. Both he and Kelsey sat in silence for a while with their thoughts. Daryl looked off at nowhere in particular, and Haley saw from his expression that Kelsey was right about him not wanting her to go back for Allen. She could also tell he didn't have a better plan in mind or else he would have brought it up by now.

Kelsey for her part watched her son fidget in his stroller. He was awake but didn't seem bothered by the raised voices in the room, if he was even aware of them. His hands fumbled around for a short time before his thumb found its way into his mouth and he settled. Kelsey's expression was tense and knotted. She didn't look distraught so much as in a battle with some kind of internal struggle.

"Dad," Haley said. "Can you give us a minute, please?"

For a brief moment, Daryl looked wounded by the request and seemed about to argue before changing his mind. Instead, he turned toward the kitchen and moved out of the room without a word. When he was gone, Haley returned Kelsey's expectant gaze and blurted the only thing running through her mind. "I don't know what to do."

"What do you *want* to do?" Kelsey asked.

"I want to save Allen."

"How do you suppose you could do that?"

Haley threw up her arms, tears finding their way

out the sides of her eyes. "Gee whiz, I don't know, Kelsey. Go back, kick some ass, and get him out, I suppose."

"Sounds good to me," Kelsey said.

"Well, I can't do that! Maybe Allen could do that. Maybe my dad could have done that. But not me."

"Why not?" Kelsey asked.

"Because I'm afraid!"

A flash of rage came over Kelsey's face, and she spoke with forced calm. "This self-doubt nonsense is so far beneath you it's pathetic."

Haley stepped back as the words hit her like a jab to the face. "You have an insult for everything, don't you?"

"I love my husband," Kelsey said, ignoring Haley's comment. "But how generous would you say he is? In all our years of marriage, I don't think I've ever seen him donate to charity. I tried to take a load of clothes and donate them when we moved into our condo, but instead, he stopped me and found some weird online business that paid for used clothes by weight. He had to ship the clothes himself and only made five bucks."

"What in the world are you talking about?"

"I'm talking about the fact that the last thing Allen ever feels is sorry for people, least of all you," Kelsey said. "He certainly doesn't pity you or stay up nights worrying if you're good enough. You should do yourself the same courtesy."

Haley glared at Kelsey. "He said the same kind of thing to me in Greenland, but I'm not going to look in the mirror and recite a book of affirmations just so I can run off and get myself killed."

"Your oldest friend is a secret hacking whiz kid,

and your father is one of the best custom tech-heads in the world," Kelsey said. "And guess what? Just because I'm a stay-at-home mom doesn't make me some ignorant slouch. We all think you're incredible, so maybe stop crapping on yourself long enough to listen to what we think." Kelsey stood up, grabbed the handle of Benjamin's stroller, and walked toward the door to leave.

Before Kelsey could get out of the room, Daryl came forward from around the corner and blocked her. "I'm not going to send my daughter on a suicide mission."

"If we come up with a good plan, she won't have to," Kelsey replied. "I'm not asking her to do anything she's not capable of, just everything she is." Kelsey maneuvered Benjamin around the narrow space to the side of Daryl and opened the front door.

"What are you going to do?" Haley called out to Kelsey.

"Do what nobody else can do," Kelsey answered, "take care of my son and work on a way to save Allen. It's that or worry myself into a nervous breakdown. But Benjamin needs his dinner and medicine, so my breakdown will have to wait." With that, Kelsey pushed Benjamin through the door then closed it behind her.

Haley sat on the couch while Kelsey's words echoed in her head. The image of the paint splatter on her bedroom floor joined the mix. Soon, Kelsey's words were overtaken by Haley's memories of painting her room rhythmically and deliberately with a paint roller. In her mind, Haley focused on the sticky sounds of paint grabbing the wall and the clicking of the roller as she changed directions at the top and bottom of each stroke. Just the mental participation in the ritual helped her put random thoughts aside. Or at least enough to help her face the reality of the problem ahead.

Daryl cleared his throat. "What are you thinking?"

Haley remained silent with her thoughts long enough that Daryl cleared his throat again. Eventually, she looked up at her father. "See if there's a way to get Allen back. Start by calling Kyle."

"Call Kyle," Daryl grumbled, "and hope that he's smarter than his codename implies."

"Okay, Dad," Haley said, annoyed.

"Seriously, 'MeatTank' is a stupid name."

"All right, I get it."

Chapter Twenty-One

Waterboard him with maple syrup and slit his throat with a craft beer bottle...

Allen's body was fully consumed by pain. Every muscle was forcibly contracted by Jodock's latest medical device, which was connected to Allen through a series of electrodes. It was designed to stress and break down muscle tissue to simulate the symptoms of several degenerative diseases. In an attempt to keep himself sane, Allen fantasized about different ways to violently kill Jodock in every US state, starting with Alabama and moving down the list in alphabetical order. The latest scenario involved how he would kill Jodock in the state of Vermont, and he desperately hoped the torture would stop before he had to think of a way to kill Jodock in Wyoming. Luckily, before Allen considered the lethal options available to him in Virginia, the pulsing electrical current stopped. The sudden lack of pain felt like the greatest sensation in the world.

"Again, I'll repeat the question," Jodock said with equal parts exasperation and boredom. "What was she wearing?"

Allen took a few seconds to catch his breath before replying. "Carol, the artificial intelligence who has no physical form whatsoever, was wearing a business casual gray skirt and white shirt."

"Why did you not simply answer the question the first time?" Jodock asked.

"Why do you care what a computer program wears? It's not real!" Allen answered.

"The program is real. We have multiple confirmations."

"No, I mean what she wears isn't real," Allen said.

"Then why do you mind answering the question? Honestly, you should try being less difficult for the benefit of time."

"I'm sorry, do you have dinner plans?" Allen asked sarcastically. He instantly regretted his tone of voice as his body was again jolted from head to toe for a minute before the device was once again deactivated.

"Still feeling clever?" Jodock asked.

Allen gagged and coughed on his own saliva and nearly vomited. His arms and legs shuddered, but it was the pain deep inside his body that was the most disturbing. Muscles he had never thought about before deep in his bowels stung and spasmed. He also noticed it was becoming more difficult to breathe.

"Getting back to this Carol individual," Jodock continued.

"I told you, she's an AI of some kind," Allen interrupted. "She's not a real person."

Jodock looked at Allen quietly for a while, and as Allen waited in terror for the punishing jolt he feared was coming, he reminded himself that it would probably be best to simply keep his commentary to himself.

Apparently deciding that further torture was not necessary, Jodock continued his questioning. "What kinds of things did you discuss with her?"

Allen struggled to understand the importance of the question. And yet there sat Jodock, a hulking figure sitting on a small stool with wheels, bent over a tablet reading prewritten questions like the most terrifying survey taker who had ever walked the planet. After considering the direness of his situation, Allen decided it was better to answer the questions than to try to understand them.

"She gave me directions to the elevator," Allen answered.

"Of the Tor building?" Jodock asked.

"Yes," Allen replied.

"How long have you lived in Chicago?"

The answer was on the tip of Allen's tongue before he realized what Jodock had done, but by then it was too late. Jodock had already seen the response he was looking for to confirm where Allen lived.

Jodock grinned as he made notes on his tablet. "What else did you talk about?"

Angry with himself, Allen didn't answer. Jodock threatenly hovered a finger above the button that activated the electrodes to make Allen speak again. "She told me to wait in the reception area," Allen said. "She also called me another time to say that Eamon wanted to meet."

"How long have you been friends?" Jodock asked.

"We're not friends, she's a computer program," Allen said.

"Not you and Carol," Jodock said before leaning up and speaking into Allen's ear. "I mean you and *Eamon*."

Allen was stunned to realize how bad he was at withholding information. A wave of despair hit him and blocked his ability to think straight until the sight of Jodock's smug, smirking face sparked enough anger to form words. "So now that I've given you such extremely valuable information, do I get a break from the torture for a while?"

"You do not deserve a reward for accidentally divulging information," Jodock said. "You deserve punishment." Jodock activated the machine again and delivered pain for another two minutes. When it stopped, Allen gasped for air as his weakened diaphragm failed to breathe deeply or quickly enough to meet his body's needs. Eventually, the burning in his chest subsided and he lay there listening to the sound of his heart pounding in his ears, remaining motionless to spare his body any more effort.

"What kind of friend does this to you?" Jodock pondered. He waited for Allen to make eye contact before continuing. "The two of you clearly don't share the same social circles, so you must have met long ago. So again, I wonder, what kind of person tricks an old friend into doing his dirty work?"

Allen turned away and looked up at the ceiling. He tried to ignore Jodock, but the man's massive size and proximity made that impossible. Returning to his mental exercise, Allen remembered the old slogan of "Virginia is for Lovers," but failed to see how that translated into any lethal possibilities worth exploring.

"You're not a young man, are you?" Jodock asked. "Neither am I, of course. But I maintain myself. You look low-average at best. Who sends a soft man into such danger?"

Focusing on his anger was taking its toll on Allen, and he couldn't keep it going any longer. As exhaustion began to overwhelm him, his mind turned to Kelsey and Benjamin. He tried to imagine what Kelsey was doing at that moment. Maybe working on the computer or running errands while angry at him for being gone. Allen mentally transported himself to those possibilities instead of in Jodock's isolated torture room. When he thought about Benjamin, however, all he could see in his mind was his son sleeping. Allen doubted Benjamin even realized he was gone.

"You're surely old enough to have a family," Jodock went on. Mentioning a family brought a flash of emotion to Allen's face that Jodock read easily. "Oh yes. A wife maybe, or maybe not. Relationships are so hard to make work. Children are more reliable than spouses when it comes to love. At least in my experience."

Allen couldn't imagine a sick beast like Jodock making first date small talk, much less changing an infant's diapers or putting a crib together. The very idea was absurd.

"No matter what happens, children always want to love their parents," Jodock said. "They're just wired that way. It's wonderful." Jodock was almost boasting about all the things he got away with thanks to a child's biological predisposition to love. "Think of your child, for example. Your eldest, if you have more than one."

Jodock's mention of Benjamin, even indirectly, brought on a new surge of rage. Jodock seemed to feed off of it as he continued. "That's right. Think of all the lovely gifts from your child that you'll never have again thanks to your friend Eamon Tor. The way your child looks at you, the love he shows in his eyes. The way he says 'daddy.' How he hugs you goodnight or laughs when you play with him."

With each of Jodock's assumed cherished moments, Allen's spirit sank more and more. He had never shared a single one of those moments with his son, and now it looked increasingly unlikely he ever would.

"And what about your moments as a father? Think about the pride you have when you look at him, or how you brag about him to other parents. Or how lucky you just plain feel to have him in your life. Eamon Tor has stolen that from you as well."

Allen's emotional state was visibly crumbling, but not for the reasons Jodock assumed. Allen struggled to remember moments where he had felt for Benjamin the ways Jodock described. Surely he must have felt that way at some point, at least before the seizures started, right? But nothing like that came to mind. When Allen thought about his feelings for Benjamin, he recalled worry, fear, desperation, and frustration. Love was there in a general sense of caring for his son, but again not in the ways Jodock referred. Not a single moment of selfless devotion came to mind that wasn't tinged with some resentment over Benjamin's condition. Allen became overwhelmed with shame.

Jodock watched Allen fall apart before his eyes, satisfied with how well things were proceeding. When Allen's emotions appeared to level off, Jodock spoke again. "Now, I hope you've enjoyed your rest," he said. "Because I have more questions."

****

Sitting at her kitchen table, Kelsey put the last of a series of medical bills on a pile that had formed over the past hour. Without having enough money to pay them all off in full, Kelsey had gone through each one, found the instructions for paying them online, and paid a portion of each one on the computer while making notes on each bill of how much money she had put against it. Kelsey hoped the busy work would take her mind off Allen, but the chore was only a harsh reminder of the other struggles she faced. At least not having money for medical bills was a familiar problem.

Kelsey fought an impulse to stand up and stretch her legs. Benjamin was strapped against her chest with a child carrier, fast asleep. The different medications he was taking to try and control his seizures had a variety of side effects, one of which was difficulty sleeping. So even though it was eleven o'clock at night, Benjamin had been writhing around in bed crying and unable to settle. Seeing as she was having problems sleeping herself, Kelsey decided to put Benjamin in the child carrier and at least be productive. The problem was, she wasn't sure how to get Benjamin out of the carrier and back into his crib without waking him. She also couldn't summon the ambition to try.

Kelsey closed the webpage she had used to pay the last medical bill. Once that window on her computer screen disappeared, it revealed her coding program open behind it, still showing the last lines she had written for Allen's armor. She had continued working on it after Allen left, even completing a series of sensor functions before being interrupted by Daryl's message of Allen's capture. Kelsey stared at the lines of code on the screen and let her mind wander. She thought about the parts and pieces of programs she had finished and still more not even started. Kelsey began to question what the point had been of even trying, much less continuing her work on it.

"No, stop," Kelsey said to herself under her breath. "I'm not going to sit here all night being sorry Little Miss Left-Behind." She opened her video call program and activated a secure line to the number she had for Kyle. If Haley wasn't going to step up, then Kelsey would have to do it herself.

The program showed a yellow calling icon for a long time as it rang, then changed to a red icon indicating there was no answer. Kelsey tried calling again with the same result. She looked at the red icon of the failed call. The longer she stared at it, the more personally offended she became.

"Screw you, 'no answer,' " Kelsey muttered, opening another program and placing its window next to that of the video call program.

After choosing a few options, the new window displayed all the programming actions the call program was making in real-time. Kelsey attempted another call and watched as her monitoring program showed her the processes and functions being used, including the servers and online locations the call passed through. Over the next forty-five minutes, Kelsey worked the problem of connecting herself from one online location to another, overcoming various security measures of encrypted usernames and virtual servers to map out a path until she was finally able to get to the internet address of Kyle's computer. Someone like Kyle would have an incredibly sophisticated firewall and security system in place to block her from accessing his system. What he probably didn't have, however, was a sophisticated system for preventing someone from forcing him to accept a video call.

Again, Kelsey activated an outgoing video call to Kyle's computer. And once again, the yellow calling icon blinked for a long time without an answer. Deciding she had waited long enough, Kelsey sent instructions to cause Kyle's computer to auto-accept.

A streaming video image popped up on the screen. It appeared to be a desk with a dim light source somewhere off camera, the image quickly falling away into darkness at the edges. She recognized the haunting glow from her own late night work sessions. The light source was from Kyle's own monitor and his camera was mounted at the top of it. Kelsey closed her eyes and shook her head at herself. It was nighttime, and though it wasn't yet midnight in Chicago, it was a realistic possibility that Kyle was asleep in bed.

Kelsey sighed and slumped her shoulders in defeat from yet another hopeless endeavor when something at the corner of the image caught her eye. There was movement in the upper right-hand corner of the screen, but only in a flash. She watched for a while longer until she saw it again. It was something physical, sweeping by the camera, coming in and out of frame. Kelsey watched for a long time more and was about to end the call again when a lanky form stumbled backward into the video frame. It was Kyle, standing and waving his arms trying to get his balance. Once he regained his footing, he pantomimed the motion of carrying a weapon and firing at some unseen foe. Around his face was a set of VR goggles with integrated headphones.

"Kyle," Kelsey called in a strained whisper, trying not to wake her son snuggled just below her chin. Kyle ducked and leaned to the side before standing up again and slowly walking forward and out of frame. Kelsey repeated his name as loudly as she dared, with no response. It was another minute before Kyle came back into frame.

Slowly, Kelsey turned in her chair, then leaned sideways toward her laptop until her mouth was just above its microphone. "Kyle," she called in a whispered bark.

Kyle turned his head to the side. "Disable chat," he called into the air.

"Take off the goggles," Kelsey commanded.

Kyle froze for a moment before removing the goggles from his face and squinting in the darkness to see who was speaking to him.

"On the computer," Kelsey said.

Kyle walked in front of his monitor. His confused expression melted as he recognized her. "Oh, hi, Missus Moran...did I call you?"

"No, I called you," Kelsey answered.

Kyle's puzzled look returned. "I don't remember accepting the call."

"You didn't," Kelsey said without elaborating.

Kyle looked around the room for whatever intruder must have accepted the call for him.

"Kyle, what are you doing?" Kelsey asked, interrupting his search.

"Playing tightrope snipers on *Annihilate*," Kyle said. "See, you and your opponent have sniper rifles, and you're both on this tightrope..."

"I get it," Kelsey stopped him.

"I can get you a copy," Kyle continued. "I have a couple spare VR sets around here I can send you, too."

"No, thanks," Kelsey said. "Well, actually, maybe yes...I don't know. Did Haley talk to you?"

Kyle sat down in front of the camera and put his goggles down on the desk. "Yeah, we talked for a little bit," he said with a deflating sigh. "I've been trying to think of some new angle. That's why I threw myself into the game. Trying to switch gears a bit, let the subconscious chew on things."

"I don't understand. You had a plan for getting out the doctor you were supposed to rescue. Just repeat whatever that plan was."

"Yeah, but we knew where we were going," Kyle said. "And we assumed they didn't know we were coming."

"Why do you think they knew you were coming?" Kelsey asked.

Kyle frowned. "I thought I was so smart breaking into their systems. But when the guards started chasing Haley, I was totally cut off. My line to the internal controls was blocked, and I lost the camera feed."

"So you think they let you hack in?"

"Yeah," Kyle answered glumly. "Pretty sure."

Kelsey watched Kyle. He couldn't bring himself to make eye contact with the camera, and for the first time, Kelsey saw that she wasn't the only one affected by Allen's capture. Still, she was the one affected most by it, so as far as she was concerned everyone else had to buck up and get to work. "What about the satellite?" Kelsey asked.

Kyle sulked and didn't answer.

"Kyle. What about the satellite? What does it show?"

"Just the roof and the perimeter," Kyle answered. "The thermal cameras can't see all the underground levels—the concrete is too thick."

"If the concrete is too thick for the satellite, how did you talk to Allen?"

"We put a signal repeater on the roof," Kyle explained. "Allen hardwired it to their system and it bridged audio and data down to them."

"Is there anything we can do with that repeater?" Kelsey asked hopefully.

Kyle put his elbows on his desk and put his head in his hands. "I don't think so. I've tried to hack back into their system, but they've rerouted the hardline so the connection Allen made doesn't work. I just...I just don't know what to do."

Kelsey knew the feeling. It was the same sense she and Allen had been living with for over two years trying to help Benjamin. The idea of accepting yet another unwinnable situation disgusted her. "Come on, there's got to be something," she said to Kyle as much as herself. While she thought, Kelsey's eyes floated around looking at nothing in particular before eventually settling once again on the snippets of code displayed on her computer. The thought of Allen's armor gave her an idea. "What about Allen's suit?" she asked.

"What about it?"

"Can you connect to it?" Kelsey asked. The excitement in her voice roused Benjamin from his deep sleep, and he squirmed in the carrier.

"Maybe, it might be possible. I mean, I can try," Kyle said as he brought his fingers to his keyboard and began working.

"Shhhhhhhhh," Kelsey shushed soothingly.

"Thank you, that's quite relaxing," Kyle said.

Kelsey thought about clarifying that her shushes

were for her son and not him, a fully grown man, but she didn't want to interrupt Kyle's work.

"Got it," Kyle reported a few moments later. "I'm getting a ready status from his suit!"

"Okay," Kelsey said. Her heart raced as she broke out into a broad smile. "Okay."

"But…what do we do with it?" Kyle asked.

"I'm not sure," Kelsey answered. "But we're going to figure it out."

"Hmm," Kyle replied, not convinced.

"Kyle, look at me," Kelsey ordered. When Kyle looked at the camera again, Kelsey continued. "We're going to figure it out."

"All right," Kyle said.

"Say it."

"We're going to figure it out," Kyle said as if making a pact.

"Good," Kelsey said with a nod. "Now let's think about how to actually go about that."

Chapter Twenty-Two

Mint, wintergreen, bubble gum, cool blast...

Allen's latest mental game was an attempt to distract himself from the foul odor coming out of Olivia Rusk's mouth as she spoke to him. He thought Rusk was at least wealthy enough to afford basic mint toothpaste, never mind more elaborate flavors. Sadly for Allen, her priorities were obviously focused in areas other than dental care as she spoke to him in the small medical room he had been returned to after his interrogation.

"Pretty hard to be a tough guy when your body is falling apart, isn't it?" Rusk asked with a satisfied grin.

Allen scoffed. "I didn't come to be a tough guy. I only came for money." Stars appeared in front of his eyes, and he was forced to lay his head on the reclined back of the medical bench he was strapped to. The severity of the weakness in his body took him by surprise.

"That's right, you're just an operator. A soldier for hire," Rusk said with feigned sympathy. "A mercenary who knows Eamon Tor personally." Rusk leaned in closer. "For all we know, you two might even be lovers."

Though it hurt every muscle, laughter rose up in Allen and wracked his body. The conflict of amusement and pain threatened to overload his brain until Allen's wave of hysteria died down.

Rusk stepped back during Allen's outburst and gave him an angry look. "What was all that about?"

Through his fatigue, Allen still managed a smirk. "Eamon Tor is a trillionaire. Being his lover sounds amazing."

To Allen's surprise, Rusk shared in his amusement with her own smile that gave her thin face an even more boney appearance. "Wealth does make it hard to stay chaste."

Allen tried to process Rusk's implication but was distracted when a pair of medical technicians entered with a new device on a cart. He stared in a cold sweat at the various components while the technicians retrieved them from the drawers of the cart and assembled them on the overbed table beside him. "What questions could you possibly still have to ask me?" Allen said.

"Oh, no more questions, this is all just extracurricular now," Rusk replied, a grin still on her face. "I am running a research facility, after all."

Watching the technicians, Allen saw that the largest parts of the device were long, curved pieces of thick plastic resembling shin guards or some kind of sport braces. On their insides were dark circles but Allen couldn't tell what they were.

Unable to stand the dreadful wait any longer, Allen closed his eyes. He pictured Kelsey's face. He thought about Benjamin and wondered if his son had suffered any seizures that day. He decided that no, on that day Benjamin had been seizure-free. The page for that day in his seizure log was blank. That possibility comforted him. He imagined that a day without seizures had made Kelsey happy, and she and Benjamin had ended their seizureless day with a long walk outside. Maybe they'd even stop for ice cream. It was a fantasy, so why not.

The sound of the door opening broke the spell and made Allen open his eyes. Jodock walked into the room and over to the cart where the technicians were finishing the assembly of their equipment. Jodock looked things over and nodded his approval before stepping away and sitting on a small wheeled stool. As he did during the earlier interrogation, Allen found the size disparity between Jodock and the stool ridiculous.

"Hey, Jodock," Allen said. "You think Rusk will ever buy you a big-boy chair to sit on?"

Jodock closed his eyes and took a deep breath to stay calm. Rusk turned to Jodock. Allen could tell by her reaction that his comment had hit a nerve of an ongoing disagreement.

"Don't you say a word," Rusk scolded Jodock. "I told you to choose between hiring more men or buying bigger stools. You made your choice."

"There's money for both," Jodock grumbled.

"Yeah, well, maybe when it's not *your* money," Rusk replied. She walked over to Allen as the technicians began attaching the thick plastic pieces of their device around the lower halves of each of his legs, using straps to secure them in place. "Especially when I have to pay for expensive things like this."

"Do I get told what this is going to do or is it some sort of surprise?" Allen asked, fighting a sudden queasiness.

The technicians finished attaching pieces to Allen's legs and moved on to his arms as Rusk answered. "They're bone resonators," she said with pride. "You wouldn't believe how many bone conditions there are.

Did you know that blood is actually made in your bones? It's crazy." Rusk took a piece of the device out of one of the technician's hands and held it close to Allen's face, showing him the dark circles he had seen earlier. "See, they're lined with tiny little speakers that use different frequencies to make your bones vibrate." Rusk handed the piece back to a technician before stepping away and doing a sort of dance as she waited for things to be ready. "I'm excited to see what kind of damage they do."

While the technicians finished their preparations, Allen watched the old woman. Something had been gnawing at the back of his mind ever since Eamon first explained the mission to him. He felt something familiar when he saw the images of Rusk in the surveillance photos. It was some personal memory that went beyond the public awareness he had of her, and as he sat there terrified of what was about to happen next, the memory came to him.

"I've met you before," he said to Rusk.

"Yeah, maybe you worked for me," Rusk said, watching the technicians as they attached wires from a control unit to the pieces strapped to Allen. "You look like a solid middle-manager."

"No," Allen said absently as his memory became clearer. "I shook your hand. It was in the auditorium. In grade school." Allen smiled recalling his youth. "There was a city-wide reading competition, and our school had read the most books in a year. I got first place because I read more than anyone else, but that was only because I read a ton of those choose-your-own-adventure books. So even though I got to the end, I had really only read half the pages of the book. Nobody else had figured out that trick so I won."

"The City Readers Scholarship," Rusk remembered. "The public schools were turning into underfunded dumps—it was pathetic. If I hadn't put up some money they all would have gone down the toilet."

"Everybody at school was so excited," Allen went on. "We were getting new computers and 3D printers, and money for tutors. Or at least my mom was excited about the tutor part."

Rusk chuckled pleasantly and smiled. "She was probably pretty proud of you," she said, her tone softer.

"Oh yeah," Allen said before closing his eyes. "Her and dad came to school for the presentation. The principal spoke, then she introduced you. You gave the biggest smile and announced the number of books we had read. You acted like you couldn't believe it, and we all giggled and yelled telling you it was true."

Rusk chuckled again. "Kids love correcting adults. They get such a kick out of it."

"Then you said you had a special prize for the student that had read the most books in school," Allen went on. "You said my name and I was instantly embarrassed. I felt like I had bricks in my shoes. But I forced myself to stand up and walk the stairs to get on stage. You held out your hand and shook mine, then you put a medal around my neck."

"It was fun giving out those awards," Rusk admitted. "I always looked forward to it."

Allen opened his eyes and looked at Rusk warmly. "You seemed like such a nice person."

For a moment, Rusk shared Allen's warm expression. Then her eyes turned hard and her mouth curled. Without warning, Rusk slammed her palm down on the control panel in front of her, which had only been finished a moment earlier.

The pain was instant and overwhelming. Allen howled in agony. The noise sounded like someone else's voice in his ears.

"Don't tell me who I was!" Rusk bellowed. She pulled her hand off the activation button. Allen lay panting as she continued. "You're just like the rest of them, taking and taking. And what did I get for all my kindness?"

Before Allen could answer, Rusk slammed her palm back down on the button. Again, Allen wailed.

"Nothing!" Rusk screamed above Allen's cries. "Sickness and suffering and disease. Husbands who only loved me for my money, children who turned out lazy and spoiled!"

Rusk removed her hand from the button again. With the device turned off, Allen melted into the chair and had a coughing fit that escalated until he vomited. Rusk stepped away from the control console and came closer to Allen. Through his dizziness, Allen saw that Rusk's face had turned red with muscles twitching randomly as she pointed a finger at him. "You were just another worthless kid I wasted my time and money on. I gave you so much, and you came here to destroy everything I care about." Rusk spun around and walked to the door. After opening it, she turned to Jodock. "Run the device until he passes out," she instructed.

After she left, Jodock nodded to the technicians. As the pain flooded his body again, all Allen could do was continue to scream and hope he would soon pass out.

****

"What about the toilets? You can't get any less

secure than toilets," Kyle offered from the video monitor sitting on Daryl's kitchen table. Kelsey looked across at him. His suggestion was logical, but not realistic.

"Somehow I don't think they have their toilets hooked up to anything computerized," Kelsey said to him. "Or at least not enough to make them all back up at once."

"But the water system may be computerized," Daryl added from his seat next to the screen. "Kyle, could we make the water system back up?"

"That only hurts us," Haley interrupted from her chair across from her father, next to Kelsey. "If water fills the hallways or floods the lower levels, it just forces everyone up and in our way."

Benjamin began fussing in his stroller behind Kelsey. A quick glance at a clock on the wall told her it was time for his lunch. Luckily, she had planned to feed him during the hastily-called meeting that she had all but demanded with Haley and Daryl. After hours of brainstorming, it had become clear to Kelsey and Kyle that they needed fresh minds to get any further in their plans to save Allen.

"I think Haley's right," Kelsey said as she pulled a container of mashed carrots from the bottom of Benjamin's stroller. "Not on the evacuation part though, that could be good for us. I just...I'm worried that if we create something actually dangerous...you know." Kelsey sighed.

"That they would evacuate and leave Allen behind," Daryl finished for her.

"Yes," Kelsey said, putting a bib around her son's neck. "I'd rather not kill my husband while trying to save him."

"What about going the other way?" Daryl asked, looking up at the ceiling trying to envision his own suggestion. "We could lock the whole place down. Everyone stays where they are and we control the doors and only fight the people we have to."

"Yeah, that would be great," Kyle agreed. "I just wish I could pull that off, but a total lockdown would be controlled by their core systems."

"And you still can't hack into those?" Daryl asked.

Kyle answered by slumping his shoulders and shaking his head.

"That's why it has to be something with basically no security," Kelsey explained as she put a spoonful of carrots into Benjamin's mouth. He mushed the food between his lips and released a steady stream of orange drool out of his mouth as he ate. Kelsey noted to herself that the stroller would probably need to be taken apart and cleaned when they got home.

"And something that's got wireless access," Kyle said. "It's the same trick I used at the Nolan Building. I can bounce a data signal down through Allen's armor and connect to a nearby wireless device, but not the main system's hardline. At the Nolan Building, I could observe the security camera footage, but the folks in Greenland have theirs behind encryption."

Haley gave Kyle a skeptical look. "So we need something that's wireless and not secured with encryption, but also important enough to disrupt the whole facility so we have a chance of getting out with Allen, all without getting killed."

"Yes, you've described the situation perfectly," Kyle said.

"The best idea I had so far was the fire alarm," Kelsey said, using her small spoon to catch some fallen carrot from Benjamin's mouth.

"Half the time a fire alarm goes off is spent looking around to see if it's real," Daryl said doubtfully.

"I know," Kelsey said. "Kyle and I went back and forth all night until we decided we needed a couple more great minds to help us."

Daryl and Haley looked at each other, both equally unconvinced they had any great ideas about the situation locked away in their heads.

"All right," Daryl said. "Let's just take a second and think about this for a bit."

"Maybe the garbage systems…" Kyle started.

"Think silently," Daryl interrupted before closing his eyes.

"Oh yeah, that makes sense," Kyle said, excited to at least have a new way to think about the problem they were stuck on.

A minute went by. Then two. Kelsey finished feeding Benjamin and put away his bib and food container. As she used a wet paper towel to wipe the food from her son's face, an electronic alert sound went off in a repeating loop. Everyone looked to the video screen where the sound was coming from and waited for Kyle to explain what was happening.

"I've picked up Allen's voice," Kyle announced as his fingers raced across his keyboard.

"How?" Daryl asked.

Kelsey dropped the paper towel on the floor and leaned in. "He used the microphone on Allen's armor," she explained. "Turned the gain all the way up and put it through a filter algorithm to try and locate him."

"The distance from the repeater on the roof to the armor puts it on sublevel five," Kyle said. "So the algorithm will locate his distance from there. We figured it was worth a try. The computer has to really crunch the audio though." Kyle made a flurry of keystrokes before continuing. "It looks like the computer picked up Allen's voice an hour ago but didn't finish processing it until now."

"Where is he, Kyle?" Kelsey asked.

"Waiting for it…" Kyle answered, looking down to his computer screen just below his video chat camera. Kelsey ground her teeth and shook her foot until Kyle finally answered. "Got it! Sublevel seven, Procedure Room Three!"

Kelsey was overcome. The confirmation that Allen was alive made her lightheaded. She smiled, looked down at Benjamin, and leaned toward him. "Daddy's alive," she said, kissing him on the cheek. "Daddy's alive." After sitting back up, Kelsey leaned in again toward the video monitor. "Can we hear it? His voice?" she asked.

"Yeah, totally," Kyle replied with a grin before returning to his keyboard. "It'll be a little compressed, but…" Kyle extended his index finger and pointed it straight down toward his spacebar with a flourish. "Here we go."

As soon as Kyle pressed the spacebar, the sound of Allen's tortured screams filled the room. Having been washed through the computer, the tone shifted and phased. But Kelsey could tell that the agonized cries were those of her husband. She retched in despair.

"Shut it off!" Daryl yelled. Kyle hit his spacebar again. The sound of screaming stopped, replaced by

Kelsey's gasps of shock. She put a hand on the table and focused on getting her breathing under control. Once it finally slowed, she sat up and composed herself.

For a long time, nobody spoke. In the silence, Kelsey calmed herself by taking a mental inventory of what she knew. Allen's scream meant he was alive, at least as of an hour before. She knew where he was being held. She knew Allen's armor could help them create a distraction. Somehow. For a moment, she instinctively moved on to mentally list the things she did not know, but her heart couldn't take it. The number of things she didn't know was overwhelming. So she moved into a third direction.

"I believe my husband is alive," Kelsey announced to the group. "I also believe we can save him. And I definitely believe we have to try."

After another long pause of silence, Daryl was the first to speak. "I agree with you," he said, "but I'm not sure what to do as far as a distraction. Even with Kyle's data signal trick, there might not be anything that's perfect."

"And I still believe there could be," Kelsey responded.

Daryl nodded.

"I don't know about a distraction," Haley spoke up. "But I might have an idea about how to get Allen out."

Everyone turned to Haley, all leaning in closer at the possibility of any kind of solution.

"But Dad," Haley said to her father, "I have to borrow something. And you might have to beg for a favor."

Chapter Twenty-Three

BP 126/70. Pulse 64. Resp. 18. SpO2 98%.

Allen stared at the monitor showing his vital signs. At first he could only see it as a multicolored blur. Over the previous hour, however, it had become easier to focus his eyes and clearly read the display. He used to think heart rate monitors beeped constantly for each heartbeat like in the movies, but multiple hospitalizations with Benjamin taught him that nurses usually only turned that sound on when patients were moved from room to room. At least when they weren't in the ER. Watching his own vital signs on the monitor, Allen fell into the same routine as he did when watching Benjamin's. He followed the heartbeat waveform as it refreshed from left to right, making a small spike, a large spike, then another small spike in a repeating pattern over and over again.

Allen didn't know if he had been asleep for hours or days. He had flashes of memory from being awake for short times before exhaustion pulled him back under. Lying in the room alone, he made a point of enjoying the quiet and lack of anyone around him. He knew it wouldn't last. Still, when Jodock entered the room a minute later, it was hard for Allen to control his disappointment.

"I'm relieved to see you awake," Jodock said brightly, somehow managing to make chipperness seem menacing.

Allen only grumbled.

"Don't be so glum," Jodock said while reviewing the results of Allen's medical tests on a tablet. "Today is a very exciting day."

"I'm going home?" Allen asked, mostly sarcastically but with a tiny bit of hope.

"No," Jodock replied as he put his massive hand on Allen's shoulder. "Today you receive your Eden Therapy treatment."

Allen felt numb. "What, you finally ran out of ways to torture me?"

"Useful ways, anyway," Jodock said, turning his attention back to his tablet.

"And what happens after that?" Allen asked, his body starting to tremble. "You test me more as I slowly lose my mind, then you kill me anyway?"

"No, no, no," Jodock said reassuringly. "Yes, we test you, but when we're done we'll send you home."

"As what, a drooling madman?" Allen said.

"Not necessarily," Jodock replied unconvincingly. "Who knows, maybe we'll find a treatment for the side effects."

"That would be nice."

Jodock smiled. "Yes," he said. "But in that case, you're right, you wouldn't go home. We'd just shoot you."

Jodock worked the rest of the time in silence, taking Allen's blood pressure and drawing blood from his arm. Allen tried to pull away, but his muscles were so weak and sore that Jodock easily held him down. Allen thought about trying one last act of defiance by spitting in Jodock's face, but it didn't seem worth the effort and might only provoke him to perform some of his less useful forms of torture on Allen. Instead, Allen decided to take advantage of Jodock's good mood.

"Can you at least sit me up in the bed?" Allen asked.

"Of course," Jodock answered pleasantly. He used the power controls to incline the top half of the bed, then placed pillows behind Allen to help prop him up. "Better?"

"Yes," Allen said. He had to stop himself from thanking Jodock. "By the way, how long was I out?"

"Almost three days," Jodock answered. "Our conditioning procedures can take a lot out of a person."

"So it's not torture, it's 'conditioning' now?"

"You are by far the most self-righteous saboteur I have ever met," Jodock said.

"I guess I don't find torture and murder to be very ethical ways of perfecting medical treatments."

Jodock scoffed. "Every new treatment requires hurting people, either through pain or by failure. You're arguing a difference of degrees."

Allen shook his head in disgust. "You're messed up."

"If I cured someone you loved, I doubt you'd say that," Jodock said as he collected the vials of blood he had drawn from Allen and put them in a plastic holder. "Besides, you're ignorant. So we'll just have to leave it at that." Jodock grinned and gave a small bow as if finishing a debate competition before making his way to the door.

Before Jodock could leave, however, an alarm echoed through the room and hallway beyond as strobe lights flashed in the ceiling. Jodock put the vials down on the counter at the side of the room before stepping to the door and pressing an intercom button mounted on the wall.

"What's going on?" Jodock demanded to know. A pair of security guards arrived in the hallway as Jodock waited for the reply.

"Carbon monoxide alarm," a voice told Jodock through the small speaker. "Sublevel seven and climbing through the building."

"Shut down the heating units," Jodock commanded.

"The system did that automatically," the voice replied. "But it's heavy on sub-seven and the whole building is filling up. It'll take a few hours to vent it out."

Jodock stood in thought without responding. Again the intercom crackled. "We need to start getting everyone out. Right?"

Instead of answering, Jodock looked at Allen. The two guards waiting outside in the hallway exchanged confused glances. With his gaze still on Allen, Jodock replied. "Get everyone out," he commanded. "Our guest and I will stay here."

"In the carbon monoxide?" one of the guards asked. Jodock looked at him and he withered under his boss' glare.

"Yes," Jodock replied flatly. The guards moved to leave, anxious to escape the threat of asphyxiation. "Wait," Jodock called to them, stepping into the hallway. He held out his hand. "Sidearm." The guard who spoke earlier jogged back and handed over his handgun before running off again. Jodock returned to Allen's room and put the gun down next to the vials of blood, then opened a cabinet and retrieved a pair of ventilator masks and tubing.

"Why don't you want to go outside?" Allen asked. "You lose your coat?"

"Seems suspicious," Jodock said as he connected the lengths of tubing to oxygen ports in the wall.

"Sounds like you should be with your men then," Allen said.

Jodock connected each of the ventilation masks, then turned dials on the wall to activate the flow of air. "I think I'll stay right here," Jodock said. "If it is an attack, this is where they are coming."

Allen wasn't sure what to make of the situation. Any sort of rescue seemed so unlikely that he immediately dismissed the possibility. He was angry at Jodock for mentioning it and torturing him one last time.

Jodock secured a ventilation mask over Allen's nose and mouth before taking the other mask and doing the same on himself. He then walked over to where he set the gun. For a brief moment, Jodock started to sit on the small wheeled stool before thinking better of it and leaning against the counter where he wouldn't be mocked. Allen was disappointed.

"So, we're just going to sit here?" Allen asked, his voice muffled through the ventilation mask.

"You're going to sit here," Jodock answered with a similarly muffled voice, picking up his tablet. "I have more work to do."

As Jodock worked, Allen fought between wanting to believe someone was coming for him versus avoiding false hope. He decided that a mental distraction was the only way to cope with the situation.

"For a glorified security guard, you have some pretty strong opinions about medical ethics," Allen said.

"Ethics," Jodock repeated with distaste. "Your ethics suppose that everyone deserves the same treatment."

"Yeah, that's generally how that works," Allen replied.

"Most people are worthless," Jodock said, still tapping away at his tablet. "They do pointless things with their pointless lives and contribute nothing to the world. While truly special people suffer by their rules and lack of imaginations." Jodock looked up from his tablet and put it aside before continuing. "And when those special people get ill and need help to survive, the only options available are primitive and small-minded. Or so new that everyone is too timid and afraid to try them. So doctors let extraordinary people die just to protect the masses."

Through the ventilation mask, Allen saw an anger on Jodock's face that didn't seem directed at him. Allen wanted to know more, who this person was to Jodock and what happened, but the hate in Jodock's eyes felt too deadly to taunt with sensitive questions. Even if the rage wasn't meant for Allen, it could certainly be taken out on him.

As Jodock held his hard gaze on Allen, a muffled boom came from somewhere in the levels above. The room shook slightly and a light cloud of dust fell from the ceiling, loosened by the movement. Jodock leaned back, grabbed the handgun from the counter, and kept his eyes on Allen as he went to the intercom.

"What's going on?" he asked in a raised voice.

"We're under fire," the voice reported breathlessly before another explosion rattled the room. The sound of gunfire came through the intercom. "Explosions from an unknown direction."

"We're surrounded by a rocky plain," Jodock shouted. "How can you not see who's firing on you?"

"Too busy trying to find cover!" the voice shouted back. Allen listened. The shots were too quick and chaotic. Jodock's men were firing blindly downrange.

"Get to the vehicle pool for cover," Jodock instructed. "See if you ca—"

A much closer explosion cut him off. The lights flickered, and Jodock stumbled before leaning against the counter for balance. He grabbed his handgun and pointed it at Allen. "If someone comes through that door, you will die."

Allen stared at the barrel of the gun, but instead of fear he felt something else. An emotion he couldn't quite place began to swell over him. It was like a tingle in the back of his mind that grew and grew.

Another explosion rocked the room, even closer. Jodock stumbled back, knocking over a table of instruments in the process. Once he found his footing again, Jodock returned to the intercom. "Get everyone back inside," he said.

"But what about the gas?" the voice asked.

"There is no carbon monoxide—it's a trick," Jodock said. "Come in. Now."

While Jodock returned to the bedside with his gun still pointed at Allen, the mysterious feeling continued to grow. It felt warm, a mixture of joy and relief tinged with a kind of sadness. It felt familiar, but it wasn't until the tears welled in his eyes that Allen fully understood what it was.

"Why are you crying?" an angry Jodock demanded to know.

"I'm just…" Allen began before becoming overwhelmed and starting over. "I'm just so damn proud."

Without warning, the wall behind Allen erupted. Concrete debris flew through the air, pushed by a billow of flame. Jodock was knocked across the room while the back of Allen's hospital bed protected him from the brunt of the explosion. He turned his head and saw a hole in the wall ringed with flame. Through the fire, a looming figure emerged like some underworld demon. The figure knocked bits of burning wall down as it passed through the hole, covering itself in a cloak of cinders. Allen's jaw dropped as he watched it draw closer, knowing without a doubt he was witnessing the single most dramatic thing he had ever seen in his life.

Allen was mesmerized until a sound of shifting debris broke the spell, and he turned to see Jodock rise to his feet. Allen noticed Jodock's empty hands and spotted the handgun on the floor. Jodock, seeing the gun as well, lunged for the weapon. He was fast, but not as fast as the mysterious figure. As Jodock dove, the figure stepped forward and cracked him with a backhand. Jodock flew like a doll and crashed against the cabinets before slumping on the floor.

Now that the figure was away from the flames, Allen got his first clear look at his rescuer. At first he didn't understand how Haley had gotten so tall. Then he recognized Daryl's robotic walker suit with its mechanized arms, curved running blades on robotic legs, and mounted heavy weapons.

"Can you stand?" Haley asked as she dropped down and removed his restraints.

"I'll sure as hell try," Allen replied, sitting up. Haley lowered so Allen could put an arm over her shoulder and together the two stood up.

"There's a place to ride on the back," Haley said, leading Allen around the robotic frame.

Allen saw that she was overselling the accommodations a bit as she hoisted him into position. There was no seat on the back, just two foot platforms, a short padded pommel to sit on, and a chest harness to keep from falling out. Allen recognized the components from different wheelchairs Daryl had owned through the years.

"Sorry, it's the best Dad could rig up," Haley said as she strapped Allen into place.

"Listen, Haley," Allen said. "We can still finish what we started."

Haley connected the final buckle and stepped down to the floor. "What, destroy the Eden tech? Allen, honestly…"

"I know I'm pretty banged up," Allen said, reading her expression.

"And how long until someone turns off the freight elevator?" Haley argued. "I didn't come through the wall for fun. The freight elevator is our only way out."

"We'll never get another chance," Allen said, pleading. "We'll hit it with a rocket or whatever this thing has and run out of here."

Haley held a clenched jaw for a moment before raising a finger and pointing at him. "If it takes anything more than that, we're gone. No matter what."

"No matter what," Allen agreed.

Haley climbed up the front of the walker's frame, secured herself, then turned the contraption back toward the way she came in, bouncing Allen against his all-too-unforgiving seat. They passed through smoldering rooms and other blasted walls until they emerged into a wide hallway. As they passed storage hangars with vehicles and large equipment, Haley sped the walker up to a light jog.

" 'Tank, I need to know which room to go through," she said. A few seconds later, she stopped. "Left or right? I have no idea which way is east," Haley said to Kyle through her earpiece. Getting her answer, Haley swung the robot to the left to face the wall. "This is going to be loud," Haley warned Allen.

Allen had just enough time to put his fingers to his ears before Haley fired up her rotating pulse minigun and blasted an improvised doorway. Haley moved through the opening, covering her and Allen with a fresh coat of concrete debris.

On the other side, they waited for the dust to clear. "Is this the room?" Allen asked.

"Supposed to be, I can't see anything yet," Haley replied. "Wait…shit," she muttered.

"What?" Allen asked.

"MeatTank, do you know anything about this security door?" Haley asked.

"What kind of security door?" Allen asked, unable to turn to look for himself.

Haley spun the robotic frame around, pivoting at the waist, allowing Allen to see for himself. "Take a look. I don't remember seeing that on the blueprints."

In front of Allen was a type of door he had never seen outside of a bank vault, mounted on a frame that surrounded the standard doors he had expected. A keypad on the side showed red to indicate it was locked. "No…" Allen said in a whimper.

"Well, can't you ID it from my video feed?" Haley asked, speaking to Kyle.

"We could put charges on the hinges," Allen said desperately. His chest heaved and he wiped sweat from his forehead.

"Allen, this is a rescue operation, not a demolition job," Haley replied. "I don't have anything like that."

"Just try!" Allen yelled.

"What?" Haley asked into her earpiece. A moment later, Haley repeated what Kyle told her. " 'Tank says he found the door model, it's over a foot thick."

"Try!" Allen shouted again.

Haley sighed before turning the robot back around. She raised the robotic arm with the pulse minigun, its rotating barrel spinning up as she took aim and fired a flurry of pale green pulse bolts toward the door. But after firing on the hinges, the support frame, and every other weak point she could think of, the door showed no signs of yielding. Activating her grenade launcher, Haley then blasted the lower hinge. The explosion was deafening in the small space but brought the door no closer to opening. "I'm sorry, Allen," she said. "This isn't going to work."

Allen didn't respond. Instead, he reached down and released the buckles on his chest harness before jumping to the ground and landing in a heap. Allen heard Haley call out to him again as he scrambled toward the security door. By the time he reached it Haley had spotted him.

"Allen! Get back here. We have to go!" she

screamed.

Again, Allen didn't answer. Instead, he balled his hand into a fist and punched the keypad.

"Allen, stop it!" Haley screamed.

Ignoring Haley, he continued to punch the door. Allen thought about how pointless all his effort and suffering had been. He was angry that Rusk and Jodock had made things so hard. And the thought of going home empty-handed, to the exact same situation with his son's health drifting further into hopelessness every day made him angrier still.

His hand bled and hurt horribly, so he decided to use his head instead. But before he could begin headbutting the keypad, there was a sharp tug at his shoulder. He spun around and found Haley scowling in a way he'd never seen before. She pulled her arm back and clocked him with a punch to the jaw, and as he fell to the floor, Allen wondered what in the world he had done wrong.

Chapter Twenty-Four

"You know what's easier than this? Anything. Anything is easier than this."

Haley chastised an unsteady Allen as she helped him walk back to the robotic walker. "Honest to God, just one time I want things to go the way we planned it. Just one easy mission. Just one time."

Haley stopped to let Allen brace himself on the robot as she climbed up onto the frame. As she did, Allen muttered something Haley couldn't make out.

"You'd better be saying 'thank you' or 'sorry Haley,' " she said as she yanked him up and guided him back into his seat.

Allen again muttered something as he fumbled with the buckles of his chest harness. Haley climbed lower to help him.

"What?" she asked, clipping his buckles into place.

"Why can't I save him?" Allen said, staring past Haley. "All I want to do is save him and nothing works. Why doesn't anything work?"

Seeing Allen distraught, Haley felt a wave of regret over her anger against him, but a sharp crackle in her ear pushed it aside.

"Twelve guys have gone back inside," Kyle said in her earpiece. "The rest are still looking for the drone."

Haley bounded back into the walker's control seat and strapped in. "How many grenades does it have left?"

"One," Kyle answered. "I was saving that for when you leave the building."

"We're heading out now," Haley assured him, grabbing the controls and turning around. As soon as she crossed into the hallway, however, she was stopped by a torrent of gunfire that pelted the front edge of the walker. Haley quickly backtracked. "I found your twelve guys!"

"You need to hurry," Kyle said. "They probably just followed the holes in the wall, but at some point they're gonna realize you used the freight elevator and shut it down."

Haley spun up the pulse minigun, poked the robotic arm attached to it around the corner, and fired blindly down the hallway. A spattering of stray bullets fired back at her, but once she pulled the arm back the gunfire toward her re-intensified.

Haley looked over her shoulder. "Allen?" she called. He did not respond, and from the slumped form Haley made out from the corner of her eye, she decided Allen was in no mental state to assist in a firefight. She reached down and withdrew two pulse pistol sidearms from their holsters, one in each hand. "MeatTank, I'm going to need you to drive."

"Rock and roll, Space Baby!" Kyle exclaimed.

"Seriously, don't play around, this is real," Haley said, checking her weapons.

"Don't worry...I got this."

Haley groaned. Kyle was acting as if it was all a video game. Then again, he was really good at video games. "You cover Allen. I'll keep eyes front. We don't stop until the elevator."

"Roger that," Kyle said.

Haley stretched her arms, rotated her head to loosen her neck, then held her pistols at the ready. "Let's go."

Controlled remotely by Kyle, the robotic walker lunged through the hole in the wall and sped down the hallway. Haley was confronted with muzzle flashes from every doorway. Luckily, Kyle's constant firing with the minigun made the enemy shots go wide. Haley blasted at every gunflash she could see until the walker passed the first set of doors. Kyle was forced to rotate the walker's minigun arm up and around to face the rear and cover their backs, the other arm following to maintain balance. Haley fired at every door she could see, filling the hallway with smoke and debris that pelted her as the walker dashed toward the elevator.

"Spin me!" Haley yelled as the walker passed the final set of doors. The top half of the walker spun on its central socket as Kyle rotated the arms up and around again to maintain his line of fire behind them. With both Haley and Kyle firing backwards, the walker came to a hard stop inside the freight elevator. Haley used her foot to kick the button for the surface level and continued to shoot down the hallway until the elevator's door finally closed.

As the elevator rose, Haley struggled to control her breathing while she returned her guns to their holsters.

"That was intense," Kyle said through her earpiece.

"Says the guy sitting at a desk," Haley replied. She rotated the legs of the walker in the cramped elevator car to face the door, then watched as the indicator showed they had arrived at the surface. "Tell my dad we're on our way out," Haley told Kyle. "I don't feel like playing hopscotch all the way to the coast."

"Already have, he's inbound," Kyle said.

Haley moved the walker into a runner's ready position as the elevator doors parted. Squinting against the low sun shining through the loading tunnel, Haley accelerated quickly and was at full speed by the time she emerged into the open.

Only four guards were left scattered outside still looking for the source of the taunting explosions. Once they caught sight of Haley and Allen, however, their curiosity naturally turned to the giant sprinting robot.

As she had done earlier, Haley spun the upper half of the walker around to protect Allen from incoming fire while the bottom half continued running to move forward. The guards fired at Haley, several shots ricocheting off the frame near Haley's head. "Looks like a pretty good time to cover our retreat!" Haley shouted over the noise of the walker and gunfire.

"I need them closer," Kyle said. "Your dad says he's ten seconds out."

Haley grumbled before firing her minigun to the outside of the chasing guards, driving them closer together. Realizing they couldn't keep up with her, the guards slowed to focus on aiming more precisely. "Now, Kyle!"

"I'm dropping it," Kyle replied.

Bullets panged around her as Haley caught sight of a tiny speck falling from the sky. The grenade exploded an instant later a few yards ahead of the guards. The blast sent soil and rock flying, throwing them back.

"Okay, Kyle, get me out of here," Haley said.

"I got ya. Your dad's in place," said Kyle.

Haley rotated the top half of the walker to face

forward again. Once it was oriented, she turned control over to Kyle. The walker began hopping from one leg to the next like an athlete performing a triple-jump. Each time the walker bounded, its curved blade legs compressed and expanded, pushing it higher into the air. After the third bounded jump, Haley braced herself as the arms and legs of the walker tucked in close to the frame while hurling forward.

In the blink of an eye, the landscape around Haley disappeared as she, Allen, and the walker slammed into a set of airbags lining the cargo hold of the cloaked hovercraft Daryl had flown into position to catch them.

With the airbags deflating and retracting into the walls, Haley heard her dad over the radio. "Catch complete, heading out."

G-forces pushed Haley into the side of the walker as the hovercraft turned hard and quickly accelerated. Once the force on her body leveled out, Haley unbuckled herself and descended the walker to check on Allen.

With a sullen expression, he looked around the cargo bay. "Where you been keeping this thing?" Allen asked.

Haley unbuckled him and helped him to the floor. "It's a loaner," she said, moving him into a narrow seating area. Allen sat down while Haley attached medical monitoring equipment to him.

"From whom?" Allen asked. "Your secret, debonair benefactor?"

"No, from yours!" Daryl yelled from the cockpit ahead. Haley and Allen watched him turn in his pilot chair and lean out so they could see him. "Mister Richter sends his regards."

Allen leaned back as Haley gave him a handful of pills and a small bottle of water. "He just let you borrow a cloaking hovercraft?"

Haley shuddered in anticipation of her father's answer.

"Not exactly," Daryl said. "He said to consider it an advance payment on the next mission."

Haley leaned back, took a seat directly across from Allen, and watched as he put all the pills in his mouth and swallowed them with a single gulp of water. "Thanks for coming to get me," he said absently.

"You're going to be okay," Haley said.

Rather than answering, Allen looked off, closed his eyes, and let the painkillers pull him down to sleep. Haley sat watching him for a long time, wondering how true her statement would turn out to be.

Chapter Twenty-Five

"It's buzzing, but it's not unlocking. Maybe you could just come down?"

Allen stood on the stoop of an apartment building speaking through an intercom. It was his fourth EatFleet food delivery of the day and he was attempting to coax its recipient, "Derek G.," into working up the strength to come down the stairs to receive his order of pad thai.

"I don't know, man, let me try it one more time," Derek G. suggested. Allen heard the electronic lock buzz to life. Once again, he tried to pull the door to the building open, and once again it wouldn't budge.

"Sorry," Allen said. "It looks like you need to turn the knob from the inside."

On the intercom, Allen heard Derek G. sigh. "Okay, I'll come down."

Allen looked at his phone to check the time. This would be his last drop-off before heading back to the children's hospital. Kelsey was already there in the surgical waiting room standing by for an update about Benjamin's procedure.

In the three months since Allen was rescued from the facility in Greenland, Benjamin's infantile spasms had not improved. His erratic brain waves made his already-limited abilities slip, including his ability to eat. Benjamin's doctors decided he needed a feeding tube surgically connected directly to his stomach to receive water and liquid food, what was called a "gastrostomy tube" or "g-tube." Allen and Kelsey reluctantly agreed. It was around the same time that Allen had also reluctantly decided he needed another source of income. Though Allen had healed enough to return to work, Benjamin's own declining health made Allen fear his son was slipping into depths he would never recover from. There were special tasks every hour just to keep Benjamin healthy, and with a g-tube and a feeding pump being added to the mix, taking on missions halfway around the world became out of the question—even if it meant earning much-needed income.

Through the glass of the door, Allen saw Derek G. descend the last steps on the other side and approach the door in bare feet and a flannel robe. He turned the doorknob from the inside, opened the door, and stuck his free hand out to receive his food.

"Here you go, sorry about that," Allen said, handing over the pad thai. He wasn't sure exactly what he was apologizing for, but he still held out hope for a tip and figured an apology couldn't hurt. After Derek G. wordlessly took his food and disappeared back into the building, Allen walked down to the street to his drone-cycle, mounted up and put on his helmet, then took to the sky.

Heading south with Chicago's skyscrapers ahead in the distance, Allen called Kelsey with the hands-free function in his helmet. He spoke as soon as the call was connected. "Hey, did anybody come out?"

"No, but the hour isn't up yet," Kelsey said.

"I'm heading home now to park the cycle and take a car to you. It'll be cheaper than parking," Allen said.

"Unless they changed their minds."

"No, they still want him to stay overnight," Kelsey said. She sounded like she had food in her mouth.

"How's the sandwich?" Allen asked, already knowing the answer.

"The best discount bologna ever," Kelsey answered. Ordering food from the hospital cafeteria had become too expensive to waste money on, especially considering they had a copayment charge for the surgery coming their way, so they had taken to packing their own food.

"Okay, I'll see you soon," Allen said. He and Kelsey exchanged goodbyes, then he navigated home and parked the drone-cycle on the roof deck of his condo building before stopping in to grab the overnight bag he'd packed earlier.

As Allen hailed a vehicle from his automated car service app and walked downstairs to the front of his building, he felt a pang of financial guilt. It was a splurge to be driven directly to the hospital and not take something cheaper like the bus, but Allen wanted to get there as soon as he could. Somehow being present for his child's surgery had become an indulgence.

Soon after confirming his destination on his phone, a small car arrived, covered with so many graffiti tags and street posters that its original color had been lost to time. It pulled up to Allen as he stood at the curb. He opened the door, sat inside, and mentally rolled his eyes as he looked across the bare dashboard and noted a loose mounting plate in the center where a map and interactive display should have been. Somebody must have gotten sick of the loud commercials usually blaring from the console.

Allen closed the door and the driverless car instantly pulled into the street and headed out. As he rode, Allen checked his earnings for the day on his EatFleet app. Sixty-seven dollars. Allen had been driving all morning and half the afternoon for that money. Back when he had been working, he could have earned that in an hour. Allen closed his eyes and took deep breaths, wishing away the start of a headache he could already feel. He didn't want more medical equipment and monthly supplies. Now he would have a feeding pump and special formula to pay for. Not to mention the fact that a hole was being intentionally placed in his son's body. As if epilepsy wasn't breaking his son down enough, now the doctors were doing it as well.

Allen stared out the window as the car headed through downtown. Lost in thought, it took him a while to notice that the car was not going in the direction it should be. Rather than heading toward the eastern outskirts of Chicago's loop, the car was heading south toward the downtown commercial core.

"Hey, wait a minute," Allen said before realizing there was no one there to hear him.

With the car's center console removed, Allen checked the app on his phone for a stop function but found nothing. At a traffic light, Allen tried opening the door but it was locked. After throwing his shoulder into the door and failing to budge it, Allen lay back on the seat and kicked the door with his legs until it became obvious that wouldn't work either. He was about to use his phone to call for help when he recognized the route the car was taking. It was the same route Eamon's automated town cars had taken when Carol summoned him to Eamon's home. Allen had tried getting in contact with both Eamon and his artificial assistant for the past three months and had been ignored every time. He wasn't sure what else he expected from a friend who lied to him, but if Rusk and Jodock were to be believed and Eamon had a perfectly working cure for Benjamin, Allen wasn't above sucking up his pride.

Still, the fact that Allen would be virtually kidnapped at that exact moment on his way to the hospital struck him as both infuriating and frustratingly typical.

As before, the route of the driverless car took Allen to an alley with an automated door that led to an underground garage and lone elevator. Once the car parked, Allen was able to open the car door. He stepped out and stood there, looking at the elevator door with contempt. Allen paced back and forth, conflicted.

He was pissed at Eamon.

He was desperate to help Benjamin.

He wanted to tell Eamon off.

He wanted to beg him for help.

The door to the elevator opened as if to say, *Well? What have you decided?* As if there were really a choice. If Eamon knew a way to cure Benjamin, Allen couldn't turn his back on it. Though that didn't mean he had to be happy about it.

Allen stepped into the elevator and waited as it made its way up, grinding his teeth the entire way. When the elevator opened again, Allen stepped into Eamon's penthouse, the light of day revealing the benefits of the penthouse's wall-less design. Allen was struck by the beauty of the sky and the city's upper skyline in virtually every direction he looked. Allen walked forward, expecting someone or something was no doubt waiting for him. As he passed the cluster of kitchen appliances, his expectations were confirmed.

"Hello, Allen," Carol's voice said from the refrigerator. Allen looked over in time to see the image of Carol appear on the door of the refrigerator through a built-in display screen.

"Where is he?" Allen asked.

"Mister Tor is tied up with several business ventures—"

"Bullshit," Allen interrupted. "Where is he?"

"He is not available at present," Carol said, looking apologetic.

Allen walked deeper into the penthouse, refusing to have a conversation with a refrigerator.

"We never had the chance to debrief after the events of your last mission," Carol said, her voice following Allen through speakers in the ceiling.

"Yeah, whose fault is that?" Allen continued to explore the open-plan penthouse, deciding he may as well see how the other half lives.

"Apologies," Carol said. "Mister Tor's schedule did not allow for a meeting."

"How is he feeling these days?" Allen asked, exasperated with Carol's verbal dancing. She did not immediately answer. Allen turned left and passed between two groupings of bedroom sets while he waited for an answer. It felt like strolling through a furniture showroom.

"I am not at liberty to discuss Mister Tor's personal health."

"He doesn't have Lou Gehrig's disease?" Allen asked. He spotted one of the few doors in Eamon's home, a bathroom door on the far wall of the penthouse, and headed for it, curious about the bathroom fixtures. "Or I should say, he used to have it but doesn't anymore, right?"

"You were doubtlessly told many things during your capture," Carol said condescendingly. "Many of which were surely not true."

"Like the fact that he actually helped build the Eden technology? Oh, and not only that, he used it to heal himself. And he found a cure for the side effects but kept it a secret. Stuff like that?"

"Captors can be very convincing under threat of torture," Carol said.

Allen approached the door. "Rusk wasn't trying to convince me of anything, she was pissed." He grabbed the door handle and tried turning it, but it was locked. "You understand 'pissed,' right? Like how getting manipulated to take out Eamon's ex-partners might also make *me* pissed?"

"Mister Tor has a new mission that he thinks may smooth things over," Carol said with fresh pleasantness.

Allen didn't answer. Why would an empty bathroom be locked? He took a step back from the door and looked up. He had assumed that the wall in front of him was like any typical wall running the length of the penthouse. But he could see ventilation ducts, data cables, and other utilities running beyond it. He had been thinking too traditionally. Eamon's home would have floor-to-ceiling windows on all four walls, not just on one, two, or three as commoners like Allen might have. There was something beyond the wall in front of him.

"It's a new mission that would offer you a second

chance," Carol continued. "With the same conditions and benefits as the first."

"I have a different idea," Allen said, turning around and trotting away until he reached a large vase. "Instead of sending me on a mission, Eamon is going to cure my son." Bending down, Allen lifted the vase from the floor. He groaned as he hefted it up and carried it back to the locked door.

"I demand that you stop!" Carol commanded.

"Now I definitely won't," Allen said, pleased she confirmed something interesting was beyond the door. Allen picked up his pace to gain momentum before pivoting and swinging the bottom of the vase into the door like a battering ram. The door budged slightly but held.

"Eamon!" Allen shouted as he stepped away. He made sure to aim where the door latch met the frame before stepping forward and heaving the vase into the door again. He heard a crack as the door moved farther in, but it still held.

"You are obviously stressed," Carol noted. "Your Healthy Helper is reading a very high heart rate. Perhaps you'd like something soothing like lemon balm tea?"

Allen bent over to rest the vase back on the floor before ripping the Healthy Helper off his wrist and tossing it away, rules be damned. "I want to talk with Eamon," he grunted, lifting the vase back up.

"I'm warning you to stop!" Carol said.

Allen readjusted his grip while he walked backward and readied to hit the door again. "You're going to fix my boy, you son of a bitch!" he yelled, running forward to deliver what he hoped was the final blow.

Before Allen made contact, the door opened and a muscular man in nursing scrubs emerged. Rather than stopping, Allen leaned his weight in and struck the man in the chest with the vase, knocking him into the wall. Allen dropped the vase and it made a hard pang on the concrete floor as he ran through the door. On the other side, another man came at him, a guard wearing the same uniform as the ones in the lobby downstairs.

The guard swung at Allen with a baton. He spun away out of instinct, grabbed the guard's wrist, and twisted it. The guard dropped the baton with a groan and Allen took it from him. After striking the guard in the back of the leg, Allen kicked him to the floor and turned to find Eamon.

Allen immediately ran into a glass wall that ran from floor to ceiling. Unable to stop himself in time, Allen hit the glass and came face to face with a screaming and disheveled Eamon Tor, pounding on the other side and bellowing at Allen with the hoarseness of an animal.

Stunned, Allen fell back and landed hard on the floor, all the while looking into Eamon's eyes. They darted around with confusion, wide and bloodshot, with no hint that he recognized Allen at all.

Allen felt a hard tug under his arms before he was turned and his face pressed into the floor. As Allen was held down by the guard, he heard a zip-tie closing and felt a sharp pinch as it tightened around his wrists. The guard retrieved the baton, pulled Allen to his feet, then put a hand on his shoulder to direct him back out the way he'd come.

The nurse who tried to stop Allen earlier quickly

walked past and entered Eamon's enclosure through an access door on the left side of the glass wall. Allen strained to watch as Eamon recoiled from the nurse and backed into a far corner away from him.

"Stop, please, Mister DelTorre," Carol's voice called out before her image materialized on the glass between Allen and Eamon. Her gaze was directed at the security guard. "Mister Moran can stay."

"Are you sure?" DelTorre asked. He looked older than Allen first assumed and carried himself more like a career professional than a typical part-time security guard.

"Yes," Carol replied, "the damage has already been done."

DelTorre sighed, seeming to take the comment personally. He took a utility knife from his pocket and cut the tie around Allen's wrists. Rubbing away the pain, Allen watched the nurse inside the enclosure try to calm Eamon down. The nurse held his arms out and spoke in a soothing voice as he approached, encouraging Eamon to sit down on a padded chair that was positioned near a bed. Allen also saw a small table with paper and art supplies like something a toddler would use, as well as a toilet and sink against the far wall.

"It's all right, Eamon, everything is fine now," the nurse said calmly as he got closer. Eamon got down on his haunches and shook his head in disagreement.

"Listen to Jack now, Eamon. He's your friend," Carol said, her image apparently visible through both sides of the glass.

Eamon looked at Carol, and his rage flared back to life. He screamed, ran at Carol's image, and pounded on the glass at her as hard as he could. Frustrated that his blows did not affect her, Eamon then slammed his head against the glass. The nurse, Jack, came up behind Eamon. Like a magic trick, he produced a prefilled syringe seemingly out of thin air and used it to inject something into Eamon's thigh.

Jack ducked with practiced skill as Eamon swung at him. Eamon tried to hit him again, and the two did an attack-and-dodge routine for a few seconds until Eamon got slower with drowsiness. With Eamon's eyes fluttering, Jack was able to put his arms around him from behind and lead him to the bed. Eamon attempted a few more woozy swings of his arms as Jack laid him down, where he went still and fell asleep.

"Mister Tor never found a cure for the side effects," Carol said, now looking at Allen.

"No cure..." Allen repeated, the air suddenly feeling thin.

"No cure," Carol confirmed. "As I'm sure you were told during your capture, the psychiatric complications of Eden Therapy are certain and, so far, irreversible. Mister Tor was confident a solution could be found, but..." Her voice trailed off.

"But why...why would...?" Allen stammered, struggling to put words in the right order. "Why would he say there was only a chance of getting them? He told me he could help Benjamin."

"Mistor Tor held on to an optimistic—"

"He said he could cure my son!" Allen shouted with venomous anger.

Carol's expression shifted to one Allen didn't expect from an artificial intelligence—sympathy. "Eamon felt that if he told you the truth, you wouldn't take the job. On the other hand, if you had a personal incentive to see the job through, you were more likely to complete it. More than a typical operator."

Allen's forehead furrowed into a knot. "Meaning I'd be so desperate that I'd do anything to get it done."

"He was feeling the effects of the Eden complications and became obsessed with destroying the technology before it could be widely abused. Not to mention prevent himself from hurting more people. That's why he created me."

"To do what?" Allen asked, gesturing toward Eamon's enclosure. "Keep him prisoner?"

"At first, my job was to prevent him from hurting anyone, either personally or through the resources of his company. In addition to handling other day-to-day logistics, of course."

Allen looked at Eamon. Even asleep, his face was frozen into a scowl. "Who did he want to hurt?"

"The complications bring out a compulsive desire for violence," Carol said. "He wanted to hurt anybody. Or everybody, depending on the episode."

"So you locked him up."

"I confined him to the building," Carol said. "Until this room became necessary for treatment."

"Because he's having more episodes," Allen said.

"His life is now one continuous episode. That's why I have full financial and medical power of attorney over Mister Tor's affairs, to execute according to my programming."

Allen looked around the room at DelTorre and Jack, neither of whom could hold Allen's gaze for more than a second before looking away. "You're keeping this secret," Allen said. "There's no way this is legit.

You're hiding Eamon's condition from shareholders and his corporate board. This is illegal as hell."

"Parts are," Carol said.

"Am I supposed to guess which ones?"

"Just like parts of what you do for a living are sometimes not strictly legal," Carol said.

Allen laughed. "Okay, computer, that's a nice threat. I want all the money Eamon was supposed to give my son."

"You did not complete the mission," Carol said with naive confusion.

"It's called blackmail, Carol, I want the money or I'm telling."

"To what end?" Carol asked. "If I don't give you the money and you expose us, you still won't get the money."

"For God's sake, then give me the money to be…kind!" Allen said, shouting face to face with Carol. "My boy is unconscious getting a hole put into him. You and Eamon could have prevented that with your pocket change. But no, I have to jump through hoops and missions and conditions. Just give it to me!"

"I can't," Carol said.

"Why not?"

"Mister Tor was clear that the Eden technology must be destroyed," Carol said.

"He was obviously sick when he said that. There's no way that the man I knew in college, who was my best friend, would not want to help my child."

"I agree."

"Then give me the money," Allen pleaded.

"There's something you have to understand," Carol said. "You are talking to me as if I am a human being, which I am not. Your argument is logical. My programming, again, is not. Even I can see that some of the rules Mister Tor gave me contradict each other, like preventing him from harming anyone yet allowing your family to suffer. But Mister Tor gave his instructions before his total loss of control, so I'm forced to obey them."

Allen walked along the glass wall of Eamon's enclosure, watching him on the bed. Even in sleep he was battling demons, occasionally twitching his arms as if fighting in a dream. Allen didn't recognize any traces of his old friend. "Why are you keeping him here, like this?"

"To keep him safe while we continue to search for a cure," Carol answered.

Allen scoffed. "You and Rusk are blowing through billions a month and you still don't have a treatment."

"But there's still hope," Carol said encouragingly. "Don't you still have hope? For your son?"

Allen stared at Eamon. Seeing his friend bear the weight of such a heavy illness gave Allen the same feeling of helplessness he often felt when looking at Benjamin. "Hope. Desperation. Need. I don't know the differences anymore." The similarities between Eamon and Benjamin evoked a feeling of dread in Allen, one he'd long since learned couldn't be cured by his rage, regardless of how righteous it was. "You said something about a mission?" Allen asked.

"Yes," Carol said. Her image in the glass faded away, replaced with a series of surveillance photos. "After your escape in Greenland, Rusk's facility was evacuated. Presumably because it was infiltrated." Several gruesome photos appeared on the glass to

Allen's unpleasant surprise. "The test subjects were discarded before heavy equipment was brought in to remove essential technology."

The pictures continued to cycle with images of the evacuation. In several close-ups, Allen recognized Jodock overseeing various steps of the operation. Allen couldn't help but let out a sigh of disappointment that his torturer was still alive.

"We tracked the equipment after it was shipped," Carol continued, "but we lost it at the port of Saint John's in Newfoundland. They used a falsified manifest, of course."

Allen eyed up the images of shipping containers being loaded onto trucks at the Greenland facility, and the same containers being loaded onto a ship. "They knew they were being watched," Allen said. "They wouldn't have unloaded at the first port they went to."

"Still, we had to track down every container," Carol said before images of containers being unloaded filled the glass in front of Allen, including ports in Newfoundland and others down the upper East Coast.

Allen looked at the images and imagined the vast amount of money and work required to track and confirm all the containers and their contents. Then he looked at an image of Jodock standing on a dock as the ship was being loaded in Greenland.

"Jodock knew you'd track them all down," he said. "That's why he never left the ship."

Carol was silent for a moment before answering. "Yes, that's what we eventually surmised as well."

It was satisfying to hear a computer be embarrassed. But Allen still had reason to scowl. "So this is the mission, board a ship on the open sea? It's just as bad as the last one."

"Allen, I..." Carol said before stopping herself. Allen looked as Carol reappeared on the glass and waited as she struggled to collect her virtual thoughts. "By the time Eamon found out about Benjamin and his condition, the Eden complications had already begun. Every thought he had focused on finding a cure for the side effects and beating Rusk to it. He felt that if he succeeded, everything would work out in the end. It would all be justified. Everything he did was filtered through that—he couldn't tear his thoughts away from it. I think, in his mind, offering money for your son while also manipulating you to get what he wanted was the only way his condition would allow him to help you."

Allen looked past Carol and beyond the glass at Eamon. "Choosing me of all people seemed kind of random."

"I'm sure it wasn't," Carol said.

Allen was overcome with a sense of loss for the friend he'd known. He walked over to the access door. Jack the nurse opened it from the inside and stepped aside to let Allen pass. He walked to Eamon's bedside and pulled the nearby chair over to him. Eamon fussed in his sleep, unable to settle. Instinctively, Allen pulled the blanket up over Eamon's body right up to the base of the chin, just as he would do for Benjamin. Under the covers, Eamon's muscles relaxed and the resemblance to the friend Allen knew returned. Softly humming absently as he did for Benjamin's bedtime routine, Allen sat down on the nearby chair and watched his friend's breathing slow to the regular pace of a peaceful sleep.

When he was satisfied Eamon had fully settled down, Allen stood up and walked back to the wide glass wall where Carol waited for him. "If I do this, I'm going to need a few things," Allen said in a whisper.

"Like what?" Carol asked.

"First off," Allen replied, "payroll."

Chapter Twenty-Six

"You owe me a cake that says 'thank you' with tiny 'thank you'-shaped candles whose flames also spell out 'thank you.' "

"That would be incredible," Allen replied to Kelsey as she finished tightening the clips on the back of Allen's armor while standing in the cramped office of Eamon's aircraft hangar.

"No less incredible than me spending months on the software of this suit," Kelsey said, grabbing her husband's shoulder and turning him to face her. "All because of my undying love for you."

"Between gaming sessions with that VR software Kyle's been sending you," Allen added.

"To clear my mind," Kelsey said, looking over the armor one last time.

"And I'm sure the fact that you plan to sell copies of the software had nothing to do with your motivation to finish it."

"To earn money to help my needy family," Kelsey countered.

"Well then, thank you, thank you, a thousand times, thank you," Allen said.

"That's just for the software though," Kelsey said, squeezing herself through the narrow opening around a small desk to get behind Benjamin's stroller. "What

286

about thanking me for even letting you go?"

"You're going to be on comms the whole time, right?" Allen asked.

"And monitoring the suit," Kelsey said. "Now that I'm on payroll it all feels so official."

Allen chuckled. "We're a regular 'Hopeless, Incorporated.'"

"Yeah, but it feels good. Still though..." Kelsey said, shifting her feet.

"What's wrong?"

"You can still back out of this," Kelsey said.

"I'm all suited up ready to go—"

"I know, I know," Kelsey interrupted. "I'm just saying that we can always find another way if it means losing you again."

"You know how much Benjamin needs this. And now that we officially got the HAPA restriction..."

"I'm just saying there's more than one path to saving him," Kelsey said.

Allen stared at his wife, unable to turn his mind away from the mission at hand. "This is the way forward. I know it."

Kelsey took a deep breath, let it out, then nodded. "Okay then. Well, you've got the suit on now, and you're on the clock. Better get out there," she said as she began pushing Benjamin forward toward the door.

"Wait a second," Allen stopped her. "I want to talk to him."

Kelsey stopped and pulled the canopy back on the stroller. Benjamin sat there looking up at the ceiling, casually moving his gaze to points of interest known only to him.

"I'll see you outside. I'll just be a minute," Allen

said to his wife.

Kelsey looked at him for a moment in surprise. "Oh, I see, a boy's talk."

"Something like that," Allen replied with a grin.

Kelsey moved around the stroller and past Allen. "Just remember everyone else is waiting for you."

"I know," Allen said. He waited while Kelsey went out the door and closed it behind her, then pulled over an office chair and sat in front of his son. "Hey, bud," he said as he tickled Benjamin on the side of his belly. Benjamin didn't laugh. He squirmed and shifted, and his breathing quickened, but if he got any amusement from it Allen couldn't tell.

Seeing drool running down Benjamin's chin, Allen grabbed a tissue from a box on the desk and dabbed the wetness. Afterward, he held the boy's hand. "You know, son, I think you're going to smile one day. You're going to laugh and play. You're going to yell and scream, maybe throw a few tantrums. When you're older you'll ask for money. You'll get mad if I don't give it to you, probably call me an asshole and wish I was dead or something else dramatic." Allen leaned in close to his son and spoke in a whisper. "Truth be told, if you learn to talk you can call me an asshole every day as far as I care."

Allen sat back. Benjamin briefly returned his gaze without expression before looking up at the ceiling. "Anyway," Allen said, "I just want you to have a fair shot at being a kid, I guess, the good and the bad. And being happy, as corny as that sounds. I wanted to make sure I told you before I left." He leaned in again and gave Benjamin a series of kisses on the cheek with a quick "love you" after each one. "Things will get better.

They've got to."

Allen stood up, grabbed the handle of the stroller, and pushed Benjamin out through the office door. Passing into the hangar, the sound of hovercraft turbines on standby filled Allen's ears. With increased support from Carol, Allen didn't have to rely on Richter's generosity for air travel this time. Instead, Allen was able to secure an unregistered Tor hovercraft from Eamon's private fleet. The aircraft resembled a kind of large, top-heavy flying turtle—its curved dome of pixel film designed to project camouflage around as much of itself as possible, with radar-absorbing material covering its adjustable turbines underneath. Everything was loaded and ready to go, waiting only for Allen to get onboard.

Kelsey stood at the bottom of the steps leading up into the hovercraft, taking the stroller from Allen as he reached her. They embraced and kissed before Allen climbed the steps, stopping in the middle and turning one last time to look at his family. As he smiled and waved, a short burst of static crackled in the earpiece he forgot he was wearing.

"Hey, Mystic, that was real sweet stuff you said to your son," Kyle said.

"Stop being creepy!" Allen shouted. In his mind he was glowering at MeatTank. In reality, however, he was looking at his wife with bitter annoyance.

"What?" Kelsey asked, confused.

"No, not you," Allen said. "Kyle's...here," he explained, pointing to his ear. He waved again to Kelsey before ducking and quickly entering the hovercraft.

"Hey, man, if the earpiece is on, I'm listening,"

Kyle explained.

"I didn't know it was on."

"Ah, okay, sorry then," Kyle said. "I thought maybe you wanted me to hear."

"Why would I want that?" Allen asked.

"I had no idea. I just thought I would…abide, I guess."

Allen reached the cargo hold of the hovercraft and moved on to the main passenger bay. He heard Haley's voice as he approached.

"I'm still confused. If you don't want people to think you're twins, why are you both wearing the same outfits?" she asked.

"Customization costs more," Allen heard one of the Zielinski brothers respond.

"Besides, we both liked the same outfit," the other brother added.

"But you had a blank check to get whatever gear you wanted!" Haley argued as Allen entered.

"Why waste another man's money?" Jacob said. John nodded his agreement. At least Allen thought it was John, the taller of the two.

"Oh, come on," Haley said, exasperated. "My dad can do something for you guys."

"That's true," Daryl replied from his seat in the cockpit. "I would love to charge you for customization. It would be my pleasure."

Haley began to speak but instead turned when Allen came in. "How's Benjamin doing?" she asked.

Allen smiled. "Good, thanks," he said, patting her shoulder as he walked past on his way to the cockpit.

"Everything ready to go?" Daryl asked him.

Allen leaned heavily against the copilot seat and

folded his arms. "Tell me I'm not making the same mistake twice."

"It's only a mistake if it doesn't work," Daryl said. "Besides, making mistakes and fixing them is pretty much how we've always done it."

"That's true," Allen said. "Good thing you're here, then."

"Oh, yeah, I'll be sure to point out every single mistake you make," Daryl assured Allen.

Allen didn't respond. He looked down, lost in thought until Daryl gave Allen a hard tap with the back of his hand.

"Come on," Daryl said. "Let's go do this for your boy."

Allen nodded to his friend, made his way back into the passenger bay, then sat down and strapped himself into his seat. Once Allen was secure, Daryl slowly maneuvered the hovercraft outside of the hangar before powering up the turbines and taking off.

Over the next four hours as the hovercraft flew to the northern Atlantic, Allen and the rest of the team found space in the cramped quarters to check and recheck their gear. After Allen confirmed the power levels on his pulse assault rifle for a third time, he noticed Haley doing the same on her pair of pistols.

"So your dad didn't have a second, miniature robotic walker just lying around?" Allen asked.

"Unfortunately, no," Haley said. "I still think we should have brought the big one."

"Well, maybe the next ship we attack will have extra wide doors and big elevators," Allen said.

"You know what I mean, though."

"You'll be great," Allen said. "There's nobody else

I would want here. Though that does remind me," Allen said, raising his hand to activate his earpiece. "Hey, MeatTank?"

"Yessir?" Kyle answered, chipper as ever.

"We have to change Specter's codename again," Allen said. "Because the original Specter is here. We can't have two Specters—it's confusing."

Haley grumbled. "We really have to do this now?"

"When I was on that medical bed, with Jodock basically about to end my life as I knew it, the wall exploded behind me. I turned my head around and saw the craziest thing. It was like a portal had opened up, ringed with fire and brimstone."

"Brimstone? Seriously, brimstone?" Haley asked mockingly.

"And then, this hulking figure comes through, like some demon from another world," Allen said with as much dramatic flair as he could muster.

"This is a new level of dad-ishness, and that's saying something," Haley noted.

"And it was you," Allen continued. "The hulking demon was you! And that's when I realized what your codename should be."

" 'Hulking Demon'?" Haley asked.

"Hellfire," Allen replied.

Haley's counterargument caught in her throat as the name sank in. Allen smiled as she paced back and forth, stammering fragments of disagreements to Allen's suggestion before stopping each time and returning to her thoughts.

"I think that's pretty solid," Kyle offered.

"Obviously it's no 'MeatTank,' " Allen said. "But it feels appropriate. To me, anyway."

"Thanks," Haley and Kyle both said simultaneously.

Allen gave Haley a nod and returned to his seat. He took a deep breath, closed his eyes, and spent the rest of the flight trying to rest and keep his mind clear. When he did occasionally open his eyes, he noted how much darker it got outside as they headed east and closer to the progression of nightfall.

As the expected time approached for them to intercept the cargo ship, the team members each made their way back to their seats to mentally prepare until Daryl broke the silence. "Fifteen minutes out. Going to ghost-mode," he announced.

The ship dropped in speed, the rumble of the turbines falling to a low murmur. That also meant the hovercraft's cloak had been activated and was now using the dynamic visual display on its surface to optically blend in with the surroundings, while also using radar absorption and other stealth technologies to stay hidden. All the same, it didn't hurt that it was a moonless night.

"Okay, let's go," Allen said, standing up. He grabbed two round, hockey puck-size objects from a compartment next to him and handed one to Haley as they made their way back to the cargo hold.

"Do I have to do anything to turn this on?" Haley asked.

"No, they're both already on standby, just waiting for Kyle to activate them," Allen answered. " 'Tank, how long will it take to map the layout of the ship?"

"The sonic imagers will send me data as soon as you stick them. Though I'll need both put in place before I get anything detailed," Kyle said.

"So before that, we don't know where we're going?" Haley asked as she and Allen reached their positions.

"Not exactly, no," Kyle said.

"Though I'm sure the Eden equipment will be as deep into the ship as possible," Allen said dryly.

John and Jacob helped one another into their matching gear and weaponry, each one equipped with a heavy repeating pulse gun that had to be supported with a sling around their shoulders.

"Five minutes," Daryl updated through the intercom. The aircraft slowed even more. Getting closer and closer to their target at ever-slower speeds was torturous, but the cloak worked more effectively the slower they went, so there was nothing to do but bear it.

"You there Ke—, er, Lovelace?" Allen asked into his microphone, nearly using Kelsey's real name instead of her codename. She chose it in honor of the world's first computer programmer, Ada Lovelace.

"I'm here," Kelsey said. "I just didn't want to make you nervous."

Allen laughed. "You're the one who sounds nervous."

"MeatTank is running ops on the rest of the mission while I focus on weapons and armor," Kelsey continued. Hidden deep within the timbre of her professional tone was a quiver and shakiness only a spouse could detect.

"This is the best way to help him," Allen said, not daring to mention Benjamin by name.

"Ten-four," Kelsey said. "Systems are green. Good luck."

Love you, too, Allen thought to himself.

"One minute," Daryl called. Allen looked down and made one more final check of his weapon before holding it at the ready and waiting for the cargo bay doors to open. Then he froze—was he expected to make some kind of dramatic speech as the team's experienced leader? But looking at the younger faces around him filled with resolve, it seemed like maybe he was the one who could use a speech from them. Each one looked set like a sprinter, staring at the bay doors as if waiting for a starter pistol to go off. Allen settled into the same posture and waited.

"Field team: final comms check," Kyle announced.

"Apollo, check," Jacob said.

"Ares, check," John said.

"Hellfire, check," Haley said.

"Mystic, check," Allen said self-consciously. *I need a more macho codename*, he thought.

"Specter, check. Ten seconds, good luck," Daryl said before turning off the lights in the cargo bay. A second later, the night vision on Allen's brand-new tactical contact lenses activated to display his surroundings.

The cargo doors opened, sending a wash of cool air and the smell of the ocean into his face. John and Jacob went out, jumping to the deck of the ship beyond with Haley and Allen following close behind.

Allen knelt and looked around. They were near the aft of the ship. Looking back, a series of cargo cranes ran to a raised platform. Toward the front, the main bridge rose up at midship, with more cranes and various lifeboats set on the deck. Nowhere did Allen see any security personnel. "MeatTank, I have zero contacts."

"Confirmed," Kyle said. "There's nothing on

thermal imaging."

"How can that be?" Haley asked. "What about the crew, wouldn't—"

A barrage of pulse fire lit up the deck in a strobe of pale green bursts, both ahead and behind them. The Zielinski brothers triggered their gun-mounted shields, each unfurling in a circle. They returned fire down the deck before realizing the pulse blasts weren't directed at them.

Instead, streams from over a dozen weapons were hitting the cloaked hovercraft.

The surface of the aircraft flashed and glitched as its camouflage system overloaded and failed. As the fully-visible hovercraft turned to flee, the enemy pulse fire converged to a single point with computer-like precision. Allen tried to warn Daryl, but an explosion burst from the side of the hovercraft, sending Allen and the rest of the team to the deck for cover.

"Dad!" Haley shouted as she scrambled to look over the rail, bits of burning debris scattered around her.

The hovercraft went down and Allen lost sight of it. "Specter, what is your status?" he asked in all but a shout. He took cover between two lifeboats where John and Jacob were doing the same. A moment later, the air was filled with the weighty sound of the hovercraft hitting the water.

"Specter!" Allen called again.

The pulse fire resumed, this time aimed at the team. Haley ran to the railing and looked down at the water. Allen jumped to his feet and ran to her. Pulse fire chased him as he reached Haley and tackled her to the ground.

"Dad!" Haley shouted again.

"Haley, I need your head here, not in the water," Allen said.

"He might be hurt, we have to get down there," she pleaded. Before Allen could respond, heavy static crackled in his ear.

"Listen to him, Hellfire," Daryl said in a pained voice, accompanied by a chorus of electronic alarms sounding in the background.

Allen spoke before Haley could get a word in. "Can you bail out?" he asked Daryl.

"No sense in that," Daryl answered. "If I can't get this thing back in the air, we're all dead."

"You want to fix it?" Allen asked in disbelief.

Daryl made sounds of effort, and Allen envisioned him pulling himself out of the pilot seat and away from the cockpit. "They blew the engine control circuits," Daryl explained through heavy breaths. "This is my problem to fix. Worry about yourselves now."

Pulse fire scattered around Allen and Haley, and they lunged to join the Zielinskis between the lifeboats.

"They're sentry-mechs!" John called out before firing back.

"That's why they didn't show up on thermal," Jacob added, joining his brother in returning fire.

Jodock finally got the gear he wanted, Allen thought. Going up against pulse weapons cut down the effectiveness of everyone's projectile shields to about a quarter of what they would be against regular bullets. And the mechs were getting closer.

"What do we do?" Haley asked.

"We make a hole," Allen declared. "And run."

Chapter Twenty-Seven

"Move a foot to your left or you'll end up in the sink."

Haley grimaced at Kyle's instruction. "Why am I the designated hole-blaster?"

"You have the most experience," Allen shouted over the pulse fire from the sentry-mechs.

Haley scrambled to the edge of the boats. "I told you we should have brought the walker," she groaned as she unholstered a pulse pistol. She tuned it to a low setting and scored a large X into the deck before backing away and pulling out her other pistol. "All right, here we go," she warned before aiming both pistols and opening fire. With each pistol on full auto, her weapons bombarded the deck and sent singed debris flying up from the ever-widening hole.

"Lovelace," Allen said as he readied his assault weapon, "I need target assist."

"Online," Kelsey confirmed. "Fire away."

Allen raised his pulse weapon up over the top of the lifeboat and pointed in the direction of the mechs. When his barrel-mounted motion sensor found a target, Allen fired in a short burst and waited for the arm of his armor to line up his next shot. "How's that hole coming?" he asked Haley.

"Got it!" Haley answered, lowering her weapons.

"Get in," Allen commanded before tapping John on

the back. "Ares, you're right behind her."

"Oh, man…" Haley said as she stepped forward and reluctantly jumped down. No sooner had Haley dropped out of sight than John Zielinski slid feet-first after her.

Allen clambered toward Jacob. "Apollo, let's go!" Jacob followed the command and disappeared below. Just as Allen moved to follow, pieces of lifeboat littered the air as pulse rounds broke their way through. Allen was hit with what felt like a pair of sledgehammers to the back as he stumbled down the hole.

Allen landed hard in a daze and lay in an inch of water. Someone pulled him to his feet and it took a moment for Haley's face to come into focus. Around them, water sprayed from damaged pipes, dousing scattered fires around the ship's galley where the team landed.

Allen's wits rushed back to him. "We gotta move."

The team ran out into the ship's narrow passageway as the sounds of metal feet approached above them. Allen locked the door behind him just before a grenade blast ripped through the galley. The door shook but held.

Haley turned around. "What about these?" she asked Allen, pulling out her sonic imager puck. Allen grabbed the device from her and slapped it against the bulkhead where it magnetically stuck.

"What are you reading, 'Tank?" Allen asked as he and Haley continued running.

"There are three cargo holds, but with only one imager I can't narrow down your target," Kyle said. "I need that second one."

"There's also another problem," Allen said,

tapping Haley on the shoulder before calling out for the Zielinskis to stop. Once they were all together, Allen continued. "If Specter gets that hovercraft back in the air, he's going to need a place to pick us up. And the best place to do that seems to be the docking bridge at the back of the ship."

"The raised platform all the way at the end?" Jacob asked thoughtfully, looking at his brother.

"We can defend it even with mechs coming from both sides. It would take some of the heat off you two," John said.

Allen leaned against the bulkhead to relieve the pressure on his lower back, which was throbbing where the pulse shots struck him. "I know it wasn't the plan to go full Alamo mode…"

"No, it could work," John replied.

"Yeah," Jacob agreed. "You're the ones they really want to kill, going after their equipment."

"Hopefully they'll only try so-hard to get us," John continued.

"As opposed to stopping at nothing for you two," Jacob finished.

"Right, something like that," Allen said. The sound of twisting metal filled the corridor from the direction of the galley.

"Time to go," Haley said, already walking away.

Allen stood up from the bulkhead, gritting his teeth from the pain in his back, and nodded to John and Jacob. The brothers turned without another word and headed for the aft end of the ship, then Allen followed Haley.

"Mystic," Kelsey broke in on the radio, "my screen says you're walking funny."

"Your screen isn't very nice then," Allen grumbled as he caught up to Haley.

"I'm turning up the assistance from your suit," Kelsey told her husband. "There's no sense in limping."

Allen's pain eased as his armor increased its support on his body, using micro servo motors to help him walk with less effort thanks to Kelsey making good on the lumbar support she had promised.

"Your shielding is at sixty-four percent after those pulse shots," Kelsey warned. "Please be careful."

Ahead of Allen, Haley took a deep breath as if steeling herself. "Specter, come in. How are things going?" she asked with forced formality.

"He's working with MeatTank to figure out a workaround for the destroyed control circuit," Kelsey answered. "I'm doing double duty at the moment. In thirty yards you'll reach the port side of the ship. That'll be a good place for the second imager."

"Copy," Haley replied, a tinge of disappointment in her voice as she checked her left down a passageway that branched off from theirs.

Allen passed by the same side passageway and was about to reassure Haley about her father when the wall behind Allen exploded. The blast knocked Allen down and he just had enough time to grab his weapon and turn before a guard came around the corner. Allen fired a quick shot that hit and sent the guard back. There was no mistaking the guard's uniform. It was the same as the security guards at Rusk's Greenland facility. Allen and Haley ran as more shots came at them from behind.

"Ten more yards and you're there," Kelsey said over the radio, her voice tinged with worry.

"Here," Allen yelled to Haley after pulling the

second sonic imager out of a pocket. He threw the puck and Haley caught it over her shoulder, then Allen turned and fired back while she ran ahead.

"I'm at the end, puck's on the wall," Haley said over the radio. Allen started running toward her before she even finished her sentence.

"I'm getting data, but…" Kelsey said. "I need a second." Allen heard the hard click of Kelsey putting her microphone on mute as he caught up to Haley and took cover around a corner.

"Great, we're on hold," Haley grumbled, firing down the corridor to keep the guards from getting closer.

"We might have to split up," Allen said.

"What?" Haley scoffed. "That's insane."

"The Eden equipment is in a cargo hold," Allen continued. "If we both go in there with the guards on us, there's no way out."

"We'll still be able to blow the stuff up," Haley replied boldly.

"No, Haley, that's suicide," Allen said sternly. "It's not that kind of mission."

"But splitting up…" Haley began.

"Just keep it in mind," Allen urged.

There was a pop of static on the radio. "Okay, I'm back," Kelsey said.

"Are the imagers working?" Allen asked.

"Yes," Kelsey confirmed. "I just didn't have access to the program to process it. And 'Tank is still busy, so I had to crack into his computer and bring it to my machine."

"You hacked into his system?" Haley asked.

"You disapprove?" Allen asked.

"No, it's just impressive," Haley answered.

"I have your images," Kelsey continued. "Based on the density of the cargo, it looks like you're headed for the center, Cargo Hold Five."

"Can you see the guards?" Allen asked.

"Not clearly," Kelsey replied. "There are fragments, but the system isn't precise enough to track people, much less people on the move."

"All right, let's get going then," Allen said, a tightness in his chest growing the longer they stayed still. "Which way?"

"Move with the hull on your left until you come to a ladder, then go down one level," Kelsey instructed. "After that I'll guide you."

Allen and Haley each fired a volley of shots before following Kelsey's directions. They reached the ladder, which was more like a narrow set of stairs on a steep incline, and descended to the level below.

"Go forward and take a right at the third passage," Kelsey said.

Haley picked up the pace. She glanced over her shoulder and stopped when she saw that Allen wasn't following. Instead, he stood in the corridor listening. "Nobody's chasing us," he explained. A scowl deepened on his face as he jogged to catch up.

After Allen and Haley turned right as directed, Kelsy updated them. "Keep going, a left at the next intersection."

Allen quickened to a run as he saw a passageway coming up on his left. He rounded the corner into the cargo entryway and locked his eyes on an access door labeled Cargo Hold Five. As he was about to open the door, Haley cried out.

"They're here!" she yelled, diving around the corner to take shelter in the entryway as a wave of pulse fire erupted behind her. In an instant, she turned herself around and returned fire.

"You need to go!" Allen yelled. "I'll cover you. Head for the docking bridge!"

"No!" Haley screamed back. "They'll flood into the cargo hold and kill you!"

"I'm not going to let you die here!" Allen screamed, a swell of panic overtaking him.

"I'm not going to let me die here, either," Haley replied before opening a quick-release compartment on her waist. She reached inside and threw something out of the entryway to the far wall of the passage. For a fleeting moment, Allen caught a glimpse of the bright yellow tennis ball before it bounced with a familiar *thunk* and disappeared out of sight toward their enemies.

"What the hell?" a male voice wondered aloud before Haley activated a button on her wrist control pad.

The explosion shook Allen off balance. He braced himself against the wall while Haley followed up her surprise grenade attack with a burst of pulse fire around the corner for good measure.

"When did you get tennis ball grenades?" Allen asked with jealous confusion.

"Once I realized I couldn't use my walker in these narrow hallways," Haley answered. "Now go."

Allen clenched his jaw. He didn't like it, but as pulse fire came at them again from down the hall, there was no time to argue. "If it gets too heavy, you blast a way through and run," Allen said. "I'll find another way out."

"Got it," Haley answered before bouncing another tennis ball around the corner, this time from floor to ceiling.

"Look out!" a guard yelled, sending them all scrambling to escape the lethal piece of sports equipment. As the grenade exploded, Allen moved the short way back to the cargo bay door, opened it, and moved inside.

Allen closed the door before surveying the cargo hold. He stood at the top of a multi-level network of scaffoldings built around the sides of the hold. Looking over the railing, Allen saw the bulk of the Eden equipment at the bottom, with various work stations scattered on different levels of catwalks. What he did not see were any guards.

"There's nobody here," Allen said, making his way to the nearest set of stairs.

"Maybe they went after Ares and Apollo," Kelsey offered.

After reaching the next level down, Allen squeezed past a computer terminal before taking the next set of stairs. The sound of his feet against metal grating echoed through the cargo hold. "Maybe," Allen said, unconvinced, as he descended the second set of stairs and reached the bottom.

Allen walked slowly toward the center of the hold where the Eden treatment chamber and other bulky equipment were arranged and headed for the main computer terminal. "I'm going to verify the data," Allen told Kelsey, pulling out a small, silver device. After searching the terminal and finding a data port, Allen removed a protective cap on the device to reveal a block of tiny metal filaments packed tightly together. Allen pushed the universal adapter in until the filaments formed to the shape of the port and made a solid connection.

"Contact, I'm getting data," Kelsey reported.

Allen felt painfully exposed while he waited for Kelsey to confirm the Eden equipment was genuine and not some kind of decoy. Allen couldn't stomach the possibility of trying to destroy it for a third time.

"It's all there," Kelsey confirmed. "Everything matches the info Carol gave us."

"Finally," Allen said, dropping to a knee. He put his pulse rifle down on the deck and removed a pouch of explosive charges from his belt. "Ask 'Tank about the hovercraft repair, maybe we can—"

Allen was struck hard on the side of the head. The force threw him a full body length away from the computer terminal. As he tried to shake the stars from his vision, he saw a massive figure looming over him.

"Allen. Thomas. Moran." Jodock's deliberate announcement of Allen's full name boomed through the cavernous room.

Allen instinctively reached for his pulse rifle, forgetting he had set it down to retrieve his explosives.

Jodock picked Allen up off the floor before throwing him like a toy against the bulkhead, his body crashing down on a workstation and medical equipment.

"Facial recognition has got to be the finest invention in the past one hundred years," Jodock said with a proud smile, casually putting his hands on his hips. He had exchanged his standard security guard fatigues for a custom suit of hardened body armor in black with subtle gold trim.

"Great work, Hanspeter," Allen said, getting to his feet. "Are we going to text each other phone numbers now?"

Jodock flashed a dark smile and walked toward Allen. "I'd rather visit in person. I have always wanted to see Chicago. I would love to meet the family."

As Jodock drew close and tried to grab him again, Allen dodged and ran toward his weapon. Just as he was about to reach it, the cargo hold was set ablaze in pale green light. The pulse blast struck Allen squarely in the back, knocking him past his pulse rifle to tumble several yards before stopping face-down on the deck. With his back screaming in pain, Allen didn't need his heads-up display to tell him that his projectile shield was completely burned out.

Chapter Twenty-Eight

This is clearly what bruised kidneys feel like.

Allen tried to take mental stock of the damage to his body as he brought himself to his hands and knees, but Jodock was far too pleased with himself to provide the chance.

"As you can see, I am no longer hampered by budget restrictions," Jodock said, returning his pulse pistol to its holster. It was much bulkier than Haley's. Allen estimated its power core was about three times normal size.

"Allen, what's happening?" Kelsey's voice shouted in Allen's ear.

Allen looked at Jodock, forced to ignore Kelsey for the moment. "You made your case and she thoughtfully approved your requests?"

"She's too far gone for that now. She chokes out words in a garbled rage," Jodock explained, making his way toward Allen. "Luckily, I was given authority to make decisions on her behalf."

"Allen, you have to get up," Kelsey commanded.

Allen forced himself to push through the pain. He scrambled to his feet and ran around the side of the Eden chamber, trying to put as much equipment between him and Jodock as possible.

"If you weren't so eager to get in here, you would have realized there's only one way in or out," Jodock said with amusement. "I'm not sure where you're running away to. It is pointless."

"I guess I'm just an optimist," Allen said, stalling for time.

"No, you're not. You're sick with desperation, and Tor knew it," Jodock said, pursuing Allen with all the urgency of a garden stroll. "Only a desperate man would think coming here was a reasonable way to help his son."

"You don't know anything about me," Allen said, moving around another bulky piece of equipment to get a better view of the nearest set of stairs.

"I know how it feels when the doctors are out of ideas," Jodock said, his voice getting closer. "And insurance says they won't try anymore. I know how it feels to watch someone suffer and wish it would finally end. That was the only relief when my wife died, much to my own guilt. I'm simply trying to save others from the same pain."

Allen considered replying with a comeback to Jodock's self-righteous monologue, but Haley was surely feeling the pressure from the attacking guards above. There wasn't time to be clever.

With a couple of obstacles between him and Jodock, Allen ran out toward the stairs. He still had the bag of charges with him, and at that moment, dropping the explosives from the top of the cargo hold before running off was the best plan he could come up with.

Allen reached the stairs, relieved to not feel the pain of a pulse blast slamming into him. His relief quickly evaporated with the sound of Jodock's gleeful laughter.

"Excellent," Jodock said, coming from around the

Eden equipment and breaking into a run. "I was hoping all this effort wouldn't be a waste."

Allen made it to the top of the first set of stairs. As he ran for the second set, he stole a look at Jodock. Rather than heading for the stairs near the side as Allen had done, Jodock was running toward the center. Fearing Jodock planned to fire straight up from beneath the catwalk, Allen quickened his pace to try and reach the top before Jodock could shoot. At any moment, Allen expected Jodock to slow and take out his pulse pistol.

Instead, Jodock leapt into the air.

The cargo hold filled with a brief roar as compressed air thrusters built into Jodock's suit launched him up and over the railing of the second level. He landed with awkward heaviness a few yards ahead of Allen, blocking his way. Allen growled. Everyone else had cool new battle-toys except him.

Allen turned, hoping to find another set of stairs to get him to the top. Behind him, Jodock's booming footsteps against the metal grating got closer and quicker.

"Allen, I'm going to tell Haley to come in to help you," Kelsey said.

"No, I'm almost—"

Allen was cut short by another pulse blast to the back. Although the intensity of the hit was not nearly as powerful as the first, it still knocked Allen off his feet and sent him crashing into the walkway. Before he could get back to his feet, Jodock was on him, grabbing him by the chest piece before lifting him up and slamming him against the hull of the ship. Jodock needed only one of his colossal arms to hold Allen in place.

"Why are you doing this?" Jodock asked. "Don't you want to cure little Benjamin?"

Allen's blood boiled at the mention of his son's name. "Your cure would kill him."

"Perhaps, eventually," Jodock conceded. "But at least, for a time, you would have a normal son. Is that not worth something?"

Allen's mind flashed back to his many times spent in the hospital for Benjamin's admissions. Other children suffered from cancer, critical heart problems, and terminal illnesses. Yet even though their conditions were considered worse than his son's, they could still talk to their parents, play games, watch television, or just plain sit up in their beds—abilities Benjamin may or may not ever master. Other parents worried about losing their "normal" children while Allen mourned the loss of the child he had expected, and he couldn't help but feel jealous. Now with Jodock suggesting Allen's feelings may have been right, he felt like a monster.

"Besides," Jodock continued, "if there was a way to stop the seizures, surely they would have found it by now. So really nothing else you do will matter."

Kelsey's voice broke through the cloud gathering in Allen's mind. "For God's sake, Allen, kick his ass!"

Summoning all his athletic ability, Allen kicked Jodock in the chest. Jodock stumbled back, and with Allen's feet once again touching the walkway, he spun and ran for the stairs. As he stepped onto the top level, Haley's voice crackled in his ear.

"Mystic, come in. How are things going in there?" she asked. Allen heard heavy weapons on the other side of the cargo bay door. "It's starting to get a little dicey up here."

"I'm coming out," Allen told her, reaching down to the explosive charges clipped to his belt. "Rigging the charges now." Allen kept his eyes fixed on the door, thinking his way through how he and Haley would blast their way out, when it occurred to him that his hand still hadn't found the charges yet. Looking down at where they should be, he only saw an empty belt clip. A quick glance behind him confirmed his fears.

"Here they are," Jodock said with a proud grin, holding the bag of charges in his hand. "I have to admit, I wasn't sure I could get them off your belt while talking."

Allen knew what Jodock wanted him to do. He just couldn't figure out why Jodock wanted it so badly. "Why go through all this planning just to fight me?" Allen asked. "Honestly, this is a lot of effort, even for a trap."

Jodock shrugged. "Three months on a ship. I'm sure you've noticed I have some obsessive tendencies."

Although he desperately needed the explosives, Allen stepped away from Jodock toward the cargo bay door. His senses of duty to Haley as well as self-preservation both encouraged him to make a run for it.

Jodock noticed Allen's intentions. "Ah yes, your partner," he said, clipping the charges onto his belt before taking out a handheld radio. "I don't want you to think I forgot about her." Jodock pushed the transmitter button on the radio. "Gerhart? Are your men ready to go in?"

Allen's heart sank. Jodock had anticipated that Haley would defend the door. Every attack Allen and his team had faced was designed to get them exactly where Jodock wanted. And now the final part of Jodock's trap was about to crush Allen's partner. He felt lightheaded as the radio crackled, dreading the confirmation of Jodock's order.

"Say again?" Gerhart's voice asked unsteadily. "Go in?"

Jodock snarled. "Yes. Send in your men."

"Sir, they went in ten minutes ago," Gerhart explained. "We're keeping the pressure up, but—watch it!" Gerhart was cut off and the radio went silent.

Now it was Allen's turn to smile. "Oh man, that's tough," he said, shaking his head in mock sympathy. "To get bad news like that *and* lose your gun…"

Jodock patted the holster on his hip and found it empty.

"You're not the only one who can do two things at once," Allen said. When pressed against the bulkhead, he had tried grabbing Jodock's pistol and shooting the man in the face. But with Jodock's long reach, Allen had to settle for kicking the pistol from its holster instead.

"*Gopfetori*," Jodock cursed in his native Swiss-German, looking over the railing and spotting his weapon a level below.

As Jodock turned back, Allen delivered a sharp blow to his face. Jodock raised his arms but Allen hammered his body before he could turn around. Finally, Jodock lunged at Allen, forcing him back. Allen only barely escaped Jodock's grasp thanks to a contorted spin move that his armor's assistive motors made feel like a stomach-lurching carnival ride.

With Jodock moving to strike, Allen's mind swelled with soaring rock music. Although he could not remember what old movie it was from, the melody came through like a choir of keytar-wielding angels. Allen dodged and counter-attacked, delivering more body blows until Jodock had noticeably slowed. Allen didn't want the rush to end, but the sound of weapons on the other side of the cargo door reminded him that Haley was still under fire.

Jodock rested against the railing, sucking in air. With a jogging start, Allen cocked his arm back to deliver a finishing strike. He aimed squarely at Jodock's jaw and swung with all the energy he and his suit could muster. But where he expected to feel bone cracking, he instead felt a sudden obstacle take hold of his arm with a pressure that made him cry out in pain.

Jodock looked up with a wicked smile. "Enough," he said, rising with Allen's arm between his hands before twisting it to an unnatural angle.

Allen screamed.

So did Kelsey. "No!" she cried. "Allen, just…just…" she stammered.

Allen's understanding of Kelsey's words slipped in and out, the intense pain overtaking everything.

"Kyle!" Kelsey continued. "Kyle, I need ship operations…"

The world around Allen slipped away. He wanted to sleep yet felt terrified at the same time. His body went cold. The sight of Jodock's bruised face snapped him back to attention.

"I've really enjoyed this," Jodock said, still holding Allen's arm. "With all my setbacks lately, it's good to have a win."

Allen kicked Jodock in the shin, hoping to reach his knee and break away from his grip.

Jodock spun to put Allen's back against the railing before drawing in closer. "No more of that now," Jodock said calmly before twisting Allen's arm once more. Allen crumpled to the metal grating, catching his breath in ragged gasps through fresh agony. Reality slipped away again. He imagined lying in bed on a Sunday morning. He thought about a hot bath.

Jodock kicked Allen in the stomach, then wrapped a giant hand around his throat and pulled Allen to his knees. Allen's attention snapped back. He couldn't breathe. Jodock looked at him blankly, waiting.

"Allen!" Kelsey cried out again. "Allen, look at the wall. The wall behind Jodock."

Allen took his wife's advice. There was no need to look into the face of his killer. He thought of Kelsey's face instead.

"There should be something written on the wall," Kelsey continued. "The feed from your contact lenses is too blurry. I need you to tell me what it says."

Allen followed his wife's instructions, too dazed to disagree. Besides, he didn't want his life to end in an argument.

"Over Jodock's shoulder!" Kelsey said.

Allen couldn't see words. He only saw letters and numbers. They would have to do. Couldn't disappoint Kelsey.

Allen silently mouthed out what he saw.

Curiosity got the better of Jodock, and he slightly released his grip. "What's that?" he asked.

Allen inhaled sharply and took several more breaths before answering in a creaky voice. "Three. Fifty. Three. A. A."

Jodock grinned. "Fabulous. Anything else?"

Only one other thing came to Allen's mind. "You're a dick."

Jodock clenched back down on Allen's neck, the grin remaining on his face.

Allen used the hand of his good arm to try and pry Jodock's hand away from his neck, but it was clasped hopelessly tight. In front of Allen's eyes, like a taunt, were the explosive charges hanging from Jodock's belt. Allen reached out and unclipped the explosives, but his quickly-weakening state made their weight too much to do anything more than pull them close on the floor.

Jodock laughed as if Allen was a puppy performing an adorable trick.

Allen looked up at Jodock's face. Even in laughter it was cruel. Allen didn't want that to be the last thing he saw, so he looked higher. He looked as high up on the hull as Jodock's grip allowed. In his mind, Allen looked past the ship to the universe beyond. He forced himself to keep his eyes open. If there was a God, Allen wanted to see it.

As darkness crept in, he kept looking. His vision narrowed to a tunnel, yet he kept looking. Finally, Allen saw something. He was convinced it was an angel coming down to rush him to heaven. Its form was unlike anything Allen had expected, and as it burst through the hull of the ship, he couldn't believe how wrong artists and theologians had been over the centuries. Allen only wished he could tell them the truth.

Angels looked just like a giant metal hook from a cargo crane.

Chapter Twenty-Nine

"*Breach, breach, breach. Deck three, frame five, compartment three—cargo.*"

The announcement from the ship's public address system brought Allen back to consciousness, followed quickly by intense pain. He opened his eyes and tried to make sense of the scene around him.

Allen was at the bottom of the cargo hold. Mangled pieces of steel railing and catwalk were scattered around him. And the air smelled like the ocean, with a light breeze brushing across Allen's forehead. He looked up and saw the night sky through a hole near the top of the cargo hold, thankfully above the ship's water line. Even if water wasn't about to flood the area, more armed guards soon would.

Allen felt his neck tighten as if being choked by a phantom hand. "Kelsey," he asked, sitting himself up against the main Eden computer unit. "What happened? Where's Jodock?"

"He's gone," Kelsey answered. "Fell out the hole."

Allen looked up again at the improvised skylight Kelsey and Kyle had made with the cargo crane. It may not have been an angel that saved him, but Allen resolved to find out who the patron saints of gravity and balance were and pay them proper homage when he could.

"Mystic!" Haley's screamed in Allen's earpiece. "I

don't know what just happened but it stirred up a hornet's nest."

Allen froze. He needed the charges. His gaze darted wildly around the room unable to focus. Allen took a deep breath as he tried to regain control of his senses. He saw twisted railings and sections of walkways on the floor, but the stairways up to the top were intact. Allen wondered what level the charges were most likely to have landed on when he had a vague recollection of them being clipped to Jodock's belt. Then he remembered Jodock's laugh, darkness closing in, and the charges firmly in his hand.

He looked down at his left hand, which he was using to prop himself up, and saw the bag of charges still clutched in his fingers. He mentally added the patron saint of tactical explosives to his worshiping to-do list.

Allen tried to stand up. "Haley, I'm coming out, just—"

Pain seized Allen's legs as soon as he put weight on them. He crumpled back down to the floor, angry at his body's betrayal. Looking down, he saw marks from multiple impacts on the legs of his armor. The same forces that had bent and twisted the metal structures in the fall had done the same to his legs as well. Allen tried to stand again.

"Just what?" Haley asked.

Again, pain gripped Allen's legs like shocks of electricity, and they buckled. Allen made an amateur medical assessment. An ankle was broken. A knee ligament was torn. His right arm was unusable. He shook his head in disgust.

It wasn't supposed to be this kind of mission.

Allen winced as he moved his left arm within a finger's reach of his right hand to access his control panel. He activated a private communication channel to Haley.

"Just get out of there," he said. "I've got another way out." Allen hoped the pain in his voice wouldn't betray his lie.

"You sure?" Haley asked.

"Yes, I'm setting the charges now," Allen assured her. "There's a door to another cargo hold. I'll make my way up top." It wouldn't be easy for Haley to get out, but with all the guards now headed for him, she could pull it off.

Allen opened the bag of charges, pulled one out, and inspected it. He shook his head as frustration set in again. It seriously wasn't supposed to be this kind of mission.

Allen turned a dial on the explosive, setting it to circuit detonation mode. If one of the explosives went off, it would activate the others. He placed the charge on the floor next to the Eden computer, then slid himself around the equipment to set the next. Considering how much Allen had gone through to get to that point, he was going to make sure the explosives were spread out enough to finish the job. It also gave him the time he needed to make a call.

Allen changed his private comm channel over to Kelsey.

"Allen, what the hell?" she asked. "Why did you mute me out, where is Haley going?"

"I'm not going to make it out, Kel," Allen said.

"Stop," Kelsey said, not having it. "Get up, set the charges, and get out of there."

319

"I can't stand," Allen said, pulling another charge out of its bag as he reached the base of the Eden procedure chamber.

"Then have Haley come get you," Kelsey replied, her anger growing. "Forget about the mission and just come back."

Allen set the charge and continued to his next spot. "There's no way I'm leaving without getting this done."

"No!" Kelsey shouted. Allen could hear her pounding on the desk. "No! No! No! You have a son, goddamnit! Benjamin needs you."

"Benjamin needs money and medicine more than he needs me," Allen shot back. "I destroy this stuff, Eamon gives him that. Nothing else I do will matter more than this."

"It won't replace his father," Kelsey argued. "He needs…we need you more than the money."

Allen stopped at the base of a power generator. "No, Jodock was right," he said. "What good am I doing him? He needs treatment and a cure, not me. That's all that matters."

"You're wrong," Kelsey told him. "You're just too desperate to see it."

Above him, high at the top of the cargo hold, Allen heard the access door slam open followed by footsteps on metal and voices reacting to the damage. "No, I'm not wrong," Allen declared, setting the last charge against the power generator. For this final charge, he activated a timer, which set itself to three minutes and instantly began counting down. "I'm sorry, Kelsey, but that's the way it is."

Kelsey was silent. While he watched the timer count down, Allen searched through his fear and pain and love for something else to say but came up short.

As the silence drew on, Allen felt the need to comfort his wife. "I'm sorry, Kelsey," he repeated. "I wish this wasn't the only way."

Finally, Kelsey responded. "No, Allen, I'm sorry."

Tears welled in Allen's eyes. "Why are you sorry?"

"Because this is really going to hurt."

Allen didn't have time for a follow-up question. Before he could speak, a red notification popped up on his contact lenses. He had never heard the term VR REMOTE COMMAND before. But in the moment that followed, as his combat armor took control of his body and stood up of its own accord, he understood he was in the midst of a stark pro/con situation.

On the pro side, Kelsey had given Allen a new toy after all. On the con side, that new toy came in the form of a severely painful physical experience.

The suit walked forward under the power of its internal motors and bent low behind the Eden equipment, forcing Allen along for the ride. "What the hell are you doing?" Allen shrieked through gritted teeth.

"Getting you home," Kelsey said, her sadness replaced with anger. In Allen's vision, the red notification was replaced by a video feed of Kelsey in the same virtual reality setup she used to play the games Kyle gave her, with VR goggles on her head and a controller in each hand. "If Benjamin fights, we fight. Even if it's just for our sanity."

Mimicking Kelsey's movements, Allen's suit stepped forward and peeked over the equipment using Allen's contact lenses. Guards in matching fatigues and energy-resistant vests had already made it to the bottom of the cargo hold while others were on the scaffolding inspecting the damage. Again, Allen wailed.

"Stop it," Kelsey chided. "They can hear you."

"Oh my God," Allen replied, gasping for breath. "I feel sick."

"You're going to feel sicker if they shoot you in the mouth," Kelsey said.

"Have to...hurry," Allen advised between retches.

A guard burst from around the corner of the equipment. "Freeze!" he commanded, pointing his pulse pistol at Allen.

In response, Allen vomited on the guard's chest.

As the guard looked down at his shirt in disgust, Kelsey took advantage of the distraction. Allen's suit followed her motions as she reached out, wrenched the guard's pistol from his hand, and delivered a kick that knocked him on his back. A pair of guards on the upper level heard the noise and looked down. Kelsey swiftly took aim and hit each one in quick succession before they could draw their weapons. Allen would have been in awe of his wife's marksmanship had he not been so busy begging her to stop.

He ended his pleading when Kelsey forced him to run forward and head straight for the stairs. The first guard Allen reached was too shocked by the screaming, sobbing man coming at him to draw his weapon. Allen could only watch as his arm punched and broke the man's nose without breaking stride.

At the base of the stairs, the next guard froze in place slack-jawed as Allen came at him in a style somewhere between a drunken master and a self-loathing marionette. Allen groaned helplessly as he spun the guard around and used him as a human shield before shooting a third guard coming down the stairs at him.

On the middle platform, Allen and his unwilling companion made their way to the second set of stairs, all the while closely watched from above by the remaining guards pointing weapons at them. While the two slowly went up the steps to the top level, joined together in a duet of panicked, off-key cries, Allen had an out-of-body experience. He felt detached as he got closer to the group of guards and time seemed to pass in slow motion as he pondered various questions:

Would Benjamin be okay?

Does love have a medical benefit?

When was the last time you told Kelsey you love her?

Wait, isn't our anniversary coming up?

Allen reached the top step and consulted his mental calendar. His anniversary was only a week away. Shouts from the armed guards broke Allen's wistful detachment and his thoughts of mysticism and love were replaced by a need for vengeance by any petty means necessary.

"I'm not getting you an anniversary present!" Allen declared to the group of armed men in front of him.

"Fine!" Kelsey replied before forcing Allen to shove his human shield ahead. While the guard collided with his nearest associate, Kelsey raised Allen's stolen pistol and took the rest of the guards down.

Allen was forced toward the door and noticed that the guards on the floor writhed in pain but were still alive thanks to their protective vests. "You better hurry!" Allen wailed as he ran. "In a minute you'll be underwater!" Once through the door, Allen moved at a full sprint through the corridor and fired on any guard coming to investigate the sound of a sobbing banshee coming their way.

"Lovelace to Hellfire," Kelsey called on the radio. "Mystic is on his way. How are things looking on the docking bridge?"

"These mechs are still being a pain," Haley answered, pulse fire in the background. "They've cut me off from Ares and Apollo. I can't get around."

"Mystic will handle it," Kelsey said to Allen's horror. "What about your dad?"

"Her dad is coming," Daryl interjected. "I'm just waiting for my new flying partner to catch on."

"Dude, I'm programming a virtual engine controller from scratch here," Kyle said defensively. It was the first time anyone on the team had heard Kyle speak with anything but extreme optimism.

"All right, I'm sorry, I'm sorry," Daryl said, his voice tinged with remorse after putting a dent in Kyle's usually unflappable chipperness. "I guess unexpected barrel rolls make me cranky."

"Sorry, 'Tank, but you're going to have to work even faster," Kelsey said.

"How come?" Haley asked.

As if in response to her question, the ship rocked from a large explosion behind Allen. He stumbled and fell, bouncing off one wall and hitting the other before landing on the floor, hammering his broken body even more.

"Why?" Allen cried with self-pity. "Why, why, why…"

A new alarm squelched out, accompanied by blinking strobe lights throughout the corridor.

"Abandon ship, abandon ship," instructed a computerized voice.

"Hellfire, Mystic will be there soon. Hold tight," Kelsey said.

Allen summoned as much toughness as he could while Kelsey brought him to his feet and he continued on. After a few more yards, he reached a set of stairs and Kelsey guided him up two decks before taking a door outside. Allen saw pulse fire ahead.

"Take cover, there," he told Kelsey, looking at a ventilation stack to his left.

Kelsey followed his lead, walking Allen over to crouch behind the stack pipe. From that position, Allen saw the remaining mechs. Two were firing at John and Jacob. The brothers returned fire sporadically, their shields apparently spent. To Allen's right, the remaining mech fired at Haley. As Kelsey forced Allen to turn his weapon on high and aim it at Haley's attacker, Allen yelled out.

"Wait, stop…"

Allen's pistol fired, hitting the mech at the waist. It split in two and crumbled on the deck. The two remaining mechs immediately turned, opened fire, and advanced toward Allen. Kelsey barely moved Allen back behind the stack pipe before it was pummeled by pulse fire.

"Yeah, we're a little stuck out here," Allen grumbled.

"Sorry, I just reacted," Kelsey said. "Where do we go?"

Allen looked around. "I don't see any other cover for at least ten yards," he said, looking at a set of metal storage containers. "The closest thing is the door we just came through. There's no way they miss before we get there."

"So what do we do, run for it?" Kelsey asked.

"They're expecting me to run," Allen replied. "So I guess…" Allen sighed. "I guess you have to do something unexpected."

"Okay, hold on," Kelsey said. She made Allen turn his back toward the containers and squat into a crouch. With his knees tucked to his chest, Kelsey made Allen launch into a backflip. Upside-down in air, Allen's pistol fired on the mech on the right, blowing its upper body into several pieces.

Allen howled in delirium, both from pain and the blood rushing to his head. But as Kelsey homed his weapon in on the final mech and his body turned upright, Allen felt he was through the worst of it. Kelsey commanded his finger to pull the trigger.

Instead of pulse fire, the pistol emitted a heavy click.

The battery of the pulse pistol was dead, completely drained by the last high-powered shot. The mech tracked its weapon on Allen as he fell toward the deck of the ship, bracing himself for the hit.

The ship lurched without warning, its balance thrown off by the sea water filling the cargo hold. The mech lost its aim on Allen and worked to secure its footing on the shifting deck. Allen wanted to cheer, but his impact with the ship cut him short. Unable to compensate for the pitching deck, Kelsey couldn't land Allen on his feet. He crashed hard on the metal surface, landing on his lower back. Immediately, Allen could tell something with his suit had changed. It went slack and the video feed of Kelsey disappeared.

"Kelsey?" Allen called. "What happened?"

There was no answer, and the fresh pain in Allen's lower back told him why. That was where the suit's main communication circuitry was located. The fall crushed it, leaving Allen helpless and unable to radio anyone. Finding it hard to think through the pain, Allen focused on the sound of his breathing and attempted to invoke patience while he waited for someone to help him. It briefly worked, until the sound of motors and mechanical footsteps broke his concentration.

Allen could move his head just enough to see the mech. It was walking in search mode, looking for a target to attack. It walked in a wide arc, and Allen was stuck in the open. The sound of Allen's own breathing became oppressive, as if he could somehow suffocate from it, and grew faster as the mech circled toward him.

Then his breathing reflexively stopped as the mech saw him. It drew its weapon into a ready position to fire. Allen looked at the barrel pointed straight at him. Would he be able to see the pulse coming or would the world simply go dark? He hoped it wouldn't hurt.

The mech moved sharply, and Allen flinched in anticipation of a pulse blast. But instead of firing at Allen, the mech turned its attention straight up into the air. Allen shifted his gaze just in time to see Daryl land the hovercraft hard on the deck directly on top of the mech, crushing it.

"Couldn't have done that five minutes earlier?" Allen mumbled out loud to himself. His vision blurred, and it took all of his effort to raise his arm to catch the beam of the hovercraft's searchlights. He heard voices yelling around him, but the words were hard to make out. Someone grabbed him under his arms and dragged him. Guards and the ship's crew made their way to bright orange lifeboats as Allen was moved inside the hovercraft. He was put down on a gurney, and the world was suddenly like a nightmare. His location seemed alien, and his memories felt like a lie.

"No, let me up," Allen pleaded, trying to sit. "I have to finish. Benjamin! God, no, I need to finish the mission!" Allen tried to run but was pushed back down.

"We did it, Allen," Haley told him, prying off his armor to make way for an IV tube. "We did it."

Allen stopped fighting as his sense returned. Something in the word "we" struck him to the core, a tightly wound universe of significance overwhelming him. Relief, guilt, exuberance, and shame filled him in equal measures as he thought about both what he'd done and almost done. The feelings continued to cycle until Allen lost consciousness, with Haley repeating her words.

"We did it. We did it…"

Chapter Thirty

"I'm so sorry your door is still manually operated. This is an outrage."

On Allen's video screen in his living room, Carol looked like she was about to go on a firing spree on every worker in the building.

"It's okay, Carol," Allen assured her. "I only mentioned it because you asked. I'm sure the work crew will get to it."

Carol shook her head in disgust. "Well, according to the original timeline, all your doors were supposed to have been converted to automatic on Tuesday."

"Every renovation has delays," Allen said. "When you bought out our whole building, we didn't know the condo downstairs had some sewer pipe in a weird place. So the work crew was trying to move that around before they blocked out the med bay and nurse's space. And the inclined wheelchair lift for the stairs was missing a bolt or something."

"Very disappointing." Carol sighed.

Allen chuckled. Compared to two months ago, a missing bolt or simply having to open a normal door may have been the best thing about his day, certainly not the worst. Though it would be nice to have the lift installed. Between his broken arm still in a cast, a brace on his knee, and a walking boot to protect his healing ankle, getting up and down the stairs was an ordeal.

"We'll be fine," Allen said. He waved his arm around toward the drop cloths and half-torn walls around him. "We know all this is temporary. On the plus side, the play space upstairs is finished."

Carol began to recite from an inventory in her database. "You should have received a stander, a swing, an activity chair, an exercise ball…"

"Yes, Carol," Allen said, laughing again. "We got all of it and it's perfect."

"Yeah, it is," a voice said behind him.

Allen turned and saw Daryl in the doorway with Haley behind him. "This new wheelchair lift is great," Daryl continued, "now I can sneak in any time I want."

"They finished it?" Allen asked.

Daryl shrugged. "I hope so because I just used it."

Allen hopped with a spring of excitement. His damaged knee buckled, not being quite up to celebratory strength. Allen clawed at the nearby reclining chair and held it with all the strength in his good arm to keep from hitting the floor. With his balance recovered, Allen turned back to Carol. Her expression had changed. She looked nervous. And whatever the reason, it was serious enough to make an artificial intelligence feel awkward.

"How is, uh…that is…" Carol stammered. "Last time you said Benjamin was on a different medication. So…"

"His seizures are down," Allen said, greeting her concern with a warm smile. "Usually two short clusters a day now, but yesterday he only had one. And the doctor said there's plenty of room to go up on the dosage." It was the first time Allen had told anyone that Benjamin's seizures were getting better. It was fitting that Carol was the first one to find out. Whether she was a real person or not, she deserved it.

Carol's face lit up. "That's very gratifying," she said. "I'll be sure to tell Eamon when he wakes up. Deep down somewhere inside, I think he would like to hear it."

"I was thinking I would tell him myself," Allen said. "I still plan on coming over this afternoon to read to him again."

"He'll like that," Carol said. "The doctors are very interested in the calming effect you seem to have on him."

"I don't know if it's me so much as the pictures," Allen replied. "I just take all the kid's books Benjamin likes. They seem to have the same taste in pop-up dragon pictures."

"That's right," Kelsey said, coming into the room holding Benjamin. "We should schedule a playdate so they can compare notes."

Carol's tension dissolved at the sight of Benjamin. "Well, hello, Master Benjamin. How are you today?"

Benjamin silently looked around the room, taking in the changes going on around him. Finally, his eyes fixed on the image of Carol on the bright video screen. He held Carol's gaze without expression.

"Come on now, Benjamin," Kelsey told him. "Can you say 'hi' to Auntie Carol?"

Kelsey fluttered two fingers against the side of Benjamin's cheek. He leaned his cheek into his mother's touch and raised a contemplative eyebrow until the corners of his mouth began to curl. Then, all at once, a broad smile spread across his face.

"Yay!" Kelsey and Allen cheered together,

continuing their family routine, as Daryl and Haley clapped their approval.

"Thank you, Benjamin!" Carol gushed.

Allen beamed. Even after two weeks of seeing his son smile, it still moved him as much as the very first time.

"All right," Kelsey said, bouncing Benjamin in her arms. "Time to go play upstairs."

"Be up in a minute," Allen said, rubbing his son on the head as Kelsey walked by toward the door. "Haley, hang back for a sec," Allen called to his partner.

Haley stepped to the side as the rest of the group went out the door, letting her dad out first to wheel back onto the flip-down platform that straddled the stairs and would lift him up one more level. Allen's gaze stayed fixed on Benjamin's smiling face until his wife and son disappeared from view.

"So, I got a call from Jacob Zielinski," Allen told Haley.

"Ugh," Haley groaned. "I thought you wanted to talk about a new job for us."

"Sorry," Allen said. "It just felt weird to tell everyone that a boy called for your number."

"A 'boy'?" Haley replied. "What am I, twelve? And why was he calling you?"

"He didn't have your number, and he was too afraid to ask your dad for it," Allen said. "And his brother said searching online for it felt creepy."

"Jacob and John were both on the call?" Haley asked, horrified.

"They sure were," Allen replied with a wide grin. "Anyway, I asked for his number instead. So give him a call back and you can, you know, crush his dreams." He pulled a slip of paper from his pocket and handed it over.

Haley opened the note and looked at the phone number. "I would rather not deal with this."

"Just do the whole 'it's not you, it's me' thing. Or meet as friends. Guys love that. They totally, completely love that."

Haley glared skeptically.

"C'mon, if you're brave enough to run into bullets, I'm sure you can handle this."

"Bullets don't try to make small talk with their brother sitting next to them," Haley grumbled.

Allen smiled. "It'll be great," he said. "Not weird in any way."

"I'm going upstairs now," Haley said, opening the door.

"See you up there," Allen said, turning back to Carol on the video screen.

The instant the door closed shut, Carol continued. "I will defer to your judgment on the doors," she said, back to business. "But moving forward, I'll insist each contractor updates me twice per day instead of just once."

"Sounds good," Allen said. "Thanks for everything—" Carol unceremoniously terminated the call before Allen finished. He chuckled. Any time Allen forgot Carol was a computer program, she always found accidental ways of reminding him.

An alert sound went off down the hall. Allen shuffle-jogged at his best speed toward it, turning into a small office he was able to reclaim now that Benjamin's therapy equipment was given its own space upstairs. He went to his desk and tapped his keyboard, silencing the alert and accepting an encrypted video call. "Hello?" he answered.

Kyle appeared in a video window on the screen. "Hey there!" he greeted chipperly. "Is this a good time?"

"Yeah, I've got a minute," Allen said.

"Okay, I'm sending the data. You should see a request to accept," Kyle said just before a new notification appeared.

Allen confirmed the request, and his computer began to download the data. "Thanks for setting this up for me," he said.

"Sure thing," Kyle replied. "I can appreciate this mystery client of yours valuing privacy. What you're seeing on your screen is the security program I gave you compiling tiny bits of data it spread to millions of online locations from the original encrypted files. The tiny remote copies of data will then delete themselves and you'll have the only copy."

"Sounds like what I need," Allen said. "Thanks again. So, am I seeing you next week?"

"Next week?" Kyle replied, feigning ignorance.

"It's not a surprise party, Kyle," Allen said. "Though I guess it will be for Benjamin since he doesn't understand that his birthday is coming up, but really it's more of a thank-you party for everyone."

"Right..." Kyle said hesitantly. "Hopefully I can make it out."

"You need to get out of that tiny apartment and explore the real world, my friend," Allen insisted. "And if you say no, I'm pretty sure Daryl or Haley will just come and drag you here."

"So either fly first class or travel in the trunk of a

car?" Kyle asked.

"Well, it's your money to spend, I guess. But, yeah, that's about right," Allen said.

"I'll be there then," Kyle said, relenting. "I'll take the chance to bring some new VR games for Kelsey to check out."

"Hmmm," Allen replied, his still-healing injuries stinging with the memory of their creation on the ship.

"Okay, that program will quit when it's finished," Kyle said. "Talk to ya later."

"Thanks again," Allen said before closing the video chat window and ending the call.

Allen turned his attention to the progress bar on the security program. He clicked an option to see the individual files that had already been downloaded, revealing a list of garbled names made up with sequences of random letters and numbers.

Allen opened the lower drawer of his desk where a safe was hidden. He entered his code on the keypad and removed a silver device, a twin of the combination data reader and transmitter unit he had used on the cargo ship to confirm the files in the Eden computer database, though the need to confirm those files was entirely of Allen's making. After some convincing, that is.

"Did he send it?" Kelsey asked, coming into the office.

"Yes," Allen confirmed, inserting the silver device into his computer's data port. A moment later, the file names unscrambled to reveal titles of various Eden Therapy protocols as well as equipment schematics, procedure notes, and program files, with more appearing by the second.

Allen felt as if Jodock's shadow loomed over him.

It was the same sense he had when he took the devices to one of Daryl's competitors to have them outfitted with hard-wired encryption and transmitters to a private satellite. Allen couldn't shake the feeling that small parts of Jodock's arguments were correct, that his cruelty had created a tool that could potentially justify the means, and it haunted him.

"We did the right thing," Kelsey assured him, reading his expression.

"I know," Allen replied. The sick feeling of agreeing with even a small part of Jodock's thinking was nothing compared to the possibility that Allen would be responsible for completely erasing what could one day be the only way to treat his son. Not to mention the thousands of other people cut off from medical care, left to suffer and die.

"Then what's wrong?" Kelsey asked.

"If Carol finds out…"

Kelsey moved closer and spoke softly. "For now, we'll just lock it up and sit on it. We don't have any money left to do more than that anyway." She moved away and headed out the door. "I gotta get back upstairs."

Allen watched the file download continue. Kelsey was right. The cost of modifying the data devices had completely wiped out their rainy day fund, leaving nothing left to pay for actually getting the data to Allen's computer. Luckily Kyle had been good for a favor.

Satisfied the download process was going well, Allen removed the silver device from his computer. The file names returned to their encrypted state, once again unreadable without the digital key. As Allen put it back into his safe, the tension in his shoulders eased as he hid away both the device as well as his concerns about having it. No sense in dwelling on worst-case scenarios.

Allen looked around his home on his way to the door and stopped at the kitchen counter. There, as always, was the worn notebook where Kelsey logged Benjamin's seizure activity. Allen carefully opened the nearly-detached cover and thumbed through the pages five and ten at a time until he reached a special page. It contained a bit of news that Allen hadn't dared mention to Carol. Hope can be as brittle as hair-thin glass and sometimes requires privacy to protect.

Allen ran his finger down the page. At the top was written the date, in Kelsey's handwriting, from three days earlier. Allen's finger passed the date and continued. Down and down it went, through every ruled line filled with nothing but blank paper. No noting of times. No descriptions of spasms. No lengths of clusters. There had been seizures after that day, and a notebook full of seizures before it, but for one day Benjamin had been free.

Grasping the top corner of the page, Allen pulled it gently away, tearing it from the spine of the notebook. He held it at arm's length and admired it as he walked into the kitchen. He rubbed the edges of the paper between his thumb and forefinger, feeling the reality of the thing he had wished for. Then, he folded it in half with the precision a sacred document deserved. As he reached the far end of the kitchen, he folded it again. And finally, he folded it a third time as he came to a stop.

Allen smiled at the crisp little rectangle in his hands. He held that smile as he pressed his foot on the pedal of the kitchen garbage can and sprang open the lid. His smile continued still as he tore the page into tiny bits and let each one fall like a tumbling snowflake into the bin. What was right and wonderful about his son would not be found on that blank page or any others yet to come in that dreaded book. It was just a log of seizures, after all. Not a log of days he loved his child.

With all the pieces fallen from his hands, Allen continued toward the door. The renovations were coming along nicely, no matter what Carol's frustrations were. Benjamin's new medicine was helping. And for the first time in years, there were real, encouraging possibilities on the horizon. It was a joy in life Allen had all but forgotten. He had always wished for things to get better for Benjamin yet never allowed himself to actually expect them to. But now, for the first time in a long time, he truly felt hopeful.

And so, with a new sense of excitement, Allen went out the door and ran up the stairs to play with his son.

A word about the author…

After graduating from film school, Matthew Wilcox worked in advertising as a copywriter penning everything from pickle coupons to national TV commercials. He eventually left full-time work to focus on raising his kids and helping his son in his fight against epilepsy. In addition to writing ads, Matthew also studied comedy at a number of Chicago's writing and satire programs. Some of his other completed works include online satire, several sketch revues, and a one-act play. He lives with his family in Chicago, Illinois.

Thank you for purchasing
this publication of The Wild Rose Press, Inc.

For questions or more information
contact us at
info@thewildrosepress.com.

The Wild Rose Press, Inc.
www.thewildrosepress.com